THE INVERNESS PROTOCOL

Joseph P. Catlett

I0565064

☙Артйом☙

Artyom Publishers
Washington, D.C.

Author's Note: This is a work of fiction. The resemblance of any characters to persons living or dead is purely coincidental. In addition, the events depicted in this novel never actually took place at the Food and Drug Administration or Georgetown University Hospital.

'…the serpent beguiled me and I did eat.'
Genesis 3:13

Prologue

Millie Beattie stood barefoot in the snow wrapped in a backless hospital gown. As the effects of the pain medication began to wane, she found herself in the midst of a skeletal forest, its branches like a fine network of capillaries against the gray of dusk. The January air was suddenly frigid, especially on her bare backside, and the redolence of snow was unmistakable. For her, winter was such a desolate time of year, the stillness almost maddening, and the sun never seeming to rise high enough.

Another contraction refocused her thoughts. It began in the small of her back and made a tight circle around her abdomen. The pain was becoming more intense, almost unbearable without the narcotic coursing through her veins. She panted until it subsided, just as they had instructed her to do.

She had been sequestered during the final stages of her pregnancy, along with the other women. There were Heather and Patti who were recovering from having their babies – babies they were never allowed to hold or even see. Then there was Tanya, the new girl, who was just starting out and seemed to be naïve about everything, a country bumpkin in the truest sense of the word. As the days lumbered by, she began to have second thoughts about The Protocol. No matter what problems the child might possess, it would be hers and not theirs. With the doors unguarded, she had simply left without clothes or shoes, a decision undoubtedly influenced by the narcotic-induced euphoria. Now she had to find her way out before nightfall.

The engine of a vehicle, a truck judging from its roar, broke the stillness somewhere in the distance ahead. Its echo became louder, then began to fade and was soon gone. The highway was not far away, probably a quarter of a mile at most. She had already covered a fair distance and in the process discovered that the beautiful wild roses carpeting the forest floor in summer were now just thorny stalks beneath the snow. Her feet were numb and bleeding, and her hair clung to her face in long, sweaty strings.

Another contraction brought her to a standstill. The contractions were becoming stronger and more frequent. Her water had broken some time back, and she knew it wouldn't be long now.

Then she heard them behind her, thrashing through the undergrowth, drawing closer as their flashlight beams danced between the tree trunks. A stab of adrenaline caused her heart to jump. She plunged into a copse of winterberry where the bare branches smacked her face and tore her skin. She ran as fast as her enormous belly and heavy breasts would allow.

She soon emerged onto a narrow lane with shallow tire treads gouged in the snow. It led to a gate of rusting bars flanked on both sides by tall brick walls. A security camera perched high over the gates followed her as she staggered forward and grabbed the cold steel.

But they were soon upon her, pulling her down into the snow. During the struggle that ensured, one of them produced a syringe topped with the longest needle she had ever seen and plunged it deep into her bare buttock. The stab of pain was followed shortly thereafter by a calm and warmth that seemed to envelop her in a blur of inner peace.

As she gently spiraled into darkness, the painful shrieks of an infant filled the air.

One

The old man limped down a sidewalk on the esplanade between the Potomac River and Rock Creek Parkway. One hand gripped a cane with which he carefully negotiated the icy and uneven concrete, while the other clutched a briefcase. Each step produced a labored breath that fogged his glasses until he could barely see. He was forced to stop momentarily to retrieve his handkerchief. After wiping the lenses clear, he pulled his fedora down lower and drew the collar of his overcoat closer.

Most of the street lamps stood lifeless in the evolving darkness, some even missing the ornate globes. To his left, commuter traffic on the Parkway formed a string of lights that flowed under the overhanging terraces of the Kennedy Center and steadily crawled across the Roosevelt Bridge into northern Virginia.

A 757, its landing lights blazing, roared over the river as it followed a glide path to Reagan National Airport. The aircraft defied gravity a little less with each passing second until it dropped from sight behind the trees on the other side of the river. In the twilight above, he could see the landing lights of incoming aircraft on final approach forming a large arc that stretched over the towers of Georgetown University all the way to the National Cathedral on Mount St. Alban.

The man shuffled over the snow to a bench facing the Potomac and eased himself onto the cold metal. A week of subfreezing temperatures had caused a skin of ice to form over the dark water, but it had fractured in places, giving the appearance of a large jigsaw puzzle. A person wouldn't last long in that water, he thought as a chill laced his spine. Memorial Bridge stretched across the river on the left, and further upstream on the right, the trees of Washington Harbor, perpetually draped in white Christmas lights, shimmered invitingly. Directly across the river, the boxy buildings of Arlington rose above the shoreline.

Just after another airliner passed overhead, he was startled by the breathy voices of two men jogging abreast down the sidewalk behind him. He reached for the handle of the pistol buried deep in the pocket of his overcoat. A splintered conversation about hedge funds drifted above the din of traffic as the men continued down the sidewalk, eventually disappearing behind a bridge pylon.

The man took a deep breath to quell the pounding in his chest. His eyes darted about as he slid the briefcase under the bench. He pulled himself erect, using the cane for balance, and returned to the sidewalk where he stood in the glow of a streetlight. Seconds later, a black Suburban pulled to the curb, and with some difficulty, he climbed into the passengers' seat, slamming the door behind him.

As the Suburban eased into the swiftly moving traffic, a stout man in a navy blue sweat suit with a toboggan covering his head, jogged over to the bench. His breath came in short quick gasps as he sat down heavily. After glancing about, he bent down and retrieved the briefcase. With the aid of a penlight, he clumsily spun the dial on the lock while still wearing gloves, his hands shaking violently. After several failed attempts, he removed the gloves with his teeth and spat them on the bench beside him. The cold dial spun easily under his bare fingers and when the proper combination had been entered, the clasp sprung up with a snap. He carefully drew up the lid and examined its contents

The briefcase contained multiple brown glass vials packed in bubble wrap secured together with masking tape. Wedging the penlight between his teeth, he gingerly unwrapped one of the vials and studied it under the bluish glow. The vial contained multiple large capsules each with a white granular substance that was iridescent in the modest light. He carefully rewrapped it and counted the others still bundled in the bulky packing material.

"More than enough," he whispered, still clutching the penlight with his teeth.

Two

Jane Riley hurried through the Hall of Nations toward the Grand Foyer of the Kennedy Center. The light snow that started hours earlier had stalled traffic across the District, bringing the most powerful city in the world to a standstill. She had abandoned a stranded cab more than a block from the center complex and trotted through the traffic in heels with her gown held high.

A sign kiosk announced the annual awards for the American Society for Cancer Research being held in the Concert Hall. Her picture had been inserted into the kiosk, below which read "Dr. Jane Riley, Commissioner of the FDA, recipient of the Society's Presidential Award." Below that was a picture of Nina Cardozo, an opera star from Milan and breast cancer survivor, who was to provide entertainment for the evening. Jane glanced at her reflection in the glass door before going into the foyer. Her auburn hair had been engineered into an elegant fold, and with her fingers, she gently brushed away the melting snow.

An arch of multicolored balloons welcomed her into the red-carpeted foyer, a space stretching 630 feet across the backside of the entire building and having a ceiling height of 60 feet. The room was one of the largest in the world, and could accommodate a recumbent Washington Monument with 75 feet to spare. Long prism lights glowed above a well-dressed crowd, noisy with the discordant hum of simultaneous conversations. Outside the floor-to-ceiling windows that comprised the exterior wall of the foyer, a silent snowfall continued to powder the brightly lit terraces that overlooked the Potomac River.

Jane checked her coat and took a program from an usher. Nina's performance would precede the awards ceremony, giving her enough time to compose a short acceptance speech. She would jot down a few salient points, but her remarks would largely be extemporaneous as she mined her memory for the details.

"Dr. Riley, you look stunning tonight!" Senator Frederick Hines intoned as he took her hand. The influential septuagenarian was chair of the Health, Education and Labor Committee before which she had often been called to testify about FDA-related issues. He had always been one of her strongest allies in Congress.

"Thank you, Senator." She leaned in and gave him a kiss on the cheek. He was about her height and sported a thick shock of white hair. "How'd your knee replacement go?"

His eyes sparkled as he smiled at her. "Well, the surgery went fine," he began, "but it was the recovery that seemed to take a while. But I'm happy to report, I'm back…"

"How about a picture for the Post?" A young man in an ill-fitting tuxedo had interrupted them. He was holding aloft a large, rather complex appearing camera. Before they could respond, he had snapped several candid shots. The flashing lights attracted several more attendees who came over to offer congratulations and have their pictures taken with the Commissioner.

When the spots had cleared from her vision, Jane recognized an old friend standing near the stucco-like bust of John Kennedy. Peter Hilson was handsome in his tuxedo, his thick hair grayer than she remembered from their days at Georgetown, but his blue eyes were just as striking. He was conversing with a thin young man with brown hair and wire rimmed glasses who Jane recognized as Josh Hanley, a former student and protégé of hers. Hilson was pounding the air with his fist as he talked.

"Peter, Josh, how have you been?" She asked, moving toward them.

Their conversation ended abruptly and Hilson kissed her on the cheek. "Congratulations Jane! What an honor!"

"Congratulations, Dr. Riley," Hanley echoed as he raised a bottle of sparking water.

"Thanks." She glanced at her watch. "The traffic was horrible. I thought I was going to be late."

"You know how Washington is. Just the threat of snow throws this city into a panic," Hilson replied.

"How is life in academia treating you?" she asked.

Hilson frowned. "It would be nice if our faculty could get their grants funded." He turned to Hanley, who rolled his eyes and looked away.

"Jane, I know there isn't much time before the program starts." Hilson took her by the arm. "But we have some catching up to do. Josh, if you could excuse us please."

He began to steer her through the crowd.

"I get the distinct impression that I interrupted something important," she remarked.

"Don't worry about it," Hilson replied curtly.

"How is Suzy?" she asked.

He frowned. "I guess you haven't heard. Suzy and I separated months ago."

Her eyes widened. Dr. Suzy Fischer had collaborated with Hilson on many important research projects and had eventually become his wife. As far as Jane could recall, they had been married almost twenty years.

"I'm so sorry."

He waved his hand. "Please, it's okay. Thirsty?"

"I think there's time for a sip or two. What are they serving?"

"Cheap champagne." He grabbed two flutes off a passing tray and handed one of them to her. The two had wandered into a less populated area of the foyer and stopped near a staircase that led to the upper tiers of the Concert Hall.

"Jane, I have a confession to make." Hilson studied his shoes momentarily. "I actually came here tonight needing to talk to you. You may find what I am about to tell you a bit shocking!"

She recoiled slightly. "Peter, what is it?"

"You must understand that what I am about to tell you must be held in strict confidence," he began.

"Of course." She took a sip of the champagne to fortify herself.

Before Hilson could say another word, a high-pitched male voice emanated from the crowd. "Dr. Riley! Dr. Jane Riley! I've been looking all over for you!"

"What the hell?" Hilson was clearly annoyed as a stocky, balding man approached them. He offered his hand, and she took it briefly.

"Dr. Dickson," she intoned. Dr. Maxwell Dickson was the last person she wanted to see that evening, or ever for that matter. "I didn't expect to see you here tonight. This is Dr. Peter Hilson. He's director of the cancer center at Georgetown."

The two men shook hands. "I'm the senior vice president at

Leeland-Crofts, in charge of regulatory affairs," Dickson announced to Hilson.

"Ah, one of the largest pharmaceutical firms in the world." Hilson raised his glass.

"The largest!" Dickson turned to Jane. "Dr. Riley, it's important that I discuss the application for our anticancer drug, LCN33." He glanced at Hilson then added, "Alone."

Her eyes narrowed but she maintained her composure. "Dr. Dickson, you know this is not the time or place..."

"It is urgent that we speak now," he persisted.

She looked at her watch. "I really don't have time for this. Besides, I doubt that your shareholders would want you discussing proprietary issues in public. You should direct your inquiries to the review division for your application at the agency."

He smiled thinly. "I am the senior vice president for a Fortune 500 company. I should be talking to someone at the agency who is on a comparable level, such as yourself, of course. And speaking of our shareholders, who include some of the most influential people in the world...."

"This conversation is over." Her voice was calm as she glanced at Hilson, whose free hand was drawn into a fist. She took him by the arm and started to leave, but Dickson blocked her path.

"Dr. Riley, please," he persisted. "How could your agency deprive cancer patients of such a promising new drug?"

Before she could respond, Hilson intervened. "You heard the lady. I think you'd better step aside, buddy."

"Peter, please. Let's not have a scene." Her face began to burn. She could fight her own battles, and Hilson was well aware of this fact. But she also knew that Hilson's type A personality and sense of machismo would never allow him to stand back while a colleague, particularly a female one, was being harassed.

Electronic chimes sounded throughout the foyer indicating that the performance was about to begin. She took one last sip of her champagne, grabbed Hilson's flute and handed them both to Maxwell Dickson. "Would you be so kind?" she said sweetly.

The man's face turned a brilliant red but before he could respond, a commotion erupted in the foyer. Several protestors held signs indicating that they were part of the 'CanActUp

Group.'

"There she is!" shouted an older woman with wiry gray hair. "Jane Riley, Commissioner of the FDA, who would deprive dying cancer patients of life saving treatments!"

"Talk about making a scene," Hilson muttered. "Who the hell are they?"

"The 'CanActUp Group,'" Jane replied evenly. She turned to Dickson who stood speechless, his mouth open, as he still clutched the empty flutes. "Did you have anything to do with this?"

"I swear to you I didn't. It's a weird coincidence," he proffered desperately.

"Murderous bureaucrat!" shouted another protester, this one an overweight man with wild curly black hair and thick glasses.

"It's a travesty that you are being given the Presidential Award from the Society! A travesty!" an unseen woman shouted from within the knot of protestors.

By now, conversation in the foyer had died and all eyes were on Jane Riley and the group of demonstrators. For several minutes no one moved. Then two security guards, both of whom appeared to be just shy of eighty, stepped in front of the protesters and gently prodded them toward exit. However, they did not leave quietly and continued to shout their slogans as the guards ejected them from the foyer. "Your time is up, Jane Riley," the wiry haired woman went on. "Your days are numbered! I speak for all those with cancer who no longer have a voice...."

The electronic chimes began to sound again, this time distinctively louder.

"What is this CanAct Group anyway? Sounds like some sort of thespian society," Hilson said sardonically. The two had left Dickson behind and began to flow with the stunned crowd into the Concert Hall.

"The CanActUp Group is, as the name implies, a cancer activist group. Their position is that cancer patients should have access to any drug, approved or not, regardless of its safety or efficacy data. They think cancer patients should have the right to take any risks they want."

"It sounds like they want to go back to the time of snake oil peddlers." Hilson straightened his tie. "By the way, is LCN33 going to be approved soon?"

Jane avoided his gaze. She wanted to tell him that it was an ineffective drug fraught with serious side effects and didn't stand a chance of approval. "I'm afraid that's confidential information."

"Oh come now," he prodded. "I just want to capitalize on a little insider information. You know, buy stock in *Leeland-Crofts* when the price is low and then when the drug gets approved…."

"The price of the stock goes up, you get rich, and of course, I go to jail," she finished.

"Details," he shrugged.

Members of the National Symphony Orchestra sat on the stage in a semicircle. The conductor stood on a rostrum at the epicenter organizing the score as the tuning of instruments floated above the drone of the audience. The two stepped aside at the back hall as the audience continued to flow in.

"Peter, what was it you wanted to tell me?" Jane asked.

"It's going to have to wait. It's too…involved."

"Can we meet after the program?" she asked.

Before he could answer his pager went off. He pulled it from under his cummerbund, and his eyes widened as he read the text message. "Damn!"

"Anything wrong?"

He nodded. "I have an emergency I need to take care of. Sorry I'm going to miss the awards ceremony. We'll need to talk soon. I'll call you tomorrow. This is something I need to talk to you about in person. Good luck with the speech." He gave her a quick peck on the cheek and disappeared into the crowd.

Feeling somewhat nonplussed, Jane found her seat in the front row of the orchestra section next to Senator Hines. The lights went down, and the audience chatter slowly fizzled. The conductor then began to sweep his baton like a magic wand, impelling the orchestra to do his bidding to brilliant effect. At the end of the first movement, a rotund Nina Cardozo, draped in a blue satin gown, moved onto the stage like a large float. She curtsied several times as the audience applauded. After the commotion died, the program began with an aria from Act I of *Le nozze di Figaro* "Non so piu." Singing the part of Cherubino, her lovely voice cast a mesmerizing spell as she complained in Italian "*Non so piu cosa son, cosa faccio.. I no longer know what I am or what I am doing.*" The audience listened and barely breathed. At its conclusion, she received a standing ovation. The diva curtsied, threw a kiss toward the applauding multitude and daintily waved. The approbation went on for several minutes.

Jane stood during the ovation but suddenly began to feel faint. She sat down heavily.

"Are you okay, Dr. Riley?" Hines asked, putting his hand on her shoulder.

She nodded. "Yes, I guess I shouldn't have had that champagne on an empty stomach."

Hines nodded then turned back to the stage and rejoined the ovation.

A tall, cadaverous man walked to the rostrum in the center of the stage and, after the applause had died and the audience was reseated, introduced himself as Dr. Franklin Pike, president of the society. After thanking Nina for a lovely performance and welcoming everyone to the gala, he introduced Jane Riley by summarizing her educational pedigree and list of accomplishments. No mention was made of the protest that had occurred earlier in the foyer.

"And now I have the distinct honor of bestowing upon her the Presidential Award."

Now in a cold sweat, Jane rose from her seat as applause filled the cavernous hall. After awkwardly negotiating past the senator, she headed for the small flight of steps leading to the stage. By the time she reached the podium, the boisterous crowd seemed to undulate before her. She grasped the podium firmly for support as Pike held up a plaque and offered his free hand. She managed a weak smile, having forgotten what it was she was about to say.

The room started to spin about her, turning the audience into a roaring kaleidoscope of colors, and she felt herself begin to fall. There was a painful blow to the side of her head as she hit the floor with a loud crack. For a fleeting moment, shadowy faces hovered around her before they all collapsed into oblivion.

Three

"I want to see my baby!" Millie Beattie said for the eighth time. It may have been the ninth or tenth, she wasn't sure. "I want to see…" Him? Her? She wasn't even sure about that either.

"Millie, please calm down," the slender blond woman replied in a soothing voice from the other side of the bed. She was clad a blue scrub suit and a white lab coat. "You know that is impossible."

"It's my baby, Jenna." Millie only knew Jenna's first name and that she was a nurse. Beyond that, she knew nothing more about her, where she was from or who her people were. She did know that Jenna was not from around these parts. Her accent told her as much.

Jenna came around the bed and moved in closer. "We told you already Millie. Your baby did not survive." She started to place her hand on Millie's shoulder, but Millie quickly pulled away.

"I'm sorry," Jenna said, retracting her hand. "We're all sorry."

Millie glared at her. "You're lying. All of you! You're a bunch of liars! I heard that baby cry."

"It only lived for a few minutes." Jenna paused then continued. "Now Millie, you knew the rules going in. Everything was spelled out in the consent form that you signed."

"I don't care about that now." As with the rest of her clan, Millie was thickly built, muscular even, with broad shoulders and heavy arms and legs. Jenna, however, was just the opposite, tall, thin and shapely. That alone caused Millie some resentment. She thought about lunging at her and grabbing her by the throat, but quickly realized that it would probably get her nowhere. "Please, Jenna, just one look. Please."

Jenna sighed. "Millie, we've been over this multiple times. I can't do that. As we told you before, the money has been deposited into the account number you gave us. You're free to leave." She walked around the bed to the door. "I'll escort you out now."

Feeling defeated, Millie grabbed her duffle bag and followed. She was about to sling the bag over her shoulder when she hesitated. "I really need to use the bathroom before I go. It's a long ride back to my sister's place."

Jenna sighed again as she reflexively looked at a door in the corner of the room. "All right, go to the bathroom. Call me when you're ready to leave."

As Jenna closed the door behind her, Millie shoved the plastic ID card, the one she was required to wear while in the research complex, between the doorframe and the lock just before it latched. She waited, holding her breath, to make sure that Jenna had not noticed that the locking mechanism had not clicked. When there was no recourse, she slowly opened the door a crack and peered out. The corridor beyond was composed of gleaming white tile floors and white walls. Wooden doors lined both sides and double metal doors with square windows set at eye level enclosed each end of the corridor. She could see Jenna walk to another door, unlock it and go in. The corridor was now deserted.

Millie gingerly stepped out of the room and looked up and down the hall, uncertain which direction to take. She took a few tentative steps into the hall as the door to her room quietly closed behind her. She was about to tiptoe past the room into which Jenna had just disappeared, when the metal doors at one end of the corridor swung open. A man in a white lab coat had entered the corridor but he was so engrossed in the contents of a manila folder, he had not yet noticed her. She slowly moved backward toward her room but when she tried the handle, it wouldn't budge. Panicked, she tried the next one over, but it was locked too.

Millie's heart pounded away as she scanned the corridor. The metal doors at the other end seemed to be the only way out. As calmly as possible, she began to walk to the doors, trying not to arouse suspicion, despite the fact that she was dressed in old blue jeans and a black Rolling Stones tee shirt.

"Ah….may I help you?" The man had finally noticed her and based on her apparel, obviously knew that she was likely not a member of the staff.

"Ah, housekeeping," Millie blurted out as she continued towards the door.

"Excuse me! Where do you think you're going? That's a sterile area."

Millie broke into a canter, plowing through the doors and throwing them closed behind her. The room was dark, save for the weak shafts of light that shone through the windows in the door. As her eyes adjusted, she frantically looked about, knowing that the man in the white lab coat would be there at any minute. Before her eyes could adjust to the dim light, she plowed into a long, metal sink on the right side of the narrow space. Changing direction, she moved to the opposite side, holding her hands frantically in front of her, groping the darkness, hoping not to run headlong into something else. Her hands found a wall, and then a door. She grabbed the handle, opened it and went in, slamming it shut just as the metal doors swung open.

"Millie? Where are you?" It was Jenna's voice.

Millie felt the wall and found a light switch. The tall narrow room was instantly flooded with the light of overhanging fluorescent lamps, and she quickly latched the door. The room appeared to be a storage space. It was lined on one wall with tall metal racks holding boxes, bottles and other miscellaneous items. A metal table stood along the opposite wall upon which sat a rectangular glass tank that resembled an aquarium and was filled with a yellowish-green liquid. There were no other doors in the room.

Jenna banged on the door and then jiggled the handle.

"Millie, are you in there?" she called. Then her voice became somewhat muffled but more urgent. "My god, she's in the holding room. Where's the key?"

Millie looked about. So this must be the holding room, whatever that meant. She scanned the room, unsure of exactly what she was looking for, until her eyes fell on the aquarium sitting on the metal table. With a great deal of apprehension, she moved toward it. Beside the aquarium was a manila folder with the words "B.B. Beattie" on the tab. The initials B.B. usually meant 'baby boy.' She knew that from when her sister had her baby. B.B. meant baby boy and B.G. meant baby girl. So she must have had her Johnny, she thought. Johnny Alan was the name she had planned to give her baby if it was a boy.

With shaking hands, Millie opened the folder and began to read, but not understanding the medical jargon, threw the folder back on the table and instead peered down into the aquarium. A fleshy mass with a tuft of dark hair at one end was floating in the caustic fluid. The vapors stung her eyes as she moved in closer for a better look. Then she saw the mask-like face of her son, scarier than any Halloween mask she had ever seen, with dark lifeless eyes and a squashed nose. But the mouth....the mouth was just a hole, and where were the ears? The sight made her feel weak and dizzy, causing a bitter brash to begin at the back of her throat. As Jenna threw open the door behind her, Millie Beattie dropped to her knees and began to vomit all over the clean, white floor.

Four

Jane Riley awoke to the drone of voices, the glare of lights, and the clang of metal. She was naked except for a hospital gown and shivered on the hard mattress of a gurney. An intravenous line had been inserted into a vein in her right hand and was attached to a bag of clear fluid hanging over the bed. EKG leads were pasted on her chest, and the electronic chirp of her heartbeat emanated from a monitor nearby.

Through the pounding in her temples and the bright overhead light, she squinted and looked about. Garish orange curtains hung directly in front of her. Metal cabinets with glass doors lined the green tiled wall to her right and a sink occupied the opposite side. Above her, a surgical lamp hung like a giant white spider from the ceiling.

"She's waking up!" A female voice spoke somewhere off to her right.

Two figures leaned over the gurney, one on her right and one on her left, eclipsing the blinding light. She tried to speak but managed only a groan.

"Dr. Riley?" The voice came from a young African American woman with close-cropped hair and oval wire-rimmed glasses. She was heavy set and wore a white lab coat. "I'm Dr. Brooks, a neurology resident, and you're in the emergency room at Georgetown University Hospital."

"What happened?" Jane asked through chattering teeth.

"You had a seizure at the Kennedy Center," the other voice replied. It was a familiar voice but she could not readily place it. "Do you remember?"

"A seizure?" She tried in vain to retrace the last several hours of her life.

"You've been given an anticonvulsant." The resident was enunciating each word as if Jane was hard of hearing. "Do you understand?"

She closed her eyes. "Could you please get this light out of my face and get me a blanket?"

When the resident reached up and swung the overhead lamp away, Jane discovered that the other voice belonged to Josh Hanley. He was standing by her gurney in a tuxedo with the top of his shirt open and the undone bow tie hanging lopsided around his neck.

"Josh Hanley?" she asked as the resident unfurled a blanket and placed it over her. "What are you doing here?"

"When you fell to the floor, you hit your head pretty hard. I rode with you in the ambulance. I was a paramedic before I went to medical school, you know," he replied.

"That was great of you," she managed.

"Have you ever had a seizure before?" Brooks asked, clipboard in hand.

"No." Jane rubbed her forehead against the persistent throbbing.

"Do you have any other medical problems," Brooks pressed.

"No, but it feels like someone hit me on the head with a hammer!"

Brooks noted that on her clipboard. "They'll be taking you for a brain scan, an MRI," she said, continuing to write. "My attending is Dr. David Wallenberg. He's a neurologist here on faculty at Georgetown, and he will be seeing you shortly."
She then left the room.

Jane reached over and felt a lump the size of a golf ball on the right side of her head, just above the ear. "Ouch."

She looked at Josh. "I can't thank you enough for helping me like that."

He shrugged. "No thanks needed."

"Do you have any idea what's going on?" she asked.

"Not yet. You've only been examined by the neurology resident so far. She will be back with Dr. Wallenberg soon."

Jane felt somewhat embarrassed. She had not seen Hanley for several years and now he was keeping a vigil at her bedside.
"I'm in good hands here. Why don't you call it a night?" She looked at her watch. "It's almost midnight. I'm sure you have better things to do."

He smiled. "Do you want me to call your family?"

His question made her realize how alone she was. With her parents and husband deceased, her family consisted of a daughter

Elizabeth, who was away at college in California, and a younger brother who lived in Manhattan. "No, thank you. I'll call my daughter later. It will be less traumatic for her to hear about all this from me."

He nodded. "Okay, then. I guess I'll be going. If you need anything, just have me paged."

As he left, her nurse came bustling in. A flowered smock draped her large frame and her short bleached hair was tightly spiked. "They're ready for you in Radiology. You'll have to remove your jewelry for the MRI."

Jane impulsively reached for her mother's pearls and breathed a sigh of relief. With shaking hands, she undid the clasp and pulled off the matching earrings. Her throat tightened as she studied the diamond engagement ring and matching wedding band. It had been two years since her husband's death, and during that time, the rings had not been removed once. Now the pain that had initially crushed her returned in sharp stabs of recollection: the sad face of the policeman at the door, the disbelief, the overwhelming sense of loss. She carefully worked the rings from her finger then took off her watch.

"Do you have a safe place for these?" The break in her voice was almost imperceptible.

The nurse pulled open a drawer, and took out a manila envelope. "Give them to me, honey, and I'll make sure they're put in a safe place." She dumped the precious gems into the envelope, licked the cover, and sealed it.

When she disappeared behind the curtain, Jane wondered if she would ever see her jewelry again. Her thoughts were then quickly refocused on the differential diagnosis of an unexplained seizure. The worse case scenario was a brain tumor or aneurysm. Aside from that, metabolic abnormalities had been ruled out. If an infection such as meningitis or encephalitis was present, she would be much more incapacitated. Then there were those seizures that occurred without an explanation. Her anxiety had peaked by the time a tall, slightly bent, elderly man with thick glasses and a bow tie opened the curtain. He was completely bald save for a rim of gray hair around his ears. The sleeves of his white lab coat were rolled up to the elbows and a black bag was firmly wedged under his right arm. Dr. Brooks followed close behind.

"Hello Jane," he said gently as he took her hand.

She looked into the grandfatherly face and instantly recognized the neurology professor who had been on faculty for over thirty years. "Dr. Wallenberg. I'm sure glad to see you."

Their first encounter had occurred when she was a medical student, but years later, even after she had joined the faculty at the university, she could never call him by his first name.

"Dr. Brooks has gone over your case with me in great detail. Do you remember anything about what happened?" he asked.

She shook her head. "No."

"Do you recall experiencing any peculiar smells or having visual problems this evening?"

"No, sir."

"Amnesia is common after a *grand mal* seizure," he said to Brooks, then back to Jane: "You may never fully remember what happened, but apparently we have plenty of...ah..well, plenty of witnesses," he replied.

Jane felt her face warm. "Oh…how embarrassing."

After removing several instruments from his black bag, Wallenberg began a thorough exam of her nervous system. The methodical and well-practiced examination evaluated every major component of the nervous system, from her head to her toes. When he was finished, he carefully returned the instruments to his bag. "I agree with your assessment," he said to Brooks. "The exam is normal."

The nurse threw open the curtain. "They're ready for her in MRI, Dr. Wallenberg."

"Jane, we'll see you after the MRI is completed," Wallenberg said as a husky orderly in scrubs moved in and grabbed the gurney.

The orderly pushed her out of the cubicle, through the noisy emergency room, and down a brightly lit corridor to the MRI suite. Save for a different color of paint, the corridor, through which Jane had first trod as a medical student, had changed very little. She recalled countless trips to the ER to admit a seemingly endless stream of patients. As a resident, she had been on-call every third night, and was expected to work straight through the night if the patient load demanded it. An internal medicine residency lasted three years, and despite all the other years spent in college and medical school, it was this relatively brief period of time that had transformed her into a physician. The brutal hours and almost overwhelming workload had been a life-changing experience, and with the retrospection of nearly twenty years, she now appreciated this as one of the most gratifying periods of her life.

Once inside the MRI suite, a technician helped her onto the narrow scanner table. He placed her head onto a saddle-like apparatus and gave her a pair of soft earplugs. "You're going to need these. It gets kind of noisy in there. You're not claustrophobic, are you?"

She mumbled "no" as she inserted the earplugs.

The technician retired to the brightly lit console that looked like it might have come from the Starship Enterprise. The lights dimmed as the mechanized table gently moved into a narrow tunnel.

"We're about to begin," the technician said through a microphone. "Please stay as still as possible."

As the table moved into the tunnel and the walls seemed to close in, a high-pitched hum was followed by knocking sounds. The table slowly moved further into the tunnel, and there were more knocking sounds followed by grinding noises that seemed to go on forever. The short time it took to do the scan seemed like hours. She was greatly relieved when the table eased out of the tunnel.

She was taken back to the emergency room and wheeled into the same bay to await the result of the MRI. By the time Wallenberg and Brooks returned, she had convinced herself that the scan must be horribly abnormal.

"The MRI is negative," Wallenberg said with what sounded like disappointment.

She exhaled forcefully. "Good!"

"Dr. Brooks will now do a spinal tap, and that should do it for the night," he continued. "We'll do the electroencephalogram in the morning. You'll be admitted to the Neuro Unit. If all goes well, you may be discharged tomorrow."

At that point, Jane recalled that she had left a pile of documents on her desk, among which was a draft of her Senate testimony on tobacco regulation that was in need of extensive editing. She also remembered that she was going to call her daughter but wondered exactly what she was going to tell her. All she had so far were negative tests. Even though a number of things had been ruled out, Jane was becoming increasingly uncomfortable with the fact that there was still no explanation for what had happened to her.

The nurse threw open the curtains again and then closed them behind her. "We'd better get moving on the spinal tap. We have a line of patients in the hallway waiting for this bed!"

Wallenberg took her hand. "Jane, I will see you in the morning."

After he had gone, the nurse helped Jane lie on her side and curl up into a fetal position to open up the spaces between the vertebrae, thereby allowing access to the spinal canal. She could feel the cold liquid being painted on the small of her back as Dr. Brooks scrubbed the skin with a solution of iodine. She then put a sterile drape over the area.

"I'm going to inject xylocaine now, and you're going to feel a sting," she warned.

Jane winced as the tiny needle entered her skin and then felt intense stinging that quickly abated. The procedure itself proved to be relatively painless and was over in a matter of minutes. As Brooks placed a small bandage on the area, an orderly threw the curtains aside. "Her bed's ready, Doc!"

Brooks followed the gurney as it was wheeled out of the cubicle. "I'll follow up on the results of your spinal tap tonight," she said.

Jane was taken from the ER to a private room in the Neurology Unit. The room contained a standard hospital bed covered with a taut white sheet tucked neatly at the bottom. In addition to the over-the-bed-table and nightstand, a chair covered in drab vinyl occupied one corner, and a large television hung awkwardly from the ceiling. An antiseptic smell pervaded the small space. Jane fished her purse out of a plastic bag containing her belongings, found her cell phone and punched in her daughter's number. It was just past one AM, but in California, it was just after ten. Beth would still be up studying. After a few pleasant exchanges, Jane gently relayed her news.

She heard her daughter gasp. "A seizure? Are you all right?" Her voice was now an octave higher.

"Yes, I'm fine. The MRI of my brain was okay and I'm now waiting for the results of the spinal tap. The EEG will be done tomorrow." She recounted the events as she knew them, but in the end had to admit that she actually did not remember anything about the whole incident.

"Do they know what caused it?" Her daughter's voice began

to crack with emotion.

"Not yet, but they may never know what caused it."

"I'll catch the first flight to Washington!"

"No, Beth! Don't go overreacting!" Secretly, she wanted her daughter there. "Your midterms are coming up. Besides, I'll probably be discharged tomorrow. I'll give you a call and let you know, okay? You need to go back to your studies and try not to worry."

After a long goodnight, Jane hung up and rolled over in bed. Before long, she was in a deep sleep and unaware of the blood that was oozing from her nose.

Five

Josh Hanley sprinted across the campus quad, dodging the undergraduates who stood in his path. A thin crust of snow blanketed the broad front lawn and had caked his black loafers. He could feel his socks becoming wet as the melting slush seeped through the seams of his shoes. He jumped onto a salted brick sidewalk that took him past Healy Hall to the Cancer Center, a modern box-like building of glass and concrete neatly tucked next to the massive brick structure that was University Hospital. The industrial appearing buildings that housed the cancer center and hospital stood in conspicuous contrast to their gracious Gothic counterparts that had been rendered in stone over two centuries earlier.

Josh careened through the glass doors at the entrance and took the stairs to the second floor where the offices of the Department of Hematology/Oncology were located. Fumbling with a multitude of keys, he unlocked the door and grabbed a white lab coat from the back of his desk chair. A buxom woman wearing a tight white sweater and short black skirt ambled down the hallway as he was closing the door behind him. Her hair was golden blond and done up in a beehive into which she had stuck a pencil. A pair of gold-rimmed reading glasses was perched at the end of her nose, and the matching chain swayed as she walked.

"Dr. Hanley, aren't you supposed to be on rounds, Hon?" Dottie Shane glanced at her watch. "It's seven forty."

Josh smiled as he thrust his arms into the coat. The competent and extremely organized secretary for the division, Baltimore-born Dottie Shane, possessed an almost Mussolini-like attitude when it came to keeping them on schedule.

"Yes, I'm running a little late. Is Dr. Hilson in?"

"He's been in his office since about five this morning. Grant deadline, you know. Disturb at your own peril, Hon."

"Thanks, Dottie, I'll take my chances."

Josh knocked on Hilson' door and hear a familiar voice telling him to come in.

Peter Hilson was seated at his desk rapidly typing on the computer keyboard with his back to the door. The computer screen was partially visible, and he minimized the text before turning around.

"Hey Peter, sorry to interrupt," Josh said meekly.

"Shouldn't you be on rounds?" Hilson asked, glancing at his watch.

"Yes, I'm running late! I just wanted to let you know what happened to Jane Riley last night. I heard you had to leave before the awards ceremony."

Hilson knitted his brow. "What are you talking about?"

Josh quickly relayed the events of the previous evening, and Hilson's eyes widened in disbelief.

"Jane had a seizure while giving her acceptance speech?"

"Her head was banging on the floor. It was awful! Franklin Pike about had a coronary, and then a dozen doctors rushed onto the stage. The place erupted into utter chaos."

Hilson pushed back from the desk and swung his chair around. "But I was talking to her just before the performance; she was fine."

Josh's beeper suddenly chirped to life. "The residents are looking for me," he said, hastily studying the message. "Anyway, I rode with her in the ambulance. She was unconscious but stable during transport. Her labs in the ED looked fine. She had an MRI but I don't know what it showed, and she was admitted to Dr. Wallenberg's service last night."

"Dave Wallenberg? I thought that old fossil retired years ago."

Josh took immediate offense at the derogatory comment about someone he greatly admired. "David Wallenberg is a brilliant neurologist, Peter. Just because he's getting on in years….."

"Look, Josh, I was kidding." Hilson shook his head. "I'll have to see her and find out what happened."

"I have to go, Peter. We'll talk later."

"Josh, wait. Something's come up and I need to leave town this afternoon. I'm on the inpatient service next month, but I'll need you to cover it for me."

"For how long?"

"At least a couple of weeks, maybe the whole month. I'm not sure yet."

Josh gritted his teeth. "That will make two months in a row of attending on the inpatient service, and I had planned to try to catch up on my research next month."

"Your research?" Hilson chuckled and rolled his eyes. "I wasn't aware that you had anything of significance going on. After all, your last grant didn't get funded."

Josh's face burned. "That's because I don't have time to get anything done. I'm always on the inpatient service."

"Look Josh, no one else is available. You're drafted."

"But…."

Hilson returned to his computer and began to type again. "Pull the door shut on your way out, please."

Josh closed the door a little harder than he should have. "You're welcome," he muttered and took several deep breaths as he headed to the hospital.

He had stayed on at Georgetown after finishing his fellowship in hopes of being mentored into a successful physician scientist. But as the years passed, Hilson began to treat him as if he was his personal servant, a fact that Josh had come to resent. The bitter truth was that Hilson placed an inordinate amount of value on educational pedigree, and since Josh had not gone to one of the Ivies, he shouldn't expect to go very far up the academic ladder, regardless of how successful he was - at least, not while Hilson was in charge.

The cancer center consisted of offices, research labs, and clinics that were physically connected to the hospital by both a skywalk and a tunnel. Patients undergoing treatment with either conventional or experimental cancer therapies were admitted to the Oncology Ward or 'Onc Ward' as it was known.

Attending on the grueling inpatient service was rotated amongst the faculty on a monthly basis. Patients on the onc ward were among the sickest and most complex in the hospital. Their treatments consisted of an amalgam of chemotherapy and biologic agents possessing an array of toxic effects that required careful management. In addition to the stress of overseeing the care of patients admitted to the ward, the attending was also responsible for the supervision and education of the trainees - fellows, residents and medical students - who rotated on the inpatient service for the month. The attending was held accountable for all the decisions and actions of the trainees and was ultimately responsible for patient outcomes.

The peripatetic rounds started at seven thirty in the morning and could go on for hours, depending on the number of patients to be seen and the severity of their illnesses. The bulk of medical education occurred during this period, when each patient was interviewed, examined and discussed at the bedside. This traditional system of 'hands on' learning was responsible for the education of generations of physicians.

The onc ward was constructed of an east corridor and a north corridor joined together at a right angle by a Nurses' Station. Both sides of each corridor were lined with patient rooms, and The Bone Marrow Transplant Unit, separated from the rest of the ward by double glass doors, occupied the end of the north corridor. This specially designed area housed patients undergoing bone marrow transplants and those whose immune systems were severely depressed.

Josh approached a group of six white coat-clad youths standing in a knot near the nurses' station. "Sorry I'm late," he said.

They all mumbled in unison something that sounded like 'good morning' but Josh couldn't really tell.

"We have twenty-five patients to see today," Marc Abelman announced. Just shy of thirty, the slender young man with graying brown hair and rimless glasses was pursuing fellowship training in hematology – the study of blood diseases. A fellowship in hematology was taken after completion of a three-year internal medicine residency and consisted of three additional years of subspecialty training. The fellow was responsible for ensuring that prior to rounds, every patient had been evaluated by the residents, and any problems dealt with before the attending ever came to the floor for rounds. Having a good fellow on the inpatient service who could skillfully manage the patients in his own right made the attending's job much easier.

"We should start with Mrs. Newman," Abelman continued. "She's not looking well this morning."

This day is starting out just peachy, Josh thought sardonically as he led the entourage down the hall where they stopped outside a room. Gloria Newman was a fifty-three-year-old woman with acute leukemia. She had received high doses of chemotherapy in an attempt to induce remission. In the process, however, her normal blood counts had been affected by the treatment and were severely depressed, impairing her ability to fight infection.

"What is going on with Mrs. Newman, Nathaniel?" Josh asked, directing his question to the intern, a thickly built African American man.

"Ms. Newman is at day 14 of induction," Nathaniel Johnson began. "She spiked a fever to 102 early this morning and is now on broad spectrum antibiotics. Her vitals are stable and the exam is negative but she does not look well. She's very weak and has lost her appetite."

"And her counts?" Josh asked.

The intern referred to a clipboard. "White count is zero point one, 'crit 22, and platelets 10. I'm going to transfuse both blood and platelets today."

"Have we added antifungals?"

The resident, Richard Hamberg, a short, stout man with red hair and freckles nodded. "Yes, sir."

Josh took a deep breath. "She's a time bomb. She could crash at any minute." He led the way into the room and found the nurse hovering at the bedside. The patient, a gaunt woman with a turban on her head, was lying in bed shaking violently. "Her blood pressure is falling," the nurse said urgently.

"Her pressure was fine when I saw her this morning," Johnson said, his eyes wide.

Josh looked at him. "I believe you. These patients are at risk for overwhelming infections and rapid deterioration. This looks like septic shock. Let's transfer her to the ICU before she codes!"

"Systolic is at 70 and O2 sats have dropped to 85%!" the nurse interjected.

The patient suddenly lost consciousness and began to turn a deep blue. Abelman felt her neck. "There's no pulse!"

"Call a code!" Josh barked. "Start CPR!"

Before long, several floor nurses had pushed a red "crash cart" into the room and broke the plastic lock. One of them produced a large bulbous ambu bag and placed the facemask over the patient's mouth and nose while Johnson pushed a board under the patient's torso and began chest compressions. EKG leads were hastily applied to the chest wall, and a jagged line danced across the monitor.

"V. fib," Josh said grimly. "Let's shock."

Hamberg grabbed the paddles from the defibrillator, positioned them on the chest and pressed a button on one of them. "Charging!" The machine emitted a short whine. "Stand clear!" He squeezed the buttons on the paddles as the others reared back from the bed to avoid being shocked as well. An electrical current went through the comatose woman and her flaccid body jumped slightly. Then all eyes turned to the monitor to see if the jolt of electricity had jump-started the cardiac circuitry and eased their crashing patient from the edge of death.

Six

Trinity Church sat on the corner of 36th and N Streets in Georgetown just one block from the main campus of the university. The cornerstone of the Greco-Roman structure was laid in 1849, and the completed church was dedicated in 1851 by Bishop Armand Charbonnel of Toronto. Following the Second Battle of Bull Run in 1862, the church was appropriated by Union forces for use as a hospital. Temporary floor boards were placed on top of the pews, and the Sanctuary served as an operating suite. The building was eventually returned to the Diocese of Washington 1863. In 1874, the Federal Government reimbursed the congregation $350.00 for use of the building during the Civil War. For over a hundred fifty years, the church served as the spiritual home for many residents of the District, from wealthy, influential Washingtonians to slaves. Noteworthy parishioners included the first mayor of Washington and President and Mrs. John F. Kennedy.

As Father George McBrien stood before a mirror in the sacristy and began to vest for the 7:30 AM weekday Mass, an elderly woman limped into the sacristy through the back door. Her white hair was done up in a tight bun, and a threadbare apron covered an equally worn floral print dress.

"Father McBrien," she said breathlessly, "there's a young man here who needs to speak with you. He says it's urgent."

McBrien felt a surge of panic as he looked at his watch. "Delores, I have to say mass in five minutes. Is there another priest at the rectory who can talk with him?"

"No, Father, the others have left for the morning. He says it's *extremely urgent*," she repeated.

The priest took a deep breath. "Where is he?"

The housekeeper went to the back door and pulled in a short stout man with shoulder length oily blond hair.

"This is Mr. Stanley Wright," she announced. "He says he's

one of our parishioners."

McBrien noted the stained light blue parka and the thick lenses framed in heavy black plastic, but there was no glimmer of recognition. "What can I do for you, Mr. Wright?"

The young man gazed at the floor.

"Well, go on," Delores prodded, "Father needs to start Mass."

He looked up. "I haven't been to church for a long time but I need to talk to you," he said, pushing his glasses up his nose. "Just you, alone."

McBrien nodded to Delores, who slowly limped out and closed the door behind her. He then turned to the young man. "Can it wait until after Mass?"

Wright hesitated. "Have you seen the newspaper this morning?"

McBrien looked at his watch again. "No, I haven't. Why?"

"I need to talk to you about what happened to Commissioner Riley."

"What happened to Commissioner Riley?" McBrien recalled that Jane Riley and her family had been parishioners at Trinity for generations.

"She got sick last night during a speech at the Kennedy Center. She's in the hospital."

McBrien sighed. "I'll have to pay her a visit. But what has that got to do with you?"

Stanley Wright shifted from one foot to the other. "I...ah....need to confess...that it's my...ah..fault that she's sick."

Seven

The EEG laboratory was a darkened, windowless maze of cubicles lined with sound proofing tiles that had yellowed with age. Each cubicle was barely large enough for a cot. A thin young man in a blue scrub suit introduced himself as Bryan, the EEG technician, and helped Jane onto a cot in one of the cubicles. He then began to explain the procedure in great detail. In order to record the electrical activity of her brain, it would be necessary to literally glue multiple electrodes over many different areas of her scalp. He had her lie down and then sat in a chair at the head of the cot. He undid the once elegant fold, now no more than a tangled mess, and her hair fell down on the pillow. She could then feel him applying the cold glue to her scalp.

"How easily will this stuff come off?" She asked, her gaze fixed upward.

He continued the methodical application without pause. "You usually have to scrub a little, but it will come off when you shampoo."

When the task was completed, he instructed her to lie still and relax as he took his place at a console where all the wires converged into a computer. The electrical activity of her brain had been translated into parallel rows of wavy lines that bobbed rhythmically across the computer screen. The lights were turned down, and with the yellowed tiles muffling every sound, Jane felt herself began to drift off. After what seem like only a few minutes, her doze was interrupted by muted voices just outside the cubicle, and the clock on the wall indicated that she had slept for nearly half an hour. She tried to raise her head only to discover that the electrodes were still attached to her scalp and imagined that she must look like a modern version of Medusa. Bryan was no longer seated at the console, and the EEG computer had been turned off. The door to the cubicle opened abruptly, and David Wallenberg stepped inside. He turned up the lights, and Jane saw the outline of his face through her squint. As always, his resident, Lynn Brooks, was at his heels.

"Oh, sorry." He immediately pushed the dimmer switch. "The EEG is normal."

"Great." She stretched. "May go home then?"

He grabbed his chin. "I'd like to get an MRI angiogram, an MRA, to see if the blood vessels in your brain are inflamed."

"You think I might have vasculitis?" She thought he was going overboard simply because she was a high profile patient who also happened to be a physician.

"It's a possibility," Brooks cut in.

"How likely?"

Wallenberg sighed and shook his head. "Doctors as patients!"

Jane realized that he was probably becoming annoyed with her. She was, after all, questioning the clinical judgment of a medical icon.

"It's in the differential diagnosis," he continued. "But I have to admit that the likelihood is low."

She had to make peace. "Okay. When will this be done?"

"There's an opening in the schedule this morning."

"And if that's negative?"

He frowned. "We may never find out what caused the seizure, Jane. We'll unhook you from the machine and send you over to the MRI suite. If the MRA is negative, you'll be released this afternoon. I can see you in the office next week for a follow up appointment."

When the MRA was complete, Jane returned to her room to find it awash in brightly colored snapdragons, carnations, roses and other cut favorites in vases, along with fruit baskets and potted plants that anchored Mylar balloons bearing salutary messages. While casually perusing the cards on the arrangements, she placed a call to Ellen Downs, her extremely loyal and often motherly executive assistant.

"Jane, you don't know how worried we've been. It's all over the papers and the news," Ellen said breathlessly. "Did you get our flowers?"

"I know, Ellen, but don't worry, I'm fine and yes, I'm sure the flowers are here…somewhere. I just wanted to let you know that I'm probably going home today, but I'm not sure when I will be released. I left a draft of the Senate testimony on my desk and would like you to drop it off at my house on your way home from work tonight."

There was a pause at the other end. "Why Jane Riley, you are no condition to work!"

Ellen's maternal disposition was sometimes more than she could bear.

"Ellen, I'm fine, really." She pulled a crusty bit of dried glue from her hair. "Gross."

After a lengthy discussion on how Jane should take better care of herself for, after all, she was a physician and should know better, Ellen finally acquiesced.

The next call was to her housekeeper, Estelle, who like Ellen Downs, required some mental handholding and wrist chaffing before she was calm enough to listen. The housekeeper's requested duty was to bring some clothes - since Jane couldn't very well leave the hospital in a urine-stained evening gown - a coat, and some much needed toiletries. With her minions now charged, she was contemplating a long, hot shower when Peter Hilson knocked on the open door. He was wearing a pressed white lab coat with his name embroidered in bold black letters just above the left breast pocket, a white shirt, and a tie striped with the university's gray and blue. A bulky manila envelope was in his hand.

"May I come in?" he asked politely.

"Peter! What a pleasant surprise!" She tried to straighten her glue-matted hair but quickly realized it was pointless.

"I heard about what happened last night after I left." He came into the room and sat down on the edge of the bed.

"Yeah, you missed all the fun."

"I think these are yours." He handed her the envelope.

She opened it and was relieved to see her jewelry. "Oh, thank you so much."

"I found out that David Wallenberg was taking care of you so I gave him a call. Everything is negative, including the MRA."

She nodded. "I figured the MRA would be normal."

He grabbed her hand and her pulse quickened. "You know that when we physicians do a lot of tests, it's because we don't know what's going on."

Unconvinced, she shrugged. "I suppose so." She broke the embrace to put on her wedding ring and then the diamond engagement ring. "Peter, I'm starting to remember some things from last night, although my memory is still quite fuzzy. I seem to recall that you were about to tell me something of dire importance."

He hesitated then shook his head. "No. Not now, Jane. Your recovery is more important."

She rolled her eyes. "I'm fine, really. I had a nosebleed last night but that seems to have cleared up."

"Look, I have to go out of town this afternoon, but I will be back in a week or so. I'll give you a call."

"Oh….okay." She wondered how something that had seemed so important the evening prior could now be put off for 'a week or so.' "Going anywhere exciting?"

"It's a research meeting…of sorts." His beeper suddenly chirped, and he got up as he read the message. "It seems as though every time I try to talk to you, my beeper goes off. I have to run. Listen, you take care of yourself, okay?"

She smiled. "Don't worry about me, Dr. Hilson. You know how tough I am."

*   *   *   *
         *   *   *

Josh finished rounds just before noon and was ravenous by the time he returned to the office. Several patients had already begun to register for the afternoon clinic, and the nursing aides were busy straightening and restocking the exam rooms.

"You want to grab some lunch before clinic?" Dr. Nick Perone's large frame filled the doorway. The former fullback for Notre Dame had joined the faculty just a year before Josh had.

Josh glanced at his watch. "We'll have to hurry. I have a killer clinic this afternoon. Let's do *Millie's*. If we're lucky, it won't be too crowded."

The sunlight glistened on patches of ice that still littered the uneven brick sidewalks of Georgetown. Despite the residual bite of winter, Josh enjoyed the brief reprieve outside the confining walls of the hospital as they walked one block to *Millie's*, a small diner popular with university community.

The bar and grill was located in a converted row house. A polished wooden bar with a row of swivel stools topped in red vinyl occupied one side of the tight space while the other was lined with tables decked in red and white checked vinyl tablecloths. The off-white walls reflected the muted light of suspended white globes. As was usual for that time of day, the diner was packed to capacity and filled with the raucous chatter of students. Although the food was only marginally better than that of the hospital cafeteria, the service was prompt.

As two coeds got up to leave, Nick dove for their seats at the bar.

"I guess it helps to go to lunch with a former fullback," Josh observed.

The two briefly studied the menus as the waitress cleared away the dirty plates and then placed their orders.

"How's the inpatient service?" Nick asked.

"Sucks!" he said glumly. "I lost a patient this morning." He briefly relived his patient's code blue and subsequent demise.

"Oh, sorry. Who was it?"

"One of the leukemics. Coded on rounds and died of sepsis."

Nick shook his head. "She had a bad prognosis, Josh. She wasn't going to do well no matter what you did. Don't beat yourself up over it."

"I know….but still." Josh couldn't help but take the loss of a patient personally. "She was such a nice lady."

There was an unintended but appropriate moment of silence.

"And guess you heard about Jane Riley," Josh said.

Nick took a sip of tea and then sat his glass down. "Bits and pieces. What happened?"

Josh recounted the events of the prior evening as Nick grabbed several packets of sugar and dumped the contents into his tea. A white mound covered the ice and he stirred the slurry with a long spoon as he listened. "I rode in the ambulance with her to the hospital."

Nick took the spoon from the now cloudy tea and briefly put it in his mouth. "Really? Why did she have a seizure?"

Josh shook his head. "I don't know what all the tests show. I've been on rounds all morning and haven't had a chance to check."

"You did some research in her lab, didn't you?"

"Yes. She was doing some cutting edge research on cellular growth," Josh replied. "She's actually a molecular biologist by training and taught me a lot of useful techniques." He took a sip of diet cola. "Apparently, I wasn't that successful at generating meaningful data. At least, that's what she told me."

"What? Those papers were published in major scientific journals," Nick said. "And your name was on several of them.

You were doing some great stuff in her lab, right up to the time she left to go to the FDA. And then you got stuck with Hilson as your mentor." He made air quotes.

Josh grinned. "Well, I was the lead author on only one of them, and it wasn't published in a major scientific journal. Actually, it was a rather obscure scientific journal. But anyway, I lost all funding to continue what I was doing when she left. We were just beginning to understand things about cellular maturation that no one else was even looking at. It was an exciting time." What might have been, he thought wistfully.

The food arrived, and they ate in silence as the collegial drone continued on in the background.

"My NIH grant didn't get funded again," Josh said abruptly. "And Hilson scoffed at my research today."

"He scoffed? Wow, what a great word. I'm going to have to use that one."

"Nick, please."

"Sorry. What did he say?"

"He just made some derogatory comment to the tune of 'gee, you're doing research? Who knew?' Anyway, he's making me cover for him next month as the ward attending."

Nick gulped. "He's dumping on you again? Two months of attending in a row? What are you going to do about it?"

Josh shrugged. "What choice do I have?"

"What about private practice, Josh? You and I could start our own practice….."

"No, no, no." Josh shook his head. Nick's solution to any troubling situation at the university was to bring up private practice and how they could make "a killing."

"But we could make a fortune!"

Josh shook his head again. "No, Nick, I do not want to go into private practice. You know how bad it is for oncologists out there with all the cuts in Medicare reimbursements. A lot of practices are folding. We'll just have to put up with Hilson until he decides to go somewhere else."

Nick frowned. "The ironic thing is that he has the nerve to disparage your research when everyone knows he's never had an original thought of his own."

"Why do you say that?"

Nick took another sip of tea. "His research is all derivative, Josh. He takes an idea from someone else, runs with it, makes it bigger and better before they know what hit them."

"That's pretty cynical of you."

Nick pounded the counter with his large fist, and the tableware clanked. Several people looked up from their lunches. "It's true," he declared. "Look at all the papers he's published. The original work was published by someone else."

Josh recalled several recent papers that had been published with Hilson as the lead author and realized that Nick had a point. They all seemed to capitalize on prior studies, be they clinical trials or experimental basic science. He then remembered seeing Hilson's computer screen before he minimized it. "When I went into his office this morning, he acted like he didn't want me to see what was on his computer screen. I caught a glimpse of it, though. The 'something Protocol.' I didn't quite catch the whole name of it. Do you know what he's working on?"

Nick sat back and grinned. "Now that's a good question. No one seems to know. And as you have noticed, he spends an awful lot of time out of the office. I've heard rumors that he has another lab off site and is doing some sort of top secret research."

Josh was intrigued. "Really? A top-secret project? Where did you hear that?"

Nick grinned. "Who else? Dottie, Hon." He wiggled his fingers to mock her legendary red nails.

"Dottie would know; she seems to know everything." He thought for a moment. "Hum, top secret, huh?" He downed the rest of his drink and put the glass on the table. "Let's get the check and get out of here. When I get a chance, I'm going to have a little chat with Dottie."

*   *   *   *
    *   *   *

George McBrien arrived on the Neurology Unit and quickly located Jane Riley's room only to find her seated in a chair reading the newspaper in a room filled with the pungent scent of fresh flowers. The newspaper accounts had highly dramatized the whole affair, and he was relieved to see that she looked so well. His heart pounded as he stood at the door, unsure of what to say or do.

Jane looked up from the newspaper over reading glasses. She had a pencil wedged between her teeth and quickly removed it. "Father McBrien. What on earth are you doing here?"

"I read in the *Post* what happened to you." He knew his voice was quavering, and he tried to steady it. He looked about in an attempt to diffuse his anxiety. "I heard you were admitted last night, but it looks like you've been here for weeks."

She smiled. "It's pretty amazing, isn't it? News travels fast as they say."

He took a seat and studied her face, unsure of what he was looking for. "How do you feel?"

"I feel fine, Father," she said. "Why so serious?"

He sat back abruptly. "Oh….um, sorry, I didn't mean to… May I ask what happened?"

She removed her glasses. "I had a seizure, but we're not sure what caused it. All of the tests are negative."

"I see." He nodded to the paper. "And it looks like you're making quick work of the crossword puzzle."

She chuckled. "I should be preparing for an upcoming Senate hearing on the evils of tobacco, but I'm doing this instead. I'm going home later today so you shouldn't waste your time on me. Go see someone who's really sick! And please smile, Father."

His guilt was almost overpowering. The recollection of what had been said in the secret of the confessional just moments earlier resonated in his mind despite attempts to expiate it. He was forced by the unseen hand of God to sit there and attempt to smile. Oh if his thoughts could somehow be read! She would see behind the feeble smile and know the dark secret he harbored. Here she was talking about an upcoming Senate hearing that she may not even live to see!

"I'm glad you're doing all right," he said weakly. "I just wanted to stop by and say hello, and give you my blessing." And what else could he do?

With a trembling hand, he quickly made the sign of the cross over her as sweat began to run down the sides of his face. "I'll pray for you."

Jane knitted her forehead. "Are you all right, Father?"

"Yes, yes….of course. Good day, Jane." A lump rose in this throat and his chest tightened as he backed out of the room. He raced down the hall toward the elevators feeling as though he could not inhale enough of the antiseptic air.

"Good morning, Father," a nurse said as he ambled clumsily past her.

"Ah….good morning," he managed.

In his desperation to get off the floor and out of the hospital, he punished the DOWN button over and over with his fist. He had to leave, to forget what he knew. That was his job. God in his infinite wisdom, would take care of the rest, right? He had continued his assault on the DOWN button before his eyes finally fell on the lighted exit sign to the stairs nearby. After throwing open the door, he burst into the dimly lit stairwell, and with sweaty hands, gripped the chipped metal railing. His breathing came in labored gasps as the door banged shut behind him, creating an excruciating boom that echoed up and down the empty shaft.

Eight

As a rule, the clinic schedule was overbooked, the laboratory backed-up, and the patients irritated from having to wait. Josh's first patient was Lloyd Wyatt, a female impersonator whose stage name was Miss Fifi LaJones. She was a twenty-eight-year-old African American transsexual in the midst of sexual reassignment. In her role as Miss LaJones, she performed in cabaret lounges in the seedy Southeast section of the city. Estrogens had softened her male features and caused gynecomastia - enlargement of the breasts - that had been augmented with breast implant surgery. The next step was to have been sexual reassignment surgery, which would transform the male genitalia into those of a female. Fifi had looked forward to this metamorphosis with much anticipation.

But Fifi had AIDS and, as a result, had developed the dark purple lesions of Kaposi's sarcoma on her face and trunk. To make matters worse, the cancer had invaded her lungs, and had caused debilitating shortness of breath. Chemotherapy had arrested the growth of the tumors and had given her a temporary reprieve. However, the planned sexual reassignment surgery had been postponed indefinitely.

Josh reviewed her progress with the clinic fellow, Dr. Ibrahim Singh, who noted that following the initial doses of chemotherapy Ms. Wyatt's breathing had substantially improved. In fact, the patient had been able to return to the stage, albeit on a limited basis. Now, however, her clinical status appeared to be more precarious.

"She seems to be in denial about her disease," Dr. Singh declared in accented English. "Her lungs sound fairly bad to me but she denies feeling short of breath, which I find very difficult to believe. She was also not very receptive to my seeing her," the fellow continued. "And she is very, very cross that she had to wait so long. She wouldn't get undressed and just barely let me listen to her lungs."

Josh waved his hand. "She has….issues with 'student doctors.' And she'd be upset if she had to wait thirty seconds. Sounds like I'll have to sweet talk her a bit."

He rapped on the door and entered. "Hello, Miss Wyatt, and how are we doing today? Why you look lovely!"

The patient was standing in the middle of the room, hands planted firmly on hips, dressed in a long tight fitting black dress with a short gold lamé jacket. A beret of silver sequins adorned her head. Multiple gold bangles encircling her forearms clanked softly with each hand gesture.

"*We* are doing fine, Dr. Hanley, just a little tired of waiting!" She then relaxed her stance and threw out a hand. "So you think I look lovely, huh? Oh, honey you're just so fine, I guess you're worth the wait."

The fellow stood silently, hugging the chart to his chest as he listened to the banter, his forehead deeply furrowed.

"Dr Singh tells me that you think your breathing is okay, but he tells me your lungs don't sound so good."

"Been fine, but I'm losing my hair from that crap you're putting in me. Luckily, I have the best wigs in town!"

Josh removed the stethoscope from the pocket of his lab coat. "Let's take a listen to you."

"Can you unzip me, darling." Fifi shimmied out of her jacket and perched on the exam table. "Your nurse wanted me to put that thing on, but I told her I wouldn't be caught dead in that little polyester frock." Using a finger adorned with a gold encrusted 'press-on' nail, she pointed accusingly to a folded hospital gown resting innocently on the exam table. "Perhaps you have a cotton sheet. This girl don't let polyester touch her body!"

Dr. Singh quickly rummaged in a drawer in the exam table and found a white sheet. "I can not guarantee that this does not contain synthetic fibers, Ms. Wyatt," he said, handing it to her.

"That's okay, Honey. As long as it's less than fifty percent, I'll be fine." Fifi let the bodice of her dress drop to her waist as she draped the sheet around her shoulders.

Josh put the stethoscope to her back. "Take some deep breaths, please."

The breath sounds were quite noticeably diminished from the exam of two weeks prior and wheezes were now present, both signs of airway obstruction. He readjusted the sheet and listened to the front of the chest, deftly maneuvering around the firm implants.

"Are you sure your breathing is fine?" He draped the stethoscope around his neck.

"Uh huh." She replied coyly.

He looked at Dr. Singh and frowned. "I think you are right." He then turned to Fifi. "You definitely sound worse to me than you did two weeks ago."

"Oh, all right, honey, maybe it is a little worse than last time. I don't know. I just try to ignore it." She abruptly jumped off the table, threw the sheet aside and pulled up the bodice. "Would you be a dear?"

"Fifi, if this treatment isn't working anymore, there's not a whole lot of point in continuing....." With great difficulty, Josh re-zipped the dress. "…the treatment."

She grabbed the gold lamé jacket and thrust her arms into the sleeve. "I think it's still helping me and I want to continue."

Josh thought for a moment. "Okay....we'll give it another two weeks just to make sure. Please have a seat in the waiting room until your blood counts come back." He and Singh started to leave the room.

"Dr. Hanley, I'd like to speak to you." She looked at Singh. "Alone."

Josh nodded and Singh started through the door.

"No offense, honey," Fifi called after him as he left the room and closed the door. "Dr. Hanley, if I am getting worse, and I might be, I don't want you puttin' me on no...what's that thing you call it.....life support machines. You hear me? When it's my time to go, I'm making a graceful exit....just like I do on stage." Her arms went out in a dramatic gesture.

Josh was silent for a moment. "Okay....I'll make a note of that in your chart." He reached for the door knob.

"Promise me one more thing," she continued.

"What's that?"

"When my time comes, you'll take good care of me...you'll make it....easy for me."

He nodded and opened the door. "I promise."

She smiled through tears. "Good. I'm glad that's settled. Now, don't keep me waiting too much longer, honey. I have a mani and pedi at five!"

"You should be out before then," he replied, closing the door behind him.

Josh knew that the disease in Fifi's lungs was becoming resistant to treatment, and the consequence of this, a slow death by suffocation, was all too familiar. No matter how hard he tried to maintain the detachment, it was nearly impossible not to feel empathic. He knew that his job was to help his patients as best he could. Some he would cure, others he would help to live longer and hopefully better, while others he would help to die with dignity. The acceptance of impending mortality was difficult for most, particularly the young. These he had to ease into the idea of dying; the idea that, despite what life expectancy should be, one's time on earth is reckoned by God, or the fates or in whatever or whomever one had faith. Most finally accepted the inevitable, which was painful but necessary. It was painful for him, too. And no matter how many times he dealt with this aspect of his art, it never became easier.

But in the end, he would take care of his patient.

Nine

The plane finally broke through a thick stratum of clouds, and Peter Hilson caught his first view of the hilly Scottish countryside. The transatlantic flight to London's Heathrow had been relatively smooth, but the sixty-minute flight to Inverness, Scotland was choppy, as the engines of the small plane that carried him and a dozen other passengers grinded against a strong gale. At that time of year, the hills were brown with patches of snow stretching between them. A long narrow lake could be seen in the distance, with a band of fog rising above its length.

"That's Loch Ness," his seatmate announced in a thick Scottish brogue. He was an older gentleman, with a graying auburn mustache and ruddy cheeks.

"It's beautiful," Hilson noted.

"Aye," the man replied.

The plane drew closer to the loch as it descended, and Hilson got a more expansive view.

"I didn't realize it was so large."

"Aye," he replied again. "Now you can understand how a monster could hide out there for so many years."

Hilson made no reply, uncertain if the man was joking or serious, and turned to the window again. The sky was various shades of gray, but Hilson found the dreariness it created across the landscape to be paradoxically quite beautiful. "I heard the winters here can be variable. Has it been very cold this year?" he asked, surveying the heavy white clouds that floated beneath them and seemed to snag on the surrounding hills.

The man chuckled. "The weather here can be unpredictable for sure but recently our winters have been fairly mild, with snow in the higher elevations and rain down below. It can be clear one minute and rainy the next."

"I see," he replied.

The plane jumped as it descended through another layer of clouds. It then banked to the side and leveled off again. Rain began to shower the windows.

"No golf today, I guess." Hilson continued.

The old man huffed. "Wouldn't stop me. I play in all kinds of weather here."

The pilot's voice crackled through the intercom, informing the passengers that they should fasten their seat belts as they were about to land and that the local time was three-oh-three. Hilson adjusted his watch as the plane began a steady descent. Soon the tops of trees and buildings rose on either side of the fuselage, following which the landing gear hit the rain soaked tarmac with a thud. The plane quickly decelerated and eventually came to rest near a whitewashed cinderblock building with a row of large windows. A man in a dark blue jumpsuit pushed a movable staircase toward the plane.

"We're here," said his seatmate as he unbuckled his seatbelt and began to rise.

"So that's the terminal, I suppose?" Hilson asked.

"Aye," said the man. "Nothing fancy but it works."

Hilson pulled his computer case and carry-on from the tight overhead compartment and donned his overcoat. He then followed the rest of the passengers out to the staircase and into the cold steady drizzle. After cautiously negotiating the slick stairs, he sprinted across the tarmac to the terminal. Just inside the spartan security area, a man held a sign with Hilson's name scrawled on it.

"Hello, I'm Dr. Peter Hilson," he said. "I suppose Dr. Willgoos sent you."

"Aye," replied the driver, taking Hilson's carry-on. He reached for the computer case but Hilson held out his hand. "This stays with me."

The man shrugged. "As you wish. Follow me, please."

He led him out to a white van parked at the curb and opened the door. Hilson climbed into the passenger's seat. After placing the carry-on into the back of the van, the driver then plopped into the driver's seat, started the van, and turned onto a broad double lane highway.

The van streaked down the highway at what Hilson thought to be an excessive speed, and his anxiety was heightened somewhat by the fact that they were driving "on the wrong side of the road." Other vehicles flew by them at equal velocity in the opposite direction, their tires spewing sheets of water that crashed onto the van's windshield, temporarily blinding him and the driver. The gusts that followed them rattled the windows and caused the whole van to shutter.

"What's the speed limit on this road?" Hilson asked, making sure his seatbelt was tight.

The driver shrugged. "I'm not sure there is one."

By the time the van arrived in downtown Inverness twenty minutes later, the clouds had scattered, and the sun glistened in thousands of bright crescents on the surface of Loch Ness.

"They weren't kidding about rapid changes in the weather here," he remarked.

"Aye," the man replied. "She's unpredictable, the weather."

The driver abruptly turned onto a narrow road, moving away from the center of town.

"Where are we going?" Hilson asked.

"Fort Augustus, of course," the driver replied.

Hilson relaxed. "Oh, of course," he mumbled to himself.

The narrow, twisting road took them down the length of the loch, careening around stone outcroppings and small inlets. Occasionally they encountered a vehicle going in the opposite direction, which required split second maneuvering and hair width distances on the part of both drivers. Hilson's driver reassured him that, since the number of tourists at that time of year was low, the chance of having a mishap was also 'relatively low.'

The road around the loch went on for miles, past tiny hamlets and larger towns until the driver pulled off unto a gravel path that took them to a walled compound with a well-guarded security gate. The van stopped at the guardhouse and was quickly waved through the gates.

"Why all the security?" Hilson asked.

His question was met with silence, leaving him to wonder if the driver heard him or just didn't want to answer the question. He strained to see through the trees as the van made its way around a curving gravel road and pulled into a spacious plaza laid out in front of a massive complex of Gothic stone buildings. Off to the side, was a structure that appeared to be a church or cathedral.

"Where are we?" Hilson asked.

"Fort Augustus Abbey," the driver replied as he vacated the front seat and went to the back of the van to retrieve the carry-on.

"Fort Augustus Abbey?" He wondered if perhaps the driver had picked up the wrong person. "What are we doing here?"

The driver opened the door. "Don't worry sir, it's not a Benedictine abbey anymore, well, most of it isn't. There are still a few monks who live in a part of it." He pointed toward the church and its attached buildings. "The rest of it used to be an abbey school but is now used by Dr. Willgoos and his team of researchers. Come on then. Follow me."

Hilson followed him through massive wooden doors into a grand hall lined with arched windows punctuated by trefoil designs, a broad floor of marble inlay and high ceilings with Gothic ribs. As they made their way further into the building, the arched doors that lined the corridor exposed forlorn rooms in need of renovation. Impressive stonework and faded oak wainscoting recalled a more prosperous era in the life of the abbey. The corridor eventually became an airy arcade of stone arches that completely surrounded a meticulously kept courtyard.

"The monks live on the other side of this courtyard so that part of the building is off limits," the driver noted. "Most of them are fairly elderly. They take strolls in the garden every morning and afternoon."

Once past the arcade, the driver stopped at a sophisticated-appearing electronic device that was decidedly out of place in the ancient building. He stood in front of it for several seconds, and Hilson noted the flash of a retinal scanner.

"That's pretty high tech stuff," he said.

"Can't be too safe these days," the man replied as a large metal door swung open. "This way, please."

The corridor beyond had been substantially renovated and modernized. Although the architecture was still decidedly Gothic, from the arched doorways and trefoil windows to the ribbed ceiling and the marble floors, the rooms that lined the hallway contained sophisticated laboratory and electronic equipment, microscopes and computers. In contrast to the other parts of the abbey, these rooms hummed with activity as scores of laboratory personnel worked at state-of-the-art lab benches or conferred over computer screens. Hilson attempted to assimilate it all as the driver led him into a great room with a high arched ceiling and a massive fireplace at the opposite end. A long wooden table dominated the space, its intricately carved chairs scattered haphazardly around, while stacks of books, reams of paper and PCs littered the surface. Several vending machines were tucked into an alcove. Young men and women in white coats were scattered about the room, some at the table working on the computers and others conversing over data sheets. A tall man with a booming voice stood at the head of the table dwarfing the woman who stood next to him. He wore a white coat over a polo shirt and blue jeans. His thick hair was red, almost orange, with a beard and eyebrows to match.

Hilson had met Richard Willgoos only once at a scientific symposium the year before, but they had corresponded on several occasions by email. He was a world famous expert on cloning and had his picture splayed on the cover of Time ten years earlier when he cloned the first farm animal. Willgoos was pointing to the piece of paper as the woman, clad in similar attire, looked on. Hilson instantly recognized his wife, Suzy.

"Dr. Willgoos, Dr. Hilson is here," the driver announced as he led Hilson toward them.

Willgoos looked up. "Ah, Peter, so nice of you to come all the way to Scotland." The Scottish accent echoed throughout the cavernous hall. He took Hilson's hand in a hearty shake.

"Yes, nice to see you again, too, Richard," Hilson mumbled. He then looked at Suzy. "This is quite a surprise. How long have you been here?" He noted that her hair was longer and somewhat unkempt, and that heavy black plastic framed glasses had replaced her contact lenses. Even in this more intellectual mode, he found her attractive.

Suzy Fischer recoiled. "And a fine 'hello' to you too, Peter."

"Sorry, Suzy, it's just that you were the last person….er…I just didn't expect to see you here," Hilson replied.

"I've been here for about three months now. It was a once in a lifetime opportunity, and I just had to grab it. I know I should have let you know, but I've just been so busy."

Hilson shook his head. "No, it's fine; it's not any of my business anymore."

"Welcome to the Abbey!" Willgoos broke in.

Hilson was suddenly aware of Willgoos' discomfort. "Quite a place you have here," he responded.

"Yes, the Benedictines were quite willing to allow us to rent it out from them. Otherwise, they were about to lose the property."

He waved his hands about the room. "This used to be the refectory."

Still distracted by the presence of his wife, Hilson refocused on the tall, arched windows, beyond which was an expansive view of the loch. "Impressive. Those monks know how to live."

Willgoos chuckled and then turned to the driver. "Harry, leave Dr. Hilson's things in my office, please." Then to Suzy: "We can continue this later." He gave her back the data sheet.

"Nice to see you again, Peter," she said. "Maybe we can get together over a cup of tea later."

"Sure. I guess we have some catching up to do."

As Suzy returned to the table, Willgoos moved toward the door, and Hilson followed.

"Would you like something to drink, ease nature, take a nap, or anything of the sort? We have accommodations here for the research staff and visitors. It's not fancy, dormitory style for the most part, but it's very comfortable."

"No, I'm fine for now. I managed to get some sleep on the plane."

"Well, then follow me." Willgoos led him outside and down an expanse of lawn that sloped to the edge of the loch. The air was crisp if not slightly chilly, which didn't seem to bother Willgoos who was still clad in a thin lab coat. Hilson buttoned his overcoat as he followed him to a weathered wooden bench that faced the water. Willgoos plopped down and motioned for Hilson to do the same. "So, how was your trip over?"

Hilson joined him on the bench. "It was okay. I'm a bit jet lagged." He looked out over the water and the surrounding hills. The sun was low in the sky and partially hidden by a veil of clouds. "This is so lovely, so peaceful. How do you get any work done?"

"Oh, believe me the novelty wears off after a while."

"Ever spot Nessie?" Hilson asked, trying to distract himself from thoughts of Suzy sitting in the refectory.

Willgoos smiled. "Not yet, Peter. But you didn't come all the way here to search for Nessie, now did you?"

He turned to him. "As I alluded to in my emails and other correspondence, I am working on a project that is of the highest security, and I need to discuss it with you in person."

Willgoos' smile faded. "So forget the small talk. Let's get down to business."

Feeling a bit nervous, Hilson stood, walked the few steps to the waters edge and grabbed a pebble. With the flick of his arm he sent it skipping across the water. He then turned to Willgoos. "No one can hear us out here, can they?"

The other man shook his head and gave him a quizzical look. "No one is listening, I assure you. Not even the monks."

Hilson nodded. "Good."

Willgoos stood and joined him at the water's edge. "So what is this secret project you're working on?"

He took several deep breaths and picked up another stone. "I'm sure my ex-wife has filled you in on some of the details." He flicked the stone across the water. "I'm sure that was the reason you chose her to work in this fabulous laboratory you have here."

Willgoos raised his thick eyebrows. "Not so fast, Peter. I didn't know that she hadn't told you she was working in my lab. She has impeccable credentials and is a cell biologist of international prominence. I was fortunate that she chose to come."

Hilson turned. "Fine. Forget it. So how far along are you at cloning a human, Richard?"

Willgoos hesitated. "Is that what you're working on? I thought you were involved in cancer research, tumor genesis or some such. Suzy never mentioned any project involving human cloning. I had no idea…."

"I'm doing this project at great personal and professional risk," Hilson interjected. "Someone somewhere is going to do it, but it's almost illegal to do such experiments in the States. And you must be in the best position with all your experience."

Willgoos crossed his arms over his chest and grabbed his chin. "You're probably right that eventually it will be done, but I would say it's a bit premature, don't you think, and somewhat dangerous. My own research has shown that even though cloned animals appear to be normal, genetically they are not. I mean, to my knowledge, no one has yet been able to solve the methylation-sequencing problem. The ethical question is should we even try?"

Hilson was well aware that a major barrier to human cloning was the issue of DNA methylation. In normal development, molecules containing hydrogen and carbon in a 2 to 1 ratio known as methyl groups, bound to DNA in specifically timed sequences and patterns to activate gene expression in a specific order, for the formation of body organs, for example. The problem with cloning was that the sequences were usually not reconstituted in exactly the same order or pattern as they were during normal development. As one researcher had noted during a conference on cloning, it was like listening to a musical composition, then jumbling the score and trying to put the notes back in the exact order and the right time. "We know what the music is supposed to sound like," he explained, "and we can reproduce it to the best of our memory, but the likelihood of putting all the notes and rests and time signatures in their exact positions is infinitesimally small."

Willgoos himself had shown that in cloned animals, 95% of the genes were expressed correctly. It was the 5% expressed incorrectly that made the clone abnormal. Hilson had been working on this problem in cancer cells for years, since after all, weren't cancer cells clones of a single malignant cell? Certainly, he had postulated, the answer must lie somewhere in tumor biology, something in which Willgoos had no expertise. Hilson knew he sounded contemptuous. "Is Suzy generating her own tumor biology data or did she just steal the work that I've already done?"

Willgoos rolled his eyes. "Peter, please."

Hilson took several breaths again. "I'm sorry, Richard. I shouldn't be acting this way. I came here planning to collaborate with you. I didn't expect to see my soon-to-be-ex-wife here. I'm just a bit miffed."

Willgoos faced the water, and the gentle waves lapped at the tips of his boots. "I can understand that. At any rate, human cloning may soon be banned in the States. Members of your legislative branch and even the Commissioner of the FDA have taken a stand against it."

Peter thought of Jane. "Yes, I know the Commissioner quite well, and am aware of her position on the subject. She's drafted a letter to all physicians in the states indicating that human cloning experiments fall under the jurisdiction of the FDA, and she has no plans to allow them to proceed, at least not in the foreseeable future. I'm not sure that would fly if challenged in court, however."

"That's pretty ironic," Willgoos said.

"Really, how so?"

The other looked down briefly. "Oh…nothing."

"So are you telling me you have not made progress on the methylation issue at all?"

The Scotsman shook his head. "Not in humans, Peter. Have you?"

Hilson hesitated. "Well, no. But don't you think your animal data may be applicable to humans at least on some level?"

Willgoos put his hands on his hips and looked out over the water. "I'm afraid that's a leap of faith, Peter. But I'm willing to collaborate on this project of yours and see what we find." He turned toward Hilson. "I would like to review your data and see what you've come up with. I think we may soon be able to conquer this problem. I must say, cloning an animal is one thing, but cloning a human is quite another. We're talking about a living, thinking, feeling human being here, and not some laboratory animal. I am somewhat unnerved by the whole concept." He paused in thought. "So, how long can you stay?"

Hilson could feel his heart pound. "As long as I need to. When can we get started?"

"I would like to see your data tomorrow. You look like you could use some rest, my friend. I'm sure you're still on Washington time. I need to get back to the lab. Harry will show you to your room and make sure you get something to eat. I have a dinner meeting tonight with a delegation of researchers from China so I will see you first thing in the morning."

He headed back up the hill toward the refectory, and Hilson watched him go. He thought of Suzy and smiled. So far, his plan seemed to be working.

Ten

Over three hundred e-mail messages crammed Jane Riley's computer, and the in-box on her desk was stacked high with documents requiring 'immediate' attention. Despite a night of restful sleep, she continued to have a pervasive sense of fatigue but had resisted the almost overwhelming urge to stay in bed that morning.

A computer-generated agenda showed that several top-level meetings were scheduled for the day. The first was an internal meeting to discuss tobacco legislation proposals and Jane's testimony at the upcoming Senate subcommittee hearing. Although a U.S. District court had upheld the FDA's legal authority to regulate tobacco as drugs and medical devices, the decision had been later reversed by a U.S. Court of Appeals. The case ultimately went to the Supreme Court, where the justices voted 5 to 4 that the Federal Food, Drug and Cosmetic Act did not give the FDA statutory authority to regulate tobacco. New legislation however, eventually granted these powers, and the proposed plan to implement the new laws was to be introduced in Congress.

Her testimony would reiterate that tobacco was directly responsible for the deaths of nearly half a million Americans annually and outline how the FDA would implement the new laws. The hearings were just two days away, barely enough time to edit the written testimony drafted by her aides. But she knew that if the hearings were rescheduled for a later date, her opponents in Congress would seize the opportunity to postpone the hearings indefinitely, and thus delay enforcement of the regulations.

"Jane, may I interrupt for a second?" A stocky man with a gray comb over stood in the doorway.

"Lee, am I so glad to see you! Come in!"

Leander Murray was Deputy Commissioner of the FDA and

second to her in terms of power. His years of experience had been invaluable to Jane, especially when it came to making controversial decisions.

"What are you doing back at work so soon?" He came into the office and sat down across the desk from her. "I called the hospital, and they told me you had been discharged already! Don't you think you should rest a few more days?"

She motioned to the pile of papers that littered her desk. "Look at all this after just one day off. I can't imagine what would happen if I stayed away longer."

He nodded. "Is there anything pressing that I can take care of for you?"

"Well, yes, Lee, actually there is. I have a conflict this afternoon and I was wondering if you could cover the meeting on bioengineered food at three."

"Sure. Anything else?"

She grabbed a red folder and opened it. "How is the shutdown of *CloneScience* going?"

Murray rolled his eyes and let out a whistle. "What a mess. They weren't even close to making babies."

The FDA had jurisdiction over research involving human cloning technology, including its use for the attempted creation of human beings. Jane had forced the closure of *CloneScience*, a start-up biotechnology company that had reportedly been involved in experiments to clone a human. The testing had been discovered by Dr. Murray himself, and after warnings to suspend operations had gone unheeded, the FDA had sent in agents to shut down the lab and confiscate the equipment.

"Everything was pretty rudimentary, not even on the level of a good college science lab," he continued. "But from what the agents tell me, they're getting pretty ugly about the whole thing and making threats."

Jane raised her eyebrows. "Threats? What kind of threats? Litigation?"

Murray shook his head. "From what I understand they haven't been that civil. They've said something to the effect of having your head on a platter."

She shrugged. "Well, they can stand in line. Was the letter on human cloning finalized yesterday?"

A letter had been drafted to physicians and scientists across the country in response to the closing of *CloneScience* and reports in the media that other researchers were contemplating human cloning experiments. It was the position of the FDA, and the policy of the current Administration, that due to major unresolved safety and ethical issues, such investigations would not be allowed to proceed.

"Yes, the letter is being sent out as we speak."

Jane put down the folder. "Listen, Lee, thanks. I've been so busy with this tobacco thing and catching up in general that I haven't even been able to think about that."

The phone buzzed, and Jane grabbed the receiver. "Yes Ellen?"

"Sorry to interrupt," came Ellen Downs' voice from the other end. "But Maxwell Dickson is here to see you. He doesn't have an appointment but has something for you."

Jane looked at Lee Murray. "Max Dickson is here!" Then back to Ellen. "Tell him I'm in a meeting, and he'll have to wait."

Murray smiled. "Dickson has a well deserved reputation for being a hound dog. He called while you were out. He was at the Kennedy Center the other night and apparently saw everything. He's very concerned about your health."

Jane rolled her eyes. "Yes, I'm sure he is!" she said sarcastically. "I ran into him there, and it was quite a scene. He's frantic over the approval of his company's drug, LNC-33. I hear he was the one who pushed the company to devote significant resources to develop it. If things don't work out, he'll probably be out of a job."

Murray sat back in the chair. "It apparently did cause some excitement in the oncology community, but I think it's gotten some mixed reviews from those in the know at the National Cancer Institute. I think some prominent oncologists would still like to see it approved, though."

"What do you suggest I do, Lee?"

He chuckled. "I think you have to rely on the judgment of the primary reviewers of the application. You don't have time to review the data yourself ,and it's not your job anyway. And I don't have to tell you that no matter how much money the company has sunk into a drug, if it doesn't work, it's not approvable."

Jane was well aware that decisions made by the FDA had broad reaching health-related and economic consequences. She had learned early on that even a seemingly trivial decision could have a profound effect on world markets. If a drug failed to win approval or was pulled off the market by the FDA, its manufacturer could lose billions in sales, the price of its stock would in turn plummet, and, as a result, investors would lose their savings and thousands of jobs could be lost.

Murray got up to leave. "I need to return a call. Sorry to leave you in the lion's den by yourself. I'll see you at the tobacco meeting in about half an hour."

"Yes, I'll see you there and don't worry, I can handle Dickson."

Just as Murray exited the office, Ellen Downs carried in a tall stack of envelopes. She was a thin, elegant woman who as always impeccably dressed and whose straight gray hair was cut into a neat bob.

"What's this?" Jane asked.

Ellen dumped the envelopes on the edge of the desk. "It's get well cards from everyone in the world, I think. Most of them have been forwarded from the hospital."

Jane grabbed a handful and briefly studied the return addresses. "You've got to be kidding."

"I saved this one especially for you." Ellen handed her a white envelope emblazoned with the presidential seal, and she opened it and read the inscription. "Dear Jane, I hope you are feeling well and back on your feet in no time. God bless." Short and to the point. So much like the President. A man of few words.

Ellen craned her neck to see. "Did he sign it himself?"

Jane handed her the card. "For heaven's sake, Ellen."

"Well it's not everyday that you get a card from the President of the United States!" Ellen handled the card with great care. "May I have it?"

"You most certainly may not!" Jane retrieved the card. "I have to get back to work. These cards will have to wait."

"Speaking of which, Max Dickson is still waiting," Ellen noted.

Jane glanced at her watch. "He can have ten minutes. That's all I can spare."

Ellen ushered in Max Dickson who was bearing a large bouquet of red roses. "Dr. Riley, so nice to see you back on your feet so soon."

"And apparently you mean that literally," Jane replied.

"Please, set those down over there." She motioned to a credenza near the door.

He set the flowers down and turned. "And I must say you're looking no worse for the wear."

Jane rubbed the back of her neck. "Please have a seat, Dr. Dickson." She sat down behind her desk. He took the chair that had been recently vacated by Leander Murray and settled back into it. She had immediately noted his fine suit and expensive shoes. Both Italian, she guessed.

"So, how are you?" He searched her face.

"Fine," Jane replied, feeling ill at ease by the scrutiny.

"Oh? Great." He almost sounded disappointed, she thought. "After what happened to you the other night at the Kennedy Center, I didn't think you 'd be back in commission, so to speak, for quite some time."

"Now Dr. Dickson you didn't come all the out here to ask about my health. If this is about LNC-33, I think we've already had this conversation."

He smiled. "I see." There was a pause as he inspected her office. "Well," he said at length. "I just want to make sure that you know the ramifications of your decision. There are a lot of people out there who may not be happy if this drug is not made available to them. In a sense, I'm just warning you of that, for your own good."

Jane's eyes narrowed. "Are you threatening me, Dr. Dickson?"

His smile quickly faded. "Of course not. I'm just concerned. Look what happened the other night when those protesters barged in like that. The things they were saying. You can't control what the nutcases will do. Who knows? Maybe they had something to do with you getting sick."

She looked at him squarely. "Really? How so, Dr. Dickson?"

"Oh, I don't know." He avoided her gaze and glanced about the room again. "Maybe the stress of it all got to you somehow."

Jane was about to explode but she remained calm. "I appreciate your concern, Dr. Dickson." She was not trying to conceal her sarcasm. "But you let me worry about that. We don't approve drugs based on public opinion or fear of retaliation." She stood, walked over to the door and opened it. "I'm late for a meeting. Thank you for the flowers."

Dickson got up and met her at the door. "You're welcome."

He started to leave but stopped. "And please, do be careful."

*   *   *   *

        *   *   *

Stanley Wright pushed a mail cart just outside of the Commissioner's office suite and peered through the glass door. Seeing that Ellen Downs was not at her desk, he awkwardly scooped up a large bundle of mail and, using his posterior as a battering ram, pushed through the door into the deserted office.

As butterflies churned in his gut, Stan hovered near Ellen's desk, all the while eyeing the closed door to the Commissioner's office. That was the one place he had not yet looked. Just as he started to the door, voices emanated from the corridor, and he quickly resumed working, placing the large bundle of correspondence in the box marked *IN*, and collecting envelops of various sizes from the box marked *OUT*. Two women engrossed in conversation over the contents of a red folder hurried past the door. Their voices quickly faded as they moved further down the hall. Stan exhaled, slid the back of his hand across his brow, and pushed his glasses back. With the hallway now quiet, he put down the outbound mail and tiptoed to the Commissioner's door, his armpits damp and his pulse racing. After one last glance over his shoulder, he stepped inside. The office was a large rectangular room, with a heavy wooden desk planted firmly in front of a row of windows. Bookcases filled with volumes of textbooks and journals lined the remaining walls and a thick blue carpet covered the floor.

His first impulse was to turn and flee this inner sanctum. As sweat rolled down his temples, he took another deep breath and forced himself to the desk. It was littered with stacks of red folders, a pile of unopened mail and several medical journals. A computer monitor occupied one end of the desk, and a flock of brightly colored winged toasters flapped its way across the screen. He stifled a chuckle, then quickly scanned the desktop with his hands behind his back. Finding nothing of interest, he crouched down and searched the floor. After crawling around on all fours, he revisited the desktop and began to sift through the clutter.

"What on earth are you doing in here?"

Stan looked up with a start. Ellen Downs stood in the doorway with her hands planted firmly on her hips, glaring at him over her reading glasses. He jumped up and in the process knocked a stack of folders off the desk.

His mind became a blank, an affliction Stan frequently suffered. "Ah, ah...nothing, I...I...!" was all he could think to say. It usually worked with his mother and he hoped it would work with Ellen Downs. He bent over to retrieve the scattered folders, and a shower of pens fell from his pocket protector.

"Now look at the mess you're making, Stanley!" Ellen came in and began to help him gather the folders.

"I....I was just collecting the mail," he said, as he attempted to restack the folders into a neat pile, since at least this excuse was in part true. "Yeah, yeah....that's what I was doin'."

"Well, there's never any mail in here that you need to worry about." Her voice was stern, teacher-like in its application. "These are important documents that contain sensitive information. You are not to disturb them again, Stanley. Is that clear?"

"Yes ma'am." He backed out of the door, grabbed the bundle of mail from the out box, and clumsily attempted to push through the glass reception door. Ellen followed and held it open for him.

"Thank....Thank you," he mumbled. The mail was unceremoniously dumped into the cart, which was in turn pushed briskly down the corridor. He thought that at any moment, Ms. Downs would run after him, grab him by the collar and demand to know the truth. Instead, she stood at the door and watched him until he rounded a corner and lost sight of her.

Eleven

The monastic cells were unadorned but not uncomfortable. Hilson's tiny room overlooked the plaza in front of the complex.

"I know this isn't real fancy," Harry nodded to the narrow bed as he put Hilson's suitcase on an oversized wooden chair, "but there really aren't any hotels in Fort Augustus, anyway."

"It's fine, really." He looked about. "Ah, where's the bathroom?"

The other man pointed. "Down the hall. It's shared."

Hilson sighed. "Just like being in college again. Oh well. Thanks."

Harry nodded and started for the door. "Good evening, sir."

Hilson closed the door and looked around. "I guess I'll take a shower, then find something to eat."

A soft rap on the door interrupted his unpacking. Suzy Fischer stood before him when he opened it.

"Suzy! What are you doing here?" he whispered.

She held her finger to her lips, slipped into the room and closed the door. She then jumped into his arms. "Oh, Peter, how I've missed you." The two kissed passionately. "You were brilliant today in front of Richard. I wish you could have seen your face when you saw me. The look of shock was so authentic."

"Believe me, he doesn't suspect a thing. I made sure that he thought I was completely disgusted by your presence here," Hilson replied.

Suzy produced a high-density memory stick from the pocket of her jeans. "Take this," she whispered. "It's all here."

Hilson grabbed the drive and held it in the palm of his hand. "Wow! Everything?"

"Aye," she mocked. The two chuckled. "The synthetic methods for all the pertinent enzymes are all there."

"Excellent! Just in time to get Tanya started on The Protocol.

Did anyone see you come in?"

She shook her head. "I almost ran into Harry but managed to duck into a closet before he saw me. You're in for a surprise, Peter. Some of the data have already been published. It's been there all along, right under our noses."

"Really? What?"

She held her fingers to her lips. "I don't have time to go into it. I'm supposed to have dinner with Richard and some other investigators." She looked at her watch. "I'm already late and they'll be wondering where I am. Once you take a look at the data, you will understand what I'm talking about."

"I can't wait to see it. Tomorrow, when I meet with Richard, I shall inform him that an unfortunate emergency has occurred at home that requires my immediate presence," he whispered.

She quickly gave him a kiss on the lips. "I miss you so much, Peter. I can't wait until this charade is over."

He pulled her to him. "I miss you, too, Suzy." He leaned forward and kissed her passionately again. He knew that she could feel his arousal.

She broke the kiss but held him close for several minutes. "I want you so bad, but I have to go." She moved toward the door then stopped. "How is Millie doing?"

Hilson looked at his feet. "Not well, but she'll be okay…eventually." He looked up. "Why don't you sneak back up after your dinner?"

Suzy hesitated. "I love you, Peter, but it's too risky. Look, have a safe trip home, and I'll see you in a couple of weeks."

She gave him one last kiss before slipping through the door and disappearing down the darkened hall. Hilson watched her go, then closed the door, grabbed his laptop and sat on the bed. After booting the computer, he inserted the memory stick and opened the first file. Hilson was pleased to see that the work was well organized with a table of contents and data sets arranged in chronological order. He perused the table of contents then stopped halfway down the page and realized what his wife had alluded to. There it was in black and white: "DNA methylation sequencing in developing hematopoietic progenitor cells of the bone marrow." He read the last part out loud: "Principal Investigator…..Dr. Jane Riley!"

Twelve

A husky young man with slicked back dark hair stood inside the Lincoln Memorial, staring up at the colossal figure of the sixteenth President of the United States. Jim Leppo then turned his gaze down the majestic sweep of the snow-whitened National Mall. In the orange and pink layer of horizon, the Washington Monument stood bathed in floodlights at the other end of the frozen reflecting pool, and the lighted dome of the Capital glowed in the distance beyond. A woman eased past him guiding the hand of a toddler bundled in a bright red coat. Leppo watched as the two cautiously navigated the steep icy steps that led down to the western edge of the mall. Only a few tourists remained inside the cavernous monument, their hushed voices and footfalls echoing off the great slabs of polished marble.

Leppo recognized a tall, powerfully built man standing alone in one corner, focusing – or at least appearing to - on the eloquent inscriptions carved into the marble walls. He was wearing a long black overcoat, with a burgundy Washington Redskins cap covering his shaved head. In his gloved hand was a white and blue bag bearing the trademark sunburst of the Smithsonian Institutions.

Leppo meandered over. "Dr Jekyll, I presume," he intoned discreetly.

"Good evening, Mr. Hyde," the man in the black coat replied.

Leppo relaxed and looked around. "So how may I help you?"

The man in the Redskins cap continued to study the inscriptions as he spoke. "I have a problem that needs to go away."

Leppo produced a small carton from the inside of his jacket, pulled a cigarette out of it with his lips and lit it in the cup of his hand "That's my specialty." He squinted as smoke billowed around the words.

Hyde continued in a hushed tone. "A bird has been singing."

"A stool pigeon, eh?"

Hyde turned and rolled his eyes. "Keep your voice down."

Leppo took another long drag off the cigarette and forcefully blew out the smoke. "And how am I supposed to find this pige…er… bird?"

Hyde continued to pan the atrium. "All the information you need is in this bag. Now listen very carefully. Before you do anything, you must first find out who all he told about the white powder." He enunciated the words 'white powder' very clearly.

"White powder? What's the 'white powder?'" Leppo made air quotes.

"That's not for you to know, but he will. This information is crucial to me, do you understand?"

Leppo shook his head. "Yeah, who did he tell about 'the white powder.' He made air quotrs. "Got it. And the money?"

"Half of the money and all the information you need is in the bag. You will be given the other half when the task is completed." Hyde set the bag down, turned and abruptly walked away.

As Leppo stooped to grab the bag, a park policeman approached him. "Hey, you!" he shouted.

Leppo grabbed the bag with a start and began to run toward the steps.

"You come back here," the policeman shouted. "Smoking is not allowed in here! Come back here!"

With the bag tucked under his arm, Leppo bounded down the steps, taking them two at a time, and narrowly missing an elderly couple precariously supporting one another on the steep descent. After throwing the shrinking butt to the ground, he raced into the stand of trees and shrubs that lined the reflecting pool. Once certain that the policeman had not followed him, he opened the bag under the light of a streetlamp and examined its contents. A bulky envelope contained a single sheet of paper and some cash. He held the paper to the light, studying the Xeroxed picture of a young man who he did not recognize. Below the picture was a paragraph of information that would have to wait for better light. He then discreetly thumbed through the stack of crisp new bills, and satisfied, resealed the envelope. "Okay, Mr. Hyde, you got yourself a deal."

By then, Hyde was moving quickly among the streets that ringed the monument until he spotted a black Suburban. He opened the door and climbed into the driver's seat.

"Well?" a voice asked from the back seat.

Hyde hesitated before starting the engine. "He'll take care of it."

"Does he suspect anything?" the voice pressed.

Hyde turned the engine and put the SUV into gear. "Fortunately, he's not that smart."

Thirteen

Peter Hilson pulled his SUV into the faculty parking deck. It was Sunday evening, and the garage was nearly empty. His plane had landed at Dulles that afternoon and he had driven the thirty miles to the university campus without bothering to stop at his home in Chevy Chase and unpack. Like the garage, the office was deserted, save for a light on Dottie Shane's desk, probably left on by one of the maintenance workers, he surmised.

Hilson hadn't slept in over twenty-four hours and was exhausted. The airplane food was unpalatable, and he had refused to eat it. On top of being hungry, he could not stop thinking about his wife and how long it had been since they had made love. Despite the gnawing in his gut, he could feel himself becoming aroused yet again and fought to ignore it.

He unlocked the door to his office and threw his briefcase on a nearby chair. He then quickly booted his computer and placed the high-density memory stick into a USB port. Upon opening his email account, hundreds of messages popped into view but he ignored them and typed in an email address in the new memo window. Just as he was about to attach several carefully selected files from the memory stick to the new memo, a voice from behind gave him a start.

"Dr. Hilson, what are you doing back so soon?" He turned to see Dottie Shane dressed in a black form-fitting sweater, the tightest blue jeans he had ever seen, and knee high spiked heel boots.

"What the hell are you doing here?" he said coarsely.

"And a fine howdy doody to you too, sir. I was catching up on some work. That's not a crime, is it, Hon?"

Hilson relaxed. "No, no, of course not, Dottie. I'm sorry. It's just that you startled me."

"Sorry Hon, I guess neither one of us expected the other to be here." She studied his computer screen. "How was your trip?"

"Very productive," he replied, trying to block her view.

"You working on a grant deadline again?" she persisted.

"No, Dottie. Look, I'm really busy and want to get out of here as soon as possible."

"Sure, Dr. Hilson. Just let me know if you need me to do anything." She started to leave.

"Thank you so much, Dottie," he said congenially. "Ah, Dottie, there is one favor I need of you."

She stopped. "Yes sir, anything."

He hesitated. "Could you...ah....pretend that you never saw me here today."

"Pretend?" She gave him a sideways glance, and he knew that she was not the type who would compromise her integrity.

"Well....just don't bring it up, okay? You see, I have to go away again for a while."

"Does this have to do with your secret project, Dr. Hilson?"

He felt his stomach drop. "Where did you hear that?"

"Oh, around."

Holy shit, he thought, who else knows about this? "What exactly did you hear?" Some of the coarseness had returned to his voice.

Her eyes widened. "Oh, nothing really."

"What exactly, Dottie?" he repeated.

"Th...that you are working on some secret project. Nobody seems to know what it is. That's all, I swear!" Her voice quavered.

He softened. "Nothing more?"

"No sir."

He knew that Dottie Shane was trustworthy. "Okay, fine. I do have this thing....this off campus research project that is of top priority, and I would appreciate your discretion. The less you know, the better."

She seemed to find this arrangement acceptable. "Sure, Dr. Hilson, you can count on me. My lips are sealed. Is there anything else?"

"One other thing. You can give all my mail to Sherry," he said, referring to his postdoctoral laboratory assistant. "She will forward it to me."

Dottie put her glasses on the end of her nose and began to write on a small pad that she seemed to carry everywhere. "Yes sir, all the mail to Sherry in your lab," she said as she wrote.

"Anything else, Hon?"

"No, that will be all thanks. And please pull the door shut on your way out," he said, dismissing her.

When Dottie had gone, Hilson resumed his memo and pressed send. He was about to leave when his pager went off. I just got back and already someone is paging me from the farm, he thought. He studied the text message from Suzy Fischer that had been forwarded from the hospital paging system: "Getting out ASAP RW knows someone stole his data."

Fourteen

The Wright home was an old brick row house that sat on a tree-lined street in the northeast quadrant of the District. The evidence of years of neglect - peeling paint and rotting wood - stood out conspicuously amongst its other modest, but well kept, neighbors.

Stanley pushed through the rusting gate and slammed it shut behind him causing what was left of the iron fence to shutter violently. He burst through the front door and entered the dimly lit front hall.

"Stanley?" Mona Wright called from the kitchen.

"Yeah Ma?" He collapsed into his favorite easy chair in the living room and grabbed the remote. The new Sony in the corner stood out prominently amidst the drab, dated furniture.

"Stanley, what are you doing home so late? It's almost seven o'clock!"

The roar of a long deceased audience emanated from an old rerun of *I Love Lucy* as the five feet tall Mona Wright, wrapped in a calico apron, stuck her graying bouffant through the kitchen doorway.

"Stanley Wright, did you hear me?"

"Yeah, I heard you. I think the whole neighborhood heard you!"

"Stanley, where have you been?"

"Out."

Mona stepped out of the kitchen, her hands resting on substantial hips. "Where out?"

He sighed and rolled his eyes. "Me and some friends stopped off at *Pobah's Arcarde* on the way home."

"Well, why in the world didn't you call me?"

His shoulders went quickly up and down.

Mona wagged her head. "Well, go wash up. Your dinner is in the oven."

"I had a burger already," Stanley replied, holding up the remote as he continued to surf the channels.

"Well, I never! Here I made a meatloaf and you don't even call and tell me you won't be home for dinner."

"I told you I was going out with the guys after work today," he replied without taking his eyes off the television.

"When?"

"Last night...er.....this morning. Yeah, it was this morning."

Her eyes narrowed. "Stanley Wright you did no such thing."

He ignored her, and Mona returned to the kitchen to put away the leftover food. She returned several minutes later to find him engrossed in an episode of *Star Trek*.

"Stanley you have seen this one a million times. Now go up stairs and get your laundry. I have a rinse and curl on Saturday so I won't have time to do it then. And I'm not about to drag that hamper of yours down to the basement, with my bad back and all." She grabbed her hip for emphasis. "Stanley, are you listening to me?"

"But this is the one where Captain Kirk is disguised as a Clingon!" He protested.

"A what?"

"A Clingon. He beams to the Clingon vessel and..."

"Stanley Wright, go get your laundry now!"

He dropped the remote, got up with a huff and bounded up the stairs, taking them two at a time. His room was cluttered with outdated computer equipment, an old stereo system that his mother had purchased at a yard sale, and a prodigious collection of comic books. Posters of female celebrities and heavy metal rock groups decorated the walls. Dust balls and dirty socks littered the floor. Stanley grabbed the hamper and collected the stray pieces of clothing from around the room. When he returned to the first floor, his mother followed him down the narrow staircase into the dingy basement where the washer, dryer, and legions of arachnids and insects dwelled.

"Now let me do this. You'll mix up the clothes and put too much detergent in," she scolded.

From birth, Stanley had been a difficult child. The years of dealing with their son's special needs had strained his parents both financially and emotionally. As a result of his desire for a normal son and a normal life, his father, Gene, had taken to the bottle, and the drinking had led to abuse of his wife and son.

During his early adolescence, Stanley himself had become violent, not understanding his emerging manhood and its hormonal urges. He had mistreated animals, was disruptive in school, and exhibited other forms of antisocial behavior, all of which served to fuel his father's fury. Due to his learning disabilities and erratic behavior, he had required special schooling and, at times, medication to control his impulses.

Gene Wright had died suddenly shortly after Stanley had turned sixteen, leaving Mona Wright alone to raise her son during one of the most difficult times of his life. Eventually, however, with the persistence of his mother and special education classes, he was able to become gainfully employed through a Federal Government program for the mentally challenged.

With the dishes done and the laundry spinning, the two sat quietly in the living room. Stanley's eyes were glued to the television while Mona crocheted multicolored yarn into an afghan. It was close to ten when a noise on the back porch startled them.

"What in God's name was that?" Mona put down her crocheting and got up to investigate. Stanley followed her through the kitchen to the back door. She flipped the switch to the porch light and peered out through the ruffled-edged knickknacks. A bare, yellow bulb cast a dim circle of light that reached just beyond the worn decking of the porch. Seeing nothing of immediate concern, Mona unlocked the door and stepped out. The backyard was narrow and overgrown with tall grass and weeds jutting up through a thin crust of snow. In the vague light, a rusting bicycle lay on its side with brown stalks of dried weeds standing up between the spokes of its wheels, and the remains of an abandoned charcoal grill crouched nearby. The garbage can had apparently been toppled from its perch at the end of the porch.

"What is it, Ma?" Stanley asked, craning his neck to see around her gray bouffant.

She jumped. "Stanley, you scared the dickens out of me!"

He squeezed past her and saw the garbage can on its side. "Must be that stray dog again."

"I thought the dog catcher had caught that mongrel," Mona replied. "Just look at that mess. Stanley, get that up!"

Stanley pulled the garbage can upright, placed the un-torn

bags back into it and secured the lid.

"Well, at least this time the bags aren't torn open. Before you know it, we'll have rats again," Mona said.

The two retreated into the house, and soon thereafter Stanley retired to his room. Mona went to the basement to put the clothes in the dryer so they would be ready for Stanley in the morning. She was about to climb the stairs when a blast of cool air stopped her. The bare 60-watt bulb dangling from the ceiling lit only the washer and dryer, leaving the recesses of the basement deep in shadow. Feeling somewhat uneasy, Mona grabbed a flashlight from a shelf near the stairs, and clicked the switch. Only a feeble light emanated from the tiny bulb.

She smacked the light in the palm of her hand. "Damn flashlights. Never work when you need them to."

Holding the weak light in front of her, she began a foray into the darker reaches of her basement. She stumbled amongst boxes and discarded toys before finding the source of the air leak. One of the narrow, ceiling-height basement windows was open the few inches permitted by the hinge mechanism. "Well, what in the world? How did that get opened?"

She grabbed an old chair and climbed up on it. Despite the limited height of the basement ceiling, she was just barely able to reach the end of the metal frame and, with some effort, slammed the window shut.

"There." She stretched further to push the latch into a lock position.

Once back on the main level of the house, she turned out the lights and headed up to her bedroom. Upon completion of her nightly rituals, including the application of a mint green face mask and hair wrap, Mona had just turned out the lights when another noise startled her. She stopped, held her breath and listened. The sound of metal scraping against metal emanated from somewhere on the first floor.

"Now I'm spooked," she whispered to herself. "The garbage can, the basement window, and now this!"

Wondering why anyone would want to break into her humble home, the shabbiest one on the block, she quickly donned her flannel bathrobe and quietly opened her door. A nightlight softly illuminated the hallway, and only the top of the staircase was visible. Stanley's room was just across the hall past the staircase. His door was closed, and the sonorous breathing coming from within indicated that he was fast asleep. Mona tiptoed across the hall, wincing with every moan and creak of the floorboards, and tried to turn the knob. The door was locked.

"Stanley!" She whispered harshly, jiggling the knob. "Stanley Wright, unlock this door at once! Stanley wake up!"

The scraping sound suddenly stopped, and she thought she heard a door creak open. The chill of panic stabbed her and she raced back to her room. In darkness, she threw open the closet door.

"Oh Gene, where did you put that?" she whispered, groping about in the darkness until her hand rested on the cold metal of the double barrel shotgun. She pulled the heavy weapon from the corner, battling dresses and coats, and finally wrenched it free. She un-cocked the barrel while cradling the wooden handle in her arm, and frantically foraged among the panties and socks in the top drawer of the dresser.

"I never thought you would ever come in handy," she whispered, pulling out a box of buckshot and filling the barrels with trembling hands. "I hope you still work."

Mona cocked the gun and tiptoed into the hall. With her heart about to leap from her chest, she listened at Stanley's door once again. The snoring continued without interruption. After hesitating for several minutes, she slowly descended the stairs, taking them one at a time. The streetlights filtered through the shears over the windows, bathing the first floor in a ghostly blue. Seeing that the living room was empty and the front door was secure, Mona crept down the hall past the dining room to the kitchen door where she stopped and listened. The scraping sound had started again, but this time the pitch was higher and it was coming from the other side of the kitchen door. Waves of adrenaline sent her heart pounding harder. Her breaths came in short, quick gasps as streams of sweat ran down her cheeks, forming narrow gouges in the facemask. She quickly wiped the stinging goo from her eyes, and, with the shotgun held aloft, kicked the door open with all her might, sending it banging against the adjacent wall.

"Who's there?" She screamed, lunging into the kitchen with the shotgun in front of her. Her hands shook violently and the hairs on the back of her neck stood erect as she swung the gun about, searching the dimly lit kitchen through its site. Her gaze rested on the window above the sink where she stopped, and slowly lowered the rifle. There in the light of a streetlamp, a branch of an old locus tree chafed against the glass as a gentle breeze rocked it back and forth.

Mona chuckled at her own silliness. "Well, for land's sake."

Then a sudden thud on the back porch startled her again. She gasped and jerked the shotgun up, this time toward the window in the back door just in time to see a human shadow flicker past the curtains. Her chest tightened, and she couldn't breathe. With her eyes closed, she held her breath and squeezed the trigger. The explosion threw her back against the wall, and the buckshot ripped through the curtains, shattering the glass panes, and sending a cascade of shards and splinters showering over the porch. For a moment, Mona could only hear ringing in her ears and smell the pungent scent of exploded gunpowder. She stood motionless against the wall, still grasping the spent weapon, not daring to move.

"What in the hell is going on here?" said a voice.

Mona Wright's heart rose into her throat. She violently swung the rifle again toward it.

"Ma, it's me! Don't shoot!" Stanley turned on the lights and stood there in his underwear, his hands held defensively in front of his chest. "What was that noise? Did you…" His voice trailed off as he inspected what was left of the back door. All of the English pane windows had been blown out and replaced with a large, jagged opening. The back porch and yard beyond could be seen through a haze of blue smoke and the shredded knickknacks. "What the hell!"

"Stanley!" Mona shrieked, dropping the gun to her side. "Call the police! I think someone was trying to get into the house!"

"What?"

Mona held a hand to her chest and plopped into the nearest chair.

Stanley took the gun from her and stood it in a corner. He then knelt beside her. "Ma, are you all right? What's going on? Why are you doing with that old gun?"

"I heard this noise but it turned out to be a branch rubbing against the house. Then I saw something…or someone outside on the porch."

"Really?" Stanley looked fearfully at the gaping hole.

"Call 911," she said with shaky voice.

*   *   *   *
    *   *   *

"So you *thought* you saw something on your back porch," the officer asked Mona Wright for the fifth time as he wrote on a small pad.

"I'm almost certain there was someone there," she replied.

"Almost certain?" The officer prodded.

"Well….certain. Yes, I'm certain," Mona said with a bit more confidence.

"Could you describe this person?"

"Well….not really. I mean I just saw the shadow of someone….on the back porch." She motioned as Stanley began to hammer a board over the broken window causing the officer to wince with each blow.

"I see. And you say the garbage can was knocked over earlier in the evening and then you found a basement window pried open," he recounted.

"Well…..I wouldn't say it was *pried* open" she noted.

The officer stopped writing. "Uh huh. So you just *think* someone was prowling around your house tonight. You didn't actually *see* anyone."

"Well….yes…..I think."

The officer nodded as he banged the end of his pen against the pad. "So tell me, Mrs. Wright, is that gun of yours registered?"

"Registered?" She looked over at the ancient firearm that was now propped in a corner of the kitchen. "I….I…don't know, Officer."

"I see." The policeman closed his notebook just as a svelte young cop came through the back door. "Anything Reggie?"

"Neal, I think you should come take a look at this," he replied.

"What is it?" Mona asked, following them out onto the porch with Stanley close behind her. By now her face mask had cracked into a mosaic and the hair wrap made her look somewhat like a shorter version of the Bride of Frankenstein. She hugged her thin bathrobe against the cold.

The blast and sirens had awakened the neighbors on both sides of the house, and they now stood on their back porches watching the drama unfolding at the Wright house.

"The neighbors see anything?" Neal asked as he followed Reggie around the corner of the house. They stopped beneath the kitchen window.

"Not that they'll admit to." Reggie stooped and positioned his flashlight over several large footprints in the crust of snow under the locus tree. "Look at these."

Neal stooped to look, then took out a measuring tape. "What size shoe does your son wear?"

"Eight and a half," Stanley spoke up.

"This is at least a ten," he remarked. "And looks fresh." The policemen stood up.

"And look at this tree branch." Reggie pointed up to a narrow limb that had a recent incomplete fracture, causing it to droop and scrape against the glass of the kitchen window.

"Looks like some moron tried to climb up this flimsy tree," Neal remarked. He then turned to Mona. "Well, Mrs. Wright, it looks like you may have had a visitor tonight."

"Oh my Lord." She grabbed her mouth with one hand and her chest with the other. "I knew someone was out here!"

"What if he comes back?" Stanley asked fearfully.

"We'll keep an eye on the house tonight, and patrol around the neighborhood. Chances are the buck shot scared him away." He paused and then added. "Ma'am, please be careful with that gun."

After seeing the police officers off, Mona and Stanley returned to the house.

"Stanley, you sleep in my room tonight, in your father's bed." Mona insisted. "We'll keep the gun on the floor between us....loaded....just in case."

Fifteen

Peter Hilson's hands shook as he drew the light blue liquid into a syringe.

"How's it look?" Suzy Fischer asked anxiously as she peered over this shoulder, hugging a clipboard to her chest. She had arrived from Scotland the week before under the guise of coming home to a family funeral. But she knew that Richard Willgoos was no fool. He knew exactly why she was leaving, and she was well aware of the eventual repercussions of her actions.

"It is a very pure batch according to the chromatographic analysis," he replied, gingerly flicking the syringe with his finger to shake the bubbles to the top. He then pushed the plunger further into the syringe to drive the small pocket of air out through the needle. A drop of the liquid oozed from the tip of the needle when all the air bubbles had been evacuated. "Five cc's, correct?"

Fischer glanced at a clipboard and flipped up a page. "Based on a weight of 185 pounds, five cc's of a 10% solution is the correct dose." She hesitated. "You know, Peter, I have been waiting for this day for a long time just as you have, but I must confess I'm a little unnerved." She paused as Hilson pushed the plunger to the 5 cc mark. "This has never been done in humans before. We don't know exactly what's going to happen when the enzymes are mixed together. Perhaps we should test it on an animal first….just to be sure."

The synthesis of activating enzymes was based on the data generated in Willgoos' lab and had been more complicated than Hilson ever imagined. He discovered that meticulously maintaining a proper acid-base balance, temperature and concentration of key elements such as potassium and magnesium had been crucial to the process. However, the purification of the final product had been accomplished in just one week with his laboratory technicians essentially working around the clock. He let out his breath and carefully recapped the needle. After handing the syringe to Jenna who had been waiting nearby, he turned to his wife. "What are you saying, Suzy?"

She hesitated, not wanting to spoil the moment. "I'm just a little nervous about all of this, that's all. I just don't want to put two lives in danger."

Hilson grabbed the bridge of his nose and began to massage it. He always did this, she knew, when he was becoming frustrated, especially with her. "You told me that Richard had tested this in humans."

"Not this formulation," she quickly said. "Not mixed together like this."

He lowered his hand. "Perhaps you should have thought about that months ago when you were working in his lab," he said evenly. "Is there any reason to believe that the enzymes will act differently when combined? After all, the native enzymes are normally combined in the blood stream, right?"

Her cheeks burned; she had managed to provoke her high-strung husband at an important moment of his career. Originally trained in obstetrics and genetics, she had first met Hilson at Harvard where she was doing postgraduate research on the molecular genetics of inherited diseases. She had instantly fallen in love with her brilliant and strikingly handsome mentor. The fact that he was married at the time had no bearing on her desires. She eventually shifted her research focus and joined his laboratory. As far as her career was concerned, it had been a conversion to the true faith, and she became a sycophant of unparalleled loyalty, doing whatever he wanted, whenever he wanted it. Her devotion went far beyond what was usually required of a postdoctoral research associate. She had kept long hours in the lab, essentially abandoning any semblance of a social life outside of his orbit, and when he left Harvard and headed to Washington, she pulled up roots and followed him. Then late one night when he complained that his wife was not giving him what he wanted, she obliged him, right on the desk in his office. Forever smitten, she was determined to have him as her own and did what she could to euthanize his already failing marriage. At her insistence, the two became husband and wife almost immediately after his divorce was final, and she became his full-time servant. She did anything he told her to, including spending a year in Scotland to purloin research data from a respected colleague. And unlike his first wife who had demanded absolute fidelity, she tolerated his occasional dalliances. It was a slippery slope for sure, but a brilliant man like Hilson had needs that should be satisfied expeditiously so he could get on with his important research. So what if he slept with other women, as long as he came back to her.

"Well, yes, I suppose you have a point," she replied, her concern still not fully assuaged.

He nodded. "Good, then we agree that additional testing is unnecessary. Besides, our patient has signed a consent form acknowledging that this particular combination has never been tested in humans before."

"But I don't know if she fully understands that. She's focused on getting her money."

Hilson shook his head. "Then you can stay here while we go in." He turned to Jenna. "Okay, Jenna, this is it. This is a very special moment. We are about to make history."

Jenna smiled and nodded. She placed the syringe on a tray and left the lab. Fischer followed Hilson and Jenna out of the lab, through double doors and into the corridor. The last thing she wanted was to be sidelined while the attractive and amply endowed Jenna shared in her husband's moment of triumph. Hilson stepped ahead and stopped at one of the wooden doors that lined the corridor. He smiled at his wife, a sign that he had forgiven her brief apostasy, rapped on the door and then opened it. He walked into the room and held the door open for the others. A young woman sat propped up in the bed with a celebrity gossip rag draped over her protruding belly. She was somewhat overweight, her face studded with acne scars, and her shoulder length blond hair was dark at the roots. Her jaws vigorously worked on a plug of pink chewing gum.

"Hi Tanya, how are you feeling today?" Hilson asked.

Tanya looked up and shrugged. "Fine."

He nodded. "Good. Are you ready to proceed with the protocol?"

Tanya put her magazine aside. "I'm as ready as I'll ever be."

"You've read the consent form and understand what we are about to do?" Fischer cut in.

Tanya nodded and continued to chomp. She then blew a small pink bubble that smacked against her lips.

"Do you have any questions?" Fischer persisted.

"When do I get my money?" she asked, scratching her elbow.

"We've already discussed that, Tanya. When the protocol is complete, you will get your money," Hilson replied.

Tanya offered her arm to Jenna. "Fine. Let's just get this over with. I need the cash."

Sixteen

The hearing on tobacco regulation was held in the Dirksen
Senate Office Building, a square, marble-clad structure located in
the shadow of the Capital. Jane entered the paneled chamber
accompanied by her assistant commissioner for legislative
affairs, attorney Donald Hart, a lanky thirty-seven year old New
Yorker, her deputy commissioner Lee Murray, and a cadre of
executive aides. The Commissioner's testimony was to be
delivered first, followed by an interrogatory by the twelve-
member senate subcommittee. A rebuttal would then follow by
the tobacco industry and its lobby. The hearings would proceed
until all business had been completed, with breaks given at the
discretion of the chair.

The subcommittee members were seated behind elevated
"choir stalls" at the front of the chamber. A long table, covered
with a floor-length, Kelley-green cloth and decorated with
nameplates and microphones, sat in front of the stalls.

Jane found her nameplate in the center of the table and sat
down, flanked on either side by Hart and Murray. While waiting
for the hearing to start, she surveyed the standing-room only
crowd and found an austere group of well-dressed gentleman
sitting behind and to her left who she immediately recognized as
highly paid tobacco company executives and their counsel.
Interspersed among the throng were members of the health care
industry, prominent scientists, and the curious public who had
come to watch. Video cameras were scattered throughout the
chamber to record the proceedings and allow live broadcast to
the world via C-SPAN. Senator Alan Levinson, a Democrat
from Minnesota, sat as chair of the subcommittee. Though small
in stature, he was a firebrand widely known for his liberal
leanings and open disdain for the tobacco industry.

With several bangs of a gavel, Senator Levinson began the
proceedings with a few introductory remarks following which he

instructed Jane to begin her testimony.

Suddenly, a woman at the back of the chamber sprang to her feet and began shouting. She had brilliant red hair and was accompanied by a small group of protestors who stood with her. "Jane Riley denies cancer patients life-saving treatments!" they shouted in unison over and over again as they held up a large sign indicating that they were members of the CanAct Group. The audience began to stare, and a generalized murmur filtered through the chamber.

"Order, order! We will have no more outbursts from the audience. The Capital Police will please remove these people from the chamber at once!" Levinson roared.

Leander Murray leaned close to Jane. "They're back!" he whispered.

Jane rolled her eyes but did not comment as the Capital Police rounded up the protestors and forcefully escorted them out of the chamber. "Your days are numbered, Riley!" a man with curly hair and thick glasses shouted as he was pulled through the door.

"Sorry for that outburst, Dr. Riley. Now, hopefully without further interruption, you may begin your testimony," Levinson intoned.

Jane's testimony was entered into the record. She began by describing the hazards of tobacco use, its well-known addictive properties and its impact on the health of Americans. She concluded by outlining her plans for the implementation of the new law and urged the members of the committee to 'do the right thing.'

When she finished, the chamber erupted with applause, most of the crowd rising in a standing ovation. The tobacco company executives and their counsel whispered to one another as the tumult took place around them.

"Order! Let's have order, please," Senator Levinson instructed. The ruckus slowly died and the chamber fell silent again. "Thank you for your informative testimony, Dr. Riley. We will now proceed to the interrogatory. I would invite the ladies and gentleman of the committee to question Dr. Riley about her proposals. The chair now yields the floor to my distinguished colleague, Senator Rawlings."

Jane leaned over and mumbled to Lee Murray, making sure she was out of range of the microphone. "Here we go!"

Senator Jeremiah Rawlings, whose family's fortune was

derived from the very same product the FDA was proposing to regulate, had limped into the chamber several minutes into the testimony and now sat back in the thick leather chair. Although just shy of eighty, he cut an imposing figure, with his square-jawed face framed by a thick white mane. Now in the midst of his fifth term in office, he had foiled the Commissioner's regulatory efforts at every turn.

He leaned over the microphone, arms folded in front of him. "Well, Miss Riley, that was quite a little speech you gave there," he intoned in an exaggerated Southern drawl.

"Excuse me, Senator Levinson," Senator Frederick Hines interrupted. "I would ask that the gentleman from North Carolina address the gentle lady by her proper title, that being *Doctor* Riley." He smiled at Jane and winked.

"Senator Hines, you're out of order," Levinson noted. "But since you're right, as you almost always are, I'll let it slide."

The audience chuckled.

"Senator Rawlings, you will address the gentle lady by her appropriate title," Levinson instructed.

"Oh, of course. The gentle lady will excuse me. *Doctor* Riley." He continued then paused.

"Senator, do you have a question for the gentle lady?" Levinson asked.

After an aid had whispered in his ear, the senator spoke up.

"Dr. Riley, do you know, or have you even thought about the economic impact this law and your proposed implementation would have on these United States?"

"Senator, we are still in the process of calculating the economic impact of the new regulations, so I don't have those data yet."

"So you don't know. Is that what you're telling this committee?" He looked up and down the dais to his colleagues.

"Yes, that's what I have just indicated, sir," Jane delivered calmly.

"I didn't think you would." He gave a satisfied nod, then leaned into the microphone, his voice now tinged with rage. "I suppose you are aware of how much this industry has spent on litigation and how much it will have to pay over the next twenty five years. I would submit to you, *Doctor* Riley, that your proposed implementation of this new law would have an extremely negative impact on our economy, and in particular, those states whose economy is heavily dependent on tobacco production! And I would also point out that this charade you call regulation will be about as effective as prohibition was! This is a free country, Dr. Riley, and some people chose to smoke."

There was a brief, but anticipated, sprinkling of applause from tobacco sympathizers.

"Order!" Senator Levinson banged the gavel. "Dr. Riley, would you like to respond?"

Incensed, Jane took a deep breath. "I would submit to *you*, Senator Rawlings, that a price cannot be affixed to the health and welfare of a nation, particularly of its children. The regulations that we are proposing would actually result in a decreased number of tobacco users and in the long run, decreased amounts of funds spent treating the diseases caused by tobacco use. This will in turn significantly reduce the burden on the Medicare and Medicaid systems, which as everyone in this chamber knows are hard pressed to meet the needs of elderly and poor Americans as it is. As a result, we would see a favorable impact on the economy in the coming years. I would also like to remind you that my job is to ensure that the public health is protected, and that is what I intend to do! I hope, sir, that I have adequately addressed your concerns."

Senator Rawlings did not reply. The great mop of white hair made his face seem especially crimson as he took a sip of water.

"Do you have any more questions, Senator?" Levinson asked.

Rawlings nodded 'no' and sat back in his chair.

The interrogatory that continued from there was more agreeable for Jane as she fielded questions from other members of the committee with her usual degree of aplomb. The session lasted for several hours, and by the end of it, she was exhausted.

"Doctor Riley, I want to thank you for coming today," Senator Levinson remarked at the end of it. "I think your statements have left quite an impression on all of us. This subcommittee will carefully consider your testimony. We will hear from the tobacco industry this afternoon. This session will now adjourn for lunch." He looked at his watch. "We will reconvene promptly at one thirty."

With a drop of the gavel, the room was set free. Reporters swarmed the chamber, their microphones held aloft on long poles as cameras flashed from every direction. Jane suddenly found herself in the middle of the horde as they buffeted her with questions and stuck their black lollipop microphones in her face. She politely answered each question as she gathered her papers, placed them in her brief case and then slowly made her way through the crowded chamber. The video lights were blinding and, with her free hand, she shielded her face from the glare.

"How's your health, Dr. Riley? You were recently in the hospital. Was it serious?" A young blond woman dressed in a smart navy blue suit shoved a microphone in her face.

"I'm.....fine....really." Jane was annoyed that personal questions were being asked and considered it highly irrelevant and unfair. She managed to slip into a nearby ladies room, leaving the swarming reporters standing helplessly outside. Once inside, she leaned against the door, praying that the young woman in the blue suit wasn't brazen enough to follow her in. But the press had already found another target and descended upon Senator Levinson as he strode down the hall toward his office.

The lavatory was long and narrow, with mirrored basins lining one wall and wooden stalls lining the other. White ceramic tile covered the floor and walls and vintage globe lights hung from the ceiling. Jane noted the image of a haggard woman in one of the mirrors and thought at first that someone else was in the room. Realizing that the image was her own, she let her briefcase slip to the floor with a bang that echoed around the room. Leaning over the basin, she inspected her refection, turning her head from side to side to get a closer look. Her hair seemed dull; her skin was pale, and dark circles ringed her eyes. She rubbed the side of her face to smooth out the fine lines that now framed her mouth.

"I look like shit!" she said to no one in particular. Suddenly, a wave of nausea seized her and she leaned over the sink for support. The burning sensation in the back of her throat told her the inevitable was about to occur, and she ran to a stall, hovering over the bowl to avoid soiling her suit. The retching lasted only a few seconds after which she felt weak. Returning to the sink, she splashed some cold water on her face and rinsed out her mouth.

"What the hell's happening to me?" She ran a quick brush through her hair and applied another coat of lipstick before noticing that a large amount of her hair now coated the basin. Feeling panicked, she ran her hand through her hair, and not finding any more loose strands, exhaled sharply. She adjusted her suit, grabbed the dropped briefcase and ambled out of the restroom. The crowd was still thick and the cavernous hall echoed with the dissonant hum of multiple conversations. Don Hart stood towering over the crowd talking with a reporter, and she gently grabbed him by the arm.

"...that is our position....oh...here's Dr. Riley." He turned toward her but she shook her head and pulled him aside.

"Did I say something wrong?" he asked.

"No, no, Don. It's just that I feel awful," she whispered. "I don't think I can stay for the afternoon session."

He studied her face. "What's the matter?"

She gave a half shrug. "I don't know. I just have to leave. Do you think you and Lee can handle it from here?"

He grabbed her shoulder and squeezed. "Sure, Jane. You've already given your testimony. The rest of the afternoon will be spent listening to the tobacco people trying to defend themselves. I don't think you'll miss anything. Do you want me to take you home?" Despite the reputation New Yorkers had for not being nice, she knew the sincerity in his voice was genuine.

"No, no, I'll be all right. I can take a cab, but thanks anyway. You and Lee stay and fly the colors. I'm sure you two can handle any questions that might arise."

He gave a knowing nod. "Sure, Jane. Go on home. You do look a little pale."

"Thanks, Don. I owe you both."

Jane drew on her coat against the February chill as she left the building and flagged down a cab that took her straight from Capital Hill to her home in Georgetown. Upon entering the house, she didn't even bother to turn on C-SPAN and opted instead for the soft leather sofa in the study. Since Estelle had the day off, the house was silent, save for the ticking of the mantel clock and the muffled roar of an occasional car negotiating the cobblestones on P Street. She pushed her shoes off onto the thick Persian rug and settled on the sofa, quickly falling into a deep sleep.

Some time after four, the telephone pulled her back to consciousness.

"How are you feeling, Jane? I hope I didn't awaken you." It was Leander Murray. "Don told me you went home."

"It's okay. I feel a little better now," she lied. "So how did it go?"

"Fine. Those tobacco guys were chewed up and spit out, no pun intended, by most of the committee members except for a couple."

"Let me guess. Rawlings was very conciliatory," Jane said.

"I think it would be more appropriate to say that his nose was firmly wedged between their buttocks."

"Oh...God that's gross." The thought made her feel queasy and she grabbed her stomach.

"Sorry....I forgot. Anyway, you didn't miss much. Same ole, same ole from them."

She shifted the receiver from one ear to the other. "Did anyone notice that I wasn't there?"

"I don't think anyone was really expecting you to sit and listen to that crap, Jane. In fact, I think it showed them that you really didn't care what they had to say....I mean, what can they say? They know they're a bunch of sleaze balls."

"Well, that makes me feel better. I really hated leaving but I was afraid I was going to barf. That would have been embarrassing."

"But think of the message it would have sent!" Murray responded.

They chuckled together.

"I'll let you go Jane. I hope you feel better. Do you think you'll make it in tomorrow?"

"Oh...yeah...I'll be okay by tomorrow."

"See you then. We can get together and do a postmortem on the whole thing."

"Right. Thanks again, Lee, and tell Don thanks, too."

She hung up the phone and realized that the nausea had subsided. She thought about the leftover chicken soup in the refrigerator and wondered if she should try to eat something. Instead, she reclined on the sofa, and before long, was fast asleep again.

Seventeen

At five o'clock that afternoon, Stanley Wright stamped his timecard and headed for home. The sky outside was overcast, portending the predicted rain that night, and despite the early hour, the street lamps were beginning to flicker. The temperature had fallen, and he zipped up his light blue parka against the chilly air.

A husky man with slicked back hair stood leaning against the building with his thumbs hooked into the pockets of his blue jeans. He was wearing in a black leather jacket and a short cigarette was wedged between the fingers of his right hand. A thin stream of smoke rose like incense from the orange glow. Without taking his eyes off Stanley, he took a long draw on the butt.

Stanley drew the collar of the parka around his neck, thrust his hands deep into the pockets, and headed toward a nearby metro station. The man followed, his thumbs still hooked in the pockets of his jeans, and the shrinking cigarette bobbing precariously between his lips. Just before entering the metro station, the man squeezed the butt of his cigarette between his thumb and forefinger, took one last drag, and held in the smoke as he flicked the butt onto the sidewalk. Stanley placed his fare card into the slot in the turnstile and was about to go through when the man grabbed his arm.

"Hey kid, you got change for a dollar?"

Stanley pulled away. "No….no I don't."

The man grabbed his arm again. "Look, kid, I really need change for a dollar."

Stanley tried to pull back but the man held him firm, his grip becoming painful. "Let go of me!" he cried.

The door to the security kiosk between the turnstiles opened and a metro guard stepped out. "Is there a problem, here?" she asked, resting her hand on the holster of her revolver.

The man let go of Stanley's arm. "No Ma'am, just need change for a dollar."

She motioned with her head. "There's a change machine over next to the fare card dispenser, sir. I suggest you try that."

He looked about. "Why, thank you, officer," he said politely. "I didn't even notice it!"

His heart now racing, Stanley went through the turnstile and down the escalator, glancing backward as he went. The underground station had a massive barrel vaulted ceiling of concrete honeycombs, and the red tiled platform was crowded with commuters. The man in the leather jacket soon came down the escalator and onto the platform. Stanley moved as far away from him as he could, and nervously waited for the inbound train that would take him safely to his home in Brookland, in the northeast quadrant of the District.

When the lights embedded in the granite edge of the platform began to blink, indicating the presence of an approaching train, Stanley felt somewhat relieved. The headlights of the metal dragon illuminated the tunnel just before it sped into the station with its brakes squeaking as it came to an abrupt halt. When the doors opened, throngs of passengers spilled out onto the platform. Stanley squeezed through the multitude and found a seat near the door as others swarmed in to fill the vacant seats. An overweight woman with an oversized purse squeezed her large frame into the seat next to Stanley. The man in the leather jacket calmly entered the car and briefly caught Stanley's gaze before settling in the seat behind him. By the time the doors closed, the car was at capacity with passengers crowding the aisles. The man's very presence caused Stanley's pulse to pound again, but the crowded conditions precluded a move to an alternate seat. Beads of sweat formed on his forehead, and he futilely wiped at them with the vinyl sleeve of his parka.

At the next stop, Stanley was determined to change seats once the train cleared out. When he got up, the man in the leather jacket rose as well, and when he sat back down, the man followed suit several rows behind him. Stanley felt his chest tighten and his heart pound harder. There was no mistake: this man was following him.

The train pulled into the station at the Naval Hospital and National Institutes of Health. When the doors opened, Stan nearly leapt out and tore into a throng of uniformed clad men and women.

"Watch where you're going," a woman with a rolling suitcase exclaimed as Stanley pushed past her, knocking the case over. "Excuse me, asshole!" another man said angrily.

Stanley raced up the moving steps, shoving his way past a multitude of commuters. By the time he reached the security kiosk, he could barely breathe.

"Help! Help! Someone's after me! Help me, please!" He began to pound his fists on the bulletproof glass.

"Stop banging on the glass!" a voice crackled through the imbedded intercom. The door at the side of the kiosk opened and an imposing guard stepped out.

"What's your problem, sir?" he grunted, wiping powdered sugar from his mustache.

"A man, he's following me!" Stan whispered hoarsely, pointing in the direction of the crowd. "He's after me, I know it!"

The guard squinted at the multitude moving through the turnstiles. "Who is after you? There must be hundreds of people here!"

Stanley surveyed the itinerant throng. "He was there….in a leather jacket. I saw him!"

"I don't see anyone coming after you, sir. Now if you'll excuse me." The guard started to close the door.

"No, no wait. He must still be down on the platform!"

The guard rolled his eyes and sighed. "Okay, sir, let's go down and check out the platform." He grabbed his cap and closed the door behind him. Stanley followed him down the escalator to the platform. By now the train was full and began to pull out of the station. Only a few commuters were left scattered about the platform between the inbound and outbound tracks.

"Well, it is any of these people?"

Stanley quickly scanned the crowd. "I…I don't see him. He has black hair and is wearing a black leather jacket and jeans."

The guard made a sweep of the platform, looking behind the escalators and around support pylons. He opened the elevator doors and closed them again. "Sir, I don't see anyone matching that description. Maybe you're mistaken. Now, if you'll excuse me."

Stanley watched the guard rise up the escalator and disappear at the top. Perhaps he was mistaken, he thought. After all, why would anyone be after him? Then he remembered his confession the other day to a crime that he was involved in through no choice of his own and realized there was a reason to be afraid. His heart began to palpitate as he also recalled the prowler that had visited them the night before, and the fact that his mother was now home alone. A bank of payphones stood in the middle of the platform, and he raced to them, frantically digging into his pockets but finding only a few pennies. "Please, please, I need a quarter!" he shouted. "Does anyone have a quarter? This is an emergency!"

Several people stared but no one offered up the needed change.

"The fare machines will give you change," one elderly woman volunteered. "But you have to put more money in than you need."

Stanley raced up the escalator to the 'add fare' machine. He grabbed several dollar bills from his wallet and stuffed them into the slot. It took several tries before the machine finally accepted the wrinkled bills. Stanley punched in the minimal amount – $1.10- and as the coins began to clank into the metal change bin, a train pulled into the station. He grabbed the change from the bin, leaving several coins behind, bolted down the escalator, and nearly dove into the departing train.

The ride home seemed interminable, and the quarters and nickels dug into his flesh as he held them tightly in his palm for the entire ride. By the time the train pulled into the Brookland station, it was nearly dark and a cold drizzle pelted the glass canopy that sheltered the open-air platform. Stanley pushed through the turnstiles and headed to the payphones just outside the station. His hands shook as he deposited the correct change into the slot, and punched in his home number. As the line at the other end rang, Stanley paced as far as the cord would allow, gulping the damp, musty air.

"Hello," Mona Wright answered.

"Ma, Ma, are you all right?" he said urgently.

"Stanley, it that you?" said the voice at the other end. "Why, of course, I'm all right. What's wrong with you?"

"I'll explain later. Just keep the doors locked and....and....don't answer if anyone knocks. I'll be home in a couple of minutes."

"Stanley, what in the world are you talking about?"

"He…a man, was following me…." He suddenly felt the jab of a hard object in the small of his back and a firm grip on his arm.

"Don't move, kid," a gruff voice whispered in his ear. "Now drop the phone or you're dead."

The stench of stale cigarette smoke stung the air, and Stanley froze with horror as his breath came in short gasps.

"Who…are….you?" he choked. "And what do you want from me?"

"Let's just say, there's something you have that I want," he whispered in Stanley's ear. "Now drop the phone."

The distant squeak of Mona Wright's voice could be heard as the receiver fell away: "Stanley! Stanley, what's happening? Stanley answer..." It made a thud against the concrete wall and then swayed limply as it dangled from the cord.

Eighteen

"I just wanted to congratulate you on your impressive remarks at the tobacco regulation hearing," Senator Levinson spoke at the other end of the telephone.

"Thank you, Senator." Despite her growing nausea, Jane managed a smile as Ellen entered her office with a fresh cup of coffee.

"I'm glad you didn't stay and listen to their garbage. We all realized that you have more important things to do."

"I appreciate that Senator, but truth be told, I just wasn't feeling well." She propped her head in one hand and held the receiver with the other.

"Let me tell you, the whole thing made me sick, too. And Jerry Rawlings! Well, don't get me started on him. Most of us are behind you, Jane, and applaud your efforts. I know this Congress moves at a snail's pace but I think now's the time to act on these regulations."

"I appreciate that, Senator. I knew I could count on you." Jane felt flushed, and the contents in her stomach began to churn.

"Are you okay?" Ellen mouthed.

Jane shook her head 'no.' "Ah…Senator….I….I really appreciate your support…I….could you hold on for just a minute?"

She handed the phone to Ellen as the burning began in the back of her throat and grabbed for the waste can. Leaning over in her chair, she began to heave.

Ellen took the phone. "Ah, Senator, ah…Sir…ah….this is Ellen Downs, executive assistant to Commissioner Riley. I'm afraid something has…ah…come up…and the Commissioner has a little emergency in her can…er…..on her hands." Wincing, she put her hand over the receiver as Jane began gagging then removed it just long enough to speak. "Oh…ah, yes Sir, she's fine, everything's fine really…and….ah….. she apologizes profusely and appreciates your support, sir. Um....she'll give you a call sometime in the near future to....ah.....further discuss these issues."

She hung up the phone. "Goodness! Jane, may I get you anything?"

"I feel much better now, but I could use a glass of water." The wave of nausea had left, and she sat back in her chair. "Thanks for covering for me," she said, dabbing her mouth with a napkin. "I need you to call a meeting this afternoon of Don Hart, Lee, and my aides so we can go over the details of the proposed tobacco legislation."

Ellen hesitated. "Are you sure?"

"Yes, I'm fine. Please, schedule the meeting. And where is Stanley? He was supposed to have made multiple copies of the testimony, and they're not on my desk as I had requested."

"I'm not sure where he is. I haven't seen him today. I'll call the mailroom and see if he's hanging out there."

Jane rolled her eyes and shook her head. "If he's goofing off down there again....just bring me some water, please."

"Right away, but first, I'm going to get rid of this." Ellen picked up the waste can and carried it out of the office at arms length.

Several bouts of nausea and dry heaves had sent Jane running to the restroom throughout the day, interrupting important meetings and conference calls. Despite dismissing her symptoms to the staff as a prolonged case of the flu, she was becoming increasingly concerned about her health. The apprehension peaked when a large clump of her hair fell on the pages of a document she was perusing. It was then that she realized the arms and shoulders of her cream-colored blouse were also coated with hair. She vigorously brushed at her shoulders as if deadly insects clung to her and then frantically ran a hand across her scalp. Several large clumps came out painlessly between her fingers.

"What in the name of......?"

Ellen Downs bustled into the office and Jane quickly hid her hands behind the desk. The last thing she needed was for her maternal-prone executive assistant going into hysterics over yet another new symptom.

"Stanley's missing!"

"What do you mean?"

Ellen handed her the front page of the Post. "He apparently left here yesterday evening but didn't make it home."

"What?" Jane grabbed the paper and skimmed the article. "It says he may have been abducted from the Brookland Metro Station."

Ellen shook her head. "What should we do?"

Jane considered the options. "Other than answering any questions the police may have, I don't know what else we can do." She paused, not wanting to conjure the possible outcome of an 'abduction.' "Maybe he just took off for a few days off. He's done that in the past," she tried to reassure Ellen and herself. "I'll give his mother a call this evening and see what's up."

She returned to the document that lay open on her desk but Ellen didn't budge. Sensing her presence, she looked up and removed her reading glasses. "Is there something else, Ellen?"

"Dr. Wallenberg called twice today wondering why you haven't kept your appointment with him. I put those messages on your desk but apparently you disregarded them."

"Oh, really." She scanned the desk, lifting several documents before grabbing two pink slips. "Oh, yeah, here they are."

Ellen frowned. "We're all concerned about you. You've been under so much stress lately, and you do not appear to be well. Why don't you call it a day?"

Jane surveyed her desk and felt somewhat overwhelmed. "Look at all this work I have to do!" She looked up. "And you can tell everyone to stop worrying." She waved her hand dismissively. "I'm fine."

Ellen sat down across from her and leaned forward, coming eye to eye with her over the desk.

"You are not fine, Jane Riley, and if you were my daughter, you'd home in bed right now!"

The thought made Jane shudder. "With some chicken soup in hand, no doubt."

"Couldn't hurt. The hearing is over now, and you can relax a little," Ellen continued.

Jane stared at her desk and hesitated. She then closed her eyes only briefly and took a deep breath. Her head was pounding and she felt as though she was going to be sick again. "Okay…okay, you win." She looked at her watch and then the clutter on her desk once more.

Ellen rose to her feet. "Jane, for your own good, please go

home!"

Jane felt that Ellen frequently overstepped her bounds. She had served several other Commissioners, all men, and Jane often wondered if they were subjected to the same maternal treatment. In the end, she was able to forgive Ellen, mainly because competent staff assistants were hard to come by and she was one of best. She also knew that her concern was genuine. The woman was, after all, a mother and a grandmother, two titles that she bore with a great deal of pride.

"Okay, okay, I'm going."

As Ellen stomped out triumphant, Jane shut down her computer and donned her overcoat. She grabbed the tote bag that contained a laptop, slung it over her shoulder, and went out to Ellen's desk.

"I'll walk with you to the garage," Ellen announced as she seized the computer tote and plopped it on her desk. "You're leaving this right here."

The combination of Ellen's audacity and feeling unwell made Jane very cross. "God, Ellen, I just want to know if you treated the other Commissioners you served the way you do me?"

Ellen stared at her over her reading glasses. "Where do I start?" She began a litany of past Commissioners and their needs, from reminding them to take their medicines to shopping for last minute gifts for birthdays and anniversaries, the dates of which she also kept track of for them. "Need I go on?"

Jane suddenly felt a lot less pampered. "No. Sorry for the outburst."

Without saying another word, Ellen grabbed her purse and nearly pushed Jane out of the office, locking the door behind them. Eventually they found themselves in the cavernous parking garage. The two stood by Jane's car where Ellen absently mindedly fixed her gaze through the window at the blue and white emblem on the steering wheel.

"Are you sure you can drive home alone? I could drive you home, you know. It's really no bother," she said eagerly.

"No, Ellen, but thanks anyway," Jane replied, opening the door of her car. "I'll be fine. I'm just a little tired."

"Okay, then, see you in the morning." Ellen started to leave but then hesitated. "If you need anything, just give me a call. I've programmed my number into your cell phone. Just go to the menu and find the directory....."

Jane stopped her. "I know how to access my directory, Ellen. That's very kind of you. Now go. I'll be fine."

Ellen's parking space was several levels down, and she headed toward the stairwell door over rows of empty parking spaces. For an instant, Jane thought of calling her back, showing her the clumps of hair on her coat, and confessing how incredibly awful she felt. Instead, she watched Ellen disappear into the stairwell. The heavy fire door closed behind her with a bang that echoed throughout the empty garage. Jane got into her car, and sat behind the wheel, too exhausted to move at first. Her home was six miles away in Georgetown. Just six miles, she thought, surely I can drive six miles.

Her head was still throbbing as she started the engine of her BMW, put it into gear, and pulled out of the garage. Both the inbound lanes into the District and outbound lanes to the Maryland suburbs were heavy with traffic. She pulled onto an inbound lane that crossed the Capital Beltway two miles later and became Wisconsin Avenue, which in turn ran through Bethesda and Chevy Chase straight into the heart of Georgetown. Four more miles, she told herself, just four more miles.

As Jane eased through bumper-to-bumper traffic, the nausea that had gripped her earlier in the day began to return. Beads of sweat formed on her forehead, and when a frantic search of the glove compartment failed to produce a paper bag, she rolled the window down hoping to spare the interior of her car.

When she approached the hill above Tenley Circle, the world outside became a blur of colors. Violent convulsions racked her body, and her foot became wedged on the accelerator. The BMW jerked with each frenzied movement, as it wove its way down Wisconsin Avenue, swerving toward the oncoming traffic. A sudden sharp turn to the left sent the vehicle plunging into the outbound lanes. It clipped the rear of a minivan before careening over the curb, narrowly missing a group of children in parochial school uniforms. After sacrificing several parking meters and a traffic sign, the car crashed headlong through the window of a fast food restaurant.

Nineteen

George McBrien stood in the sacristy of Trinity Church when Delores Del Torto burst in wielding a newspaper in her uplifted hand. "It's on the news and in The Post," she announced breathlessly, handing him a newspaper. "Did you see this? The young man who was here the other day has gone missing!"

McBrien's hands shook as he skimmed the article. A picture of Stanley Wright, ostensibly an ID photo judging from the quality, stared back at him with a serious, almost pained look. McBrien's stomach burned, and he began to feel faint. "Jesus, Mary and Joseph," he whispered. The story noted that Wright had mysteriously disappeared from the Metro station in the Brookland section of the city the evening prior. The piece went on to describe him and what he was wearing when last seen. It also mentioned that he had voiced concern to his mother, Mona Wright, in a phone conversation earlier that evening that someone may have been following him. The piece went on to say that he was a federal employee with the Food and Drug Administration. A number followed for anyone having information about the missing man.

McBrien's mind raced as he trotted back to the rectory. His years at the seminary had not prepared him mentally for what was now happening. These situations were not entirely unfamiliar to him, as they had been discussed and dissected, but it had been in an abstract or historical context. In medieval times, confessors were regularly tortured or thrown off bridges for not disclosing to jealous kings what their queens had confessed. Now he was on his own, bound by the seal of confession, a sacred vow he had taken at his ordination, and could not divulge Stanley Wright's confession to anyone. His hands shook as he fumbled to unlock the door to the rectory and when he had finally conquered the stubborn mechanism, nearly stumbled into the front hall. The other priests with whom he shared the rectory were out on other duties. Save for the ticking of the old clock in the reception room, the rectory was quiet.

He raced to the kitchen where a small television used by the housekeeper sat on the counter. He pressed the on button and the television came to life just as the weatherman was completing his forecast. "Come on, come on," McBrien whispered. Next came the sports report, and he paced up and down nervously, watching the scores flash across the screen. After the business report, the anchor finally intoned the words he was waiting to hear. "And now to recap our top stories….." And there it was, the story of Stanley Wright's disappearance. The piece was essentially a repeat of what was in The Post. The camera abruptly cut to a short, stocky woman with her gray hair done up in a bouffant style. The script at the bottom of the screen indicated that her name was Mona Wright, the mother of the missing man. She was sobbing and intermittently dabbing at her eyes with a lacy handkerchief.

"Do the police have any leads?" An unseen reporter thrust a microphone into her face.

"As I told the police, my Stanley thought someone was followin' him."

"You say he thought someone was following him?" the reporter repeated.

"Yes! Yes, that's what I just said."

"Did he describe that person to you?"

"No. I just dismissed it as his imagination!" she wailed.

"How do you feel about you son's disappearance?" The reporter had pressed for the obvious emotional response and was not disappointed.

"Oh, I'm just beside myself!" the woman wailed again.

The screen then flashed to the familiar haunting picture of Wright as the reporter requested that anyone with information on the whereabouts of the man should contact the number at the bottom of the screen. When the clip had ended, McBrien switched off the television. He then bounded up the stairs, taking them two at a time, to his room, where he picked up the phone. He could feel the galloping pulse at his temples as he punched in a familiar sequence numbers.

"This is Father George McBrien," he said breathlessly to the voice at the other end. "I need to speak with Father Patterson right away."

Sweat flowed in steady streams down the sides of his cheeks, and a wave of nausea had gripped his stomach. He nervously paced behind the desk waiting for what seemed like hours for his friend and seminary classmate to pick up at the other end. Father Edmund Patterson was currently pursuing a doctorate in theology at the Catholic University of America. In the challenges inherent in preparing for a life in the priesthood, this brilliant but humble individual had been a true friend and confidante.

"Hello George? To what do I owe this pleasure?" Patterson's voice was serene, as always.

"I need to talk to you Ed as soon as possible." McBrien's voice cracked. "I think I may have really screwed up."

Twenty

The window exploded into thousands of fragments as the BMW came crashing into the lobby of the restaurant, sending glass, bricks and orange plastic furniture hurling in every direction. The stunned employees cowered below the counter as debris rained down around them. In a cloud of thick, black smoke, the car stalled in the lobby just shy of the counter where its engine wheezed and died.

A crowd began to gather outside the restaurant as a police cruiser blinked and blared to the curb. Two patrolmen jumped out, pushed through the crowd, and clambered over the rubble into what was left of the lobby. The wrecked car sat covered with mortar dust and bits of glass.

"Hey!" a tall, powerfully built patrolman shouted as he waded over the debris toward the car. The driver's side window was down, and he could see Jane Riley's body resting limply over the now deflated air bag of the steering wheel. "Lady, can you hear me?

He put two fingers to her neck and hesitated. "She has a pulse!" he shouted to his partner then turned toward the kitchen. "Is anyone hurt back there?"

A fair-skinned red-headed young man covered in dust peeked above the counter. "Everyone's okay back here," he replied with a quavering voice.

"Paramedics are on the way," the other officer shouted as he put down his phone. "Get these people out of here. I smell gas!"

Four youths dressed in orange and brown uniforms scampered from behind the counter. The officers helped them through what was left of the front window of the restaurant. Multiple police cruisers converged on the scene as the patrolmen cordoned off the area with yellow tape. Several fire engines had arrived, and the firemen immediately began to douse the inside of the wrecked building with foam. Other policemen were redirecting the flow of traffic down Nebraska Avenue, away from the crash site, and the onlookers, fearing an explosion, had quickly dispersed. A news van from Channel 4, with its large antenna elevated above the traffic, had parked across the street, and a female reporter spoke into a microphone using the crash scene as a backdrop.

When the ambulance finally arrived, a team of paramedics leapt from the truck, and after quickly gathering their equipment, awkwardly climbed through the debris while hauling a stretcher and a bag of life support equipment. By now, the smell of gasoline was pervasive, and the medics quickly went to work. After placing a hard, plastic Philadelphia collar around Jane's neck to stabilize the cervical spine, they carefully extracted her from the car. She began to stir as they worked at securing her to a backboard. She tried to move her head but found that it was wedged between two large pieces of foam rubber secured to a board by a broad piece of tape that wrapped her forehead. She then tried to pull off the irritating oxygen mask that was affixed to her face, only to discover that her arms were firmly bound to her sides.

"Ma'am, are you in any pain?" a paramedic asked as he used a light to check her pupils.

"My...head..," she moaned. "What happened?"

"You've just been in a serious accident, and we're taking you to the hospital."

A brightly lit menu hanging over the counter suddenly caught her attention.

"Where am I?" she muttered.

"Let's just say you tried to get carry out the hard way," the paramedic quipped as they carried her out over the rubble.

*   *   *   *
        *   *   *

"Dr. Riley. We finally meet again." David Wallenberg stood at the end of the gurney in the emergency room along with the ever-present neurology resident, Lynn Brooks.

"Dr Wallenberg! What happened?" She had been cleared of any spinal or internal injuries by the Trauma Team and lay on a gurney once again, in a flimsy hospital gown.

"It appears that you had another seizure, only this time while driving your car."

Her reply was a barely audible slang term for feces.

"I'm awaiting your phenytoin level, but I have a suspicion that it's sub-therapeutic. Jane, you're lucky to be alive!"

"What's happening to me?" She was sure this moment would be one of her most embarrassing ones.

"I wish I could say. Have you been taking the phenytoin that I prescribed?"

She hesitated. "No, Dr. Wallenberg, I haven't. I thought it was making me sick."

He glared at her over his glasses with Dr. Brooks standing behind him, her arms folded across her chest. "Dr. Riley, noncompliance is not going to do you any good. Why didn't you call me? You could have been killed, and you could have killed someone else!"

Sufficiently chastened, she became quiet. Much to her relief, the triage nurse suddenly opened the curtain and walked in. It was the same nurse who had cared for her before, only this time, her hair had been dyed bright red.

"Dr. Wallenberg, I have her lab results." She thrust a piece of paper in front of the neurologist and gave Jane a disapproving look.

He briefly studied the paper before sharing it with Lynn Brooks. "Good Lord!"

"The lab repeated it twice. They say the results are accurate," the nurse intoned.

"What's wrong?" asked Jane.

The neurologist thought for a moment before responding. "Just as I suspected, your phenytoin level is undetectable. But your blood counts…..Jane your blood counts are extremely low. You could….die at any moment!"

Twenty-one

With the doors closed, Father Edmund Patterson sat quietly in the musty parlor of the rectory, under the watchful portraits of Saint Ignatius Loyola and Bishop Charbonnel, as George McBrien paced back and forth. The worn but sturdy antique furniture rested firmly on soft oriental carpets that absorbed most superfluous sounds. Plastered walls were lined with mahogany bookcases overfilled with classic works of literature, religion and philosophy, and the grandfather clock soothingly ticked away the minutes.

Patterson watched the remainder of his brandy swirl in the snifter. He was a diminutive man, with close-cropped hair and a full beard. "Well, George?"

McBrien hesitated. "I have to make this a matter of confession."

Patterson raised his eyebrows. "This is going to get complicated, isn't it?"

"Yes. Are you willing to hear my confession?"

He placed the snifter on a side table. "Of course."

McBrien knelt down. "Bless me, Father…"

Patterson held up his hand. "Forget the pleasantries. Just get to the good part."

McBrien began to talk quickly, reliving the encounter before he lost his nerve.

*   *   *   *
        *   *   *

"So you would like to make a confession?" McBrien asked, adjusting the purple stole about his cassock. Despite having already seen him, his penitent seemed to prefer to kneel behind the screen rather than sit face to face. McBrien would accommodate whichever way made him feel most at ease.

"Yes." The voice was a harsh whisper.

"Go on," McBrien pressed. "When was your last confession?"

"Uh, my last confession? I don't know."

McBrien gave a knowing nod. "I see…so it's been a while." He held up his hand to make the sign of the cross. "You begin by blessing yourself and say 'bless me Father for I have sinned.'"

"I think I'm going to kill someone," Wright whispered, ignoring the very specific instructions.

McBrien stopped in mid blessing, his hand still held aloft. "Go on."

After some hesitation, the man continued. "Well…someone's real sick now and might die."

McBrien slowly lowered his hand. "The Commissioner?" The pace of his heartbeat quickened. "And how is it your fault?" He could hear Wright shifting his weight from one knee to the other, causing the somewhat fragile divider between them to shudder again.

"I'm the one who made her sick."

McBrien leaned in closer to the screen. "And what have you done?"

"I…I… put something in the food. Some sort of white…powder. I…I….don't even know what it was," he stammered.

"You…poisoned her?"

"Yeah…poison." The man's voice began to quake. "I poisoned her."

Beads of sweat gathered on the young priest's forehead and ran in streams down the sides of his checks. The stiff, clerical collar suddenly seemed too tight, and the armpits of his cassock had become damp with sweat. His gut tightened.

"If you knowingly did this then you've committed a grave sin. You must listen to me very carefully." He had only read about such cases in the seminary, but the recommended instructions were still fresh in his mind. "If you did something wrong *intentionally* that has caused serious harm or death to another person, you *must* go to the police, and turn yourself in. That is the only way to gain absolution for such an act. Do you understand?"

"Yes," came the sniffled reply.

"But why would you do such a thing?" McBrien pressed.

The man hesitated. "They know something about my past. They threatened to tell the police. They also said they would harm me….and my family….my mother if I didn't do as I was told."

The priest sat back and pulled a handkerchief from the pocket of his cassock. He mopped his brow and wiped the sides of his face. He thought of his own saintly mother at home in Baltimore and a lump rose in his throat. "Who are they and what do they know about your past?"

Wright was silent.

"Stanley, who are they?"

"I can't....I can't tell you. There're powerful people...and they're dangerous.....very dangerous."

"And what do they know about your past that is so troubling?"

"I've already confessed that a long time ago," he answered quickly. "I don't need to tell you about that now."

McBrien leaned into the screen again, his voice now with a measure of urgency. "If the thing in your past is so terrible and the police don't know about it by now, does that mean that you didn't turn yourself in for that crime?"

Wright hedged. "Well, no."

"Then how were you granted absolution for that?"

"I didn't confess to a priest back then."

McBrien rubbed his forehead. "Okay, fine. Look, you must turn yourself in for all the crimes you've committed, past and present, and receive your just punishment. That is the only way to obtain absolution."

"But I can't. I don't want to go to jail. Who will take care of my mother? What will she do if I go to jail?" He began to weep softly. "Besides, they'll kill her anyway."

McBrien gave him a moment before continuing. His prayer for inspiration was immediately answered. "You don't have any idea what you gave her?"

Wright sniffled. "No."

"Do you still have any of it left?"

"Yes....yes, I do. Somewhere."

"Somewhere?"

"Yes, the little brown vial. I still have some of it. I think I know where it is."

McBrien sighed. "Then please find it, and when you do, bring it to me, Stanley. Bring it to me, and we'll go to the police together. We need to figure out what you gave the Commissioner before it is too late!"

    *   *   *   *
       *   *   *

When McBrien had finished, Patterson propped his elbows on the arms of his chair and intertwined his fingers in front of his chest. "This was a sacramental confession?"

McBrien shrugged. "I treated it as such."

"Do you think you can convince him to go to the authorities?"

McBrien rose and sat down on a nearby chair. "He's....gone."

"Gone?"

"He's missing."

"Missing?"

"Yes. He may have been abducted from a metro station. It was in the news. You probably read about it or heard about it on the television," McBrien bowed his head. "And I'm afraid this is all my fault."

Patterson shook his head. "No, George, it is not your fault. He was involved in this and apparently other crimes long before he ever involved you in this. As our Lord said, 'those who live by the sword....'"

"'Shall perish by the sword.'" McBrien took a deep breath and blew it out. "It seemed like such a good thing to do at the time, but after I thought about it for a while, I realized that I may have put his life...and the life of his mother....in danger."

Patterson shifted in the chair and thought for a moment. "I don't know what else you could have done. You followed the recommended advice. You told him to go to the police and turn himself in. Now it's up to him."

"But what if I put his life in danger? In a sense, I've doubled the problem. Now there are two...three lives in peril." He looked down at his feet. "The guilt is killing me. I feel so powerless." He looked up and sat forward, resting his elbows on his knees. "What are we supposed to do if we know the identity of a serial killer? Or, what if someone told you about a bomb planted in a school. You wouldn't let innocent children die, would you?"

"For this I need a drink!" Patterson swallowed his last gulp of brandy, and put the glass down on a side table. He then removed his thick, wire-rimmed glasses and pinched the bridge of his nose between the thumb and forefinger of his free hand. "No, of course not." He paused again. "I would alert the authorities somehow. I know that I could not allow innocent people, especially children, to die. Unfortunately, the bottom line is that you can't break the seal of the confessional. You would be stripped of your priestly duties and probably excommunicated. Priests have gone to their deaths before revealing what was said in confession."

The thought made the hairs on the back of his neck rise. He stood and went over to the portrait of Saint Ignatius Loyola, founder of the Society of Jesus, the official title of the Jesuit Order. The saint was depicted in full eighteenth century liturgical vestments, looking heavenward with a thin, gold halo barely visible around his head. In one hand, he clutched a bible and with the other held up a cross. The words A*d Majorem Dei Gloriam* - All for the greater glory of God - were emblazoned in gilded letters across the bottom of the portrait.

"The only thing you can do," Patterson continued, "is hope this person comes back in again, then you could convince him to turn himself into the authorities." He stood. "Sorry to run like this, but I'm afraid I have an early day tomorrow. And, I must confess, pardon the pun, that I'm very uncomfortable with this conversation."

"Confession," McBrien hastily added. He opened the doors to the parlor and escorted his friend into the hall. "Look, I'm sorry I put you in this awkward position…."

Patterson held up his hand again. "It's always a pleasure to see you, George. We should go out for a beer one of these days."

He turned to leave, but McBrien stopped him. "You didn't give me my penance."

Patterson smiled and patted him on the arm. "Pray for me, my friend, and I shall pray for you."

The two embraced and bid each other good night. McBrien bolted the front doors and returned to the parlor to collect the empty glasses, feeling worse than he had before Patterson's visit. He now wished that he had never burdened his friend with what was essentially his own, private issue. In fact, he tried to rationalize that it wasn't his issue at all. But that assertion failed to assuage his anxiety, and as he passed by the office, the computer on the desk caught his attention. He suddenly realized that there was one option that he hadn't even considered.

Twenty-two

In the third precinct headquarters of the District of Columbia Police Department, Detective Grace Love sat amid the clutter on her desk surrounded by stacks of papers and manila files. A thick folder occupied the epicenter of this chaos, one for which she had specially cleared a space. She paused at one page, then the next, reading carefully and jotting notes on a yellow legal pad. The gruesome photos of the murder scene were spread on the desk just beyond the folder.

She raked a hand through her close-cropped Afro and shook her head. "Um, um, um! How could anyone do this to another person?"

It was just before seven, and the office was empty. Grabbing her cracked and stained mug, she sauntered amongst the empty desks in the large open office to the coffee pot and filled the mug with the black fluid. She took a sip and shivered.

"Yuck! Must be left over from lunch"

She dumped her mug in the nearby sink and set a new pot to brew. An aromatic steamy black line trickled from the hissing machine. Her stomach growled in protest as she savored the smell, reminding her yet again that she had skipped lunch, opting instead for caffeine. Her bathroom scale had indicated that twenty extra pounds had appeared seemingly out of nowhere and had attached themselves to her buttocks and thighs. Skipping meals and light workouts were a strategy that she had adopted to make it disappear, but it was one that had not been good for her demeanor. She had lost about seven and a half pounds in several weeks but had a long way to go to shed the unwanted mass.

Al King, her partner, walked into the office carrying a brown bag with large oily blotches. The sweet aroma activated her salivary glands, and her mouth began to water. "Hey, Grace, want dinner?"

"Are you trying to torture me, Al?" Her stomach rumbled

again.

"Well I figure if we have to be here this late in the evening, we may as well enjoy it. You still on that diet kick of yours?" He reached into the bag and pulled out a large chocolate covered pastry.

"Yes, and you're certainly not helping matters," she snarled.

"Uh huh. Just think how hot you'll be when you lose that weight," Al continued as he absentmindedly surveyed the glistening brown chocolate. "Billy Dee will want to take a ride with you!"

"Go to hell, Al," she said, going back to her desk and plopping in the old vinyl chair. "Billy Dee's old enough to be my grandfather. Besides, you could stand to lose some of that spare tire of yours, you know. And your wife would kill you if she knew what you were having for dinner."

Al King had just turned thirty-five and any evidence that he had once played tight end for Howard University had long since vanished.

"Oh come on, Gracie Mae, don't you love me anymore?" He took a large bite of his donut for emphasis.

"Who said I ever loved you?" she snapped back. "And don't call me that. My mother's the only one who's allowed to call me that! Now stop stuffing your face and get over here. We need to rehash some of the info on the Ting case."

He rolled his eyes. "Not again, Grace! We've been over that case a million times."

"Look, Al, I can't help but think that we're missing something, and I want to make sure we haven't left any stone unturned. I'm going to catch this monster if it's the last thing I do!"

The case of My Ting was perplexing. Dr. Ting had been a promising young researcher at Children's Hospital in the District. On her way home one night, someone had apparently followed her from the Metro station to her home in the Shaw section of the city, brutally raped and then bludgeoned her to death with a blunt object. The perpetrator had left not one clue and apparently either did not ejaculate during the act or had worn a condom. And not one foreign hair had been found at the scene, leading Grace to speculate that the perpetrator had been completely shaved from head to toe. There was a small amount of foreign skin under the fingernail of her left pinky, but for some unknown reason, the DNA was degraded. No similar murders had been reported, ruling out the possibility that a serial killer was on the loose. The knowledge that the perpetrator was still free to rape and murder some other unsuspecting woman angered Grace so intensely that she was beginning to lose sleep over the matter. The death of Dr. Ting had been a great loss to the scientific and medical communities, not only of Washington, but of the world. She was a brilliant physician who had offered the world so much already, and God only knew how much more she would have done. Grace had faith that some clue was going to show up eventually. If there was a God, something would show up.

But it had now been nearly a year and there were no new leads. The trail appeared to be as cold as the killer. She threw the file back on her desk. It had been one of those days when she just wanted to walk out of the door and not look back. The journey to her present position had been a circuitous thirty-six years. She was the youngest of six children in a family headed by a single mother. Her father, a police officer, had been killed in the line of duty shortly before she was born, leaving her mother to raise her family alone, often working two jobs. This left little time for her children. By default, the older children had assisted in raising the younger ones. All of Grace's siblings had excelled in school and had managed to garner scholarships for themselves. Grace had been different. She had been the rebel of the family, determined for reasons inexplicable to her mother, to follow a different path. Perhaps it was because, as the youngest, she had tended to get away with more than the other children. Or maybe it was the crowd she chose to associate with in high school. Whatever the reason, Grace found trouble wherever she could.

Her first encounter with law enforcement came after her arrest for shoplifting. Her devastated mother thought it would be good for her to spend a few nights in jail before bailing her out. Grace's limited association with inmates whose crimes far eclipsed hers had proved to be effective therapy, and she vowed never to be incarcerated again. As a first offender, she was sentenced to community service, and during that time, met some of the first female officers on the District police force. Their bravery and commitment had inspired her to pursue a career in law enforcement and continue her father's legacy. After graduating from the police academy, she accepted a position with the District of Columbia Police Department, and was on the force for five years before becoming a detective. Because of her knowledge of the streets, she had proven to be an effective law enforcer and a formidable detective. And she took the inability to solve crimes very personally.

"So of all the people who were on the Metro, why her? Why would the killer single her out?" Grace asked rhetorically. She had actually ridden the Metro several times at about the time the victim had, and scanned the crowd for suspicious faces.

King wiped his mouth with a crinkled napkin. "Maybe he digs Asian chicks. Bad luck, maybe. Look, Grace, we've been over and over this. We need a break and it doesn't look like one's coming our way. It's been too long."

Grace toyed with her pencil. "There's got to be something. There's no such thing as the perfect crime."

King frowned. "Look, the only thing we have is incomplete DNA that doesn't match anyone in the database. It must've been someone she knew, a fellow researcher maybe."

"We've already explored that angle, Al." She got up, went to the window and looked out over a city that had already slipped into darkness. The Washington Monument, illuminated by the giant floodlights at its base, could be seen for miles around rising above the other buildings in the city and piercing the evening sky. She loved living and working in Washington with its historic and cultural attractions. It was a beautiful city with a dangerous underside. She turned to look at King. "We need to approach this case in a different way. For example, why was the killer's DNA so degraded? There's something we're missing. I know there's going to be a break in this case soon. I can feel it."

King rolled his eyes. "Okay, Grace, whatever."

She turned back to the window. "I know you're out there somewhere, you bastard," she whispered. " And I'm coming after you."

Twenty-three

Jane sat up. "What do you mean?"

"Your blood counts are low," Wallenberg repeated sullenly. "You're at risk for serious infection….bleeding…..I'm not sure what's going on."

"May I see them?" she asked calmly.

With a shaking hand, he gave her the paper. "The lab has repeated the tests."

"Twice!" The nurse nodded.

Jane scanned the report. "But there *must* be some mistake! You must repeat them again!"

He thought for a moment then finally acquiesced. "All right, I'll have them repeated again." He turned to the nurse. "Please have the blood work done again STAT."

A second sample of blood was drawn and, after what seemed like hours later, Wallenberg came back into the room.

"I'm afraid there's no mistake, Jane." He handed her the paper. "I'm going to have to call in one of the hematologists. This isn't my area of expertise."

Jane stared at the second report, trying to control her emotions. She had been healthy all of her life, had exercised regularly, never smoked, and only had an occasional glass of wine. A gnawing ache began in her abdomen as she continued to stare at the numbers, hoping a decimal point was in the wrong place, or the name at the top of the paper was not hers after all.

She then began to look at the numbers from a physician's point of view. The white blood cell count was 1000. A normal white count was 4500 to 9000. A low white count, of course, would place her at risk for life-threatening infection. And her hemoglobin level, the component of her red blood cells responsible for carrying oxygen to her brain, muscles, heart, and every organ in the body, was only 8.0, normal being 12 to 14. This, undoubtedly, had accounted for her extreme fatigue. And finally, the platelet count, the small cells that helped the blood to clot, was at 25,000 with a normal range of 150,000 to 350,000. A low platelet count would put her at risk for serious and potentially life-threatening hemorrhage.

Intense anxiety surged from within her, bringing with it a whirlwind of fears. In the deepest regions of her subconscious, she had always thought of herself as invincible, indestructible and had no doubt that she, like her mother, would live a very long time. Now she was being dragged across a fragile divide from health to sickness, 'the other side' that, as a physician, she had never experienced first hand. She did not belong there and had no intention of staying. She thought of her daughter and of the grandchildren that she did not yet know. Fear and anxiety quickly morphed into anger. She would demand that someone get to the bottom of all this and soon, or else….yes…of course she could die, and die very quickly, but that was something she had no intention of doing.

*   *   *   *

  *   *   *

"Her platelet and white blood cell counts certainly are low," Josh Hanley said to David Wallenberg as he gazed down the microscope at the Commissioner's blood smear. The two were seated at a multi-headed teaching microscope in a laboratory in the cancer center. Dr. Wallenberg had called from the emergency room just as Josh was about to leave for the evening. They had agreed to meet in the laboratory to look at the blood smear, and Josh had sent Marc Abelman to the ER to do the preliminary consultation on the case.

"Is she on any medications that could do this?" he asked.

"She's being treated with phenytoin for unexplained seizures, but she was taking it only sporadically. In fact, her levels are actually undetectable so she obviously wasn't compliant," Wallenberg replied.

Josh continued to scan the slide, his eyes fixed to the binocular lenses. "As you are aware, bone marrow suppression has been reported with the anticonvulsants in general."

"Yes, that's well documented in the medical literature."

Josh finally looked up from the scope and rubbed his eyes. "This is most likely an idiosyncratic drug reaction and hopefully she will recover soon. The hematology fellow has arranged for her to be admitted to my service to one of the isolation rooms in the transplant unit."

"Good!" The relief in Wallenberg's voice was obvious.

"I'm going over to see her now that's she's settled in." Josh yawned and looked at his watch. It was nearly ten o'clock, and a gnawing discomfort just below his ribcage reminded him that his evening meal was long overdue.

"I've switched her to phenobarbitol to control her seizures," Wallenberg noted as the two got up. "I'll have the neuro resident keep an eye on her levels."

Josh had been in training at the university when he first encountered Jane Riley. She was a highly regarded educator and clinician who rewarded extraordinary behavior but who was merciless to those whose performance she deemed substandard. Fortunately, Josh had been in the former group, but nonetheless she had left him quaking in his shoes on more than one occasion. The years he had spent doing research in her lab had been productive, despite the fact that the data he had generated had not been 'clinically useful' according to Riley.

Josh assumed that, as Commissioner of the FDA, Jane was probably acquainted with most of the top specialists in every field, including his own. From his past experience of working in her lab, he knew that she would want answers, and she would want them now. He also suspected that she would want one of the more experienced faculty members handling her case. His apprehension began to build as he approached her room. He was relatively young and not nearly as experienced as some of the other members of the faculty. After all, Dr. Wilton Roth, section chair, was an internationally recognized expert in the field of hematology and had done extensive research on bone marrow disorders. He was, however, approaching seventy and no longer attending on the inpatient service. Then, there was Ricarda Mayer, a seasoned hematologist in her early sixties who had pioneered the treatment of many hematologic malignancies. And the list went on and on, reflecting the prestige of the university and the accomplishments of its faculty. If necessary, he would call upon the expertise of his colleagues and see to it that all the best minds of the university would be involved in her care from the outset. He took a deep breath as he walked out of the elevator. Marc Abelman had seen and examined her with intern Nathaniel Johnson, and the two were waiting for him on the transplant unit.

"So how's the new admit?" he asked wryly.

"She's stable and looks fine considering that she single handedly trashed Tenley Circle this evening," Marc said flippantly. He then reviewed her case in detail, which included the history and physical exam findings.

Josh grabbed his chin in thought. "So what do you think is going on?"

Marc closed the chart. "I'm not sure. The bone marrow suppression could certainly be secondary to phenytoin, but it was undetectable in her blood, so she hasn't even been taking it. I'm not sure why she's having seizures in the first place and why her hair is falling out. I just can't seem to tie it all together."

"Her hair is falling out?"

Marc nodded.

"And the urine tox screen?"

"Negative."

"Professor Wallenberg can't find a reason for the seizures," Josh continued. "But as far as her bone marrow suppression, I'm operating on the premise that it has to be the phenytoin. However, we will need to do a bone marrow biopsy tonight."

Marc nodded. "I've ordered a biopsy tray to her bedside."

"Good. Let's go see her."

Josh led them down the corridor to one of several isolation rooms on the unit. The three dutifully washed their hands with a disinfectant soap and entered the room where they found Jane sitting up in bed watching the late news.

"Good evening, Madam Commissioner," Josh said with feigned formality.

She smiled. "It's Déjà vu all over again, as they say. I didn't realize that our paths would cross again so soon." She motioned toward the television bolted to the wall. "As you can see, I made the evening news. 'Jane Riley, Commissioner of the FDA, gives all new meaning to the term 'fast food!' Video at ten.'"

Despite her predicament, she was in a better state of mind than he had anticipated. He glanced up at the television bolted high on the wall opposite her bed. On the screen, a reporter stood in front of the damaged building, with a microphone in her hand, recounting the incident in dramatic detail. The other hand held a small notepad to which she frequently referred and with which she made sweeping motions to describe the accident.

"I managed to contact my daughter Beth before the news

broke into the national media, thank goodness," Jane remarked as they watched. "She's on the red eye out of LA."

The news clip ended, and when the anchor went on to the next story, Jane used the remote to turn off the television.

"How do you feel?" Josh inquired.

"Exhausted and nauseated, but the nausea seems to have gotten a little better. I've had it for several days now and have not had much of an appetite. And look at this!" Using a hand, she raked her scalp and easily pulled out several large clumps of hair. "I thought this was probably due to stress but now I'm not so sure."

Josh examined her scalp. "How long have you noticed the hair loss?" There were several patches of baldness with thinning of the hair in general.

"Just today," she replied then stopped. "I think it actually started yesterday, but I really noticed it just before I left work this afternoon."

"Have you noticed anything else out of the ordinary?"

"I feel as though I have the flu, and it just won't go away. I start to feel better and then I get sick again. I've had two seizures, and Dr. Wallenberg doesn't know why. And now my blood counts are depressed. I certainly hope someone at this prestigious institution can tell me what the hell is happening to me!"

"Well, I have looked at your blood smear," Josh quickly added, sensing her mounting frustration.

"And?"

He took a deep breath. "There's really nothing diagnostic about it, but I think the most likely culprit is the phenytoin."

"That may explain the low counts, but it doesn't explain the hair loss," she challenged.

"That's true," he acquiesced, feeling his face become warm. Jane Riley had already begun to second guess him.

"You know, to be completely honest with you, I haven't even been taking it." She managed a weak smile. "Can you image? The Commissioner of the FDA is noncompliant with her medication."

"Yes, it was undetectable on testing. Why weren't you taking it?"

She shrugged and pulled a strand of hair from the front on her gown. "I thought it was making me sick....and I guess I just felt that I really didn't need to be on it in the first place."

"I think we call it denial," Josh countered.

"Touché." She nodded. "We doctors are so good at that, aren't we?"

"When was the last time you took it?"

Her forehead furrowed. "I don't know...a week ago, I guess."

Josh raised his eyebrows. "I see. I've reviewed your case with the fellow and the intern." He nodded to Marc and Nathaniel who up to that point had been silent. "They tell me you have no other medical problems."

"No. I've been as healthy as a horse."

Josh considered this. "Okay then, let me examine you."

He performed a thorough physical exam, and aside from the partial hair loss, known medically as alopecia, found no other abnormalities. "We need to do a bone marrow biopsy tonight."

She winced. "I figured you would."

"We'll need to have a conclusive answer as soon as possible," he explained. "Dr. Abelman will be performing the procedure under my direct supervision."

Jane nodded and looked at Abelman. "You look pretty young. I hope you've done at least one before."

Josh chuckled. "He's done plenty and does a good job."

After the nurse had administered a mild sedative, Josh had her lie on her side in the fetal position in preparation for the bone marrow biopsy. Abelman donned sterile gloves and opened the biopsy tray. He carefully sterilized the skin overlying the posterior iliac spine, the knob of bone that protrudes just above each buttock, with an iodine-containing solution, starting in the center and making large concentric circles outward. He repeated this two more times, then placed a sterile drape over her lower back such that only the cleansed area of the skin, made brown by the iodine, showed through a precut opening. He proceeded to numb the skin with a local anesthetic, which was then carried down to the bone. After making a small incision, he took a hollow needle with a stylet in the center, and carefully pierced the skin, embedding it into the bone. After removing the stylet, he attached a syringe to the needle and withdrew a small amount of what appeared to be blood. Jane flinched, and then relaxed.

"We've gotten the aspirate," Josh assured her.

With slow, twisting movements, Abelman pushed the needle further into the bone by about two centimeters, and then removed it in the same manner. The small core of bone marrow was then pushed out onto a glass slide. It was half an inch in length and about as thick as a toothpick. The specimen was then plunged into a small cup of formalin.

Before it could be studied, the little sliver of marrow would be placed in a special solution to decalcify the bone. It would then be embedded in paraffin, cut into slices only a few microns thick, mounted on a slide, and stained. The aspirated specimen would be smeared onto slides and also stained. The specimens would be ready for review the following day. When they had finished, the three bid her good night. Once outside the room, Josh instructed the intern on call to notify him of any major changes in her condition. The last thing he wanted was for the Commissioner of the FDA to crash while he was the attending of record.

Twenty-four

An icy wind lashed his face as he made his way down the
mountain. It may have been the Matterhorn or his favorite
mountain in Jackson Hole. Or it could have been neither; he
wasn't sure. A gray mist hung in the air, and nightfall was
quickly descending. He couldn't really see where he was going,
but when he tried to slow himself down, the turns only made him
go faster. A feeling of panic turned into terror when the snow
under his skis suddenly gave way to nothingness as he slid over a
cliff. An expanse of fields and rolling hills stretched beneath
him, like the view from an airplane. He began to fall, and a stab
of adrenaline ripped him from gut to throat. Then the feelings of
dread, of helplessness, of surrender......BEEP! BEEP! BEEP!

Josh awoke gasping for air, his heart pounding and his head
and neck damp. It took several seconds to figure out where he
was and what the sound of his beeper meant. He groped the top
of the nightstand and his hand inadvertently nudged the still
chirping pager off the edge, sending it clanging to the floor.

"Damn!"

With a groan, he hung over the side of the mattress and spied
the telltale flashing red numbers somewhere under his bed. His
outstretched hand found the pager, and he brought it up to study
the message.

"6-7-0-2. The ER."

He reached for the lamp switch and squinted against the
sudden burst of light. As his pupils slowly adjusted, he grabbed
the handset of his telephone and punched in the numbers.

"Emergency Department. May I help you?" The voice was
pleasant, and very much awake for four ten in the morning.

"Dr. Hanley," Josh grunted, lying back on his pillow. "I was
paged."

"One moment, Dr. Hanley."

With the telephone receiver wedged between his head and the

pillow, he had begun to fall back to sleep listening to the soft muzak when a voice on the other end re-awakened him.

"Dr. Hanley?" It was the voice of Nathaniel Johnson.

Josh bolted upright in bed. "Nathaniel? Has something happened to Jane Riley?"

"Oh…no, Dr Hanley. I'm seeing one of your patients here in the emergency room. His...er....her name in the medical record is Lloyd Wyatt but he...she says it's now..um...Fifi?"

He lay back down. "Yes."

"Oh, okay. Anyway, he...ah....the patient needs to be admitted."

Josh grabbed the bridge of his nose and closed his eyes as he spoke. "She has KS that has spread to the lungs."

"Right," came the reply. He could hear the shuffling of paper as the intern sifted through the voluminous medical record. "The patient comes in tonight with increasing shortness of breath and hasn't really responded to treatment. I'm afraid she's tiring out and may need to be intubated soon. The oxygen levels in her blood are dropping rapidly."

"Damn," Josh whispered.

"Sir?"

"Ah, sorry. There's not much more we can do for her. Her disease is progressing rapidly, and she's no longer responding to chemotherapy. She doesn't want to be put on life support; she's made that clear to me and it's documented in the chart. She has a living will."

"Oh, yeah, here it is," said the intern. "He's….she's a DNR all right."

DNR stood for 'Do Not Resuscitate,' which meant that, because of the terminal nature of the illness, no attempts at resuscitation would be made in the event of respiratory failure or cardiac arrest. In effect, nature would be allowed to take its inevitable course.

"She wants a dignified and pain free death," said Josh, remembering their last encounter. "Give her some morphine to make her comfortable. It sounds like she's really going downhill fast."

"Okay, Dr. Hanley. We'll make sure she's comfortable," the intern replied.

"Thanks, Nathaniel." He hung up the phone, turned off the lamp, and lay back in bed. After shifting from one position to

another within in the course of only a few minutes, he threw back
the blanket and swung his legs over the side of the bed. The
digital readout on his clock indicated that is was now 4:23. He
got up, and went into the bathroom. The bright fluorescent lamp
above the mirror hummed and flickered to life, revealing his
reflected haggard image.

"Poor Fifi," he said aloud.

After quickly shaving and showering, he headed for the
hospital. The city was nearly empty at this hour, populated by
only a few newspaper trucks and taxicabs, and the commute to
the hospital was accomplished in record time. After parking in
the physician's garage, he went directly to the Emergency
Department. Two security guards were posted at the entrance,
and they nodded him through as he flashed his I.D. badge.
Nathaniel Johnson was standing at the nurses' station, and he
looked up as Josh approached.

"Dr. Hanley! What are you doing here so early?" he asked.

"Where's Fifi, Nathaniel?"

"Number three."

"Thanks."

He pulled back the curtain, and the intern followed him into
the bay. Fifi was sitting up on a gurney, with her hands grasping
the side rails, struggling to breathe. Gone were the stunning wig
and the sophisticated make-up. A plain hospital gown replaced
the stylish clothes, and the hairless head glistened in the harsh
fluorescent light. The only vestiges of the 'sublime' Miss
LaJones were the intricately designed press-on nails.

"Well...look what...the..cat..done...brung in," Fifi struggled.
Her voice was muffled by the mask and the hiss of oxygen.

Josh walked over and took one of her cold hands.

"When did you become this bad?"

"It's..been happening...all along...I..tried to ...ignore it...as
..long..as I could." Her voice trailed off.

Nathaniel scanned the notes on a clipboard. "Her oxygen sats
have been steadily dropping since I called you."

Josh pulled a stethoscope from the pocket of his jacket and
listened to Fifi's lungs.

"I...don't...think...I'm going to...make it!" She gasped, as the
struggle to breathe intensified.

"There's not much more we can do but make you
comfortable," Josh said, squeezing Fifi's hand. "The only thing

left to do is put you on a breathing machine but it would only prolong things and I know you don't want that."

Fifi shook her head no and whispered to Josh.

"Remember...when the time came....you promised to....to take care of me..."

Josh nodded his head and turned to the intern. "Has she received any morphine?"

"I've given her two milligrams every four hours. I was concerned about respiratory suppress...."

"That's not enough! You need to start a morphine drip. Begin with two milligrams an hour and titrate up as needed."

"But Dr. Hanley won't that suppress her breathing?"

"Do as I say....now!"

"Yes sir, Dr. Hanley, right away sir." He quickly scribbled the order and disappeared behind the curtain.

"Where's your mother?"

Fifi motioned toward the opening in the curtain where a short black woman had appeared, clutching the drape with one hand and holding a handkerchief in the other.

"Ms. Wyatt." Josh went over and put his hand on her shoulder.

"Is there anything you can do, Dr. Hanley?"

"We've done everything we can." He pulled her to the bedside. "We need to make her more comfortable now."

"Oh, Dr. Hanley, I hope God will forgive him for this thing he's done to himself."

"Let's not think such thoughts." His grip on her shoulder tightened. "She needs you now more than ever. Are there any other family members we should call?"

"There's a friend of his, Ray, in the waiting room, and me, that's all the family he has."

"I'll be right back. I'll get Ray; you stay with her. We'll move her to a private room on the floor as soon as possible. That way you can stay there with her."

Though usually crammed with sick adults and crying children, the waiting room was surprisingly quiet. Only a few people were scattered about, some drinking coffee and watching CNN on a television that was bolted to the wall, while others were attempting to sleep on the uncomfortable chairs. A well-dressed young black man was seated in a corner, his chin resting on his intertwined hands, as if in a trance.

Josh approached him. "I'm Dr. Hanley. Are you Ray, Fifi's friend?"

"Yes. I'm her main man."

Josh sat down beside him.

"Ray, Fifi's condition is rapidly deteriorating," he began as gently as possible. "She's getting worse by the hour."

"She's not going to make it this time, is she?" Ray asked somberly.

Josh frowned and shook his head.

"Oh...." He softly sighed and looked up at the ceiling. Tears began to flood his eyes. "I knew there would come a time when the cancer would get worse. It's just happening sooner than I thought it would."

"Right now we're going to give her some morphine to make her more comfortable. I think you should go back and be with her."

"Fifi's mother doesn't approve of her lifestyle...or me for that matter." He wiped his eyes with the back his hand.

"Now is not the time to think of those things. Her mother will understand. I'll try to help with that. In the meantime, if there is anything I can do..."

"You've done all you can, Dr. Hanley, and Fifi thinks the world of you."

A knot rose in Josh's throat. "I appreciate that....I only wish things could have turned out better."

He escorted Ray to the emergency room bay then expedited Fifi's admission to the oncology ward where he knew that she would be more comfortable and have the privacy needed for a dignified death. The eastern horizon had begun to turn a fiery pink as Josh sat at the nurses' station on the Oncology Unit, while the intern wrote admission orders. The patient was to be kept comfortable with oxygen and morphine. Since Ms. Wyatt would probably live for only several more hours, no extraordinary measures were to be taken to prolong life.

As an oncologist, Josh regularly made decisions such as these for patients dying of cancer. Despite his years of experience, it never became easier, regardless of the age of the patient, but it was especially difficult when a patient was so young and full of life. He sighed and looked out the window as the intense pink horizon gradually brightened to a brilliant orange.

"Dr. Hanley, is there anything else I should do?" Nathaniel

looked up from the chart.

"No, I think that will do." He studied the intern's face and suddenly realized how boyish he looked. He recalled an instance in his own life when he was but an intern and wondered if he had looked as young to his superiors and his patients. *Where did all those years go?*

Suddenly, Fifi Wyatt's nurse came bounding out of the room and ran up the corridor.

"Dr. Hanley, come quick! Miss Wyatt is asking for you!"

Josh jumped up and ran down the hall with Nathaniel at his heels. By now, a crowd of close friends had joined Mrs. Wyatt and Ray for the death watch. They stood around the room, some obviously fellow drag queens now in muted dress, their murmured condolences drowned out by the hiss of oxygen.

"Fifi do you need something? Are you in pain?" Josh bent down and grasped her hand while Nathaniel stood frozen at the foot of the bed.

"Josh...you're a fine...human being," she began haltingly and with great difficulty as she struggled to breath. "You... done..your best...and...I thank you."

"It was my privilege to take care of you," Josh replied, fighting back tears. Then he whispered in her ear: "I'll always remember the fabulous Fifi LaJones."

The glimmer of a smile appeared on Fifi's face through the foggy mask and she turned to Ray: "Baby...you take...care...of...yourself...and make...sure Mama's looked after..."

"Oh Fifi," cried Ray, grasping the other hand. He began to sob. "Don't leave me, baby."

The labored breathing worsened, and Fifi became restless and anxious as she struggled to breath. Josh quickly gave another bolus of morphine and increased the rate of the drip. After several minutes, her respiratory rate gradually decreased and she slowly slipped into unconsciousness. Ray was seated at the bedside, squeezing the hand of his dying friend in both of his and sobbing uncontrollably. Suddenly, Fifi's mother walked around the side of the bed and placed her arm around Ray.

"Son," she said, as tears rolled down her cheeks, "we have one thing in common, and that is that we both love Lloyd with all our hearts. And he loved us back unconditionally. And now he's going to Jesus and all we have is each other."

Ray leaned into the woman, resting his head on her bosom as she stroked his head. At that moment, the labored breathing slowed, becoming shallow and then less frequent. After several minutes, it stopped altogether, and Fifi became very still. Josh bent down and checked the pupils with a pen light. They were dilated and unresponsive. He then felt for a pulse, and finding none, he looked at Mrs. Wyatt and Ray who were still embracing. He reached up and turned off the oxygen valve. The room became completely still.

After composing himself, Josh broke the silence. "I'm so sorry."

Mrs. Wyatt cried softy as she clung to Ray.

"I'm so very sorry," Josh said again. Ray nodded as he continued to embrace Fifi's grieving mother.

Josh left the room and walked down the hall to the nurses' station, Nathaniel not far behind, and sat down. The two were silent and after a while, Josh could sense Nathaniel's growing discomfort.

"Is something wrong, Nathaniel?"

"I….I've never seen anyone die like that before. Usually we're doing CPR and running a code."

"Oh. You mean like with Mrs. Newman."

"Yeah…and…ah...Dr. Hanley, I noticed that you turned up the morphine...."

"Yes...Doctor....and....?"

"Was that like...euthanasia?"

"Nathaniel, she was dying...she was suffocating...drowning....I did it to alleviate her suffering. She was going to die soon...I just made the dying more bearable. That's part of our jobs as physicians...to alleviate pain and suffering."

Nathaniel nodded in agreement, although his expression indicated that he had not found the argument very convincing. Maybe in time and after more experience he would more fully understand that his role as a 'healer' came in many forms.

"It's been a busy night, Nathaniel. Why don't you go shave, take a shower and get some breakfast," he said in a fatherly way. "I'll dictate the Death Summary."

Nathaniel raised his eyebrows. "Really? Are you sure?" Such menial tasks usually fell to the lowly interns.

Josh smiled. "Sure I'm sure, kid."

"Oh...okay, you're the attending, Dr. Hanley. I do what you say." He saluted offhandedly. "Thanks. I'll see you on rounds." He got up and nearly sprinted down the corridor to the elevators.

After the intern had gone, Josh sat in silence, pondering his own inevitable demise as was his ritual after the death of one of his patients. What, if anything, lay beyond the great divide between the here and the hereafter? Was there a heaven or a hell? Or had Lloyd Wyatt just passed into oblivion. As he picked up the chart to begin his dictation, he was struck by sudden warmth and turned to see the first rays of the sun filter through the window as it peeked over the horizon. He paused for a moment and closed his eyes, finding comfort in the warm embrace.

Twenty-five

Dr. Sara Wong was a highly regarded specialist in bone marrow pathology whose official title was 'hematopathologist.' In addition to her impressive academic credentials, the diminutive Dr. Wong had a passion for ballroom dancing, was an accomplished pianist, and loved a good party. She was of the third generation of successful Chinese immigrants and therefore, had no trace of an accent. Her office was furnished with black lacquer furniture, and bookcases stuffed with a jumble of textbooks, journals and manuscripts. Several abstract paintings were hung too high on one wall and a simple Chinese arrangement of silk flowers graced the top of a file cabinet. She sat gazing down binocular eyepieces at the epicenter of a multi-headed teaching microscope that resembled a large metallic insect.

When Josh and his entourage appeared in her basement level office, she looked up only briefly at the small invasion. "I see the gang's all here. Come children, gather around the scope."

Josh sat down across from her, and she looked up briefly again.

"You look…oh what's the word I'm looking for….ah…disheveled, yes, that's it. You look disheveled. Are you going for a new look or something?"

"Aren't you the funny one. No, for your information, one of my patients died this morning."

"And I thought you were used to that by now."

He had known Wong since she was a Pathology resident years prior and by now was used to her wicked sense of humor.

"Great...thanks," he replied, not in the mood for fun and games.

She looked up again and smiled. "I'm so sorry, I shouldn't have. I know how personally you take these losses." Her smile quickly faded. "I'm afraid I have more bad news, though.

You're not going to like the looks of this."

The teaching microscope had several sets of binocular lenses for individual viewing, all of which converged at one powerful lens and below which rested a microscope slide on a movable stage. A thin slice of Jane Riley's bone marrow biopsy had been fixed to the slide, and stained with blue and red dyes to highlight its structure.

Josh removed his glasses and peered into the eyepieces. "It's aplastic," he noted, then added for the benefit of the students: "Meaning that the marrow is empty. There aren't any blood-making precursor cells. We refer to the generation of blood making cells as hematopoiesis. At this point, there is very little hemopoietic activity."

Sara nodded in agreement, her eyes staying fixed to the scope.

"Is there any evidence of regeneration?" he asked.

She carefully scanned the slide. "No....not really."

"What would cause this?" Nathaniel asked.

"Drugs are a major cause of this type of thing," Josh remarked. "We're operating on the premise that it was her exposure to the anticonvulsant drug that did this." He pulled his eyes from the scope and sat back. "It just doesn't all fit. There's got to be something else. I've been wracking my brains trying to tie all her symptoms together, but I'm not coming up with anything. Anticonvulsants don't make your hair fall out."

Sara Wong finally tore herself away from the scope. "If it is the anticonvulsant, how long do you think it would take for her to recover?"

"She could turn around any day or she could be aplastic for another week. Most aplastic anemia that cannot be explained on the basis of drugs or other causes is probably autoimmune in nature. In other words, the body destroys its own bone marrow."

"So what do you think we should do, Dr. Hanley?" Marc asked.

"I want you to search the medical literature and see if phenytoin has ever done this before. For now, we'll have to sit tight and monitor her counts." Josh knew that so far, Jane Riley had been stable. The night before had been uneventful and her exam was still benign. Her executive assistant had brought in her laptop computer, and Jane seemed to be running the FDA from her hospital room. "We'll try bone marrow stimulating drugs...growth factors....that might help her marrow recover more quickly. She will probably require transfusional support before it's all over. In cases of idiopathic or autoimmune phenomena, immune suppressing drugs can be tried. However, when those don't work, a more drastic approach is necessary.

"Such as a bone marrow transplant," Abelman stated more than asked.

"Well….yes, of course…but I don't think that will be necessary." Josh put his glasses back on. "Thanks, Sara." He stood, and the team followed him out the door.

"Josh," Sara called after him. He stopped at the door and let the team pass out of the room. "Let's do dinner sometime," she said softly. "Call or text me, okay?"

Josh nodded and smiled, knowing that this was unlikely to happen.

They headed to the unit where Jane and her daughter Beth, who had arrived early that morning, anxiously awaited the results of the biopsy. The discussion was somewhat anticlimactic since the working diagnosis had not changed. Beth was tall, with straight blond hair pulled back in a ponytail, and wore bell bottomed blue jeans and a thick white sweater. It was immediately obvious to Josh that she had been endowed with her mother's confidence and intelligence.

"This whole thing has me really scared." Beth said as she held her mother's hand.

"That's understandable, Beth," Josh replied.

"Don't worry, honey, I'm in good hands." Jane gave her a reassuring smile.

He was relieved when he finally stepped out of the room. Despite confidence in his clinical judgment, he could not shake a nagging feeling that he was missing something. Something that was obvious and right under his nose. Something that if not discovered soon, would cost Jane Riley her life.

Twenty-six

Jane Riley's condition was showing signs of deterioration.

"She spiked a temp to 102 last night but quickly defervesced," Nathaniel Johnson began during rounds. "And something else also developed."

"What now?" Josh asked, trying to hide his exasperation.

Nathaniel pointed to his mouth. "She has developed ulcers in her mouth."

Abelman nodded. "She has mucositis."

"Mucositis!" Josh replied, referring to inflammation and ulceration of the membranes, known as the mucosa, which lined the mouth and gastrointestinal tract. In its severest form, the condition could prohibit adequate intake of food and water. "Does she have a rash, too?"

"No." said Johnson.

Josh looked at Abelman. "Did you find anything on your literature search?"

Abelman shook his head. "Nothing that would tie all of her symptoms to a reaction from the anticonvulsant."

"At any rate, we did cultures of her blood and urine," Johnson continued. "Her chest x-ray was negative and we started her on antibiotics."

"Is she better this morning?"

"A little."

"And her lab values?"

"They're worse today."

Josh felt his gut tighten. "Hum. Let's go see her."

Jane was asleep, and Beth sat in a chair by the bed reading the morning paper. She put down the paper and grabbed her mother's arm. "Mother, the doctors are here."

Jane awoke with a start and rubbed her eyes. "Oh, sorry."

Josh looked over the vitals sheet, noting the temperature curve. "I hear you're not doing too well today."

Jane nodded. "Yes, I started to have a sore throat last night, and this morning my whole mouth is sore. I'm really tired. I was up half the night because of all the testing. I don't think I'll be able to do much work today."

He put the bedside vitals sheet back in its slot on the wall. "I think you should just rest today." He examined her mouth and noted the diffuse redness of the oral cavity and the small ulcers that dotted the insides of her cheeks and tongue.

"Do you still think it is the phenytoin doing all this?" she asked after he had finished his exam.

Josh took in a deep breath and exhaled, hoping some brilliant thought would pop into his brain. When none came, he opted for honesty. "I'm not sure. I'm honestly not sure. It just doesn't all fit."

Jane studied his face. "So what else could it be?"

He shook his head. "I don't know. Are you sure you weren't exposed to anything else? Any other drug or chemical or source of radiation, perhaps? I suppose you're not exposed to anything like that at your job are you?"

"Roses," she said after some thought.

"Roses?" he asked.

"One of my harshest critics, an odious man if I ever saw one, brought me roses the other day," she replied.

"What?"

She waved her hand. "I'm sorry, I'm just joking. No, nothing I can think of."

"No recent trips out of the country, to Russia or China, for example?"

"No, none recent."

He nodded. "Okay. Well, right now, we'll have to continue what we're doing, regardless of the cause. It's a little too early for the bone marrow stimulants to be working just yet. You'll need a transfusion soon if your red count continues to drift downward."

"And if the counts don't come back soon?" she persisted.

Josh demurred. "We'll cross that bridge when we come to it."

Jane struggled to compose herself as tears welled in her eyes. "I just want this nightmare to be over."

Beth sat down on the bed and embraced her. "Mother, it will be all right," she said softly. "You're going to get better."

Josh was silent for a moment. He looked at Abelman, who

knowingly escorted the residents and students out of the room.

"Jane, I assure you we're going to do everything possible to get you well again," he said firmly. "We're going to present your case at our conference today and get input from all the other faculty members just to make sure we're not missing anything. We're not going to leave any stones unturned."

Beth had handed Jane a tissue, and she dabbed at her eyes. "I'm sorry, Josh, I didn't mean to break down in front of everyone. I've known you since you were an intern. I know how your mind works, how analytical and thorough you are, and I know you will get me through this."

Josh smiled and nodded, but as he left the room, his level of anxiety was mounting. From an intellectual standpoint, he was convinced that the anticonvulsant was not enough to explain Jane's spectrum of symptoms. He hoped that whatever he was missing would come out when her case was presented to the other faculty members.

*   *   *   *
   *   *   *

The white-bearded Dr. Wilton Roth, whose official title was Director of the Section of Hematology and Medical Oncology, sat in a starched white coat and bow tie at the opposite side of the table. Dr. Sara Wong was in the back of the room near a computer while Nick Perrone and other members of the staff filled the remaining seats around the table.

Josh approached a lectern near a large projection screen at the front of the room, and the pre-meeting chatter died. "We have a very challenging case for your consideration today. Our hematology fellow, Marc Abelman will present the history."

As Josh sat down, Abelman approached the lectern. A computer generated slide appeared on the screen as he began to speak. "This is the case of a fifty three year old female physician who initially presented with a seizure approximately two weeks ago." From there, he relayed in detail the saga of Jane Riley's illness in slide after slide, from the first seizure, to the second seizure and accident, and her current problem with low blood counts, alopecia, and mucositis.

"Dr. Wong will now present the bone marrow pathology," he said at the conclusion of his presentation.

Abelman sat down and Sara Wong came to the lectern. The lights were dimmed as a computer-generated slide of Jane

Riley's red and blue stained bone marrow specimen, magnified a hundred-fold, filled the screen.

"This is the patient's bone marrow specimen, and as you can see, there is extensive marrow aplasia," she began, referring to the large empty fat globules between the pink stained bone fragments. As she discussed the results of the bone marrow biopsy in great detail, she showed several more images that demonstrated various areas of the specimens at different levels of magnification and used a red laser pointer to highlight her findings.

"Any questions?" she asked, at the conclusion of her presentation.

Dr. Richarda Mayer, who was sitting next to Roth, lifted her hand. Considered an authority on leukemia and other bone marrow cancers, she was a tall, thin woman with a long, gray mane wrapped in a bun at the nape of her neck. "What did the chromosomal analysis show?"

"The chromosomal analysis was normal, Dr. Mayer," Wong replied.

"These findings are not specific for any one drug or disorder, are they?" Theodore Pittsnogle, IV, the scion of a prominent New England family, began in his usual patrician style. "Is there any aspect of the biopsy specimen that would point you toward one diagnosis versus another?"

Wong shook her head. "Not really, Dr. Pittsnogle. The findings are nonspecific, that is, this picture can be seen with a wide variety of disease processes such as idiopathic aplastic anemia, chemotherapeutic agents, viral infections like hepatitis, and others. Just based on the specimen alone, I cannot pinpoint any specific cause."

There being no further questions, Dr. Wong returned to her seat. Marc Abelman then resumed his place at the lectern and proceeded with a lengthy discussion on the various causes of bone marrow failure syndromes. In the end, however, he noted that they were not sure what was causing marrow failure in this case.

"I must admit that this is a somewhat unusual reaction for an anticonvulsant," Dr. Roth began in his professorial style. "But that appears to be the only plausible explanation."

Mayer broke in. "I'm having a hard time tying in the alopecia and the mucositis. Where is that coming from? Have there been any other exposures that she might not be aware of?"

"The tox screen was negative both times she came into the ER after the seizures, and she denies any other known exposures," Josh replied.

"The tox screen only checks for commonly abused drugs and only certain chemicals such as lead," Mayer remarked after some thought. "You could check for chronic arsenic poisoning since that has been found recently in the soil of some areas of the District as a result of munitions dumping after WWI."

Nick broke in. "But Dr. Mayer, arsenic usually doesn't cause this degree of bone marrow suppression."

Mayer nodded and shrugged. "You're right, Nicholas, it doesn't. It's been reported to cause only mild anemia and a slight depression of the white count."

"She doesn't live in those sections of the city, but we can certainly send a hair sample for analysis," Josh remarked.

Pittsnogle rubbed his forehead in thought. "Do you think she could be taking something surreptitiously, maybe for secondary gain?"

Josh quickly shook his head. "I've known her for a long time, and I think that's highly unlikely."

He grinned. "Anything's possible. Anyway, it was just a thought."

The participants grew silent as Dr. Roth began to pontificate. "In my opinion, I think you should just sit tight for now. This will be short-lived and should reverse itself. You should wait it out. Continue with the growth factors. That's all you can do."

Pittsnogle nodded in agreement. "I don't think you have any choice. Since we aren't certain exactly what is going on with this patient, it's difficult to make an intelligent recommendation. I would agree with Wil."

"Give it a couple of more days, Josh, then repeat the marrow biopsy and see if there is any regeneration," Mayer added.

Josh turned to Nick. "What are your recommendations?"

"I have to agree with that approach. I don't have any more words of wisdom beyond what's already been said."

When the conference was over, all the participants began to file out of the room. Josh started to leave but Marc Abelman caught his attention. "Dr. Hanley, my I have a word with you?"

He nodded. "Sure, Marc, what's up?" The two sat back down at the table as the room cleared. "As you know, I'm about to finish the second year of my fellowship and have to develop a research project with one of the attendings for this coming academic year."

Josh had offered Abelman a place in his own lab and immediately felt flattered. "And you want to do come work in my lab?" he said with enthusiasm.

The young man shifted in his seat. "Well, not exactly, Dr. Hanley."

"Oh."

"It's not that I wouldn't want to work with you," Abelman quickly added. "It's just that Dr. Hilson was very adamant that I work in his lab."

"Hilson wants you in his lab?" Josh recalled Nick's assertion that Hilson was engaged in a 'secret project' of some sort. "So what project does he want you to work on?"

Abelman hesitated. "Well, it involves cellular differentiation, but beyond that I can't really say."

Josh's curiosity was peaked. "You don't know, or you're not supposed to say?"

"Well, a little bit of both."

"I see. Have you talked to Dr. Hilson recently?"

"Oh no, not for a while. He's been out of the country, you know."

Nick Perrone stepped into the doorway but then stopped. "Oh, I hope I'm not interrupting anything."

"No, we were just finishing up here." Josh then turned to Abelman. "That's sounds great, Marc. I'm disappointed that you didn't want to get involved with one of my projects since I think you'd do a great job. But I understand you have to find the right fit."

The two stood. "I'm heading back to the ward. I'll talk to you later, Dr. Hanley," Abelman said.

Perone followed Josh as he made his way back to the office. "What was that all about?"

"He's going to work in Peter's lab for his research year."

"Poor kid. Does he know what he's getting himself into?"

"Oh, there's more to it," Josh continued. "You apparently were right about Peter being involved in some sort of secret project."

He pulled Josh aside. "What are you talking about?"

"Well, apparently, Peter would not tell Marc exactly what the project entailed, something to do with cellular differentiation, but he also didn't want Marc talking about it."

"Interesting. Have you asked Dottie about it?"

Josh rolled his eyes without breaking his stride. "No, Nick, that's not exactly at the top of my 'to do list.' Right now my number one objective is to keep Jane Riley from dying."

Josh walked into his office and Perone followed, plopping down in a chair. "Did you hear what happed to one of Riley's office assistants?"

"No, what happened?" he asked, sifting through some of the mail on his desk.

Perrone's eyes widened. "Don't you read the newspapers or listen to the news anymore?"

"I don't have time right now. Just tell me what happened to her office assistant."

"He's missing. The police say he was abducted from a Metro stop. He's been missing for several days now."

Josh stopped and looked up. "No, I didn't hear about that." He had read a while back in the *Post* that crime in the District was on the rise. "It is an odd coincidence, though." He sat down heavily at his desk. His head had been aching all afternoon and his stomach was upset.

"You okay, buddy?" Perrone asked.

Josh closed his eyes and began to massage his temples. "No, Nick, I'm not okay. If you want to know the truth, I'm scared to death. I can't understand what is happening to Jane Riley. There is no one single diagnosis that can explain her illness."

Perrone frowned. "So you're not convinced it's the phenytoin, are you?"

Josh stopped rubbing and opened his eyes. "How can it be? It just doesn't make any sense. Phenytoin shouldn't be causing all these symptoms, and I've never read where phenytoin causes this degree of marrow suppression. It just doesn't fit. And Nick, I'm afraid she's going to die real soon if I don't do something, but I don't have a clue as to what that is."

"But Roth and the other brain trust told you to wait it out."

Josh stood and began to pace. "That's easy for them to say. They're safe in their labs and offices. I'm on the front line. I'm responsible for what happens. I'm responsible for Jane's life, not them. Do you know the President called the other day?"

"The president of the hospital?"

"No Nick. *The* President."

Perrone raised his eyebrows. "As in *The* President of the United States?"

Josh nodded and sat on the edge of the desk. "That would be the one, yes."

Perrone let out a long, low whistle. "Wow. I read in the Post this morning that he named an acting commissioner. You must have told him that she was going to be out for a while."

"Something to that effect."

"Wow, that sucks, but what can you do?" Perrone looked at his watch. "I hate to cut this short, but I have to get out of here. I'm meeting my wife for dinner and then we're going to a show at the Kennedy Center."

"What are you going to see," Josh asked enviously.

Perone got up and stretched. "Shear Madness."

"How appropriate. Well, have fun while I'm stuck here," he replied ruefully.

"You should get out more, Josh. You know what you need? You need to take a long vacation, like maybe two or three weeks. You know, maybe one of those cruises where you meet lots of chicks. You're a real catch, Josh. Why aren't you married yet?"

Josh grimaced. As the product of an Irish Catholic father and a Jewish mother, he was used to the double dose of guilt. "Did my mother pay you to ask me that?"

"I can fix you up with one of the nurses. Hey, how about Carol.....ah, Carol what's her name. She's pretty hot."

"No Nick, Carol is trying to get her MRS degree. Not interested."

Perrone chuckled and headed for the door. "Okay, Buddy, see you Monday."

Josh heard the door shut as Perrone left. The offices and clinic were now quiet, dark and deserted. He sat down in his chair and put his head in his hands, feeling very much alone. Jane Riley was not his only patient. There were twenty-nine other souls under his care who also had complicated illnesses and were undergoing complicated treatments. And he was in charge of their fates. He decided who got treated and who was sent home with hospice care. He was responsible for all the decisions, large and small, that were made by him or by someone under his supervision. And he was responsible for the consequences of those decisions. "I need a new job," he muttered.

Then something struck him as very odd. He, and all the others at the conference for that matter, had been focusing on the symptoms that occurred after Riley was started on the anticonvulsant. Perhaps what they should be focusing is what happened before that. She had suffered with the first seizure about two weeks prior to the second one - a seizure that had never been fully explained. He thought of the roses she had mentioned earlier that day then turned to his computer screen and began to type away, plugging search terms into a Poison Control Center database. Page after page of data filled the screen as he anxiously narrowed his search, typing in the sequential terms of convulsions, alopecia, and all the other symptoms and signs that Jane Riley had suffered in the order in which they had occurred. After all the search terms had been entered, what finally appeared on the screen gave him pause. He stared at it in disbelief. "No," he said aloud. "It can't possibly be that."

Twenty-seven

Josh Hanley jogged along the C and O Canal towpath before
going to the hospital to make rounds. The long hours and stress
were beginning to take a toll on his health, and he decided that
the time had come to restart a fitness program for his own well-
being. The air was crisp, just the way he liked it, and the mist
rose off the canal like incense. His pace was slower than it had
been two months prior, but he knew that it would take time to
ease himself back into higher speeds and longer runs. By
concentrating on his breathing pattern, he tried to take his mind
off the patients in the hospital, if just for thirty minutes, but his
thoughts kept circling back to them. Was his lung cancer patient
in bed 3 on the right antibiotic coverage or should he add
another. Then there was the leukemia patient in 12 named Rose
who possibly needed more days of a specific vitamin preparation
to counteract the toxic effects of chemotherapy. Rose needs
more days of the antidote, he thought. Rose. Roses. He
remembered the roses again that Jane Riley had mentioned. If
only there was an antidote for Jane Riley's condition. The
thought amused him briefly until he remembered his search of
the Poison Control Center. He jogged on but couldn't stop
thinking about the roses. What if the unthinkable had happened?
He came to a fast walk and after several minutes stopped to hold
his aching side. What if she was poisoned by someone? He
shook his head. Josh, you need a vacation, he told himself. That
only happens in the movies. Right?

*　　　　　*　　　　　*　　　　　*

　　　*　　　　*　　　　*

"Dr. Riley spiked another temperature this morning,"
Nathaniel Johnson began rounds with what had become a litany
of woe each morning.

Josh scanned the chart feeling somewhat less stressed out
after his morning run. "Has her condition changed significantly

overnight?"

"She's continuing to complain of nausea and had some loose stool last night. We sent it for analysis."

Josh flipped through the pages of her chart. "It's probably related to her mucositis."

"Speaking of which, the mucositis in her mouth is definitely worse," Johnson added.

He frowned. "And her blood counts?"

"Also worse."

Jane's ashen body was lying stiffly in bed, her hands clasped over her stomach with the curtains drawn across the window. Somewhat unnerved by the funerary scene, Josh approached her bed. "Jane?"

She awoke with a start but did not say anything.

"I see you had another fever last night," he continued.

"Yes," she managed. The painful ulcers in her mouth had gotten markedly worse causing great difficulty with speech. Her mouth was now full of saliva that was too painful to swallow.

"Are you able to eat anything?"

She shook her head.

He turned to the intern. "We'll have to start intravenous feeding until this gets better."

"You mean, if it gets better." The bitterness in Jane's voice was palpable. Tears began to fill her eyes. "I'm scared."

He wanted to tell her that he was scared too but instead he said calmly: "I can understand that, Jane." He took her hand gently into his. "You have to believe we're going to get you through this."

"I….hope…..so." She could manage only a few words at a time. "But you….don't even know…..what's going on."

Josh suddenly felt queasy and swallowed hard. She was right, of course. He remembered his search of the poison control center, and the conclusion that he had come to. There was no way she could have received what he thought was causing her illness. Or could she have? Roses, he thought. "Do you have any enemies?" he blurted out.

Her eyes widened and she looked at him. She was about to say something but stopped, closed her eyes and gently nodded her head. "I'm….Commissioner….of the FDA. I have….lots of…..enemies. But….why would…..you ask….such a thing?"

"Anyone in particular who would like to see you, ah…."

She opened her eyes. "Dead?"

"Well, yes."

"What….are you….saying, Josh? "

He remembered Citizen Kane and his sled named Rosebud. It was racing down a slippery slope with him on it and was now impossible to stop. "That maybe someone tried to," he paused. "Um, maybe poison you?"

The residents began to look at one another in stunned silence.

"Dr. Hanley!" Abelman whispered harshly.

Jane folded her arms across her chest and looked away. "I think….the notion….is absurd."

Josh could feel the eyes of his trainees on him, probably wondering what could come out of his mouth next. Perhaps he was going crazy or becoming burned out. Maybe he just needed some time off.

"I was just covering all possibilities," he finally said. She was still avoiding eye contact as he continued. "We presented your case to all the other faculty members, and they all recommended waiting it out." He was unsure how to make her feel better, or at least more confident in the plan of care.

She finally looked at him. "And what....do you think?'

The question caught him off guard. He didn't want to question the accumulated wisdom of the faculty; the same faculty that he considered far superior to him in so many ways. Did he seriously think she had been poisoned or was he just groping for an explanation? And if he did believe it, should he actually act on his assumption? If he were to do so, the treatment would be radical and potentially harmful – fatal even.

"At this point, we have no other choice but to wait it out," he said rather perfunctorily, then added: "And we'll get you through this Jane."

He wasn't convinced that waiting was the right thing to do, but the alternatives were few based on the information available to them. As they left her bedside, he sensed that she was loosing confidence in him and the institution. They had barely made it out into the hall when Abelman spoke up. "What was that all about, Dr. Hanley? You think someone poisoned her?" The residents had gotten behind Abelman as if presenting a united front against the insanity of their attending. His tone bordered on sarcasm.

"Well, it's a possibility," he replied, detecting a hint of

mutiny.

"Based on what?" Abelman continued. His question was not out of line, but his demeanor was becoming confrontational.

"Based on..." He stopped. What was he going to tell them? That he had done a search of the Poison Control Center database and found an implausible answer? "Nothing. Just drop it."

He was growing weary of repeating the same mantra to the residents, Jane's daughter Beth, and Jane herself: 'wait it out, you're going to get better.' He imagined himself on a lifeboat in the North Atlantic shouting encouragement to those still on board the Titanic after all the other lifeboats had been deployed. An insidious lack of confidence seemed to be boring its way into his decisions. He dreaded making rounds each day, an exercise that he once enjoyed. And despite the input he had received from his colleagues, he still felt very much alone in his fight to pull Jane Riley through her puzzling illness. He tried in vain to exorcise the growing sentiment that he was not going to get her out of the hospital alive.

Twenty-eight

By the time George McBrien entered the Oncology Ward
bearing his case of holy oils, visiting hours were nearly over.
The corridors were bereft of physicians and generally deserted.
He headed for Jane Riley's room, nervously fingering the
envelop in his pocket. When he entered the room, he was not
prepared for the change that had come over her in just two short
weeks. She was lying in bed emaciated and pale, with a turban
covering her apparently bald head. Her hands held a book that
she had become too weak to read. When she saw him, she
managed a weak smile but did not speak. The sight of her
expiated any doubts about what he had planned to do. Now was
the time for him to act and stop this nonsense at whatever cost.

"Jane," he said trying to maintain his composure. "I've come
to anoint you."

She nodded her ascent, and he approached the bed. He placed
the case on the bedside table, carefully opened it, and placed the
thumb of his right hand into the blessed oils. Leaning over her,
he made a small cross of oil on her forehead. When he reached
for her hands to do the same, he was taken aback by their skeletal
appearance.

"Through this holy anointing may the Lord in his love and
mercy help you with the grace of the Holy Spirit." He made a
cross of oil on each hand. "May the Lord who frees you from
sin, save you and raise you up."

By the time he was finished, Jane Riley had fallen into a deep
slumber. He quickly collected the oils and exited the room.
Without hesitation, he went into the nurses' station and found
Riley's chart in a rack with other charts. He was just about to
pull the envelop from the pocket of his jacket when a voice from
behind startled him.

"You're here awfully late, Father." He recognized one of the
ward nurses that he had encountered before but could not

remember her name.

"Well, duty calls," he said nervously.

She studied the nameplate on the chart. "So you're seeing Jane Riley."

"Well….ah….yes, I administered the Sacrament of Anointing of the Sick." He tried to sound as calm and as official as possible. But all the while he was yearning to blurt out what he knew.

"Oh, I see," she replied.

"How is she doing?" he asked. "She looks pretty sick. What exactly is wrong with her?"

The nurse raised her eyebrows and blew out a breath. "Well, I don't think the doctor's know exactly what's wrong with her."

"Oh….really?"

The nurse nodded and moved in closer. "And just between you and me," she whispered, "I don't think she's going to make it."

McBrien recoiled. "What do you mean? How much time does she have?"

She shrugged. "You know as well as I, that's up to the man upstairs." She looked upward only briefly. "Well, I have patients to see. Good evening, Father." The nurse continued on her way and quickly left the station.

McBrien glanced nervously about before opening the chart. He started to document in the medical record that he had administered a sacrament, as was the standard procedure for the clergy, but then thought better of it. Instead, he quickly removed the envelope from his pocket and placed it between the pages with enough of it sticking out to be easily noticeable. He closed the chart, carefully placed it back in the rack, and quietly left.

Twenty-nine

The note was found by Judy Sterns at the end of her night shift. The morning shift was arriving on the unit and Nursing Report, or just 'report' as it was known, was about to begin. It was during this time that the nurses going off duty passed on information about their patients, events that had occurred during the previous shift, order changes, problems, etc., to the nurses coming on duty, thus maintaining seamless continuity of care. This sacrosanct ritual occurred at the change of each shift, and interruption by anyone, including physicians, was not well tolerated. Only a dire emergency could flush the nurses out of their conference room during this crucial fifteen minutes.

It had been a busy night for the seasoned fifty two year old nurse. In addition to the usual workload, one of her patients had arrested and, after a successful code blue, was transferred to the ICU. Another had died, albeit expectedly, and it had taken her several hours to prepare the body for the morgue. In addition, she had cared for Jane Riley, one of the sickest patients on the unit. Exhausted, she grabbed Riley's chart to finally complete her nursing assessment. As she pulled it from the rack, a long, business-style envelope slipped out from between the pages and glided to the floor.

She signed and shook her head, then doggedly stooped to retrieved it. "What now?" She asked herself. The inscription, "*For Dr. J. Hanley*" was written across on the front with the word "*CONFIDENTIAL*" inscribed below it in capital letters.

She quickly handed it off to the nurse taking over her shift for the day. "Hey Adele, this slipped out of Riley's chart. See that Dr. Hanley gets it when he comes in, will you?"

Adele was taking over the care of her patients; she took the envelope and dropped it in her pocket of her smock. The medical team had just assembled to make rounds, and the residents were gathering the charts. Josh Hanley strode into the nurses station, nodding his good mornings and headed for the phone to answer a page. Adele approached him as he picked up the phone and dialed.

"This is for you, Dr. H." She quickly handed him the envelope and went back to her duties.

"Thanks," he mumbled, taking it with his free hand. While waiting for an answer, he casually studied the envelope, holding it up to the light to inspect its contents. The caller at the other end, the ICU attending, was giving a status report on the patient who had coded earlier that morning. With his mind now focused on the critical patient, Josh stuffed the envelope in the pocket of his lab coat.

Rounds lasted over four hours that morning. Jane Riley had continued to spike temperatures and her blood oxygen levels were beginning to drop. It appeared that she was developing a lung infection that was not responding well to antibiotics, and might soon require mechanical ventilation, i.e., the use of a breathing machine, to assist with breathing. In addition, her blood counts had not budged, despite the use of bone marrow stimulants, and she was becoming weaker.

"So, what should we do now, Dr. Hanley?" Marc Abelman asked as they stood outside her door.

Josh thrust his hands deep into the pockets of his pants and looked at the floor as he spoke. "I discussed her case with Dr. Roth again last night. He has a lot more experience, and he thinks we should keep plugging away."

"But she's not getting any better," Abelman countered.

Josh looked up. "I know that Marc. If you have any brilliant ideas I'd be happy to listen to them."

"But you're the attending….."

"I'm well aware of my position, Dr. Abelman." Josh scanned the faces of the house staff, wondering if they too were losing confidence in his decisions.

Abelman's voice softened. "I'm sorry. I didn't mean to upset you."

Josh nodded. "It's okay, Marc. I'm just as frustrated as you are."

It wasn't until after rounds, when placing his stethoscope back into his pocket, that Josh remembered the envelope. He grabbed it from the pocket of his lab coat and briefly regarded the inscription of the outside before ripping it open. The enclosed note was neatly typed and only two sentences long. He read it again.

Seething, he searched the nurses' station and saw Abelman talking to one of the residents.

"Is this your idea of a sick joke?" he said stomping over to where they were standing while waving the piece of paper. "How dare you mock me!"

Abelman reared back against a nearby chair. "Whoa, what are you talking about, Dr. Hanley?"

Josh waved the note again. "Don't play dumb. One of you wise guys wrote this, and it is the height of unprofessionalism!"

"I...I'm sorry...I don't know what you're talking about!" Abelman stammered.

He thrust the letter to Abelman, who quickly took it in his shaking hands and began to read. By now all the residents and students had gathered around to see what the commotion was about. "I want to know which one of you wrote this," he said evenly, scanning the stunned faces. The shaken residents began to quickly read the letter over Abelman's shoulder.

"But Dr. Hanley," Abelman said after some length. "I didn't write this letter."

The residents quickly nodded in unison. "I sure as hell didn't write it," Johnson said innocently.

"Well, if you didn't write it, then who....?" He stopped, grabbed the letter from Abelman and scanned the corridor. Nurse Adele had just emerged from a patient's room with medicine tray in hand and was making her way toward another. "Adele!" he shouted.

Startled, she stopped in mid stride, nearly dropping her tray of medicine cups. "What's wrong, Dr. Hanley?"

He sprinted toward her, waving the letter above his head. "Where did you get this?"

"Where did I get what?"

"This." He thrust it in front of her.

"What?"

"This letter." He saw her blank expression. "It was in the envelope you gave me this morning."

"Oh, was that what was in the envelope?"

"Yes, where did it come from?"

"I...I...don't know," she stammered. "Judy Sterns gave it to me. She said she found it in Dr. Riley's chart. Why? What's wrong?"

"Is Judy still here?"

"No, she left hours ago."

"I need to talk to her. Do you have her home phone number?"

Adele put the tray down on the medicine cart and started for the nursing station with Josh at her heels. "It should be in the nursing office. She's probably in bed asleep by now. What's so urgent?"

He handed her the note, and she read it while she walked.

"Oh my goodness!" She handed it back to him, and quickened her pace. "I'll get her number right away."

Abelman stood frozen with the residents near the nursing station. "Where did it come from?"

Josh threw his hands up in a dramatic gesture. "I don't know, Marc. Your guess is as good as mine, but this may be the explanation we've been looking for!"

Adele returned several minutes later with a sheet of paper and handed it to Josh. He grabbed the phone and quickly punched in a series of numbers. Judy Sterns was roused out of a much-needed sleep and grudgingly reported just what she knew. She did not know where it came from, how it had gotten there, or how long it had been there.

"Damn!" Josh hung up the phone.

"It says that Jane Riley has been poisoned," Abelman said. "But you had already suspected that." He readjusted his glasses. "Do you really think we should put much credence to this note, Dr. Hanley?"

Josh looked him squarely in the face. "Look, I don't know when this letter was put in the chart. It could have been there for days for all we know and no one saw it. There's no date on it. Besides, visitors come and go here all day long. Anyone could have left it." Josh began to pace. "I didn't tell you this earlier but I think I know what is causing her problem. This just confirms my theory." He led them over to a computer terminal. "Marc, sit down and go to the Poison Control website." Abelman sat down tentatively and began to peck away at the keyboard. Josh stood behind him as the house staff and students huddled around. "Type in seizures or convulsions first," he instructed.

Abelman pecked away at the keyboard and after several seconds had passed, a seven-page list of chemicals and drugs flashed up on the screen. He scrolled through the list. "Geez, there must be hundreds here!"

Josh leaned over his shoulder to inspect the screen. "Now cross reference this list with alopecia."

Abelman typed in the new search term and smacked the 'enter' key. Several seconds later, another list flashed on the screen. "That narrowed it down somewhat," he announced. The list was still three pages long.

Josh straightened up. "Put in bone marrow failure or myelosuppression."

Abelman put in the next search term and they all waited in silence with eyes fixed on the computer screen. The list narrowed to one page with a single entry. "Busulfan?" he said.

"Precisely," Josh replied.

Abelman turned in the chair. "What are you saying?"

"It's got to be the chemotherapeutic drug busulfan."

Abelman drew his face into a disbelieving squint. "But how?"

"Go to the PDR website and look up busulfan," Josh instructed confidently.

Abelman hesitated then turned and punched the keyboard again. The letters PDR stood for *Physician's Desk Reference*, a book that was updated every year and contained information on every prescription drug on the market. Since physicians in practice had no way of knowing or remembering the intricacies of every drug, the enormous tome was used extensively in medical practice as a handy reference manual. Fortunately, its contents were now computerized and had become available online.

Within seconds, pages of data flooded the screen. The whole group was now leaning over the fellow, trying to peruse the voluminous information.

"Its chemical name is 1,4- butanediol dimethane-sulfonate," Josh noted. "Now, look at the pharmacokinetic section.

"No analytical method has been found which permits the quantification of busulfan or its metabolites in biological tissues or plasma," Abelman read. "So if someone wanted to commit murder without a trace...."

"It would be the perfect drug," Josh finished.

"And the patient would die, and the docs would think it was just another case of idiopathic bone marrow failure," Abelman said.

"And no one would suspect a thing," Johnson finished. He then let out a low whistle.

For several minutes, the group silently digested what had just been said.

Abelman suddenly broke the silence. "So you suspected this all along, didn't you Dr. Hanley?"

Josh shrugged. "Well, not from the beginning certainly. I mean, how would she have gotten busulfan for crying out loud? That's not exactly an easy thing to do." Josh re-read the letter yet again. "It's smart, though. Real smart. So, someone real smart, with a medical or pharmacy background must be in on this, and someone went to a great deal of trouble to tell us about it. And the Commissioner's looking real bad. I'm not sure she's going to make it unless...."

"We do a transplant?" Abelman asked.

Josh nodded solemnly. He thought of Rose and the antidote. "Unless we do a transplant."

"So you think we should act on this shaky piece of evidence and *transplant* Jane Riley?" Johnson asked.

Josh took a deep breath and hesitated. He could feel all their eyes on him, awaiting words of wisdom from their obviously frazzled attending. "I don't think we have a choice, Nathaniel. If Jane Riley has received a lethal dose of busulfan, she will not recover without a bone marrow transplant. In order for it to be successful, she will have to have a perfectly matched donor, or at least, a near perfect match. As to how she got it, right now, is not a priority to me. That's a matter for the police or the FBI, I suppose, to figure out." He then realized that multiple people had handled the letter, which would be a prime piece of evidence and evaluated for fingerprints; he laid it gently on the counter. "Nobody else touches this letter!"

"What's all the commotion about?" Beth Riley stood behind them with a hand in the back pocket of her blue jeans.

Josh turned with a start and looked at her. "Oh, Beth, ah....you're just in time!" he blurted out.

"Why?" she asked, glancing around at all the physicians who now surrounded her. "Is something wrong with Mother?"

"She's holding her own for now," Josh replied quickly. "Beth, does Jane have any siblings?"

"Just one. I had called him when mother was admitted, but

they're not really close. They've had….issues in the past.
Anyway, his secretary said that he would be out of the country
for several weeks."

Josh winced and looked at the floor. He then caught her eyes
again.

"Then they need to make nice with each other right away.
You must have him located immediately. We need to get him to
Washington today!"

Thirty

Grace Love stood at the nursing station in the oncology unit pouring over the contents of the letter. Its text was simple: '*For Dr. J. Hanley. Dr. Jane Riley has been poisoned with an unidentified substance that is in the form of a white dust or powder. This crime has been perpetrated as part of a conspiracy to murder her.*'

"So you found this stuffed in her chart?" Grace asked, using the tip of her pen to move the letter around.

Josh shook his head no. "Judy Sterns, one of the night nurses, found it early this morning, but I didn't read it until about twenty or thirty minutes ago."

"So a nurse named Judy Sterns found it early this morning." Grace jotted her name on a pad.

"Yes."

"And no one saw who put it there."

"Right."

"And no one came onto this unit who wasn't supposed to be here."

Josh shrugged. "That I don't know. At least, no one has mentioned it."

"And you think this is real? You don't think this is some kind of hoax."

She noticed him hesitate and then nervously run his hand through his thick brown hair. His face was unshaven, and the open collar of his shirt revealed a tuft of chest hair. He was thin, but well built, and appeared to be very fatigued. Although not usually attracted to Caucasian men, she found him appealing nonetheless. He didn't look much older than the residents and students around him, and she marveled that someone so young could have such daunting responsibilities.

"Yes, I think it's real….I think."

She looked him in the eyes. "You think?"

He nodded. "Uh huh."

"Okay, fine. And where is this Judy Sterns now?"

"She's at home. She worked all night. But she'll certainly be available to answer any questions."

"Uh huh," Grace said. "Is there a roster of who comes and goes in this unit?"

"No, we don't keep a record of that. There's really no reason to," Josh began. "I mean, there's nurses, food service people, housekeeping, physical therapists, visitors…the list goes on. It would be impossible to track everyone who comes and goes."

"I see," Grace said thoughtfully. "And everyone has access to the charts?"

"No, not everyone."

"Who then?"

"Well, all sorts of medical personnel, physicians, nurses, physical therapists, social workers. The list is fairly extensive."

Grace reread the letter. "So when are visiting hours?"

"They begin at eleven and end at eight in the evening."

Grace jotted some more notes on her pad. "Do you have any idea what she could have gotten?"

She noticed him hesitate again. "I have an idea but there's really no way to prove it at this point. I think she may have gotten a drug called busulfan. Her symptoms are certainly consistent with that."

Grace stopped writing and looked up. "Bu...what? Could you spell that, Doc?"

"B-U-S-U-L-F-A-N."

"Busulfan." She wrote it on her pad and studied the word. "Now what is that?"

"It's a chemotherapeutic agent. In high doses, it causes seizures and can cause severe bone marrow suppression."

"Bone marrow suppression?"

"Yes."

"Lay terms, Doc."

"Oh. Um, it wipes out the bone marrow and causes the patient not to make blood cells properly."

Grace nodded thoughtfully and arched her eyebrows. "I see. We'll need to reconstruct a list of all the nurses who were on duty last night and this morning. I need to know if anyone saw anything out of the ordinary. And I think the FBI will be very interested in this letter."

"The night nurses and nursing supervisors will be more than happy to cooperate with your investigation," Josh replied.

After spending several hours at the hospital talking to nurses, housekeeping personnel, respiratory therapists and others, Grace and Al notified the chief of police, Ramsey Powell who instructed them to call the FBI field office as soon as possible. By the time Grace and Al drove to his office downtown at Judiciary Square, two agents had already joined him in his office.

"This is Special Agent Bill Dugan." Chief Powell motioned to a husky, Caucasian male with close-cropped dark hair, seated in a leather wing chair across the desk from him. He rose and extended his hand.

"And Special Agent Jeff Cochran." Grace's eyes fell to a tall, handsome African American man with salt and pepper hair standing near the window. Like his partner, he was dressed in a dark suit and starched white shirt. Her heart jumped when she took his hand. "This is Detective Grace Love and her partner Detective Al King." Chief Powell then motioned for them to help themselves to the chairs near his desk. "I've briefed these two agents of the situation, but you two can give them the specifics of this case."

"Gentleman, glad you could join us so quickly," Grace remarked as they all sat down.

"May we see the letter?" Dugan asked abruptly.

She handed him both the letter and envelope, which were by now sealed in separate plastic bags. "These haven't been dusted for prints, yet, but several people at the hospital have already handled them."

Dugan read the brief note and passed it to Cochran who put on wire-rimmed reading glasses. "We'll need a print check and a writing analysis on the envelope." He removed his glasses and put them back inside a pocket of his jacket.

Grace nodded.

"Any leads as to where this letter came from?" Dugan asked.

"We've compiled a list of all the nurses, station clerks, orderlies, and so forth who worked on that unit during the past twenty-four hours," she remarked, handing him a sheet of paper. "It's as near complete as we can get right now. The squad is beginning to interview some of them to see if anyone saw anything out of the ordinary."

Dugan surveyed the list and nodded. "Good. And you said

on the phone that a Dr. Josh Hanley found the note?"

"A nurse found the note in the chart," King remarked. "But Hanley is our point man."

Dugan wrote on a small note pad, using his left hand in an awkward curl. "I see. And how can we contact him?"

"He's still at the hospital and eager to talk to you," Grace replied.

Dugan closed the pad and put it and the pen in an inside pocket of his jacket. "We'll pay him a visit, then."

Cochran picked up the bags containing the letter and the envelope. "We'll drop these off at the FBI Crime Lab on our way to the hospital."

"We welcome your expertise," Powell noted. "We'll continue the investigation from our end."

They all stood. Cochran looked at Grace then to King "Is there anything you'd like to add?"

Grace nodded. "One other thing. Dr. Hanley thinks the victim may have received a type of drug…what did he call it?" She pulled out her own pad and flipped through the pages. "Busulfan. B-U-S-U-L-F-A-N."

Dugan quickly pulled out his pad again and scribbled the name of the drug. He clicked the pen and returned it and the pad to his pocket again. "Good. Thanks for the info. We'll be in touch."

Grace was relieved that the FBI had stepped in so quickly. She figured this particular case could become very complicated.

Thirty-one

Beth Riley was fast asleep, lying fully clothed across the bed in her old room when the cell phone chime wrenched her to consciousness. She had spent most that day trying to locate her mother's only brother, but had somehow drifted off amid the comforting wallpaper of pink roses that surrounded her lace canopied bed. After releasing the old stuffed teddy bear from her embrace, she frantically searched the duvet and found the phone wedged between a fold.

"Hello? Hello?" She held the phone in one hand and raked the hair out of her eyes with the other.

"Hello...Beth?" The caller's baritone voice sounded as if it was far away.

"Uncle Alex? Where are you?"

"New York. I got this urgent message from my staff assistant while in Bangkok yesterday and cut my trip short."

"Thank goodness she got in contact with you. Uncle Alex, you must come to Washington immediately!"

He hesitated. "Why?"

"It's mother. She's desperately ill and needs your help."

"My help? What's wrong with her?"

"It's hard to explain over the phone, Alex." She could not hide the desperation in her voice. "You need to be tested to see if you're a suitable bone marrow donor for her."

There was another prolonged moment of silence. "A what?"

"Something's wrong with her bone marrow." Beth could feel herself began to shake. As tears flooded her eyes, she fought to maintain composure. "It's all very complicated. You need to get here as soon as possible. The doctor will explain everything. She will die without your help." She began to cry softly. "I'm sorry, Uncle Alex. I know you and mother have had your differences, but now she needs you more than ever."

She could hear him heave a sigh. "You know I'd do anything

for Jane. Look, we have the best hospitals in the world in New York. Maybe we should arrange to have her transferred."

"No…no…she's too unstable to move right now."

"Okay, Beth, don't worry. I'll catch the next flight to Washington. I'll be there tonight if I have to drive."

"I love you, Uncle Alex!"

"I love you, too, Beth."

Thirty-two

Leander Murray spoke into a blue tooth earphone as he sat behind the desk in the office of the Commissioner. Donald Hart was on the other end expressing his concern that the proposed tobacco regulations had become mired in congress. The momentum that Jane Riley had built was evidently waning in her absence. For reasons that were unclear, the subcommittee had now tabled all plans for implementation.

"It's almost as if Jane's illness came at the most opportune time for the tobacco industry," Hart lamented. "The bastards are probably relieved that she's sick!"

Murray's voice was calm. "We'll just have to pick up where we left off."

Hart hesitated. "When, Lee? When are we going to start having meetings again about this agenda? We've put so much work into it already I'd hate to have to start from scratch again."

"Right now, things are in a bit chaotic around here without Jane. I've stepped into problems and issues I didn't even know existed, Don. I'm hoping I can pull everyone together again."

Hart's tone softened. "I understand, Lee, I didn't mean to go ballistic on you, but we have to get moving…."

Their conversation was interrupted by a commotion that had suddenly erupted just outside the Commissioner's office.

"Hold on a second, Don. Something's going on. Let me call you right back." He pulled off the earphone as he walked to the door and opened it. To his surprise, the reception area was filled with several staff assistants talking excitedly amongst themselves. Ellen Downs sat behind her desk, dabbing her eyes with a handkerchief.

Murray put his hands on his hips. "What in the world is going on?"

Ellen looked up. "Deb was just in the cafeteria on break watching CNN. They're saying that a report has leaked from

Georgetown that Jane was poisoned!"

Lee Murray froze. "What?"

Deb, a tall, thin African American woman with short hair and oval black-framed glasses spoke up. "It's on CNN, Dr. Murray. They're saying that Dr. Riley was poisoned!"

"Poisoned?"

"Yes, poisoned!" Ellen repeated. "And there's another rumor that someone may have cut her brake lines the day she had that accident!"

Murray wrinkled his forehead. "Someone leaked that story from Georgetown? It just sounds so ridiculous. Why would anyone want to kill the Commissioner of the FDA?"

"Jane had enemies, believe me," Ellen rose from her chair and came around the desk. "She got threatening letters and phone calls on a regular basis. CanActUp, tobacco sympathizers, you name it."

"Oh, Ellen, really! How would anyone do such a thing in the first place?" Murray asked. He pulled away from her and turned to the group. "Excuse me. Everyone, listen up. I'll look into this rumor and see if there's any truth to it. The very notion is absurd. Now, let's all get back to work."

When the reception area had cleared, Murray looked at Ellen Downs and shook his head. "It's just a rumor, I'm sure."

Ellen sat back down and wiped her nose. "First Jane gets sick and then Stanley disappears. And now this thing about Jane being poisoned. What's going on around here?" She thought for a moment. "You know, Max Dickson came to see her just before she had her accident."

Murray frowned. "That doesn't mean he poisoned her."

Ellen nodded and shrugged. "It was just a thought."

"Let's not jump off the deep end, here. I think you should keep those theories to yourself. I don't want this office to be responsible for any false accusations," he said.

"Of course not, sir," she responded.

"Good, then. Let's consider this matter closed." He retreated into the Commissioner's office and remerged several minutes later with his brief case in hand. Ellen was seated at her desk on the phone.

"Dr. Murray!" She whispered with her hand over the mouthpiece. "It's channel four! They're wondering if you have any comment on the story about Jane."

"What? No! Tell them that the rumors are unsubstantiated, and that I have no comment at the present time."

Ellen relayed the message and then put her hand back over the mouthpiece. "Do you want to do an interview tomorrow?"

He hesitated. "Why?"

"They want to know how things are going at the Agency since Jane's been out, if there's been any slow down in the approval process, or if there's any connection between Jane's illness and Stanley's disappearance."

He exhaled forcefully. "You're kidding! This is getting out of hand, and I need to set the record straight. They can come tomorrow morning if my schedule will permit it."

Ellen offered them a time slot, then hung up the phone. "They'll be here at ten."

"Fine. Now I have an emergency meeting downtown on the tobacco regulation issue. I'll be on my cell phone if anyone needs to get in contact with me," he said, hurrying out of the office.

Once the door had closed, Ellen thought for a moment and then remembered an incident that had occurred several days before Jane's accident – an incident about which she had almost forgotten. She picked up the phone and punched in a series of numbers.

"Hi Deb, I need a little favor from you that involves a personnel file."

Thirty-three

Alex Byrne had settled into the first-class section of the MD-80 reading the *New York Times*. Because of heavy air traffic around New York, the flight to Washington had been delayed. Alex had learned long ago not to worry about things that were beyond his control. Ordinarily, he would have enjoyed the respite after a hectic day, but because of his need to get to Washington, he felt anxious.

He had returned after three weeks in Thailand to a desk piled high with work. Sleep deprived and exhausted from jet lag, he had spent the entire day tying up loose ends, dictating quick memos to his staff assistants and returning phone calls. His efficient and competent executive assistant, who saw to it that he was in the right place at the right time, had booked a late afternoon flight to Washington. After throwing a few things together, he had raced to LaGuardia only to sit on the tarmac for over an hour waiting for the air traffic around the city to clear. With the help of some gin and a whiff of vermouth, he was hoping to catch a brief nap on the plane.

"Would you like a pillow, sir?" the flight attendant asked pleasantly. She had been instantly attracted to the tall, handsome traveler in seat 3B, taking note of the thick black hair, graying just around the edges, the intense blue eyes, and the strong, broad shoulders. She had helped him with his custom-made suit jacket, savored the expensive cologne, and, noted with a great deal of interest, the lack of a wedding band. She wanted to believe that the eye contact being made was not so much for coffee or tea, but "me."

He glanced at her nametag. "That would be lovely, Melinda."

The balding, overweight man behind Alex in 4B raised his hand. "Ma'am, I could use a pillow, too."

She gave him a quick glance. "Just a second, sir." She then turned back to Alex, "Here let me help you with this." She positioned a small pillow behind his head as her well proportioned bosom dangled dangerously close to his face.

"There, is that better?" she asked.

"Quite nice," Alex smiled, inspecting her cleavage.

"Good, now you just let me know if I can do *anything* for you," she purred.

"I certainly will." His smile revealed two rows of perfect, white teeth, and she nearly melted.

"Now, what did you want, sir?" she asked the gentleman in 4B, trying to regain her composure.

"A pillow, please." He smiled, his eyes fixed to her breasts.

She reached into the overhead bin and tossed a pillow into his lap.

"Here you go!" she said with practiced cheeriness.

When the plane was finally ready to taxi to the runway, Melinda did a final sweep through the first class cabin to ensure that everyone was tucked in for takeoff.

"Make sure your seatbelt is securely fastened around your waist," she almost purred to Alex.

The plane finally left LaGuardia at around eight and landed at Reagan National nearly sixty minutes later. Alex had managed to bring only one carry-on, and Melinda made sure that it was quickly retrieved.

"You live in New York?" she asked, helping him with his overcoat.

"Yes," he replied, straightening the collar.

"So do I! What a coincidence," she answered. "How long are you going to be in D.C.?"

"Not sure," he said brushing past her.

"Well, have a nice stay! Ba-bye," she deadpanned with disappointment, realizing that Mr. 3B apparently had no interest in her after all.

Alex fought his way through the crowded airport terminal but escaped the battle at the baggage claim area. With the help of a twenty-dollar bill to the taxi steward, he was quickly placed into a waiting cab and twenty minutes later found himself standing, bag in hand, before the nursing station of the Oncology Unit at Georgetown University Hospital. Having been informed by the station clerk of Jane Riley's room number, he entered the Transplant Unit where Beth was waiting for him.

"Uncle Alex!" She hugged him then reared back. "You look

exhausted."

"I'm okay, Beth. It's nice to see you again." He gave her a tight squeeze and kissed her on the cheek. "Now tell me what exactly is going on with Jane."

Beth bit her lower lip, and Alex noted that her eyes were tearing. "It's awful but it's going to have to wait. I'll explain it all to you after you've been to the lab."

He held her again, his mouth close to her ear. "It's okay, Beth, I'm here now," he said gently. "We'll get her through this together." He released his grip. "How are you holding up?"

"Better, now that you're here." She kissed him on the cheek. "May I see her?"

"Only for a minute. I'll let the nurses know that you're here so that the appropriate paperwork can be done for you to have your blood taken," Beth said, turning toward the nurses' station. "Don't forget to wash your hands and be careful, her resistance to infection is very low."

When Alex opened the door, the person lying in bed was a stranger. She was emaciated and bald, barely able to move. Multiple IV pumps surrounded her bed, and oxygen seeped into her nose through a clear tube.

Jane lifted a hand. "Alex!" Her voice was but a whisper, but he noticed that she was smiling.

He cautiously approached her bed, not even sure he wanted a closer look. "Jane, my God!" he mumbled. "What has happened to you?" He sat beside her bed and looked at her hand, wondering if he should touch it.

"The doctor will explain," she whispered. "I'm so glad to see you; it's been too long."

"Jane, I'm so sorry..." A lump caught in his throat.

"They need some blood from you," she whispered.

"Yes, I'm going to go as soon as they're ready." He gently grasped her hand. It was cold, and he could clearly see the contours of her bones.

"Beth looks, great." He wiped away a tear with his free hand. "You've done a fantastic job with her. She's at Stanford now, huh? You must be proud of her."

Jane nodded, still smiling.

"Wow, time does fly." His voice cracked with emotion. "Look, Jane, I'm going to go find the nurse and get to the lab as soon as possible for whatever it is they need."

He got up to leave and stopped. "I want you and Beth to
know that I'm not leaving here until you are better," he said
confidently. But once outside the room, he had to lean against
the wall for several minutes before heading to the nurses' station.

Thirty-four

With Nathaniel Johnson at his side, Josh came onto the unit. He instantly spotted the tall, dark-haired man standing at the nurses' station with an overcoat draped over one arm, and the sleeve of the other rolled up, revealing a band-aid at the crook. He was well dressed and from the side looked vaguely familiar.

"I need to speak with Jane Riley's doctor," he was saying to the station clerk.

"Sir, I'm Jane Riley's doctor," Josh said as he approached the nurses' station. When the man turned to face him, he stopped in mid stride and his heart began to pound. "Alex?" His voice was just above a whisper. Before him stood a former friend he never expected to see again. His mind suddenly went blank. He was too exhausted and too preoccupied to recall all the details of their past, both good and not so good.

"What are you doing here?" he blurted out, somewhat harsher than intended.

Alex reared back. "Josh Hanley?" He surveyed the white coat and nameplate. "So you became a doctor just like you said you would."

"Yes I did." Josh's eyes fell to the band-aid. "Wait a minute. You're not.....you can't possibly be...."

"Jane's brother," Alex finished. "And I'm here to be typed, whatever that means, for reasons that are unclear to me."

"I don't believe this." Josh stood speechless and for a while the two just stared at one other. In all the years Josh had known both Jane and Alex, he never once heard them speak of the other by name. He had worked in Jane's laboratory for several years and tried to recall a time when she ever mentioned that she had a brother, especially one that had gone to the same college as he. But among physicians, the place of one's medical education was better known than one's undergraduate institution.

"So you two know each other?" Nathaniel cut in, breaking

the uneasy silence. "How weird is that?"

"We met in college," Josh said. "We were…" He stopped, searching for the right term. What exactly had they been? "Classmates," he finally managed.

"Right, classmates." Alex rolled his eyes and rubbed the back of his neck.

"This is Nathaniel Johnson. He's the intern who is taking care of Jane," Josh said quickly. The two men shook hands.

"You look like you may have played football," Alex said. "College?"

"No, just high school," the intern replied.

He turned to Josh. "So what the heck is wrong with my sister, Dr. Hanley? She looks like she's about to die."

"Nathaniel, go check on your patients," Josh said curtly. "I can fill Mr. Byrne in on Dr. Riley's condition."

The intern nodded. "Okay. Nice meeting you, Mr. Byrne."

Alex grinned. "Mr. Byrne! Please, call me Alex." He turned to Josh as the intern left. "So?"

Josh rubbed his forehead. "Where do I begin? It's a long story." His headache told him that he hadn't eaten since breakfast. He then realized that Alex was now here to stay and would likely be integral to Jane's recovery. Regardless of what had transpired between them years prior, the past would have to be quickly forgiven and forgotten. "Have you had dinner yet?"

Alex shook his head.

"If you don't have any objections, could we discuss this over dinner? I'm starving."

"It's fine with me if you don't mind." Alex lowered his voice. "I hope this forced reunion has not upset you."

Josh grabbed a clipboard from the counter and flipped up a page. "Why would I be upset?" he said nonchalantly after realizing he was looking at the nurses' vacation schedule instead of a patient's chart. "In fact, you don't know how glad I am to see you." He put the chart down. "Would I be inviting you to dinner if I was upset to see you?" Damn, I'm rambling, he thought.

"But as I recall, the last time we spoke, you said you never wanted to see me again."

Josh held up his hand. "Forget what I said then. It's ancient history."

"Okay, fine." He paused. "You know, you haven't changed a

bit, Josh. You look great!" Alex grabbed him around the shoulders and gave him a loose hug.

"You do too, Alex." He stiffened and then broke the embrace.

"Hell, Josh, I look like crap! I haven't slept for two days!"

The elevator doors opened and Beth Riley exited. "Uncle Alex, you're back from the lab."

He nodded. "And you're never going to believe this, but Dr. Hanley and I were classmates in college."

Her eyes widened. "Really? Wow, what an incredible coincidence."

"Yes, classmates," Josh repeated.

"We were about to go to dinner to discuss Jane's case," Alex interjected. "Would you like to join us?"

"I ate a long time ago, and I want to stay with mother again tonight." She reached into the pocket of her jeans. "Here's the key to the house. Mother's car was totaled in the accident so I've been using cabs for transportation. It's much easier and you don't have to worry about parking."

"Accident?" Alex asked.

"Oh, that's right, you don't know about that, either," Beth replied. "I guess Dr. Hanley can fill you in on that, too."

Alex looked at Josh and raised his eyebrows. "This all sounds so complicated."

"I'll explain it all to you, Alex. The hospital cafeteria is closed and, believe me, that's a blessing. We can go to an all night place I know in Georgetown and then I can drop you off at Jane's house. It's not far from mine."

*   *   *   *
    *   *   *

"So when will you get the results of my test?" Alex asked as he followed Josh down an uneven brick sidewalk of Georgetown.

"Your blood sample has been given the highest priority. The tissue-typing lab has essentially dropped everything else. I owe them big time. Here we are." Josh held open a heavy wooden door with a large glass window in it.

Bogart's occupied a narrow slice of M street just south of the main campus, on a sloping street overlooking the Potomac River. Well worn wooden booths lined one wall, and a polished rosewood bar occupied the opposite one. The pale yellow walls were decorated with old movie posters advertising long forgotten

Humphrey Bogart films, and Billie Holiday's voice crooned in the background. The booths were filled to capacity with Georgetown students and tourists, but the two found a place at the counter where a large African American woman greeted them with menus.

"Evenin', Doc. Late night tonight, huh baby?" She wiped the counter in front of them with a towel.

"Yeah, Ethel, it's been one of those days."

"What you can I get you tonight?" She threw the towel under the counter and picked up her pen and pad.

"I think I'll have the club sandwich on wheat, hold the mayo." Josh handed her back the menu.

"I'm starving, Ethel. What would you recommend?"

Josh noted that Alex still treated everyone as if he'd known them for years.

"This late a' night, baby, I think you bettah have th' western omelete wit' some toast and milk," she replied, writing it on her pad.

Alex handed back the menu. "Sounds good to me, Ethel. I'll let you be in charge tonight."

She looked at him over her glasses and winked. "'Be in charge o' you every night if you want me to be, baby." They heard her cackle as she sauntered toward the kitchen.

Josh shook his head. "I've been coming here for years, and Ethel has never once flirted with me."

Alex rolled his eyes. "Don't sound so disappointed."

The two men then sat staring straight ahead at their reflected images in the greasy mirror behind the counter.

"So all this stuff with Jane is pretty unbelievable. The FBI is involved. It's all so surreal. You think this letter is legit, huh?"

Josh removed his glasses and rubbed his eyes. He realized that Alex was completely exhausted, more so than himself, and wondered how much of what he had told him on the way over had registered. "If I didn't think it was real, you wouldn't be here."

"Do you think she's going to make it? She looks real bad."

For the first time in many days, Josh's confidence had returned. Not only had he solved the mystery of Jane Riley's illness but hopefully had the antidote sitting right next to him. "We will get her through this no matter what it takes," he replied to the image in the mirror. He turned to Alex. "So yes, she's going to make it."

"That's all I needed to hear," Alex replied.

"So why have you and Jane been estranged?" Josh asked.

Alex reared back. "Estranged? Who told you that?"

"Well, Beth did, in so many words."

"Oh. I don't think we were ever estranged. Pissed off with one another is more appropriate I think. Anyway, it's a long story. I'll tell you about it one day. But rest assured, I'll be here for her no matter what she needs."

"Great, that's all I needed to hear," Josh replied, placing emphasis on the 'I.' The two were silent for several more minutes.

"So, how long has it been?" Alex asked at length.

"I would say close to twenty years, I guess."

"Geez, how time does fly," Alex continued. "I still can't believe I'm sitting here...having dinner with you. I guess we should talk about what happened between us, but with this business with Jane and all, I'm just not in the right frame of mind. I guess I owe you some sort of explanation." He lowered his voice. "And that night we drank…"

"The bottle of Dom Perignon," Josh finished. A fractured memory edged the surface of his consciousness but he chose to ignore it.

Alex's face brightened. "Do you still think..."

"Now's not the time to dredge all that up," Josh cut him off. He hesitated before continuing. "It's...it's not important anymore anyway," he lied, feeling his face warm.

"Oh...okay," Alex replied.

An uneasy silence followed as Josh sipped the musty-tasting tap water, and Alex fiddled with the silverware.

"So, are you married?" Alex asked.

"No." He replied simply and took another sip of water. He carefully returned the glass to the coaster, making sure that it was perfectly centered. "Are you still married to....what was her name?"

Alex's gaze was fixed upward. "That's really a weird color for a ceiling."

"What?"

"The ceiling. It's Christmas tree green. Have you ever noticed that before?" He motioned with his eyes.

"Changing the subject, are we?"

Alex chuckled. "Oh please Josh, you really don't expect me to believe you don't remember my ex-wife's name. Nancy. It was Nancy."

"Ex-wife? So you're divorced. I'm sorry to hear that."

Alex concentrated on realigning his knife and fork. "Right. That is also a long, sad story, and when this is all over, I'll tell you about it sometime, over a couple of martinis."

"Remarried yet?"

"No. Not ever."

Ethel reappeared with plates of food, and both men tore into them eagerly.

"You two boys done et like you haven't seen food for a year," said Ethel a few minutes later, collecting the empty plates. "Coffee?" She winked at Alex again. "Dessert?"

Josh interrupted the peculiar chemistry. "The check will be fine, Ethel." He looked at Alex and shook his head again.

"What?" Alex asked with feigned innocence. "You jealous of me and Ethel?"

"You and Ethel, for crying out loud."

Ethel returned and laid the bill on the counter. Alex grabbed the check and reached for his wallet. "My treat." He laid several bills on the counter.

"Thanks, Alex," Josh said as the two got up to leave. "Next one's on me."

"You boys have a nice evenin'!" Ethel glowed as she collected her generous tip.

The two walked up the sidewalk to Josh's SUV.

"Jane still lives in my parent's old house in Georgetown," Alex remarked as he settled into the front seat, resting his head against the doorframe. "3303 P Street."

Before Josh put the key into the ignition, his passenger had become nearly comatose, grunting slightly at the end of each inspiration. Josh sat back in the seat before turning the engine and watched the man sleep, recalling their first encounter on the campus quad. During a game of pick up football, Alex had thrown an errant pass that landed squarely in Josh's lap as he sat on the lawn eating lunch, spilling soda all over his books and trousers. From that random incident an unlikely friendship was forged between the bookish introvert and the gregarious athlete. He stared at the sleeping man with a mix of admiration and disdain as his mind drifted back to those days.

*   *   *   *
      *   *   *

Matriculation had occurred on a sultry day in August. The elegant campus of Shepford College was graced with mature oaks, dogwoods, maples and festoons of boxwoods. A manicured expanse of lawn formed a green carpet from the steps of Founders Hall, a stately eighteenth century building constructed of fieldstone, to the banks of the Potomac River. The sward was littered with scores of students who had converged on the liberal arts college to begin or continue the quest for a degree. The air was full of energy as they chatted excitedly in groups, dozed in the sun, read, formed circles for hacky sack or played touch football.

Josh Hanley had found refuge from the heat in the shade of a towering oak and began to eat a hurried lunch before his afternoon biology class. With a tuna sandwich clenched loosely in his jaw and a soda balanced between his legs, he pulled out a new textbook from his knapsack. Its cover was decorated with drawings of various microorganisms, and the virgin binding cracked as he opened it for the first time. The acerbic but familiar aroma of fresh ink wafted from the pages as he surveyed the table of contents.

"Should be an interesting semester," he noted. His studies would take him from the simplest organisms, to those which were more complex, but still comparatively primitive. Study of higher vertebrates would occur in the second semester.

"Heads Up!"

His textbook scrutiny was abruptly interrupted when a stray football bounced into his lap, knocking the sandwich from his hand and splashing the sugary soft drink all over his shorts.

"Damn!" he bellowed as he dabbed at the sticky mess with a flimsy cafeteria napkin.

"Oops! Sorry about that!"

A stocky young man with a flaming red crew cut came trotting across the lawn toward him. The fair skin of his freckled face and exposed upper body had been roasted to a brilliant pink by the intense summer sun and was being basted with his abundant sweat.

"Look what you did to my shorts!" Josh stood up, and the foamy carbonated concoction ran down his legs.

"It was an accident! He threw it over my head." He pointed

to a young man standing at a distance down the lawn, who like his friend, was sweaty and shirtless.

"This is just great!" Josh seethed, unable to control his anger. "I have a class in ten minutes."

"What happened?" Alex Byrne strode toward them with a confident swagger. Unlike his friend, he was tall and handsome, and his body, tan and well defined. "Nelson, you could've caught that one if you'd have stretched that fat ass of yours a little more!"

"Fuck you, Alex!" Nelson's face became even redder.

The two tussled a bit, then the more powerful Alex grabbed Nelson around the neck and scraped his knuckles across the red crew cut.

"Owwww! Let go, you asshole!" Nelson whined as he wriggled free.

Alex looked at Josh and laughed. "Whoa, direct hit!"

"Look what you did to my shorts!" Josh exclaimed, continuing to wipe at the mess with the disintegrating napkin.

"Sorry! It was an accident, okay?"

"I have a class now, and I don't have time to change!"

"Well...so do I...so, can I, like, have my football back?" Alex asked without even a hint of compunction.

"Here, take the damn thing!" Josh gave the ball a healthy kick, and it scudded over the grass down the lawn.

"You don't have to be a prick about it," Alex murmured as he and Nelson trotted off in pursuit of the ball.

"What a Neanderthal!" Josh grumbled as he began to gather his books.

"Do you always talk to yourself?" The voice seemed to come out of nowhere, and he quickly turned to see a short woman standing just behind him. She was solid but not fat; her long auburn hair was parted in the middle, and round wire rimmed glasses were perched on the end of her slightly upturned nose. A tight white tee shirt with 'Shepford' wavering across her chest in bold, blue letters accentuated her ample bosom.

"Well, no..."

"Correct me if I am wrong, but did I hear you refer to Alex Byrne as a Neanderthal?" She grabbed her chin in mock concentration.

"Ah...well...no," he lied.

She wagged an index finger at him. "No, no, now I distinctly heard you refer to him as a Neanderthal." Her speech pattern was precise and swift, almost pressured.

"Well, okay, yes," Josh replied meekly, certain that he had encountered one of the man's friends.

The woman shook her head. "I'm afraid you have it all wrong. Do you know why?"

Josh winced. "No, why?"

"You see, by calling Alexander Byrne a Neanderthal, you risk maligning every cave person who ever lived," she continued, as if giving a lecture before an austere group of anthropologists.

Josh wrinkled his nose. "What?"

"You could, perhaps, call him an asshole, but then again, you face yet another dilemma."

"And that is?"

"You risk maligning every anus of the world."

"I see." Josh realized that he had totally misjudged this strange and interesting woman.

She continued in her mock professorial manner. "And we depend on our ani, that's the plural of anus in case you didn't know that, for a very important bodily function. That, of course, being the evacuation of fecal matter, also known as…shit."

Josh nodded. "True. Very true."

"I see that you are now enlightened. Now, how about Shithead?"

"I beg your pardon?"

"Shithead. I don't think we'll risk offending anyone else with that name, and it happens to be my favorite nickname for Alexander Byrne."

"I see," he replied.

"And it is a well known fact that Alex does indeed have shit for brains."

"Okay, then Shithead it is."

Good. Now that that's settled, I'm Joanie Cranberi." She extended her hand. "That's C-R-A-N-B-E-R-I. And you are?"

"Josh Hanley." He briefly took her hand.

She surveyed his pile of books that were now scattered in the grass. "I can tell by your new textbooks that you are a freshman."

He stooped and began to collect the books, placing them one by one back into his knapsack. "Yes. I'm pre-med."

She leaned over to help. "So am I. On both accounts."

He took the last book from her, and the two stood up.

"You're pre-med, too! Great! Nice to meet you, Joanie. You seem to know that guy quite well."

"Shithead, you mean. Yes, we went to high school together. He got accepted here to play some sport. Baseball, I think. Can you imagine a college of this caliber actually worrying about sports? It's such a travesty. May I help you with your things?"

"No, I'm fine, but thanks anyway." Josh grabbed his knapsack and slung it over his shoulder.

"You should get out of those shorts." She winked, looking him up and down with approval.

"I can't." Josh blushed. "I have my first bio class in…." He looked at his watch. "Five minutes. Snyder Hall."

"So do I! We probably have all the same classes. Come on, let's go!"

The freshman science majors biology course was officially entitled 'Advanced Biology I,' to distinguish it from the less difficult Biology 101, which was for non-science majors. Joanie and Josh entered a large, open laboratory classroom with tall English pane windows and found seats together at one of the soapstone topped laboratory benches. At precisely 1 PM, Professor James Woodward, a cadaverous man with thick white sideburns entered the room. He was wearing a starched white shirt and red bow tie beneath his white lab coat. The banter abruptly died as he scribbled his name across the blackboard, announcing, as he did so, that "there is a lot to cover before the end of the semester." Then, without ceremony and without bothering to take roll, he began to lecture at an alarming rate of speed, leading his students to believe that he intended to cover the entire textbook before the end of the hour. He was well into his lecture, when the door suddenly opened and in strode Alex Byrne. He had donned an old jersey but his hair was still wet with sweat. One hand held a half eaten apple, and the other cradled a football against his forearm.

Professor Woodward abruptly stopped the lecture and calmly removed his small, round glasses.

"This biology course is for science majors only," he intoned.

"I am a science major," Alex replied, giving the football a short toss into the air. Josh thought that at any moment he was going to tell the good professor to "go long!"

"I see. And your name is?"

"Byrne. Alexander Byrne."

Dr. Woodward put his glasses back on and scanned the roster.

"Ah, yes, Mr. Byrne. Well then, in that case, would you kindly dispose of your apple?" Then to the class: "Ladies and gentlemen, you are now adults, and I expect you to act as such. I usually don't have to promulgate instructions to my classes but in this case I see I will have to make an exception. There are two things of which you should be aware. One, I expect all students to be on time for my lectures, and two, for your own safety, absolutely no food or drink is ever allowed in this laboratory." He pointed to a large sign with big red letters for emphasis. "Have I made myself clear?"

"Yes sir! Loud and clear." Alex saluted, and a soft snicker rippled through the class.

"Good. I see that Mr. Byrne has become the self-appointed spokesman for the whole class. Would you please take a seat now?"

Alex dropped his apple in a garbage can near the door, scanned the room, then headed toward a bench.

"Oh no! He's coming this way," Joanie whispered, using a hand to shield her face.

Alex grabbed a stool and plopped next to Joanie. "Hey Joanie," he whispered.

"What are you doing here, Alex?" she whispered back, looking around at her fellow classmates to see if anyone had noticed.

"I'm a pre-med major."

"You've got to be joking." She looked at Josh and rolled her eyes.

"Hey, my father's a doctor and my sister's in med school!" Alex announced proudly.

"So? You're a moron," she countered.

"I love you too, Joanie."

"Ah…I'm so sorry, I didn't mean to interrupt you." Professor Woodward glared over his glasses as he stopped the lecture once again. "Miss….ah….?"

The whole class was now staring at their lab bench. Joanie looked about and then pointed to herself with as much innocence as she could muster.

"Yes, you my dear. The one in the tight tee shirt."

"Cranberi." Her voice was just above a whisper.

"I'm sorry, my dear, what did you say? Please speak up! Why do you suddenly have so little to say when just a moment ago you couldn't keep your mouth shut?" Professor Woodward had plunged the knife deep and was now twisting it. "I'm sure the whole class wants to know who is wasting their time and money."

Joanie cleared her throat. Her face seemed to mirror her name. "Cranberi. Joanie Cranberi, sir."

"Ah, yes, Miss Cranberi." Professor Woodward removed his glasses. "Am I boring you?"

Joanie frantically shook her head. "No sir! Not at all, sir!"

"Good. Now, if you will permit me, I'm sure the rest of the class would like to hear the lecture. After all, their parents are paying a premium price for this education, and I'm sure they'd like to get their money's worth."

"I'm so sorry, Dr. Woodward, it won't happen again." She then glared at Alex.

The lecture began again, and Josh feverishly scribbled, trying to script every word that gushed forth from the verbose Professor Woodward's mouth. Halfway through the lecture, he put his pen down to soothe the acing cramp in his hand and glanced around the room at his equally fastidious classmates. Alex Byrne, however, sat with his head resting in his hand, fast asleep.

Sleeping, Josh said to himself. He is a moron.

When class was over, a collective sigh of relief arose from the students as pens were dropped, and the accumulated hand cramps of a new generation of freshman were finally eased. Many left the room vowing to bring a tape recorder for the next class. Joanie rose quickly and began to collect her books.

"How dare you embarrass me in front of Professor Woodward on the first day of class, Alex! He yelled at me! Can you image that? No teacher has ever yelled at me!"

"He didn't yell at you," Alex shot back.

"What would you call it?" She put her hand on her hip. "And what in the hell are you doing here anyway? Shouldn't you be down the hall in kiddie bio?"

"Didn't you hear me? I'm a pre-med major," Alex replied.

"Bullshit!"

"Ah…I think we'd better keep it down." Josh noted that many of the students were beginning to stare as they slowly left the room "You're making a scene."

"Alex, how could you possibly be majoring in pre-med?" Joanie continued, her voice now lower. "You're not cut out for this."

"My father wants me to be a doctor, like him and my sister."

Joanie shook her head and rolled her eyes. Then to Josh: "What do you have next? I have chemistry."

"I have chemistry, too" Josh replied.

"I have physics," Alex interrupted.

Joanie looked at him only briefly. "Like we care! Josh, I'll catch up with you in chemistry."

She abruptly stomped out of the room.

"She's probably going to hunt down ole' Professor Woodford so that she can tell him it was all my fault. She's such a brown-noser."

Josh shrugged and began to collect his books. "It's Woodward. Professor Woodward."

"Whatever. I'm Alex Byrne." He extended his hand.

"Yes, I know." Josh shook it briefly. "I'm Josh. Hanley. Josh Hanley."

"Nice to meet you Josh Hanley, Josh Hanley. Is that kind of like Mary Hartmen, Mary Hartmen?"

Josh tried in vain to contain a grin. "Very funny."

Alex cocked his head. "How did you know my name?"

"You said it....in front of the class....to Professor Woodward."

"Oh, right."

"Plus, we kind of met already." Josh pointed to the stiff, sticky shorts that had been clinging to his thighs all through class.

"Right. The shorts. Sorry about that. Nelson's such a dork. I just met him yesterday. He's my roommate. He said he played football in high school, but I have my doubts."

Josh slung the knapsack full of books over his shoulder and heaved it into a comfortable position. "He sure doesn't look very athletic to me."

Alex followed Josh out of the laboratory and down the crowded, noisy hall. "I've known Joanie since middle school, and she thinks I'm just a stupid jock."

His statements elicited another shrug from Josh, this time accompanied by an acknowledging wince.

"She's a genius, you know," he continued as they walked

down a stairwell and out the doors into the August heat. "She has a photographic memory or something like that."

Josh nodded. "She does seem pretty smart."

"And she's got those enormous tits." Alex nudged Josh and held out his hands in front of this chest for emphasis. "She's like the Dolly Parton of the bio lab."

Josh wasn't sure how to respond because it was in fact true. Alex Byrne apparently pulled no punches.

The two stopped at an intersection of the sidewalk, and Alex put his hand above his forehead to block the glare of the sun.

"God, what a scorcher. Hey, let's go get a Coke before our next class. My treat."

Josh hesitated and looked at his watch. "I only have a few minutes before chemistry class, and I don't want to be late."

Alex rolled his eyes. "Jeez, are you like a worrier or something?" He draped his arm over his new friend's shoulder and steered him toward the campus canteen.

As the first semester progressed, Josh soon realized that Joanie's predictions were coming true. Although Alex did possess athletic talent, he was by no means a star in the classroom. His struggle to pass was all too evident, and the constant barrage of abuse by Joanie Cranberi had only made matters worse.

"Maybe you're not studying right," Josh offered one day after class as the three of them sat at the lab bench gazing down their microscopes.

"Maybe you shouldn't be in this class." Joanie stood and placed a vinyl cover over her scope. She then began to collect her things. "Maybe you're not cut out for this. Perhaps you should think about changing your major to like ditch digging or garbage collecting."

"Joanie, give it a rest," Josh said wearily as he stood and began to cover his own microscope.

She stopped what she was doing and placed a hand on her hip. "So what's this now? Did he brainwash you or something? If I recall correctly, you're the one who called him a shithead!"

Still sitting between them, Alex looked from Joanie to Josh. "You called me a shithead?"

"I called him a Neanderthal," Josh said, ignoring Alex. "You're the one who called him a shithead!"

Alex winced. "You called me a Neanderthal?"

Joanie reared back and crossed her arms. "So now you're taking his side."

"I'm not taking sides. I didn't realize there were sides to take."

Alex put a hand up between them. "Wait a minute, here. When did you call me a Neanderthal, and when did you call me a shithead?"

Joanie threw the last book into her knapsack and heaved it over her shoulder. "If you only knew."

Josh threw his hands in the air. "If I only knew what?"

She forcefully pushed her glasses back up her nose. "I thought you were my friend, Josh Hanley."

"I am your friend, Joanie. I'm also Alex's friend."

She glared at them, her eyes moving first to one then the other. "You men are all alike, you know that?" Without another word, she stormed out of the lab.

"What did I say?" he called after her. He turned to Alex who was quietly seated on the stool staring at him.

"You called me a Neanderthal?"

Josh waved his hand. "It was a long time ago when you trashed my shorts. It's ancient history. Forget about it."

Alex shrugged. "Okay, whatever." He then returned his gaze down the microscope. "I wouldn't worry about Joanie. She's probably on the rag or something. She'll get over it." He stopped and looked up. "My slime mold looks…dead. I mean, it's a mold! They grow in dorm shower stalls, but I can't grow one when I feed it…slime mold food or whatever this stuff is."

He leaned back on the stool and blew out his breath such that it caused the hair above his forehead to flutter. "You know, I hate to admit this, but maybe she's right. Maybe I'm not cut out for this."

Josh sat down next to him. "Don't give up so easily. Maybe you just need a little help."

Alex stood and began to collect his books. "I need help, all right. I need help with biology, chemistry, and God help me, physics." He paused as if he wanted to say something else, then just shook his head. "Anyway, I'll see you later. I have to make a pit stop before my next class." He started to leave, but Josh grabbed his arm.

"Wait…Alex. Look, maybe….maybe I could help you."

"Oh yeah? How?"

"We can study together. I can tutor you. I used to do the same thing in high school."

Alex frowned. "Oh, I know your type. You tutored the dumb kids, right? So you feel sorry for me, is that it?"

Josh stood. "No…no…not at all." He studied Alex's face and his heart jumped. Embarrassed, he looked away.

"Something wrong?"

He quickly shook his head and began to collect his books. "No…nothing."

"Well, I guess it wouldn't hurt to try."

Josh looked up and smiled. "If it doesn't work out, we'll call it quits."

Alex thought for a moment. "So what's in it for you?"

Josh felt his face warm and he swallowed hard. "Why does there have to be anything in it for me? Can't I just help a friend?"

Alex smiled and gave Josh a playful punch on the shoulder. "All right, I'm game. Let's see what happens."

Despite the protestations of a very verbal Joanie Cranberi, a regular study routine was established in the evenings after class. Alex initially had trouble finding time to study between workouts and parties, but Josh managed to help him realign his priorities. He soon realized that all Alex really needed were lessons in time management, and the rest seemed to fall into place. Toward the middle of the first semester, their efforts had begun to pay off as Alex's grades took a remarkable turn for the better.

"I still can't believe you're helping that moron," Joanie pronounced one day in chemistry lab a week before final exams were to begin. She was stationed at a bench directly across from him such that they were facing one another with a rack of water and gas lines between them.

Josh shrugged, weathering yet another diatribe against Alex as he stirred his solution in an Erlenmeyer flask perched over a Bunsen burner.

He looked at her through a blur of scratches in his well-worn safety glasses. "Can't we just drop it, Joanie? I mean, what has Alex ever done to you?"

Dressed in an oversized white lab coat, she peered at him through her own well-worn safety goggles. "Nothing."

"Well then why do you hate him so much?"

This time she shrugged and looked away. For a second, Josh

thought she was going to cry. The solution in his flask began to boil, and he turned down the flame. "What? What did I say?"

She kept her head down as she worked on her experiment. "Nothing."

"Look, Joanie, it's none of my business, okay?"

She thought for a moment. "Has Alex mentioned anything to you about me?"

He pursed his lips in thought. "Um, just that he knows you think he's a dumb jock. Oh, and that you're real smart. 'Genius' was the word he used." He decided to leave out the part about Dolly Parton.

Her face remained frozen in thought as she poured over her lab manual. "Who is he dating these days?" She was apparently trying to ask nonchalantly, but Josh noted a distinct unsteadiness in her voice.

"Some girl named Nancy."

She looked up, and he noted the slightest hint of a smirk.

"Nancy Valone. A cheerleader."

Josh shrugged. "Yes."

"That figures. How many girlfriends has he had this year?"

"Several. His relationships don't seem to last long."

She rolled her eyes. "Relationships? I think 'conquests' is the more appropriate term." She filled a flask with distilled water and set it on a tripod above the flame of a Bunsen burner.

"And does he brag about his conquests to you?"

Josh recalled the details of numerous ribald stories over the preceding weeks. He shook his head. "No, not really."

Joanie went back to reading her manual. "I'll bet."

He knit his brow. "So, did you have a thing for him? In high school?"

She forced a thin smile. "You're too smart, Josh Hanley." She looked about then leaned forward. "You see, every girl in my high school had a thing for Alex. I was stupid enough to think I had a chance with him, and I...well, I sort of..." She quickly glanced around the room again.

"What?"

She heaved a sigh. "I asked him to the Sadie Hawkins Day Dance."

"The what?"

"It was a dance where the girls got to ask the boys instead of the other way around, and, well, I asked Alex."

"Oh," Josh intoned.

"Yeah, it was totally embarrassing. He essentially laughed me out of the room. I nearly died. And, I never lived it down. Me, the science geek, asking the captain of the football team. It was a nightmare."

"Sounds pretty awful," Josh whispered.

"Thank goodness I'm now at a place where no one, but you and Alex of course, know about that."

"And you still hate him for it."

"Yeah, well, there is that." She then redirected the conversation. "So what are you getting out of this tutoring bit? I mean, Alex isn't exactly your friend. He has a whole different set of jock friends that he hangs out with. Outside of the classroom, he doesn't give you the time of day, does he?"

Josh kept his head bowed, studying his lab manual. "Why is that so important?"

"It's almost as if you…" she hesitated.

He looked up. "What?"

She took a deep breath and adjusted her glasses. "I just don't want you to get hurt, that's all."

"Hurt?"

She shook her head. "Never mind."

"No. What?"

She leaned back and grabbed the neck of her flask with a pair of tongs. "I don't want to get into it. Now, if you'll excuse me, I have a distillate to decant."

"Wait a minute. What did you mean?"

She put the flask back down on the tripod over the flame.

"Okay, fine. You're not dating anyone, are you? I mean, you know, like a woman?"

A hint of panic stirred in the pit of his stomach. His face warmed, and his heart thumped. "No. Why?"

She looked around the room yet again and leaned forward. "People are talking, Josh."

His knees became weak and his neck and armpits had suddenly become damp with sweat beneath the polyester lab coat. "About what?" his voice cracked.

"You and Alex. You mainly," she whispered.

There was now a slight sense of nausea. "What are they saying?"

"You know." She let her wrist drop.

His throat tightened as he turned down the flame to keep his solution from boiling over. "Who said that?" he whispered harshly.

She put a finger to her lips. "Shhhhhh. I overheard that moron Nelson talking in the cafeteria this morning."

Josh leaned forward. "What did he say?"

She hesitated again. "He was sort of implying, I guess, that *you* might have a thing for Alex."

His mouth went dry, and he swallowed hard. "That jerk!"

Sensing his uneasiness, she came around the bench and stood next to him. "Look, I'm sorry, Josh I just thought...."

"Ah....Ms. Cranberi, contrary to the fact that you think this is your social hour, I kindly request that you return to your bench as your solution is about to boil over." Professor Herbert, the chemistry instructor, was glaring at her through thick safety glasses from across the room.

Joanie scurried back to her bench. "Yes sir. Sorry sir." She quickly removed the flask from the flame and then looked up.

"We'll talk later," she mouthed.

Later that evening, Josh was waiting in the library when Alex finally came bounding in.

"Where've you been? It's almost nine o'clock?" He held up his wristwatch for emphasis.

"We need to talk," Alex growled.

"What's going on?" Josh asked nervously.

Several shushes came from the surrounding carrels where students were perched with open books. He motioned for Josh to follow him into the large, open common area. Once they were out of earshot, Alex grabbed Josh by the arm and pulled him close. "We need to go somewhere and talk in private," he whispered.

Josh felt a stab of fear. "Now?"

Alex nodded. "It's very important."

A feeling of dread arose in his mind as he recalled his conversation with Joanie that afternoon.

"What about?" he asked innocently. "I mean, finals are next week and...."

"Grab you coat and let's go. I'll meet you on the quad."

"But my books and notes are back there."

Alex rolled his eyes. "They'll still be there when you get back. No one's going to bother them. Besides, the library stays open till midnight the week before finals."

Josh returned to the stacks and grabbed his coat. He found Alex standing on the quad in front of the library with a brown paper bag wedged under his arm. Josh motioned toward the bag.

"What's that?"

"You'll see."

Josh looked back through the glass doors of the library where scores of students sat with their heads bowed in deep concentration over notes and textbooks. The press of guilt seemed to pull him back into that warm, book-lined cocoon, and his first impulse was to retreat inside where it was warm and safe. He turned to Alex, whose pull seemed to be even greater.

"Where are we going?"

"To the McMurran Hill monument," Alex replied, referring to the 150-foot granite column with a ball atop that commemorated the founding of the college in the early nineteenth century. It was perched on a cliff overlooking the river.

"McMurran Hill? Why all the way up there?"

"Privacy." He started off across the lawn then stopped and turned. "Are you coming or not?"

Throwing one last glance back toward the columned library, he pulled the collar of his coat around his neck and followed Alex into the shadows.

*　　　　　　*　　　　　　*　　　　　　*
　　　*　　　　　　*　　　　　　*

Josh was roused from is thoughts when Alex stirred. His mouth was dry and there was a distinct knob in his throat. As he turned the engine, he suddenly realized that he hadn't talked to Joanie in ages. He would have to send her an email, or maybe even give her call. She had become a urologist, one of the few females in the profession. Where was she in practice? Columbus, Ohio maybe? She was not going to believe this.

He wiped a tear from his cheek as he put the SUV into drive and pulled out onto the street.

Thirty-five

It was 6:45 in the morning when Wes Shipley pulled into the parking lot at Gravelly Point Park. Located at the end of the main runway of Reagan National Airport, the seven acre park was sandwiched between the George Washington Memorial Parkway on its west side and the Potomac River on its east side. The Point offered a panoramic view of the Washington skyline, with the dome of the Capital off to the east and the obelisk of the Washington Monument to the north. It was the perfect place to launch a boat or begin a bike trip on the fifteen mile trail along the river to Mount Vernon. Other popular activities included soccer or softball on its broad flat greens, or fishing on its rocky banks. Many, however, just enjoyed watching the airplanes take off and land at Reagan National.

At this hour, the parking lot was empty, and Wes was able to pull his old Dodge into a choice space. His dog, a golden mix of Labrador and beagle, jumped up and wagged his tail excitedly.

"C'mon Max, it's time to go catch dinner," he said, slowly extracting his bulky frame from the driver's seat, causing the rusting vehicle to spring up and briefly shudder.

The dog's tail was a fluffy blur as he jumped to the pavement. Wes slowly limped around the car and opened the trunk, revealing a wide variety of fishing rods and tackle. This morning, his seventy-year-old body was somewhat stiff, and he pulled out a flask of Jack Daniels from the pocket of his overcoat and took a slug. Alcohol was prohibited in the park, but he knew it was easy to take liberties with libations at such an early hour. Max jumped up excitedly, his ears standing at full attention.

"No, Max, this is Daddy's medicine." Wes recapped the flask and shoved it back into his pocket.

He slowly assembled his fishing rod and strung it with a heavy nylon monofilament. Grabbing the tackle box, he trudged toward the water's edge while Max kept pace with his stride.

The riverbank was grassy and wet with dew. It gently sloped to the river, and Wes carefully negotiated it, fearing another fall and hip fracture. He eased himself on a flat rock, and Max took his place beside him. With ears erect, he looked up at this master expectantly.

"Okay, time for a treat." Wes pulled out several dog biscuits and tossed them one at a time into the air. Max leapt up eagerly and caught each one as strings of saliva hung from the corners of his mouth.

"That a boy!" Wes rubbed the dog behind the ears. "Now sit and watch Daddy catch dinner."

He reared back and, with one quick jerk, cast his line. The red and white float flew out over the water and slowly descended to the surface where it bobbed gently in the current. With Max at his side, he watched the morning mist rise above the water and savored the crisp morning air. As the commuters sped down the parkway behind him, the retired postman felt sorry for the poor bastards who still had to go to work, especially those with hellish commutes.

Max began to grow restless and started to whine. With his nose pressed to the ground, the dog trotted along the riverbank, stopping intermittently to paw the earth and sniff the air.

"Don't go too far Maxie," he warned. "The Park Rangers may be comin' around soon and you're off your leash."

At seven sharp, a 757 began to roll down the runway at National Airport. The huge aircraft slowly lifted into the air, and its landing gear cleanly disappeared into the fuselage as it roared overhead, causing the ground to shudder. Wes cupped his hands over his ears and cocked his head to watch the soaring plane. A straight flight path would have taken the 757 directly over the National Mall and the White House, but because Federal regulations prohibited civilian air traffic from flying directly over the White House, the plane veered sharply to the left, following instead a course over the river as it climbed. A second plane, then a third, and a fourth, roared overhead in succession, following the same flight path as the first.

As another plane initiated its roll down the runway, Max began to bark hysterically. Wes scanned the riverbank and spotted the dog jumping up and down near a stand of trees at the river's edge. He placed his thumb and index finger at the corners of his mouth and blew. The ensuing high-pitched whistle proved ineffective.

"Max! Get over here!" he finally shouted.

The dog continued the fracas, his bark now more of a whine.

"Max, damn it, what are you yapping about? If you're chasing rats again so help me...."

Wes propped his fishing pole against the rock, slowly pulled himself up, and began to limp along the riverbank toward the over-excited canine. The plane roared overhead, momentarily drowning out the dog's yelps and the cries of his master as it lifted into the sky. Wes approached the riverbank and saw that the dog had discovered a pale blue mound that was strikingly conspicuous in its drab surroundings. Whatever it was had become wedged in the scrub brush that lined the river's edge.

"What the hell is that?" Wes took out his glasses and propped them on the end of his nose. The mound was bulky and rounded, but had no distinct markings. He moved closer, his boots now in the muck at the edge of the river, and bent over to get a better look. His heart leapt and he reared back, slipping in the mud, as the lifeless face of a young man stared back at him through the cold, clear water.

Thirty-six

"Alex, you and Jane have identical haplotypes!"

"Oh...great." The muscles in Alex's forehead formed an unknowing wrinkle. Despite nearly ten hours of sleep, he still looked exhausted. "That's a good thing, right?"

Josh held a hand in front of him as if stopping traffic. "Allow me to explain. Body tissues express certain antigens or proteins, fingerprints if you will, that help the immune system identify self from non-self - that being foreign bodies, such as bacteria or viruses, for example. When the cells of the immune system encounter a foreign body, a complex defense system is activated, ultimately resulting in the destruction or containment of that foreign body. This system of recognition is controlled by the HLA system, which stands for Human Leukocyte Antigens. Your HLA type matches that of Jane's. In other words, both of you received an identical set of antigens or cellular fingerprints from your parents."

Alex nodded. "Okay, I'm following. Please go on."

"Because your antigens match, your bone marrow cells will be less likely to see Jane's body as foreign, and therefore will not attack her tissues as severely as if they were not completely matched. We call this reaction graft versus host disease."

"Graft versus host disease?" Alex asked. "My cells would attack Jane's body?"

"That's right. Your cells are the graft, and Jane's body is the host. Alternatively, Jane's immune system, what little is left of it, could potentially attack your cells because it sees them as foreign. This would result in rejection of your cells, and they would fail to engraft in her bone marrow. Now we can't check for every antigen because there are still many unknowns about this whole process. We can however, control graft versus host disease with immune suppressing drugs."

Alex nodded. "Okay, I'll take your word for it. The bottom

line is that I can be a bone marrow donor for Jane, right?"

"That's precisely what it means," Josh replied.

"Oh....great," Alex repeated with some hesitancy. He then looked at Josh and winced. "Now what do I have to do?"

Josh began a protracted explanation of how the needed cells were procured from a bone marrow donor. First, Alex would be given a subcutaneous injection of a medication that would stimulate the release of blood forming cells, known as "stem cells," from the bone marrow into the blood stream. This phase of the process was known as "mobilization," since these cells were "mobilized" from the marrow into the blood. When the number of these cells had risen to adequate levels in the blood, they would then be collected or "harvested" using a technique known as aphaeresis.

"You see, Alex, you'll be hooked up to a machine that will filter the stem cells out and then return the rest of the blood to your body."

"Now, what are these stem cells again?" Alex asked.

"Stem cells are the seeds, if you will, of the bone marrow. They're capable of making all the other blood cells, those being the red cells, the white cells, and the platelets."

"Why aren't you taking them directly from my bone marrow, then?"

"Well, that's a good question. We used to do that but we usually don't have to do it that way anymore."

"Can I spare these stem cells? Won't my blood counts go down after you take all my stem cells?" Alex asked.

"We're not taking that many stem cells. You'll still have plenty to spare and you'll just make more, anyway," Josh reassured him.

"So I really won't be losing that much blood, then?"

"No," Josh replied. "You won't need a blood transfusion if that is your concern."

"Is the harvesting of stem cells painful?" he asked.

"Once the stem cells are mobilized, you may have some bone pain from the growth factor injections. That usually responds to mild analgesics."

Alex nodded. "Okay, then when would you start all this?"

"Right away. We'll give you a dose of the bone marrow stimulant now. We'll probably do the harvest in a few days, once your counts rise," Josh stood. "It shouldn't take long."

Alex took in a deep breath and blew it out. "Okay, Dr. Hanley, I'm in your obviously capable hands!"

Thirty-seven

As part of the National Park System, Gravelly Point was controlled by the Department of the Interior and under the jurisdiction of the United States Park Service. Captain David Saunders of the Park Police had notified the District police that a body matching the description of Stanley Wright was discovered along the banks of the Potomac River at Gravelly Point. The crime scene was secured, and the park closed to the public while officers combed the area for clues.

Trying to ignore the strong stench of decomposing flesh, Grace Love stood over the body of Stanley Wright as a multitude of park police officers searched the riverbank. By now, the sun was above the horizon and through the mist appeared as a large orange disk. Grace gazed at it with a certain sense of awe and fascination before she crouched down to study the remains. The exposed skin was ashen, and the body itself appeared to be inflated. In fact, when Grace first saw the light blue parka, she couldn't help but think of the Donald Duck balloon at the Macy's Thanksgiving Day parade. The body was that of a young man, probably in his late twenties, although it was somewhat difficult to tell. He had stringy hair that was now matted down with a mixture of blood and silt. A large bloody gash furrowed the right side of his head, and rats had nibbled the left ear and tip of the nose. When Grace could no longer hold her breath, she stood just as Al King trudged up behind her, his hands and shoes covered with mud. He pulled a handkerchief from his pocket and began to wipe his hands.

"What's it look like, Gracie?" King asked.

"Dead boy," she replied. She looked eastward to the dome of the Capital glistening through the early morning haze. The day was predicted to be unseasonably warm for March.

King snorted in acknowledgement and kept wiping. "Looks like Mona's boy, doesn't it?"

"I'm sure it is. Did you find anything?"

"A lot'a mud," he replied, continuing to wipe his hands on the now soiled handkerchief. A tall park policeman with a white goatee soon joined them.

"Detective Love, Captain David Saunders of the U.S. Park Police," he said. "I already met your partner here, Detective King."

"Captain Saunders, nice to meet you," Grace said taking his hand.

"I think my people are just about done here. We're now waiting for the Arlington County coroner."

"Great. Thanks for giving us a call about this one." She pulled out a handkerchief and, covering her nose and mouth, crouched down again to get a closer look. "Let's see what we have here." She inspected the deep, red gouges in the wrists.

"By the looks of these burns on the wrists, we figured he must have been tied up pretty tight at one point," Saunders noted. He remained standing.

Grace got closer to the head wound. "It would take a great force to put this hole in his skull. He probably hit his head on something, pier of the bridge, a rock maybe."

The wound started at the right temple and ran posteriorly, exposing part of the brain.

"The significant amount of hemorrhage would indicate that it occurred before he died," Grace noted thoughtfully. There were a number of small raised welts with dark centers on the back of his hands and on the face. "And these marks look like cigarette burns."

"The poor bastard must have been tortured before he died," King remarked.

"Apparently someone was trying to get some information from him," Saunders stated.

Grace thought for a moment and then remembered the letter. "Someone's apparently trying to poison the Commissioner of the FDA and then her office assistant turns up dead."

"I guess it doesn't take a rocket scientist to figure out that the two are related," Saunders said.

Grace nodded. "Something really smells, and it's not just poor Stanley here."

A black van bearing the emblem of the Chief Medical Examiner for the Northern Virginia District pulled into the parking lot. A park policeman waved the van into a space, and a short, bearded man jumped out of the driver's seat. He was dressed in a black overcoat, and white pants. An identification badge attached to a chain dangled around his neck. After a brief conversation, the park policeman pointed him in the direction of the body. He toted a large black bag and walked with a rather pronounced limp due to a congenitally shortened left leg.

"Mornin' Captain," he said in a thick Southern drawl as he eyed the body.

Saunders introduced the detectives.

He extended a hand to both of them. "I'm Dan Sherman, from the ME's Office for Northern Virginia. Can you tell me anything about the deceased?" he began, recorder in hand.

"The precinct got a missing person's report on him," Grace replied. "The only thing else I can tell you is that he was apparently abducted from a Metro Station in the district. No one seems to know anything else. He was employed at the FDA, and his mother lives in Brookland. And that's about all we know for sure, right now."

After they had finished, Sherman performed a thorough exam of the crime scene, speaking into the recorder as he went. When he was finished, he collected multiple samples of soil, water and surrounding vegetation, then set up a video camera and recorded images of the body and crime scene. Several hours had elapsed before the remains were finally placed in a black body bag and loaded into the van.

"We'll need to get his next of kin in to identify the body. I guess you know where the ME's office is out in Fairfax, on Braddock Road." Sherman threw his bag into the passenger's seat of the van and hopped in.

King closed the door. "We'll find it."

"We'll be out there as soon as we can with his next of kin," Grace said.

Sherman nodded as he started the engine. "The gross exam will be done sometime today, but micro will take about a week. We should have the tox screen in a matter of days, though. Catch ya later."

He pulled the van out of the parking lot just as another plane roared overhead.

*   *   *   *
      *   *   *

It had taken George McBrien several days to work up the courage to go to the house in Brookland, but he was determined to find out who else was involved in the conspiracy to murder Jane Riley. He had obtained the Wright's address on Fifth Street, a narrow street lined by 1920's row houses, from the parish registry. This section of the city had been undergoing a gradual renaissance in recent years with the influx of families tired of long commutes from the outer suburbs. Dilapidated houses were being beautifully restored, and drug infested neighborhoods were now only a bitter memory to many of the long-term residents.

The Wright home was a simple detached brick row house, painted white with fading pink trim, juxtaposed between a similar red brick row house on the left and a bright yellow one on the right. The overgrown front yard, enclosed by a rusted, sagging chain link fence, hosted a concrete cone atop which sat a shiny blue gazing ball.

McBrien walked through the rusting front gate, and up the cracked concrete sidewalk. He mounted the steps but hesitated at the door, having no idea how he would approach the situation. He took a deep breath and knocked. Moments later, the curtains at the front windows moved, and then the door opened as far as a security chain would allow.

"Who are you?" the voice asked.

McBrien could see the edge of a gray bouffant.

"I'm Father George McBrien from Trinity Church in Georgetown," he replied. "I know that you and your family are registered parishioners."

"How do I know you are who you say you are? Recite the twenty third psalm."

The priest flawlessly obliged her.

"Well, I guess that's close enough. Now let me see your driver's license."

McBrien hadn't counted on this level of security, but in light of recent events, realized that Ms. Wright was being appropriately cautious. "Okay," he said, opening his wallet. He slipped the plastic card through the opening and could see her study it through reading glasses perched at the end of her nose. The door opened. "Please come in, Father," she said. "I used to work over to the Department of Motor Vehicles. I can spot a fake driver's license from fifty feet."

As McBrien stepped across the threshold, the scent of mothballs and mildew immediately greeted his nose. On the right side of the entry hall, a staircase rose into darkness. The front parlor to the left was decorated with two recliners and an overstuffed sofa with doilies on the arms and back. The mauve velveteen material was worn but unstained. In one corner of the room, a late model television emitting a game show rerun, sat conspicuously among its drab surroundings, and an old upright piano, covered with framed photos, dominated the far wall.

"Have a seat." Mona Wright motioned toward one of the recliners. "I was about to have a cup of tea. Would you like some?"

"I don't want you to go to any trouble," McBrien replied, sitting on the edge of the sofa.

"No trouble. The water's 'bout ready," she said. She turned off the television and sat on a chair adjacent to the sofa. "I'll be able to hear the kettle when it boils."

They surveyed each other.

"So, what can I do for you, Father?" she began.

"Well, it's what I can do for you, I suppose. We heard of your son's disappearance and of course we are concerned." McBrien could not shake his cloud of guilt but knew there was nothing else he could say.

"Stanley's all the family I have, except for my sister who lives out in Maryland. She's not well, herself." She paused then continued. "You know, we stopped going to church years ago. I can't drive, what with my bad back and all." She grabbed her left hip for emphasis.

"I'm sorry to hear that," he replied. "So, Stanley works for the government, doesn't he?"

"He works over to the FDA." She motioned with her hand as if it was located in the kitchen behind them. "My Stanley loves his job." Tears began to well in her eyes, and she dabbed at them with a corner of her apron. "I'm just hoping he's gone off somewhere- fishing or whatever-and will be back soon, and this story about abduction was all in his imagination."

"I'm so sorry. I know you're upset," the priest said gently.

A high-pitched whistle suddenly emanated from the kitchen.

"Oh, the water's a boilin'" She got up. "I'll be right back."

McBrien scanned the room. Photos on the piano caught his attention, and he stood to examine them. There were photos of the Wrights at the shore and in front of the White House. A faded photograph of a crawling infant Stanley was set in a tarnished brass frame. In a more recent photo, Stanley stood dressed in a shiny blue cap and gown holding his diploma with a beaming Mona Wright at his side. McBrien picked up the frame and attempted to read the document.

"That's Stanley's graduation picture." Mona Wright entered the room carrying a small tray. It held two teacups with hot water, each having a tagged string dangling over its side, a bowl of sugar and a cruet of cream. "He didn't pay attention in class very well and had to take some of them special education classes."

McBrien carefully returned the photo to its original position. "You must be very proud of him."

"Oh yes! Ever since his daddy died he has taken care of me." Her voice cracked. "I just don't know what I would do without him!"

"I have been praying that he is found safe and sound," McBrien replied. He sat down, this time on a recliner and leaned back, instantly finding himself in a horizontal position.

"Whoa!"

"Oh, sorry, Father." She rose and helped him sit upright again. "That's Stanley's chair, and he's flopped down in it so much that it just wants to recline all the time. It's a Lazy Lad, you know," she said earnestly, referring to its provenance.

"I see," he replied.

As the chair snapped back in place, a small object fell from between the folds of the worn fabric. It bounced off McBrien's shoe and ricocheted under the sofa.

"What was that?" Mona asked.

"I don't know." McBrien got up and crouched down on his hands and knees to peer under the sofa. "I can't see a thing under there."

"Here, let me get the broom." She left the room and returned shortly carrying a broom with frayed ends. Shoving it under the sofa, she swung it back and forth. In addition to accumulated dust balls, a small object shot out from under the sofa and hit the adjacent baseboard with a thud. McBrien stooped over and picked it up. It was a brown glass vial of about two inches in length and one half inch in diameter, with a black twist cap. He held it up to the light and noted the granular powder inside. His heart began to pound. "My God, this must be it," he mumbled.

"It must be what?" Mona took the bottle and gazed at it through her bifocals. "Hum, I don't know what this is. It must be Stanley's, and it must've fallen out of his pocket while he was in the recliner." She started to open the vial.

"Ah....I wouldn't do that!" McBrien realized that his voice was louder than it should have been.

She jumped. "Why, it's probably sugar or something like that."

McBrien thought quickly. "It could be…dangerous!"

"Dangerous? Well why on earth would you say a thing like that? You think my Stanley goes around carrying poison in his pocket?"

"Yes!" he blurted out. "I mean…I...I.....don't know…um of course not! But…but maybe you should take it to the police anyway, just to be on the safe side."

"Take it to the police?"

"Why, yes, Mrs. Wright. Ah…Stanley's missing, after all and you just never know what could turn up. It could be a...a....clue to his whereabouts."

Mona Wright looked at him with a wrinkled forehead, and he thought she was going to throw him out. Instead, she studied the bottle and sat down. "You think this might be drugs or somethin' like that?"

Relieved, McBrien picked up the line. "Why, of course, I mean, possibly."

She then recoiled. "My Stanley would never take drugs, Father. I know my son. He is not a drug addict." She paused and cocked her head. "At least, I don't think so. He does stay out late some nights, and I don't know where he's been!"

"Really? Well, I didn't mean to imply that he's a drug addict, Mrs. Wright. It's just that we shouldn't leave any stone unturned." He imagined himself wrestling it out of her hand and scampering to the car with her in pursuit, swinging the frayed broom after him. "Why don't we take it right down to the police station?"

"The police station? I don't drive," she countered.

"I'll drive," he offered.

She thought for a second. "I don't know about that. I don't like getting into cars with strangers."

McBrien thought this very peculiar, since, at that very

moment, she had a stranger standing in her living room, and had his intentions been malevolent, she would have fallen victim to them long before this. He sighed. Wrestling her for it was looking more and more likely.

"I have an idea. Why don't you call the police and have them come over here and pick it up. You can show them where you found it. They might even find some other clues in the house."

She thought for a moment. "All right then, Father. That's sounds like a reasonable idea." She put a finger to her lip. "Now let's see, where did I put that woman's card."

"What woman?"

"That detective woman. What was her name?" She put the vial down next to her empty tea cup and rummaged through the pockets of her floral print housecoat, pulling out several crumpled tissues before finding a white business card. "Here it is." She looked at it through her bifocals. "Detective Grace Love. She came to see me just yesterday. She wanted to know about Stanley's job and his relationship to his boss, that Jane Riley woman who wrecked her car a while back. This is her cell phone."

McBrien was relieved that the police were connecting the dots. "Where's your phone?"

"It's in the kitchen." The two walked into the kitchen where an old turquoise phone with a dial hung on the wall. Mona picked up the receiver and dialed.

"Yes, Detective Love? This is Mona Wright here," she yelled into the receiver, then listened for a response. "Well, you know, one day at a time." She paused to listen. "You were?" She held her hand over the receiver. "She's on her way over here, now." She took her hand away. "Oh? You need to speak to me? Oh okay. Well, I have something to show you. I've found something in the house...this little bottle of powder....might be drugs or something. It might have something to do with Stanley's disappearance." She looked at George and nodded. "Yes. Yes. I'll show it to you when you get here. Okay....okay. I'll see you then." She hung up the phone. "Well, how about that! She was on her way over here."

"Good. Now I have to leave, Mrs. Wright. Will you join me in a prayer?"

"Of course, Father."

The two returned to the living room, sat down on the sofa and prayed silently for several minutes. Then McBrien spoke. "Lord, please return Stanley unharmed to his family and friends."

"Amen," Mona intoned.

He was helping Mona to her feet when a bang on the front door startled them.

Mona went for the door. "Is it Detective Love already?"

After she disappeared into the darkened hall, McBrien heard a scream as the door swung open with a bang, and Mona was thrown back against the banister. A tall man dressed in black and wearing a ski mask forced his way into the hall wielding a revolver in front of him.

"Okay, bitch, where is it?" he growled, grabbing Mona by her housecoat and putting the gun to her neck.

"Wh....where's what?" she gasped.

"You know what I want! That thing you wanted to show the cops!"

"How….how would you know about that?"

He tightened his grip on her housecoat and she cowered. "Never mind, bitch. I know you have it."

He dragged her into the living room with the gun still pressed against her neck. McBrien stood near the piano, shaking with fear. "Give it to me and no one will get hurt."

"Is...is this what you want?" McBrien held up the glass vial with a shaking hand.

"Yeah, that's it! Give it to me, motherfucker or I'll blow her brains out!" he hissed.

"Let her go and I'll give it to you!"

"Hey, motherfucker, I'll blow you both away. Now bring that shit over here and don't try anything funny!"

McBrien did as he was told, and with trembling hands, held it out in front of him. The man snatched it, and threw Mona into the priest's arms. He then held the gun at arms length, just inches from them.

"Now, get down on the floor, face down! Both of you! Do it now!"

With shaking legs, McBrien helped the whimpering Mona to her knees and then the two slowly prostrated themselves on the floor.

"Goddamn, you two are slow as molasses!" the man growled.

"He's going to kill us," Mona sobbed into the rug. "Oh Father, he's going to kill us."

McBrien lay with his arm over Mona, trying to calm her, all the while whispering silent prayers. He could hear the click of the automatic as it prepared to release its firepower and wondered who would be the first to die.

"Shit!" the man nearly spat. He abruptly jumped over them and raced toward the kitchen. The swinging door cracked against the wall, followed by the metallic bangs of pots and pans crashing to the floor.

"Police! Freeze!" Grace Love shouted as she jumped through the front door, her revolver held at arm's length in front of her, using the wall between them as a shield.

"Don't shoot!" Mona cried, raising her head slightly.

"Stay down, Mona!" Grace shouted. "Where is he?"

"In the kitchen!" McBrien pointed as he pulled Mona back to the floor.

Grace edged past them and stood with her back to the wall near the kitchen door. Then, with one quick kick, she snapped the door open and peered around the corner. "Police! Freeze!" she shouted again. The man was at the back door and opened fire, forcing Grace against the wall again. The bullets whizzed past her and flew into the living room, striking the plaster with heavy thuds and shattering the front windows. The piano yelped discordant notes as gunfire smacked through the ebony veneer, splintering the wood beneath, and shredding the framed photographs on top of it.

"Oh, Lord help us!" Mona screamed as glass and debris rained around them.

When the shooting stopped, Grace took several deep breaths, then swung around, firing into the kitchen, sending pots and dishes flying in every direction. But the room was now empty, and the back door hung limply on one hinge, the molding splintered and the newly restored glass panes shattered. Grace raced to the door, just in time to see Al King running through the backyard in pursuit of the gunman, jumping over the rusting bicycle and veering around the charcoal grill as he went. The gunman deftly jumped up and hooked the top of the six feet high board fence that enclosed the yard. It shuddered as he kicked over it and was gone. King tried to do the same but fell on his rear in the grass, his hands full of splinters.

"Owwwww!" He limped to his feet just as the screech of brakes sounded on the other side of the fence. A door opened and closed, and through the cracks in the boards, he saw a large, black vehicle speeding past down the alley.

"That was one big mother!" Grace shouted coming up behind him. She pulled a radio handset clipped to the waist of her slacks. "We need back up over at 303 Fifth Street, Northeast. Be on the look out for a large male, about 6 feet five, wearing black, race unknown, last seen in the alley between fourth and fifth streets northeast. He is wearing a ski mask and is armed. I repeat, he is armed with a semi-automatic weapon, over."

King held the back of his right leg, wincing in pain. "He's in a black Suburban."

"And he's in a black Suburban," she continued into the phone. "I repeat, a black Suburban heading east between Fourth and Fifth streets, northeast, over." Then to King: "Are you okay?"

He nodded. "I'll survive."

"Did you get a look at the plates?"

He nodded again. "Just a glimpse."

"And?"

He hesitated. "This is going to sound weird, Grace, but I'm fairly certain they were U.S. Government issue."

Thirty-eight

"Josh, may I have a word with you?" Wilton Roth stood in the doorway of his office, supported by a cane. He looked very much the part of an old professor, clad in a neatly pressed white lab coat and wearing his signature bow tie. Round wire frame glasses were perched on the end of his nose.

"Dr. Roth, please have a seat," Josh stood and motioned to a chair. Josh had trained under Wilton Roth, one of the 'greats' of hematology, and even though they were now considered colleagues, he still couldn't bring himself to call him by his first name. "How's the leg?"

The elderly professor came in with a limp and slowly sat down. "About the same, not any better or worse. Stupid of me to get on those skis at my age; this fracture is taking such a long time to heal."

Josh sat down behind his desk. "Sorry to hear that. So what brings you into the salt mines?"

Roth smiled but it was almost a grimace. "Well, I've been hearing some rumors through the grapevine about the Riley case."

"Oh? What rumors?"

"Crazy rumors." He stroked his beard. "Rumors to the effect that you're going to transplant her based on some letter that a nurse supposedly found in her chart."

"Well…yes, Dr. Roth. I'm not sure there is anything else to do." He paused. "What would do if you were in my shoes?"

Roth shifted in his seat. "I'm just not sure that doing a transplant is the right answer. As I said at the conference, I would wait it out."

"But, I think the evidence points in only one direction…."

"This is such a high profile case," he continued, ignoring Josh's remarks. "It would be a disaster for the University if anything went wrong."

"But, Dr. Roth, she's going to die if I don't."

"I paid her a visit on the unit. She's very weak. I'm not sure she can withstand the rigors of a transplant, especially since the decision to do such a highly morbid procedure is based solely on some anonymous letter."

Josh's armpits were now damp. The fatherly mentor was questioning one of the most important medical decisions of his career. "Yes, I know how weak she is. I've been taking care of her every day. My decision was not based solely on the letter. The letter just helped push me toward a unifying diagnosis. She's going to die if I don't do something drastic!"

"Unifying diagnosis? She was poisoned? That's your unifying diagnosis?" Professor Roth pulled himself up with the help of the cane and took a deep breath. "Okay, Dr Hanley, you are the attending on the case and the final decision is in your hands."

Josh stood, keeping his anger well concealed. "Dr. Roth, I don't mean to sound glib, but you didn't answer my original question. What would you do if you were in my shoes?"

Roth seemed to glare at him. "I'm just trying to be helpful."

Josh was now shaking, his emotions somewhere between fear and fury. "Would you transplant her or not? Yes or no?"

Roth hesitated. "I would think long and hard before transplanting her."

"And you don't think that I have? This isn't being helpful, Dr. Roth. I have lost many nights of sleep over this. I think I may even have an ulcer." He knew that his voice was louder than it should have been. The door was open, and Dottie Shane could be seen down the corridor with an inquisitive tilt of the head. "And the only advice you can give me is to think long and hard before transplanting her?"

Wilton Roth stood more easily than he had sat down. "Such audacity!" he thundered. With that, he turned on his heel and limped out of the room.

Josh stood there for several minutes, wishing he had never opened his mouth.

Thirty-nine

Grace trotted back to the house while King limped behind her at a slower pace. The wrecked kitchen was enveloped in a blue haze and smelled of gunpowder. Bullet holes dotted the walls and ceiling. The refrigerator had suffered a direct hit, its crystal clear blood seeping out from under it onto the floor.

She found Mona Wright and a man in black amid the debris in the living room, still lying face down on the rug, trembling with fear.

"Mrs. Wright?" She bent down and put her hand on the woman's back.

"Detective Love!" Mona whimpered, rising to her knees. "Oh, thank goodness. Are you okay?"

"Yes, Mrs. Wright, I'm fine. Are you?"

"I..I just don't know," she cried, running her hands over her trunk. "Is there any blood?"

"No, honey, there's no blood." Grace helped her to her feet and then to the sofa.

"This man in a ski mask," she continued breathlessly. "Broke down my door, and, and, he had a gun!"

"I know, dear," Grace replied calmly. "We saw that your door had been broken in and heard him shouting."

"You okay, Father?" King asked helping the priest to his feet.

"Yes," McBrien replied, straightening his collar and dusting chalky white plaster dust off his suit. "Thanks for being here. If you hadn't come when you did, both of us would have been killed."

Grace looked at McBrien. "And what is your name, Father?"

"George McBrien of Trinity Church in Georgetown." He extended a trembling hand. "We...we were having tea, and I found this little vial made of brown glass."

"In Stanley's chair," Mrs. Wright interjected.

"Yes. In her son's chair." He motioned toward the Lazy Lad.

"And it had some powder in it."

"And Father McBrien here thought it might have something to do with Stanley's disappearance," Mona interjected again.

Grace raised her eyebrows and looked at the priest. "Oh?"

"Ah....yes, drugs, or something of that nature," he replied quickly.

"And Father McBrien here gave the bottle to man," Mona said, close to hysterics. "He...he had no choice! That man held a gun to my head and threatened to blow my brains out! Oh Detective Love, it was horrible."

Grace cradled the distraught woman in her arms wondering how on earth she was going to tell her about her son.

"Now we'll never know what it really was!" Mona wailed.

"Actually, we will," McBrien replied. He rose, walked over to the coffee table and carefully retrieved his teacup. "You see, when the man broke in I dumped some of the contents of the brown vial into my empty teacup. Thank goodness it somehow survived all the gunfire."

"I see." Grace took the teacup in her free hand while still embracing Mona with the other, her suspicions mounting. "Quick thinking, Padre. And just how did you know that he would be after this?"

The priest hesitated before answering. "He said something to Mrs. Wright about wanting what we just found," he said weakly.

"I see." Grace scrutinized the powder. It had no smell and looked very granular, but not as fine as refined sugar or salt.

"I wouldn't get too close to that," McBrien warned.

"Don't worry, I have no intention of tasting it, Father," she replied. "We'll have this powder analyzed." She handed the cup to King. "Any other clues as to who this guy might be? Did either of you recognize his voice?"

Mona made no reply and McBrien shook his head. "No, I didn't."

"Okay. Ms. Wright we need to talk to you about something else." Grace took in a long breath. She just wanted to get this over with so the investigation could proceed and since a member of the clergy was already present to pick up the pieces, the time seemed right. "Now, Mrs. Wright, I know this hasn't been a good day for you, and it's about to get worse." She looked at McBrien. "And I sure am glad the good Padre is here with you."

"Why?" Mona's blood shot eyes widened.

"Mrs. Wright, the body of a young man was found this morning," she said without emotion, squeezing the woman closer to her.

"Oh my Lord!" McBrien crossed himself.

"A body?" Mona Wright's voice was a whisper.

"I know this is difficult for you, especially after what just happened here," Grace continued gently, continuing to give her a motherly squeeze. "But you're going to have to come with us and let us know if it is…your son Stanley."

"Oh, I can't," Mona sobbed. "I just can't."

Grace motioned for King to bring something to drink, and he returned shortly thereafter from the kitchen carrying a tall glass of water. With shaking hands, Mona Wright took a sip and gave it back. She then put her head in her hands.

"It must be someone else, Detective Love. It can't be my Stanley!"

McBrien retrieved a box of tissues from an end table and Mona took several.

"What happened to him?" she sobbed.

"We're not sure what happened yet, Mrs. Wright. We're going to have to do further investigating," she replied. "We found him in the river."

"In the river? You're not going to cut him up, are you?"

"Your son may have been the victim of murder, and we have to collect all the evidence. And yes, an autopsy will be done by the Medical Examiner's office. We really have no choice."

"Oh, my poor Stanley!" Mona Wright began to sob softly and laid her head on Grace's shoulder. The two began to rock back and forth. Grace frequently had to comfort the family members of murder victims and often wondered how the male detectives managed to just stand by without as much as a hand on the shoulder.

"You can't stay here. It's not safe. Is there someone we could call?" Grace asked.

"I have a sister in Gaithersburg. Lelia. Lelia Miller. Her number is by the phone in the kitchen," she managed between sobs. "She's not well herself."

"I'll call her," McBrien offered, retreating to the kitchen.

"Here, Sweetie, why don't you lie down for a few minutes," Grace said, helping the near catatonic woman recline on the sofa as she brushed away bits of plaster. "There now, you just rest a bit."

She then motioned to King and they stepped into the front hallway.

"We need to get an ID on this ASAP," Grace said in a low voice as they surveyed the teacup.

"So how do you think they knew she had something?" King asked.

Grace shrugged. "She did make that phone call to me. I suppose the phone lines could be tapped; we'll have to check that out. Or they could have been monitoring conversations with listening devices." She lowered her voice to a whisper. "If these guys are tapping phones or using sophisticated listening devices, we're not dealing with some two-bit drug dealing amateurs. And now there's a black suburban with government tags thrown into the mix. Something big is going down."

King nodded and looked behind him. He then added: "I think the priest knows something."

"Un huh. There's no doubt he knows more than he's letting on. I mean, what was he doing here and how did he know what that guy wanted?" Grace thought for a moment, then pulled out her pad and flipped it open to a page where the name of a drug had been scrawled in big block letters. "And I bet I know what's in that teacup."

Forty

After rounds that morning, Josh was sitting at his desk, finishing up with paperwork when a knock on the open door caused him to look up.

"We need to talk."

Alex stood in the doorway with his hands thrust deep into the pockets of his jeans. His voice was stern, almost menacing, and Josh notice that he was uncharacteristically disheveled with dark circles under his eyes. He was unshaven and his hair uncombed.

Josh took off his glasses. "Okay, come in and have a seat." He motioned toward a chair near his desk.

Alex came into the office but stood in front of the desk. "We need to move faster on Jane," he began, his voice low and harsh. "You…you're not moving fast enough. She's sick as a dog and you're….you're just sitting there."

Josh got up, went to the door and closed it. "Alex, are you all right? You look exhausted."

"I'm just great," he said sarcastically. "How the hell do you think I feel?"

Josh took a deep breath and went back to his desk. He motioned to the chair again. "Please, have a seat," he repeated.

Alex reluctantly sat down.

"Let's get one thing straight," Josh began calmly. "I am not the enemy. I did not make Jane sick. I got you here as soon as I could, and I'm doing my best to keep her alive and make her well."

Alex sat back, and for a moment, Josh thought he was going to cry. "I'm just worried and stressed out."

Josh gave a knowing nod but did not reply.

"I was just wondering if you'd heard anything from the lab," he went on.

A laboratory report lay on the desk, and he held it out in front of Alex as if showing an exhibit in court. "I just got the result this morning. Your white count has started to rise but not enough to do the harvest yet. You should be ready soon, though."

Alex forced a contrite grin. "You make me feel like a field of alfalfa."

Josh nodded. "Right now, you actually look like a field of alfalfa."

The two chuckled together.

"I'm sorry, Josh, I didn't mean to dump on you like that."

He shrugged. "Hey, I'm used to it. It's part of the job."

"How much longer do you think it will be until I'm ready?"

"Tomorrow or the next day, probably."

Alex leaned forward and started to say something but then stopped.

"Are you sure you're okay?" Josh asked.

Alex sank back into the chair. "My bones are beginning to ache like you said they would."

"Is it bad?"

"It's nothing compared to what Jane's going through," he said glumly. "How much longer can she take this?'

Josh toyed with a pencil but did not look up. "Well…she's holding her own." He suddenly wondered where that phrase came from.

"Nice try, Dr. Hanley, but that's not what I asked. Now cut the doctor-speak and tell me."

Josh looked him n the face. "Okay, Mr. Byrne, not much longer."

Alex looked away when his eyes became glassy and then changed the subject.

"Have you heard anything from the FBI?"

"I haven't heard a peep from anyone."

Alex frowned. "What in the hell are they doing? Don't they realize how urgent this is? Have you told them how sick Jane is?"

"They are aware of how sick she is, and I'm sure they're working very hard on the case," Josh said calmly. "But that doesn't really change what we're doing here."

Alex wiped one eye with the back of his hand. "I'm going to give them a call!" He hesitated and pointed at Josh. "No, no, I'm going down there! Yeah, that's it. I'm going down there to see if they have any leads." He nervously ran a hand through his tousled hair.

"Alex, when was the last time you slept," Josh asked quietly.

He shrugged. "I think I may have dozed last night. I sat up in a chair all night next to Jane. I was afraid she was going to…" His voice cracked and he stopped.

Josh nodded. "That's what the intern told me. Have you had anything to eat today?"

He shook his head.

"I see. Do you feel like getting some lunch? I don't have clinic this afternoon so why don't I take you to lunch. My treat."

Alex cast about then nodded. "Sure."

Josh got up, took off his lab coat and hung it on the back of the door. "I'll take you back to *Bogart's*. Perhaps your friend Ethel will be there today."

He led Alex out of the cancer center into a pleasant, sunny afternoon. They took a stroll for several blocks down the brick sidewalks of Georgetown to the old converted row house. The place was jammed, but Josh was able to grab a booth near the window from a couple of departing students.

"We're all pretty stressed out," Josh remarked, after the table had been cleared and their orders placed.

Alex took a sip of water. "This waiting game is driving me crazy. I didn't know where to go or what to do. I wanted to do something to help but I'm just sitting here, helpless…watching her slowly…" He hesitated then began again. "I'm trying to conduct business over the phone. I can't concentrate, and I only sleep a couple of hours at night." He sat back. "I'm really scared. If she goes through all this, she'll make it, won't she?"

"Of course she will," Josh said softly, knowing that he was not convincing even himself. "I'm going to do everything in my power to get her well."

"Life is fragile," Alex waxed. "And short."

"Yes, life is short," Josh replied. The cliché had always depressed him.

"What I'm also trying to say is that I really need to talk to you." Alex's voice was suddenly devoid of emotion, almost business-like.

"About what?"

Alex took a deep breath. "About what happened in college."

"Not now," he replied. Not while Jane was so close to death, he thought.

Josh noticed how blue his eyes were in the natural light that filtered through the window and how attractive he was despite his unkempt appearance. He quickly diverted his gaze to the window and squinted at the street beyond where a well-dressed woman walked her poodle down the sidewalk. As he watched the poodle dawdle, sniffing this than that, his mind began to wonder.

*   *   *   *
     *   *   *

The late autumn air was chilled with the early bite of winter and seasoned with flurries as Josh followed Alex to the McMurran Hill Monument. Up lit at night so that it could be seen for miles around, the monument, a polished granite pillar sitting atop granite slabs that formed a series of steps at its base, stood on a cliff overlooking the river. It was accessed by a circular drive that enclosed an expanse of meticulously trimmed turf. Separated by only a low stone wall that surrounded the monument, the river valley yawned below brilliantly illuminated by the light of a gibbous moon.

Alex mounted the steps, sat down at the base of the pillar and motioned for Josh to do the same. After Josh sat down, Alex opened the bag and produced a six-pack of beer.

"Here, take one."

Josh hesitated. "We're not supposed to be drinking; we're not old enough."

Alex thrust the can into his hand. "Just take one, damn it!"

He opened his own with a hiss and promptly downed several gulps.

Josh picked up the can, opened it and took a sip. He then pursed his lips and put the can down. "Kind of bitter, isn't it?"

Alex did not reply. Instead, he continued to drink in silence, gazing out over the river valley bathed in the soft light. The view was majestic, with tree-covered hills stretching endlessly in the distance and a silver sliver of river zigzagging between them.

Alex took one gulp after another. When he had finished, he crushed the empty can in his hand and gave it a toss over the wall. He then opened another and took several more gulps.

Josh finally spoke up. "What's this all about, Alex?"

"Nancy broke up with me," he said bitterly. "She accused me of fooling around behind her back!"

"Oh." Josh took another sip then put the can down.

"But….you kind of do, don't you?"

Alex continued to drink. When he had finished with the second can, he crushed it and opened another.

"You really should stop. You're going to get sick," Josh cautioned. "I think we should be getting back; it's cold up here."

Alex turned and stared at him in the moonlight. "Do you have a thing for me?"

A spasm of adrenaline shot through Josh's gut, and he instinctively reached for his can. "A….a thing?" he slurped.

"Yeah. I mean, Nelson seems to think you're queer, and well, you don't have a girlfriend or anything. I know Joanie's not your girlfriend."

"Whoa, wait a minute!" he replied. "What does that moron know?" He paused. "It's getting late, and we still have a lot to cover before finals."

He got up to leave, but Alex grabbed him by the arm.

"Don't change the subject. I just want to know."

Josh pulled free. "Is this the part where you beat me up or something? What do you want from me, Alex? All I've ever done is tried to help you!"

"You haven't answered my question," he challenged. "Besides, there are other kids in the class who are struggling but you're not helping them."

Josh wanted to run away from this conversation as fast as he could. "It's not like I have all the time in the world to tutor every student who's struggling, do I? I'm going back. Now."

Before he could leave, Alex staggered to the stone wall and jumped atop it.

"What do you think you're doing?" Josh called. "Get down from there before you fall!"

"Someone could easily jump off this wall," Alex began dramatically. "Someone did, you know. Legend has it that a young woman threw herself over the cliff because her boyfriend broke up with her. You'd think they would put a fence up or something after that."

Josh slowly moved toward Alex. "I think that's just a rumor," he said gently. "Now, would you please come down? You're making me nervous."

Alex looked over the edge. "If I died, would you be sad?"

The thought of Alex plummeting to his death brought tears to his eyes. "Yes…yes, of course I'd be sad," he said, his voice cracking. At that moment, he knew for certain that he was indeed in love with Alex. "Please get down."

"I will on one condition," he replied. "Tell me if you have a thing for me."

Alex inched closer to the edge so that the tips of his sneakers jutted out over the wall. He held his arms aloft as if preparing to take flight and teetered precariously in the breeze.

"Yes!" Josh's voice was just a hoarse whisper.

Alex looked back at him. "What did you say?"

"Yes, damn it, yes!" he cried, choking on the words. "I have a thing for you, all right! Now please get down!"

Alex pitched forward as he lost his balance, but Josh lunged, grabbed him around the waist and pulled him back with all his might. The two fell together to the granite base, and Alex began to laugh hysterically.

"You asshole!" Josh spat, as he got up, holding onto his right arm, which had taken much of the impact. "Don't ever do that again!" He grabbed the nearly full can of beer that Alex had left nearby and hurled it over the wall sending it on a trajectory that the fabled young woman must have taken.

"Hey, that's good beer you're wasting!" Alex managed between gasps as he got to his feet.

"Whatever!" Josh seethed. "You almost got both of us killed."

"There's like several feet of solid ground between the wall and the cliff. I wasn't anywhere close to the edge," he said, continuing to laugh.

"You're such a jerk! I hate you!" Josh bounded down the steps toward the circular drive.

"Hey, you just said you have a thing for me!"

"Fuck you!" It was not something he often said and usually not to someone else. But for this occasion, he was willing to make an exception.

He started across the expanse of lawn that surrounded the monument. Just as he stepped outside the rim of light cast by the decorative lamps that ringed the drive, he heard the beating of feet on the ground and turned to see Alex bounding toward him through the shadows. The sight made the hairs on the back of his neck stand up, and he broke into a run. He soon heard the panting breath just behind him, and then felt the grab at his waist. In an instant, the two hit the ground and were sliding together in the cold, damp grass.

"Help!" Josh gasped as the wind was squeezed from his lungs.

Alex pulled him close. "I'm not going to hurt you."

He could feel Alex's weight against him, his face so close their foggy breaths intermixed as they panted in unison. His first impulse was to push away, that is, until Alex forced their lips together. Josh began to wonder if perhaps he had dozed off in the library and this was all a dream as Alex's soft, wet tongue pressed and wallowed against his own.

Alex then abruptly broke free, fell on his hands and knees and began to vomit in the grass.

Josh sat up. "Are you okay? Was it the...?"

Alex shook his head as another heave seized him.

Just then, a car pulled into the circular drive, its headlights catching them in the glare. Josh attempted to shield the light with his hand. With the engine still running, the driver's side door opened and someone got out.

"What's going on here?" He recognized the gruff voice of Officer Malcolm Biddle, captain of the campus police force. As if the high beams weren't enough, he pointed a flashlight first from Josh and then to Alex.

Josh scrambled to his feet and began to brush himself off.

"Ah, nothing Officer."

"What are you two boys doing up here this late at night?" He took several steps forward, continuing to shine the light on Alex. "Is that boy sick?"

"Ah, yes, he's...ah...sick," Josh stammered.

"Have you two been drinking?" he thundered. "You know underage drinking is not tolerated here!"

"No, Officer," Josh replied. "He's infected with...with..."

"A slime mold," Alex managed to say.

The officer took a step back. "A what?"

"A...a slime mold," Josh said. "He was exposed....in the lab, and....oh, it's very contagious."

Alex nodded, still huddled on the grass. "Yeah, contagious." He spat out the last of the vomitus.

Officer Biddle took several more steps away and shone the light on Josh's face. "And what about you? You infected?"

"Oh, me? Oh...no...I've been...vaccinated. Yeah, vaccinated. And Alex...well, he hasn't."

"Does he need an ambulance?"

By now Alex was seated on the ground with his arms resting across his arched knees.

"No! He'll be all right now. He was just in the ah…"

"Puking stage," Alex finished.

"Yes, the puking stage. Now that that's over, he'll be fine."

"That so?" He eyed them suspiciously. Josh could tell that the seasoned Officer Biddle was not convinced. He was certain that scads of students' bullshit had been thrown his way over the years. "Are you going to be all right, son?"

"Yes, sir, I feel much better," Alex replied.

Biddle shook his head. "Get in the car. I'll take you both back to campus."

The three of them rode in silence on the short drive back to the main campus with Officer Biddle in the front seat and Josh and Alex in the back, like two hardened criminals being taken to the big house. As requested, Biddle would drop Josh off at the library but take Alex to his dorm.

"Thank you Officer," Josh said as he got out of the car. He then turned to Alex. "I guess I'll see you tomorrow, then?"

Alex nodded but did not speak. On a night full of surprises, there was an unexpected pang of separation as he watched the car drive away, realizing for a second time that evening what it felt like to be in love.

*　　　　　　*　　　　　　*　　　　　　*

　　　　*　　　　　　*　　　　　　*

"Two large salads and iced tea," the waitress interrupted as she sat the food in front of them. "Will that be all for now?"

Josh looked up with a start. "Ah…yes…yes, thank you."

Alex leaned across the table. "Are you okay? You look distracted or something."

"No, I'm fine."

"Look, I don't want to burden you will all this. I hope I'm not disrupting your busy schedule."

Josh shook his head. "You're not disrupting anything."

Alex eyed him suspiciously. "You were just thinking about it, weren't you?"

Josh tried to stifle a grin. "What?"

"Uh huh," Alex gasped. "You were. You were thinking about the time we drank the bottle of Dom Perignon, weren't you?"

Still grinning, Josh picked up his fork. "No." The word 'no' had been stretch out playfully.

"Or maybe that night on McMurran Hill."

Josh took a bite of salad, and still grinning, began to chew.

Alex nodded and smiled. "You were, weren't you?"

"Well…"

"Josh, here you are! Why didn't you come get me for lunch!" It was Nick Perone.

"Oh! Sorry!" he replied with a start. "I thought you were still in the clinic. Ah, Nick, say hello to a good friend of mine from college, Alex Byrne. He's Jane Riley's brother. Alex this is one of my colleagues, Nick Perone."

Alex offered up his hand, and the two men shook. Nick then squeezed in beside Josh. "Mind if I join you?"

"No…not at all," Josh mumbled as he scooted closer to the wall.

Nick signaled the waitress and ordered a Bogie Burger with fires.

"I thought you were watching your waist?" Josh asked.

"I'll let my wife watch it…get bigger, I guess." Then to Alex: "So you and Josh went to college together?"

Alex was just about to put a large forkful of salad in his widely patent mouth when he paused. "Yes. But Josh was much smarter than I was."

The small talk continued through lunch, wherein they purposefully avoided any discussion about Jane's condition. When they had finished eating, the waitress reappeared and placed their ticket on the table. After paying the bill, the three stood outside the restaurant in the warm sunshine.

"We need to get back to work," Josh said to Alex. "You need to go home and get some rest. We'll see you tomorrow for your repeat lab draw. Who knows? Tomorrow may be the day."

Forty-one

Days later, Marc Abelman sat at a computer terminal in the Transplant Unit, scrolling through the laboratory log contained in the hospital mainframe. Although Jane Riley had remained relatively stable for several days, her window for receiving a transplant appeared to be closing rapidly. Blood had been taken earlier in the morning from her brother, and the results were eagerly awaited. Abelman typed in *Byrne, Alexander* and in an instant, the lab data flashed on the screen.

He let out a low whistle. "Wow!" After making a printout, he found Josh Hanley sitting in the nurses' station busily scribing notes in the patients' charts, meticulously documenting what was discussed on rounds. "Dr. Hanley, you may want to take a look at this."

Josh abruptly grabbed the paper and scanned it. He handed it back to Marc and resumed writing. "Looks like he's ready to harvest."

Abelman took the page. "I thought you'd be excited about this. Is something wrong?"

Josh stopped writing and took off his glasses. "Let me ask you something, Marc. Do you think I'm nuts?"

"Nuts?"

"Yeah, nuts, bananas, have a screw loose, whatever. Do you think I'm jumping the gun on this letter thing? Do you think my decision to transplant Jane Riley is crazy?"

Abelman sat on the edge of the counter near the computer. "No, not at all. I think it's the only option."

Josh nodded thoughtfully.

"And so does Dr. Riley," Ableman added.

"She does?"

"Yes. She's really glad you're her doctor. Of all the people in the section, she said she trusts you the most, even more than…" He stopped.

"Than who?"

Abelman scanned the nurses' station before answering. "Well, I shouldn't say this….but she trusts you more than she trusts Dr. Roth."

Josh's eyes widened. "She said that?"

Ableman half shrugged and nodded. "In so many words."

"Really? Why is that?"

"I didn't have to ask why."

Josh grabbed the phone and punched the keyboard. "This is Dr. Hanley. Alexander Byrne is ready for harvest." He looked at Ableman and winked. "Let's roll."

*   *   *   *
  *   *   *

An hour later, Alex Byrne lay stiffly on a hospital bed staring up at the ceiling. Despite the 'easy listening' music being piped into the room, he could feel his heart pounding while beads of sweat studded his forehead, and rolled down his temples. He ached from the growth factor treatment with the pains in the bones of his lower spine and pelvis being the worse. The stem cells had finally been coaxed from the bone marrow into the bloodstream by the subcutaneously injected growth factor, and the circulating cells would now be 'harvested' by a procedure known as aphaeresis. Blood would flow from an intravenous line in one arm into a special machine that would isolate the desired cells from the rest of the blood by centrifugal force. The remaining blood would then be returned to the bloodstream through another line in his other arm.

The nurse performing the procedure looked as though she had stepped out of the nineteen sixties. Her straight, dark hair was curled up at the ends, and she wore a starched white dress, white hose and white pumps. An old fashioned nurses' cap was pinned atop her head, appearing to defy the laws of gravity. As she approached him with a small tray of needles that looked way too big to stick into anyone's flesh, his stomach started to flutter. "What are they for?"

"Not to worry, love. I'm just going to start your IV's so we can hook you up to the machine." Despite his nervousness, he found her English accent appealing. She placed a tourniquet around his upper arm and tightened it. The constriction caused several large veins to become engorged. She swabbed the overlying skin with alcohol. "Oh, this is a good one." Grasping a large needle with her fingers, she held it close to the surface of the skin.

"You're going to feel a little pinch," she said as the needle entered the skin.

Alex turned away and stiffened as the needle entered his arm. He bit is lower lip but his mind screamed 'ouch!' The pinch lasted only a second.

She secured the needle with gauze and tape. "Does it still hurt, love?"

He exhaled. "No, it's okay now."

She repeated the procedure on the other arm and began to prime the machine with sterile saline.

Josh came bustling into the room. "Ready for the harvest?"

Alex did not reply.

He turned to the nurse. "How's he doing, Clara?"

"He's a bit nervous, Dr. Hanley. His blood pressure's up a little," Clara replied. "I think he could use a mild sedative."

"Hum," replied Josh, surveying the record. "Your blood pressure is up. Have you ever had problems with it before?"

Alex stared at the ceiling and did not move, hoping that Josh Hanley would not think him a total coward. "Only when I'm about to have the blood sucked out of my body, put through a machine, and then forced back into me. Other than that, I've been fine."

Josh handed the chart to the nurse. "Give him a milligram of lorazepam."

"Good choice, love," she said, drawing up a syringe she had already ordered from the pharmacy.

"I'm sorry. I'm just a little stressed out," Alex said. "I'm worried about Jane and trying to keep my business going over the phone."

Josh rested his hand on Alex's shoulder. "I understand. But believe me, you're going to do just fine."

Clara injected the syringe into the IV tubing. "This will calm you down."

Alex clasped his hands over his abdomen, and remained very still as the medication flowed into the tubing.

"Stop acting like you're the guest of honor at a wake," Josh said to him. "You should read the paper or watch some T.V."

The two men watched as Clara attached the IV lines to the machine. As the blood began to slowly drain from the IV in his left arm and circulate through a clear, plastic coil in the machine, Alex felt a bit queasy but kept his eyes on the IV tubing. The blood flowed like a roller coaster into a spinning glass container where the machine began to separate the stem cells from the rest of the blood. A red line soon emerged in the tube on the other side of the machine at the outflow value. It slowly crept up the IV tubing attached to Alex's other arm, on its way back to his bloodstream. His eyes wide, he watched it flow toward his arm like a red snake.

"The blood coming back is okay, right?"

Clara nodded and smiled. "Not to worry, love, it's just what we want."

Alex had become immobile, frozen by the fear that even the slightest movement would disrupt the process. But soon the sedative began to take effect, and he could feel himself slowly relaxing.

"It looks like you're doing okay," Josh remarked. "I've got to go back to work. I guess I'll see you later."

"See you doc." A grin spread across his face, and he tried to salute.

Clara winked. "He'll be fine, Dr. Hanley."

Alex gazed at a small television suspended from the wall by a mechanical arm. An attractive female anchor for CNN began a report on how the world markets were faring that day. His eyelids became heavy, and before long, he had drifted off into a light sleep. In that twilight zone between sleep and consciousness, time seemed to pass quickly.

"He's tolerating the procedure very well, Doctor Hanley," Alex heard Clara say.

"Great!" Alex felt Josh grab his shoulder and squeeze. "If your harvest is adequate, we may only have to do this once. We'll do a count of the stem cells we've collected today and determine if we have to repeat the procedure tomorrow."

Alex heard only the last phrase and raised his head. "I have to do this again tomorrow?"

"We'll see, Alex. Just relax for now, okay. You're doing fine. It's not that bad is it?"

"As long as you give me some more of that 'happy medicine' I'll be fine."

Josh rolled his eyes and threw Clara a glance. "I'll see what we can do."

"He's nearly done Dr. Hanley," she noted. "All I have to do now is take him off the machine."

Alex watched her remove the IV needles from his arms and then carefully remove a bag of what of what appeared to be blood from the machine. "Are those the stem cells?" he asked.

Josh nodded. "Clara will take the cells to the laboratory for processing and count to see if we have enough."

"When will you give them to Jane?" he asked.

"If we have enough cells, we'll give them today."

It only took an hour to determine that the harvest had been a success with more than enough stem cells collected on the first run. The cells were then separated into multiple bags and several bags were delivered to the Transplant Unit. The rest were "snap frozen," that is, they were frozen very quickly following the addition of a preservative known as DMSO, and placed in a liquid nitrogen tank for future use if needed.

"Let's do this," Josh said to Marc Abelman. *Before I change my mind*, he thought.

They followed the transplant technician, who bore several bags of the cells, into Jane's room as if entering a church for a funeral. Alex and Beth were seated on either side of the bed and stood as the entourage entered.

Josh took Jane by the hand. "Are you ready for this?"

She nodded weakly but said nothing. Josh looked at the nurse. "She's been pre-medicated?"

"Yes, Dr. Hanley."

He arched his eyebrows and gave a single nod. With that, the nurse carefully attached one end of a clear plastic tube to the bag and the other to an IV line. The red liquid ran from the bag down the tube.

"The cells are going into her blood. Shouldn't you be putting them directly into her bone marrow?" Alex asked.

Josh shook his head. "The cells will circulate in the blood stream and make their way to the bone marrow where they'll find a suitable environment and begin to grow, much like seeds in good soil. The seeds are the cells, and the soil is the bone marrow."

"How long will it take them to get to the bone marrow?" Beth asked.

"They get there almost immediately, but it will take about ten to fourteen days for them to actually grow up enough to reconstitute the bone marrow, if we're lucky," Josh said. He looked at Jane. "How do you feel?"

She shrugged and whispered: "Fine."

"Good. It looks like there hasn't been any adverse reaction to the infusion. I will check back on you later." Josh walked out of the room and headed to the nursing station. He found Jane's chart and began to write. Alex soon joined him. "Josh, I just wanted to say how grateful I am that you're taking care of Jane. You're one hell of a doctor and I...." His eyes began to well with tears. "Damn, I'm sorry."

Josh stopped writing and looked up. "It's okay, Alex. I think there's a box of tissues here somewhere."

Alex quickly wiped his eyes with the backs of his hands. "I'm okay; don't worry about me."

Josh began to write again.

"You know, they pay all those movie stars and athletes multimillion dollar salaries," Alex continued. "But it's you doctors who are the real heroes."

"Well, I don't know about that." Josh suddenly recalled his encounter with Wilton Roth and put the pen down, hoping with all his heart that he had just done the right thing.

Forty-two

It was after 9 pm when the rectory telephone rang. Delores Del Torto retrieved the call. "Trinity Church Rectory," she said into the receiver.

"Ah, yes, I, ah, need to talk to a priest, Father George McBrien. Is he there?"

She shifted the receiver from one ear to the other ear and sat down, pen in hand. "May I ask who is calling?"

"I'm a friend of a member of your church. He's in a hospital in Arlington and he needs the Last Rites."

"Last Rites? You mean "Anointing of the Sick?" she corrected. "What's his name?"

"Ah....Smith...ah...Smithson....Richard Smithson."

Delores wrote his name but didn't readily recognize it. There were, however, over three thousand families registered at the parish, and many didn't attend Mass on a regular basis.

"I really need to speak to Father McBrien," the caller continued. "Mr. Smithson has specifically requested Father McBrien's presence."

"Yes, of course. And who may I say is calling""

"John Smith....ah....Smithson."

"John Smithson?" Delores repeated. "Are you related to him?"

"Yes, I'm his...ah...son."

"I thought you said you were his friend?"

The man on the line hesitated. "I'm sorry. I meant my father not my friend."

"Okay...one moment please, Mr. Smithson."

Delores found McBrien in the study. "A Mr. Smithson on line one. He says it's an emergency and has specifically requested you."

He picked up the phone. "Father McBrien." He listened as the caller repeated the request.

"Which hospital? Arlington Hospital, yes, I know it. Room 333. Yes, I'll be right there." He hung up the phone. "I need to make an emergency sick call." The holy oils were in a case near the back door, and McBrien grabbed it on his way out.

"I'll leave the lights on for you, Father," Delores called after him.

McBrien pulled out of the church parking lot and maneuvered the battered station wagon down narrow 34th street to M Street, the still congested main artery that ran through the center of Georgetown. He stopped at a light just before the Francis Scott Key Memorial Bridge, which spanned the Potomac between the District and Arlington. As he waited, a black Suburban with tinted windows pulled up behind the station wagon. When the light changed, the Suburban followed as he made a left turn onto the six-lane bridge. In the distance, the multi-layered Watergate Complex could be seen sitting on the north bank of the Potomac with the white rectangular Kennedy Center squatting next to it. As a testament to the architectural aesthetic of these two landmarks, the running joke among Washingtonians was that the Watergate Complex was a multi-layered sheet cake and the Kennedy Center was the box it came in. In contrast, the up-lit white obelisk of the Washington Monument pierced the night sky behind the two buildings.

As the station wagon began to cross the bridge, the black Suburban pulled abreast into the passing lane, nearly making contact with it. McBrien frantically palmed the horn of the station wagon. "Good Lord! Watch where you're going!"

The Suburban maintained its proximity, and the two cars began to swerve together in a deadly dance down the bridge. The passenger side window of the suburban was slowly lowered, and in a flash of light and brief thud, the driver side window of the station wagon exploded into countless fragments of glass. In that same instant, McBrien felt a searing pain pierce the left side of his chest with a force that hurled him across the seat. As the Suburban sped past, the station wagon swerved out of control and struck the iron railing that separated it from the 150 feet drop into the Potomac, producing a shower of brilliant sparks. The station wagon then banked off the railing, sideswiped another car and nearly collided with oncoming traffic in the opposite lanes. It spun around and stalled in the middle of the bridge causing traffic in all lanes to come to a complete standstill.

"Are you crazy!" A tall, husky man had abandoned his Jaguar and was screaming into the shattered driver's side window.

McBrien lay across the front seat, gasping for breath and holding his left side as blood bubbled between his fingers. "Please....I...I think I've been shot!"

"Good God!" The man pulled the door open with one hand and with the other grabbed for his cell phone. He quickly punched in three numbers, then cradling the phone with his shoulder, he spoke to the 911 operator, while ripping the black clerical shirt to expose the bloody, hissing wound. "I'm a surgeon. You're going to be all right. You hang in there, okay?"

"Thank you," George gasped. "You.... must call the rectory.... of Trinity Church. Te... tell them that .....there is a parishioner...in Arlington Hospital. His name is ..Smithson."

"Don't try to talk, Father." The surgeon knew that his patient was about to lose consciousness.

"You....you don't understand," he continued. "He needs....annointing.....he's...dying."

"I'll call as soon as I can, Father, but right now you need to be taken care of more than he does."

By now a small crowd had gathered around the scene, and the surgeon began barking orders. "You and you, give me a hand. Let's get him out of this car." Then to a young man who happened to be jogging by: "I need that tee shirt. Now!" With the help of several people, McBrien was lifted out of the car and gently laid on the pavement. The surgeon continued to apply pressure to the wound and instructed the others to raise the feet. Finally, two District police motorcycles meandered through the maze of stalled traffic, with lights flashing and sirens whining.

"This man's been shot," shouted the surgeon. "We need an ambulance immediately!"

"It's on the way," a patrolman shouted back over the roar of the motorcycle engine. "But it's stalled in traffic on M street."

The wail of an ambulance siren could be heard somewhere in the distance. The elevated bridge gave an expansive view of the center of Georgetown. Soon, flashing lights could be seen in the distance flickering through the clot of vehicles stranded on M Street.

"It's going to take too long to get through all that traffic!" the surgeon shouted, glancing from his vantage point. "He's not going to make it. Call the chopper!"

"Chopper!" A patrolman fired back. "On the bridge? Are you crazy?"

"Look, it's his only chance. I'm a surgeon at University Hospital. Tell them I said to send the chopper! Now!"

"I can hardly breath!" George managed to gasp.

"Clear the bridge! Get these cars as far back as possible!" the surgeon shouted again waving his free arm.

"This guy's nuts," one patrolman mumbled to the other as they ordered the bystanders to return to their cars and began to wave the traffic back.

Within minutes a Medivac chopper, with lights ablaze, came whizzing over the water through the night sky. When it reached the bridge, it stopped and began to hover. While still kneeling over his stricken victim, the surgeon motioned frantically with his arm as a search light nearly blinded him.

"This is Medivac one." The pilot's voice crackled through the radio to the patrolmen on the bridge. "What's he want me to do, over?"

The patrolman put the receiver to his mouth. "Land on the bridge! Over!"

"He wants me to what? Over."

"Land on the bridge! Did you copy that? Over.

"Ah, Roger that. He wants me to land on the bridge? Is he crazy, over?"

"There's no other choice! There's a man down here who's going to die unless we can get him to the hospital ASAP. The ambulance will never get through this traffic in time, over."

"Roger that! We may all die! Over and out."

Then, as the craft tittered in the crosswinds, the pilot gingerly lowered it onto the bridge, just clearing the ornate streetlamps that lined both sides. Once on solid concrete, the paramedics scrambled from the chopper under the roaring blades and descended upon the scene. They worked frantically, to bind up the wound and stem the loss of blood. After two large bore IV lines were inserted and an oxygen mask affixed to his face, McBrien was placed on a stretcher and loaded into the waiting chopper. The surgeon jumped into the chopper with the others.

Gradually, the craft began its delicate ascent. A sudden crosswind sent the chopper bucking to and fro, its blades only feet away from the shuttering streetlamps. The pilot firmly grasped the joystick with both hands.

"I can't get out, there's too much of a crosswind!" He yelled. "I'm putting her back down."

"This man is going to die!" The surgeon shouted above the roar of the engines. "We have to take him out now!"

"Look, I have a wife and kids! I don't want to die tonight!" The pilot replied through clenched teeth. His knuckles were white as he continued to hold onto the joystick with all his strength.

At that moment, despite being secured to the stretcher, McBrien managed to raise his palm upward.

The paramedic looked at his assistant. "What's he trying to say?"

At the same time, the chopper smoothly rose straight up, just clearing the swaying lamp posts.

"What the…?" the pilot gasped as he continued to clutch the joystick.

As the young priest's life slowly ebbed away, the chopper made a wide turn over the river and headed back toward the city.

Forty-three

The J. Edgar Hoover Building sat on E Street between 9th and 10th Streets and occupied an entire city block. The fortress-like edifice, once described by J. Edgar Hoover himself as "the ugliest building I've ever seen," appeared to be constructed of gigantic concrete slabs stacked on top of one another. Its prodigious security more than compensated for its lack of aesthetic value, however.

Grace and Al checked their firearms at the main entrance and obtained visitor passes from the guards. They then met Dugan and Cochran in an expansive lobby of polished granite which sported an enormous seal of the Federal Bureau of Investigation embedded in the floor.

"Thanks for coming over on such short notice," Dugan remarked. "Follow us, please."

"Thank you for analyzing the tea cup powder and the metro surveillance tapes so quickly. Your lab makes ours look like something out of the Stone Age. It's nice to see our tax dollars at work," Grace noted as she and Al followed the agents' brisk pace. "Besides, yesterday was one day I'd like to forget."

She recounted the scene at the morgue the day prior. Upon seeing her son's bloated body, Mona Wright had collapsed and was admitted to a nearby hospital under heavy sedation and police protection.

"I guess we won't be talking to her any time soon," Cochran said.

The agents escorted them to a bank of elevators that took them down several floors to the FBI crime lab. When the elevator doors opened, they found themselves in another granite covered lobby softly lit with recessed lighting. A different seal was embedded in the floor, this one containing a microscope, a flask and an artist's palette surrounded by stars. The words *Federal Bureau of Investigation Laboratory Division* encircled the seal.

The crime lab itself was divided into a series of labs, each with a specific mission. The agents led them down a long corridor past laboratories for DNA analysis, Evidence Response, Explosives, Firearms, Trace Evidence, Latent Prints, and many others. They stopped in front of a lab marked 'Chemistry' where Dugan inserted his identification badge into a receptacle by the door. A green light flashed and he opened the door into a cavernous brightly lit room with rows and rows of soapstone topped lab benches and hordes of white-coated lab technicians busy at work.

Grace let a low whistle. "Quite a place you have here."

Cochran nodded. "These lab technicians are working on material from around the country and the world."

"Um, um, um," was all she could say in reply.

The agents walked past several of the benches before stopping at one that was manned by a diminutive African American man in a white lab coat. A rust-colored solution simmered in a beaker perched over the flame of a Bunsen burner.

"This is Russell Waite, one of our leading chemists." Cochran introduced Al and Grace. "We hear you have a prelim on the powder we sent you."

Waite looked up and removed his round wire rimmed glasses. His white lab coat contrasted sharply with his dark skin, and his white hair swirled about his head in disarray. "Yes, I was just going over the findings of the Mass Spec."

Waite pointed to a large, box-like apparatus on the counter next to him. "This is a Mass Spectrophotometer. It is capable of identifying the fingerprint of every chemical known to humankind." He then turned to Cochran and handed him a clipboard. "Here take a look."

Cochran studied the report, and then handed it to Dugan, who in turn handed it to Grace. "So Russ, you found something called 1,4-butane...dimeth...."

"1,4-butanediol dimethane sulfonate, Jeff. That was what was found in the teacup. It's a drug known as..."

"Busulfan," Grace finished for him as she handed the clipboard to Al King.

"Why, yes, young lady. Busulfan." He put his glasses back on and studied Grace through his bifocal lenses. "It's commonly used as a chemotherapeutic agent for the treatment of certain types of cancers. There's also a significant amount of ascorbate in the powder."

"Ascorbate?" Cochran asked.

"Vitamin C," Grace replied. "What was that doing there?"

"That, I can't tell you," the chemist replied.

King studied the clipboard. "Now all we have to find out is how in the hell Stan Wright got a hold of this and how he knew how to use it. It's not exactly something you usually pick up on the street."

"You can get anything on the street if you know whom to ask, I suppose," Cochran replied.

"Well, I'm sure you can," King countered. "But you have to know what to ask for, right? And from what we know of this Stan Wright, he wasn't exactly a rocket scientist."

Grace turned to Cochran and Dugan. "So this is what he somehow managed to slip the Commissioner of the FDA?"

"According to Dr. Hanley, the Commissioner's illness is entirely consistent with the side effects of this drug. Now we have to find out where he may have gotten it," Dugan replied.

Jeff Cochran had been leaning against the counter, quietly studying his shoes. He then looked up. "I think we need to talk to Dr. Hanley again. Maybe he'll have some insight into all this. We're obviously dealing with a conspiracy here. Stan Wright couldn't possibly have known about this drug." He turned to the chemist. "Well, Russ, thanks for all your help."

"Yes," Grace added. "I'd like a copy of this report, if I may."

Waite smiled at her. "Certainly, young lady."

The foursome left the Chemistry Laboratory and headed for the Forensic Audio, Video and Image Analysis Laboratory. Once outside the lab, Dugan swiped his card through the slot again.

They entered a darkened room with rows of computer terminals. The agents led them to one of the technicians seated at a computer terminal busily pecking away at the keyboard. His long straight hair, pulled back into a ponytail, complemented his 'uniform' of a tee shirt, blue jeans and tennis shoes.

"Hey, Paul, how's it going?" Dugan asked as they approached.

The man looked up. "Hey, guys!"

Dugan introduced Grace Love and Al King. "Show us what you have on the Wright case."

"Come take a look." The technician took a big bite out of a red delicious apple and stared at the screen through thick glasses as the tape began to roll.

"I had to go through all the tapes to find the best ones, but I was able to digitally re-master the pertinent parts from each film into one for easier viewing." A digital counter in the lower right hand corner of the film recorded a date and ticked away the hours, minutes and seconds. The first sequence showed the Bethesda Metro station from various angles with commuters and trains moving about at rapid speeds. As the timer approached 19:50, Paul slowed the tape. The grainy black and white film showed commuters exiting the metro cars. When a young man with shoulder length hair, thick glasses and a light-colored parka appeared, Paul stopped the film.

"Here is the victim, Stanley Wright."

Grace surveyed the screen. There was Stanley in the same clothing he had been wearing the day he washed ashore on the banks of the Potomac. A chill went up her spine as she vividly recalled how the inflated parka made him look like a parade balloon. The film then continued for several seconds as they watched Stanley race up the moving stairs, knocking other commuters to and fro.

"Ouch!" Grace interjected. "I'll bet that lady wasn't too happy."

The film went on to show a visibly shaken Stanley Wright make his way to the kiosk where the Metro guard was on duty. The silent film continued to roll as Stan frantically pounded the window of the kiosk with his open hands. Several moments later, an overweight guard dressed in the dark uniform of the Metro Police opened the door. He leaned against the frame of the doorway while Stan frantically pointed behind him.

"Our victim is obviously quite distraught," Paul remarked. The film showed the guard grabbing his hat and leading Stanley back down the platform. As the guard inspected the platform, Paul sped up the tape.

The film then changed abruptly. "Here he is racing up the stairs to the fare card machine. It looks like he was adding fare or getting change. I'm not sure what was going on there, but he almost missed his train. At any rate, the next sequences will be of even more interest to you. Here we see Stanley Wright getting off the train at the Brookland stop and...as you can see, he gets on the escalator..." He pointed to the grainy black and white image of Stan Wright in a small sea of pedestrians. The image changed abruptly again, this time showing the upper platform which housed the turnstiles and guard booth. "Here we see our victim coming off the escalator and going for the turnstiles," Paul said, pointing to the figure of Stan Wright. "Now, let's take a look further on in the film." The sequences sped up and then slowed. "Here's where the victim went to the phone booths but one can barely see him because he's almost out of the range of the camera."

A man lingered behind Stanley as he talked on the phone but he kept his back to the camera. He then drew closer, nudging Stanley beyond camera range.

Paul reversed the film and ran it again in slow motion. "This is the person who must have abducted Mr. Wright." He slowed the tape down to a halt.

Grace leaned into the screen. "Hum, you get the best look at him in profile but it's not that clear. Can you get a close up of his face?"

With the mouse, Paul made a series of clicks. They watched silently as one enhanced frame slowly followed another, each one enlarging the image of the man's profile, and with it, more and more definition. "I went back through the tapes to see if I could find him and get a better picture of his face, but in every one, he has his head down, or his hand over his forehead, or some other movement that shields his face. It was as if he was trying to evade the cameras. It's uncanny."

Grace scrutinized the image. "You're a slick one, Mr. Slick," she said, endowing him with a name. "It's a bit fuzzy, but can we print that?"

Paul punched the keyboard again and several minutes later, a photograph slowly squeezed its way out of the laser printer. Grace snatched up the digitally created image.

"This doesn't look anything like the bruiser that broke into the Wright's house," she remarked. "The man that tried to make a colander out of me was much taller. Less fat. This guy has a beer belly. Unfortunately, it's not of the best quality."

"Yes, unfortunately the Metro surveillance system is hopelessly out of date. Digital technology has not yet been installed," Paul remarked ruefully.

"I think we should at least send the photo to the press.

Someone may recognize him, even though the quality is pretty poor," Cochran said.

"Speaking of the bruiser, have you gotten any leads on the black Suburban with government issue tags," King asked. He looked at Grace and rubbed his butt.

Dugan raised his eyebrows. "Do you know how many black Suburbans there are with government-issue tags? Secret Service, Congress, Supreme Court, the list goes on and on."

Cochran nodded. "You have to be sure of this. After all, you're implicating that someone in the upper echelons of the United States Government is involved in a conspiracy to commit murder. "

King pondered this before speaking. "I'm ninety-nine point nine percent sure they were U.S. Government plates."

"It would help if you could remember any of the numbers," Dugan added.

King blew out his breath and scratched his head. "I fell on my butt before I knew it. There may have been a three and a five but I really can't remember much else."

Dugan jotted a note on his pad.

But Grace had had enough talk. She put both hands on her hips. "Look guys, there is something big going on here. I think we all know that poor Stanley Wright didn't come up with a plot to murder Jane Riley all by himself. Somebody is behind this and that somebody drives a black Suburban with government tags! If I were you guys, I'd be taking this case to the Director today!"

Forty-four

Suzy Fischer got the call at midnight. Tanya had started to have contractions but was not due for weeks. Fischer knew that many of the organ systems of her fetus were not fully developed yet, the most important of which were the lungs. She found Tanya lying in bed with two small boxlike sensors attached to her swollen abdomen by wide straps that encircled her waist. The sensors were in turn attached to two different bedside monitoring devices by long white cords. One was to monitor the fetal heartbeat while the other was for recording contractions. The fetal heartbeat, sounding much like a muffled drum, emanated from one of the monitors and filled the dimly lit room. The digital readout on the monitor indicated a fetal heart rate of 160 beats per minute. A contraction was recorded on the second monitor as a large spike on the graph paper that slowly rolled out of the machine. Whenever this occurred, Tanya would moan and begin to pant through pursed lips.

"She's not ready to deliver yet," Hilson warned from the other side of the bed as Tanya began to moan and pant again. "She still has several weeks of injections on the protocol yet to go before she will be ready. You need to stop this before it goes too far."

"More importantly, the baby will not survive at this stage, Peter," Fischer replied tensely. "At least the fetal heartbeat is normal and there are no signs of fetal distress." She turned to the Jenna, who stood at the foot of the bed and was bleary eyed from lack of sleep. "Start a magnesium drip as soon as possible." She turned back to Hilson. "If this is true labor, we are in trouble. Hopefully, we're just dealing with Braxton-Hicks contractions."

Hilson instantly recalled the term from his days on the obstetric service as a medical student and knew that this term meant that the contractions were not real labor pains. These types of contractions were also known as 'false labor.'

"I hope you are right."

Fischer then instructed Tanya to roll on her side. With their help, Tanya awkwardly shifted her large frame, along with the monitors, to the left. "Sometimes, changing position helps," Fischer noted.

Jenna returned several minutes later and began to prepare an IV site on one of Tanya's arms. She then inserted the intravenous needle and began the drip.

"That stings," Tanya remarked when the fluid began to flow into her arm.

"It will be okay," said Jenna. "It won't last long."

The three watched expectantly as Tanya lie on her side. Before long, she drifted off to sleep as the fetal heartbeat droned on in the background.

"The contractions have stopped for now," Jenna said, studying the monitor after several minutes had elapsed.

"We're not out of the woods yet," Fischer added. "We'll need to monitor her for several more hours before we can be sure."

"She's due for another enzyme injection tomorrow," Hilson said.

Fischer hesitated. "I'm not sure we should give it, Peter. As you know, we are in unchartered territory here. There are no published data to tell us the best course of action in this situation."

Hilson nodded. "We are generating the data that will be published about this, and I think we should go for it. We don't really have a choice."

Fischer reared back. "I think we should err on the side of caution and hold the injection. I'm not sure what the effect will be on Tanya or the baby. What if the enzyme injections are causing the contractions? I'm just a bit concerned…."

"Look, Suzy, I'm growing tired of your lack of faith," Hilson interjected harshly. "Tanya signed on for this protocol knowing full well the risks involved."

"My lack of faith?" she replied. "I'm thinking of the safety of my patient….in this case patients. And honestly, I don't think she did understand all the risks involved. How dare you…"

"Shhhh," Jenna interjected. "You will wake up Tanya and probably upset her. And that could start the contractions all over again."

Fischer was irritated that Jenna had chosen to interrupt her but not Hilson. "Fine," she whispered. "We will give the injection tomorrow as planned."

Hilson yawned. "Okay, good. I'm going back to bed and leaving her in your capable hands, Suzy. Call me if the situation changes."

As Fischer watched Hilson go, she wondered what was happening to him. During the time of their involvement with the protocol, he was becoming a different person, so unlike the man she had fallen in love with. Was the prospect of fame and fortune so blinding that he now didn't even care about the fate of his patient and her baby? And what of all the failures, like Millie Beattie's pregnancy? Fischer had gone to great lengths for Hilson to ensure the success of the protocol, even to the point of stealing data from another researcher, something she would not have dreamt of doing a year ago. And now with this latest development, she was growing increasingly distressed by what she herself was becoming.

*   *   *   *
*   *   *

Josh was in the middle of a busy clinic when the two FBI agents appeared at the reception desk. He quickly showed them into his office.

"Thanks for taking time to talk with us again," Jeff Cochran said as he and Bill Dugan settled into the two chairs across from Josh Hanley's desk. "I know you're busy so I'll get right to the point. As I told you on the phone, a powder was found in the possession of a now deceased member of Dr. Riley's staff, one Stanley Wright." He referred to a small notepad. "And that this powder has since been identified as 1,4-butanediol dimethane sulfonate known pharmaceutically as busulfan."

At that point, Josh was relieved that the identification of the powder had vindicated his suspicions and his decision to treat Jane Riley with a transplant. His fatigue however, allowed only a measured response. "As I said from the beginning, that was my suspicion. It certainly would account for her constellation of symptoms."

"There were also large amounts of ascorbic acid found in the powder. Could you comment on that?" Dugan asked.

Josh leaned forward. "Ascorbic acid? Well, let's see. It's Vitamin C, and it's harmless." He paused then added. "But I'm not sure why it would be there."

"Would there be any reason to mix vitamin C with this drug?"

Josh thought for a moment but could not come up with a firm answer. "It's not something we routinely do. Maybe you should check with a pharmacist....wait...." He was staring at a lemon/lime soda on his desk. "From what patients tell me, busulfan has a bitter taste." He read the contents of the drink on the can. "Hum, citrate. Maybe that's it. Perhaps it was given to mask the taste of the drug."

Dugan wrote on his pad. "Interesting thought."

"Can you tell us anything more about busulfan?" Cochran asked.

"Well, let's see. It's a fairly difficult drug to use. Bone marrow suppression occurs about a week or two after administration but the seizures happen immediately, which is why bone marrow suppression was not evident when Jane had the first seizure. It causes prolonged suppression of the bone marrow which can be unpredictable, and it can't be assayed in human tissue."

Dugan continued in his familiar claw-like writing then looked at Cochran. "So someone had done some research on the use of this drug."

"Or knew about it already," Josh said. "Someone reformulated the drug with vitamin C or maybe some sort of flavored substance. Or simply mixed it in."

Cochran raised his eyes. "Stanley Wright would not have known that it was bitter."

"He would have to have a working knowledge of this drug," Josh remarked. "Someone with a medical or pharmacy background must have helped him out."

Dugan nodded as he jotted a few more notes.

"There was the one thing that these guys either forgot or didn't know about," Josh continued. "Busulfan can cause seizures in large doses, but this is relatively rare. However, we routinely put patients on prophylactic anti-convulsants when they're receiving large doses of the drug. The seizures were important clues to its identity."

"Can you think of any way he could have gotten it?" Dugan tapped his pen against the pad.

Josh thought for a moment. "I guess the easiest way would be to forge a prescription."

"Can any physician prescribe it?" asked Cochran. "Or does

one have to be an oncologist?"

Josh shrugged. "I don't think a pharmacist would routinely check to see if the physician prescribing it was an oncologist, and as far as I know, there is only one company that makes it."

"We're already pursuing that angle, and the manufacturer has been very accommodating in this case," said Dugan.

"With the Commissioner of the FDA involved, I can only imagine!" Josh forced a smile and then became serious again. "May I ask you two why there is a conspiracy to murder the Commissioner of the FDA?"

"We're not at liberty to discuss the specifics of the investigation," Cochran said.

Josh nodded. "Good FBI answer. I can understand that."

"So how is Dr. Riley doing?" Dugan asked.

"She has received a transplant from her brother and hopefully she'll pull through. It's still early, though."

"I see," Cochran replied. "By the way, do you know a Father George McBrien?"

"Yes, he's frequently on the Oncology Unit visiting members of his parish."

"Do you know that he's the victim of a drive by shooting?"

"Yes, he's in the ICU here. Why do you ask?"

Dugan looked at Cochran and the other nodded. He then continued. "I'm telling you this in strict confidence. He is probably the author of the letter you received."

Josh raised his eyebrows. "Really? How did you figure that out?"

"One small print on the edge of the envelope. He was careful, but not careful enough," said Dugan.

"But how would he have known about all this?"

"We're not really sure yet. The circumstances are unclear," Cochran replied.

"Wow, who knew?" He looked at his watch. "Gentlemen, are there any other questions I can answer? I have patients waiting in the clinic."

"No, but thanks for your time." The two agents got up to leave.

Josh stood up and extended his hand. "If you need any further information, please don't hesitate to call any time of the day or night. I'll be available."

After the clinic was over, Josh headed to the Surgical

Intensive Care unit to see how George McBrien was doing. Following extensive surgery, he was sedated and still dependent on a ventilator for life sustaining respiratory function. A large bulky dressing covered his left chest, from which a tube emerged and drained bloody fluid from the chest cavity. The tube was connected to a calibrated plastic container where the output was recorded by the nurses.

The nursing station was situated in the center of the unit, and Josh found the surgical resident busily making notations in a chart.

"How's McBrien doing?" Josh asked.

The resident looked up. His hair was tousled and his eyes bloodshot from lack of sleep. "Oh, the 'drive by' in three. He's stable." He then began a monotone litany: "He underwent surgical repair of the pulmonary artery and some lung tissue had to be resected but he's a lot more stable today. The output from his chest tube has decreased considerably, and we may be able to take it out tomorrow or the day after. His oxygenation is good and we'll be starting the vent wean within a day or two."

"Sounds like he's going to make it."

The resident nodded and yawned. "Yeah, he has youth on his side."

"Is he awake yet?"

"Negative. We'll lighten him up tomorrow when we begin the weaning trials."

"Okay, then, I'll stop by tomorrow when he's more alert."

He went past cubicle three and saw a man with close cropped hair and a full beard standing by the bedside. He was wearing a clerical shirt and blue jeans, below which his feet could be seen sticking out of well-worn sandals. He had taken McBrien's hand into his own.

Josh entered the cubicle. "Hi, I'm Dr. Josh Hanley." He extended his hand.

The priest looked up, his eyes red and puffy. "Father Edmund Patterson." He briefly took Josh's hand.

"You must be a colleague of his."

"Yes, but we're also very good friends. How's he doing, Doctor?"

"He's heavily sedated, but it looks like he's going to make it."

Patterson crossed himself. "Thank the good Lord and you wonderful doctors."

"Do you know why anyone would want to shoot Father McBrien?"

The priest studied the blue tile floor. "I…I can't say, doctor."

Josh moved a bit closer. "You can't say because you don't know, or you can't say because….you're not allowed to?" His voice was just above a whisper.

Patterson's head bounced up. "What? Why would you ask that?"

Josh shrugged. "I'm just wondering. You're his good friend. Did he mention anything to you about being in danger of any kind?"

Patterson was silent.

"You see the FBI seems to think that he might know something about a particular crime that's been committed, Father, and any information he might have told you may help them a great deal."

"The FBI?" His eyes widened. "I can't talk to them about matters of confession."

Josh looked away and heaved a sigh. "Oh, that makes sense. It was a matter of confession."

Patterson frowned. "I've said enough already, so please don't ask me any more questions. And please don't tell anyone where you got this information."

Josh grabbed his shoulder. "Don't worry, Father, your secret is safe with me."

Forty-five

A memorial service for Stanley Wright was to be held that afternoon at the FDA campus, and Ellen Downs had worn a black suit for the occasion. Most of the other staff assistants had come to work in subdued clothing, and the mailroom staff all sported black armbands. Ellen was on the phone when two well-groomed men in dark suits came into the reception area. She quickly finished her conversation and stood.

"May I help you gentlemen?" She released her reading glasses allowing them to dangle from a chain around her neck, straightened her suit and then patted her hair.

"Ms. Downs? I'm special agent Jeff Cochran of the FBI and this is my partner, Bill Dugan." The two extended their badges. "I spoke with you on the phone."

"Yes, of course, gentlemen, and you're right on time." She handed him a manila folder. "Here is Mr. Wright's personnel file as you requested. Please, have a seat."

She offered them chairs and then sat behind her desk.

"We were informed by your superiors that you probably interacted with him more than anyone else in the Commissioners' office," Dugan said as Cochran opened the file and began to read.

Ellen toyed with her pearls. "Oh, I see. Well, quite honestly, we didn't interact that much."

Dugan opened his pad. "How well did you know Stanley Wright?"

She thought for a moment before answering. "Well, let's see. He has worked here…or should I say, had worked here for about five years. He also worked for Dr. Riley's predecessor. He was a staff assistant and in that capacity did things around the office such as copying, filing. He liked the mail runs...it would get him out the office so he could goof off with his buddies in the mailroom." She put a hand to her mouth and winced. "Oh, forgive me. I shouldn't talk about him that way."

Just then, Lee Murray came bustling into the office. "Ellen I'll need to see Jane's Senate testimony on tobacco regulation. Do you have the edited copy?" He paused and eyed the agents. "Oh, I'm sorry, I didn't realize that I had any meetings scheduled this afternoon."

"Oh, these gentlemen aren't here about drug approvals. They're from the FBI." Ellen introduced the two agents as she reached into a file drawer near her desk. "They're investigating Stanley Wright's ah….murder." Her voice cracked slightly.

"Great to see you gentleman here," Murray said taking their hands in succession. "That Wright case is so tragic, so shocking."

"Yes it is. How well did you know the deceased?" Dugan asked.

"Oh, not well," Lee Murray replied, taking the document from Ellen. "I think Jane knew him much better than I did."

Dugan nodded. "I see. Well, if you think of anything out of the ordinary, please give us a call. Ms. Downs has our numbers."

"Thank you, I will, and please if there is anything else you need, let us know. Now, if you'll excuse me, I have an important meeting to get to." He turned to Ellen. "Impromptu tobacco regulation meeting on Capital Hill with some of the committee members."

"Oh, I didn't hear anything about that." She paused. "What about the memorial service?"

"I should be back in time for it, barring any unforeseen problems. Gentlemen, good day."

With that he exited the reception area before Ellen could respond. "I sure hope he gets back in time. He's supposed to say a few words on Jane's behalf."

Cochran flipped a page of the file. "What was Mr. Wright's relationship with Dr. Riley?" he asked.

"Well, quite honestly, I think Jane found him to be...oh how shall I put this delicately...somewhat inefficient, but she understood his mental limitations. She really didn't deal with him personally like the rest of us did."

"Can you tell me what sort of access he had to Dr. Riley?" Dugan asked.

"Access?" She knit her brow. "Well, he would come and go freely just like everyone else who works here. But, I mean, it's not like he saw her on a daily basis."

"And, did he ever handle her food?" Dugan pressed.

"Sometimes."

"How so?"

"Well, he usually did the lunch run."

Dugan looked up from his pad. "Lunch run?"

"Well, yes, Stanley was in charge of bringing lunch to the office. He liked doing it so much because we gave him tips."

Cochran exchanged a glance with his partner.

"Every day?" Dugan asked.

"Well, just about. Stanley did take some days off, usually Fridays. He loved to go fishing, that boy did."

"Where did these lunches come from?" Dugan asked.

"From different places. The deli down the street. Sometimes we ordered Chinese. It varied."

"So lunch came from different places everyday?" Dugan continued to write.

"Yes, usually, unless we found a place that we particularly liked."

"But Stanley picked it up?"

"Usually."

"And the Commissioner ate those lunches?"

Ellen nodded trying to remember the times she did eat the brought in lunches. "Sometimes. She really didn't eat much of a lunch, though. I'd get on her every day. She just looked like she was going to blow away in the wind."

"What did she eat?" Cochran pressed.

"Most of the time she brought food from home, if food is what you want to call it. Often one of those diet shakes, you know, those fruit-flavored things. I don't think she ate anything else, maybe a salad here and there. A cup of yogurt, some cottage cheese. She was just so busy so much of the time that she barely had time to eat."

"Where did she keep this food that she brought from home?" Dugan asked. She noticed some urgency in his voice now.

"In the refrigerator in the lounge where everyone else keeps lunches. She didn't have a refrigerator in her office, if that's what you're asking." Ellen stopped abruptly and grabbed her pearls again. "Oh my goodness! You're making the same connection I did. You think Stanley might have poisoned her food!" She began to talk quickly. "I had pulled his personnel file and went through it. I know I shouldn't have done that. Then Dr. Murray later assured us that that story about her being poisoned was untrue. That is was a rumor."

"How did he know that?"

She shrugged. "I'm not sure. I just felt so guilty about the whole thing when Stanley turned up...well, you know."

"I see. Do you think Stanley Wright harbored ill will toward Jane Riley?"

"Ill will? I don't think so. I think he was more afraid of her than anything. Jane was...is such a perfectionist. She demands the best from everyone, regardless of who they are or what they do."

"Did you notice any behavior recently that was out of line for him?" Cochran asked.

"No." Then a vivid snapshot of Stanley came to mind, and she recalled the contents of his pocket protector all over the floor. "Oh wait, I did find him in her office one day while she was in a meeting. He seemed to be snooping around."

"Snooping?"

She nodded. "He was looking through the things on her desk. I found out later that he was looking for the President's get well card. He was going to show it to his buddies in the mail room."

"He didn't tell you he was looking for the President's card the day you caught him?" Dugan asked.

"No. I guess he was so shaken when I walked in on him."

Dugan flipped the pad to a clean page and continued to write. "And he told you later that he was looking for the card?"

Ellen shook her head. "No, I think Dr. Murray told me that, too."

"There's not much in this personnel file that would arouse suspicion," Cochran noted as he threw the folder back on Ellen's desk. "His performance reviews were okay, but far from stellar."

Ellen picked up the folder and opened it. "What about the psychiatric history?"

Cochran looked squarely at Ellen. "What psychiatric history?"

"Apparently as a child, he was diagnosed with attention deficit disorder, and then growing up, during adolescence, he misbehaved in school. He'd talk back to teachers, skip school, smoke in the restroom. They referred to it as 'sociopathic behavior.'" She looked up as she continued to flip through the chart. "It should all be in there."

"There's not even a medical section to the file." Cochran said.

She closed the file and placed it carefully on her desk. "I don't understand this. There were several years of reports in the file. Some of them were written just before he started working here. It was all in here just a couple of weeks ago."

"What else do you remember about the missing information, Ms. Downs?" Cochran asked. "Do you remember who submitted the reports?"

"Let's see, what was that name?" She bowed her head in thought for several moments then looked up, her face bright. "Ah, yes, it was a Dr. Sizemore. Dr. Phillip Sizemore."

"Phillip Sizemore?" Dugan wrote the name on his pad.

"Yes, the letterhead was from a practice in the District, on 19th Street, I think."

Dugan stopped writing. "I see. Can you remember anything else, Ms. Downs?"

She frowned. "I wish I would have copied those reports now. I had no idea someone would remove them. I'm so sorry. I don't know what to say. I'm afraid your trip out here was for naught."

"Not at all," Dugan said, putting away his pen and pad. "On the contrary, you've been very helpful. May we see the refrigerator where Dr. Riley kept her food?"

Ellen shrugged. "Sure. I don't think there's anything in there that belongs to Jane."

She led them down the hall and into a brightly lit lounge that contained banks of blue lockers and modern brass and vinyl furniture.

"This icebox has not been cleaned out for quite some time," she warned them, pulling open the door.

The refrigerator was stuffed with bags and Tupperware exhibiting the various eating habits of the large number of employees in the Commissioner's office. Dugan donned a pair of surgical gloves and began taking them out one at a time, placing them on a nearby countertop.

Ellen shook her head. "I don't think you'll find any of Dr. Riley's food there. She hasn't been here for weeks, you know."

Undaunted, he continued to carefully remove the containers.

"Do you remember what type of container the Commissioner usually brought?" Cochran asked.

"Let's see." Ellen grabbed her chin. "I think she usually brought one of those plastic things. You know, the kind you can throw away without opening when the food goes bad."

"You mean, like this?" Dugan asked. He took a square plastic container out of a brown bag marked 'J. Riley.'"

"That's it!" Ellen exclaimed. "Now I remember that the last day she was here, she didn't eat all of her lunch because she didn't have an appetite."

Dugan opened the lid and quickly closed it. "Whew, bad cottage cheese and rotting fruit."

Cochran chuckled. "We'll have to take this to the lab. Russ is going to love us."

*　　　　*　　　　*　　　　*
　　　*　　　　*　　　　*

"We got the autopsy report on Stan Wright," Grace began later that afternoon. She, Cochran, Dugan and King had just sat down for coffee at a shop on Connecticut Avenue. "He died of massive head wounds - no surprise - but there weren't any drugs or toxins in his system. And so far, the picture of Mr. Slick hasn't generated any legitimate leads…a bunch of crackpot calls, but no leads. I hope you guys made out better in Rockville."

"We talked with some of the staff over at the FDA offices," Dugan replied. "The Commissioner's executive assistant was very helpful. We managed to get a sample of Jane Riley's uneaten food."

"Some of her uneaten food?" King asked.

Grace shot him a look. "To test it, of course. If it comes back positive for busulfan at least we have the mechanism." She then turned to the agents. "Impressive detective work, gentlemen. When will you know anything?"

"Probably a day or two," Cochran replied. "We just dropped it off at the lab yesterday."

"And did you find anything else of interest?" King asked.

"We found out that Stan Wright was no saint. He apparently had some issues with antisocial behavior and was being seen by a psychiatrist at one point. We got this information from the executive assistant in the Commissioner's office. Apparently these records have mysteriously disappeared from his personnel file."

"Really?" Grace asked.

Dugan took out his pad. "Have either of you heard of a shrink by the name of Dr. Phillip Sizemore?"

Grace smiled widely. "Phil Sizemore? Of course we have. He's done some forensic work for us."

"How convenient," Dugan replied. "We'd really like to get our hands on those psychiatric records."

"No problem. We can have them to you in a day or so," King replied.

Forty-six

Barely conscious, Jane Riley struggled to take each breath. An oxygen mask was affixed to her face, and an ominous hiss from the oxygenator filled the room. Alex stood at her bedside caressing Beth, who was crying softy. Jane's condition had significantly deteriorated over just one hour. Her body temperature had risen dramatically, and the increase was accompanied by fierce rigors. A rare strain of virulent bacteria had invaded her bloodstream because of her weakened immune system. Despite aggressive fluid resuscitation, her blood pressure was dropping.

"Dr. Hanley, she looks awful," Beth cried.

"Is there anything else that can be done?" Alex asked, his voice cracking.

"She is on maximum therapy," Abelman said quietly. "But despite that, her blood cultures are still positive, and her blood oxygen levels are dropping. She needs to be put on a ventilator."

Josh recalled his leukemic patient who had recently succumbed to an overwhelming infection but remained calm. "It's too early for the cells to engraft. She needs at least several more days, perhaps a week, maybe even longer." He knew that it was time she did not have. He turned to Beth and Alex. "She needs to be moved to the intensive care unit now. She will need to have a tube placed in her throat and be placed on a machine called a ventilator to help her breathe. We're going to have to do something very heroic to save her life. We will have to transfuse white blood cells until she can make her own."

"I'll call the ICU and make the arrangements." Abelman quickly left the room.

"White blood cell transfusions?" Beth asked through tears.

"Yes. It's only done in certain situations, this being one of them. It's really her only hope, at least until the transplanted stem cells can engraft. We really have no other choice."

Alex fell to his knees and took Jane's hand. "Sis, you have to hang in there." His voice was hoarse with emotion. "You're going to make it. You know how hard headed I am. Well, my stem cells are the same way. They're going to go to your marrow and kick butt! I love you, Jane. I know I haven't said that in a long time, but I mean it!"

As a tear ran down his cheek, Jane managed a slight nod.

Beth grabbed her shoulder and leaned closer. "You heard Alex," she said, her voice now stronger and more determined. "I know how tough you are Mother. You're going to get through this!"

The door opened, and Abelman entered with a team of nurses and a physician in scrubs bearing what appeared to be a toolbox. "The anesthesiologist is here to intubate her, and the ICU transport is on the way," he said.

Josh nodded. "Ah, Alex, Beth, I'm sorry, but you're going to have to step out for now. You can see her once she's transferred to the ICU."

Alex got up and grabbed Beth around the shoulder. Together, the two left the room.

Once the tube was placed and the ICU transport arrived, Josh went out into the hall where he found Alex and Beth seated together on a sofa at the end of the corridor. Alex was stroking Beth's hair and whispering in her ear as she leaned on his shoulder.

"Ah, excuse me," Josh said quietly. They both looked up and started to stand, but Josh put his hand out. "Please, don't get up. I just wanted to let you know that the intubation went fine, and Jane is now more comfortable. The white cell transfusion has been ordered and will be done as soon as she gets to the ICU." He sat down in a chair bedside them. "It's really difficult to predict how she will do over the next 24 hours, but I just wanted to let you know that things are not looking good right now."

Beth nodded stoically, her eyes puffy and red, as Alex looked at the floor.

"Can I stay with her in the ICU?" Beth asked.

Josh shook his head. "I'm sorry, but visiting hours are more restricted there. You can stay as long as you like during the day in the waiting area but the duration of your visits throughout the day will be limited. We can't let you stay in the room all night like you did on this ward."

"Then I'll camp out in the waiting room."

"Beth, that's just going to exhaust you," Alex said tenderly.

"I want to be here…in case….something happens." Her eyes began to fill with tears again, and Alex held her tight.

Josh rose from the chair. "I will let you know immediately if her condition changes at all."

Alex looked up, still caressing his favorite niece. "We appreciate all you're doing."

"Yes, Dr. Hanley," Beth said as she wiped her nose with a tissue.

Josh made a subtle bow but could not manage a verbal acknowledgement of their gratitude. He then turned and walked down the hallway, hoping that Jane Riley would at least make it through the night.

Forty-seven

Jeff Cochran walked into Bill Dugan's office bearing a huge ream of paper and dropped it on the desk with a loud thump.

"This arrived by Fed Ex this morning," he announced.

Dugan briefly flipped through the pages of the document as it lay on the desk. "What's this?"

"That, my friend, is a computer printout from the drug manufacturer that makes busulfan. It's invoices of all the pharmacies and hospitals that ordered the drug in the last year." Cochran fell into the chair in front of Dugan's desk and loosened his tie. "I also have the food analysis on Jane Riley's bad cottage cheese." He waved a folder and then threw it on top of the ream.

Dugan took the file. "Let me guess," he said as he opened it and began to study its contents. "Busulfan and vitamin C."

Cochran pointed at him. "You, sir, should be an FBI agent!"

Dugan rolled his eyes. "Please, let me think about it." He began to scan the list of invoices. "There must be hundreds here."

"There apparently isn't a big market for the drug in general," Cochran noted. "Only certain pharmacies actually stock the stuff, usually hospitals or cancer centers. These invoices cover all orders."

"I assume pharmacies keep records of prescriptions?"

Cochran nodded. "Oh yeah, and it's all computerized." He threw one of his legs over the arm of the chair. "If we knew the name of the person on the prescription, we could just go to an area pharmacy chain and plug it into the computer. I tried plugging in Jane Riley's name just for yucks. Nada."

Dugan sat back in his chair and took a sip of coffee. "So, where do we start with all this?"

"What we'll have to do is go through this list and see who has ordered it. See if anyone has ordered an unusually large amount who may not be affiliated with a hospital or cancer center."

"I guess if we knew who prescribed it we could plug that doctor's name into the computer, right?"

"That's correct."

"We should also investigate those places that order a lot of it and take a look at who's getting it."

"And who's prescribing it." Cochran hesitated. "You know, this could take a while and may be a wild goose chase."

Dugan flipped through the printout again. "This could take hours, maybe days." He looked at his watch. "I told my wife I'd take her out to lunch today. She's going to divorce me."

Cochran smiled. "Just blame me. To make things go quicker, I've narrowed it down to the Washington Metropolitan area."

He leaned across the desk and pulled out a much thinner ream from the printout. He then tore it into roughly two equal parts, and handed one half to Dugan. "Let's divide and conquer."

The two began to scan the lists and make notes. It appeared that most of the orders for larger quantities were taken from tertiary care hospitals with large cancer centers. A number of pharmacy chains were represented, with several stores repeatedly ordering the drug over the course of a year. The agents painstakingly scrutinized the invoices, working through the morning and well past noon.

"Hey, take a look at this one." Cochran pointed to an invoice using a half eaten tuna fish sandwich.

Dugan came around the desk and took a sip of coffee as he surveyed the listing. The invoice had been generated for a prominent drug store chain, Consumer's Pharmacy, on Capital Hill, for several grams of busulfan. He looked at Cochran and nodded. "A pharmacy on Capital Hill? We're getting closer. Excellent, my friend." Dugan downed the last of his coffee and gave the spent cup a pitch in the waste can. "Now all we have to do is find out who got it and who prescribed it."

Cochran stood up, checked his firearm, and grabbed his jacket. "Have them send a car around."

*　　　　*　　　　*　　　　*
　　*　　　　*　　　　*

The pharmacist at Consumers Pharmacy was standing behind a raised, glass-enclosed cubicle when the two agents entered the store.

"I'm Special Agent Dugan and this is Special Agent Cochran. We're from the FBI." They showed him their badges.

"FBI?" the pharmacist asked, peering over the counter to examine the badges through his bifocals. He had graying close-cropped hair and a thick gray mustache. "My goodness! Is something wrong?"

"We just need some information concerning a drug that was prescribed several months ago," Cochran responded.

"Just a moment." He walked down several steps and stood behind a low counter, revealing a height of five feet two inches. His blue smock bore a nameplate identifying him as 'L. Cobbly, R.Ph.' Cochran handed him the invoice, and he squinted at it through his bifocals.

"Okay, this is a chemotherapeutic agent. We don't get many prescriptions for this these days so we don't even stock it any more. We have to order it from the company and that usually takes a few days."

Dugan unfolded a piece of the printout and showed it to the pharmacist. "The invoice is dated earlier this year, in February. We need you to look into your files and find out for whom this drug was prescribed for."

"Well, let's see." A computer monitor sat on the left side of the counter with its screen facing away from the agents. Cobbly began to peck away on the keyboard. Several minutes later, a printer under the counter hummed and clicked as it spat out a sheet of paper. He pulled the paper off the printer with a loud rip and returned to the counter.

"We received only three prescriptions for that one in the past six months," he said looking at the list. He handed it to Dugan who showed it to Cochran. The drug had been prescribed to an Ethel Wheeler, Zelda McFarlane, and Rupert Olson.

"Mrs. McFarlane and Mr. Olson have been coming here for years," the pharmacist noted. "I don't recall ever meeting Mrs. Wheeler though. Our prescriptions are computerized so one can see what dose was prescribed and who the prescribing physician was." He went back to the computer and began to peck away. The printer soon began to hum again.

"You see here Ms. Wheeler was prescribed…." He paused, brought the page closer to his face and let out a low whistle. "Whew, that's quite a bit. I didn't fill this one, but an amount that size may have been shipped from the company directly to her home."

Dugan took the printout as Cochran scanned it over his

shoulder. "Is 300 capsules an unusual amount to receive all at once?"

Cobbly nodded. "Yes, in my experience, it is."

"A Dr. Peter Hilson prescribed this medicine for Ms. Wheeler," Dugan noted.

The pharmacist thought for a few minutes. "I believe he is on faculty at Georgetown University Hospital."

Cochran showed the paper to Dugan. "I see the dates of birth and addresses are here, too."

Mr. Cobbly nodded affirmatively. "Yes, we keep that information on file."

Cochran continued. "McFarland and Olson live in D.C. Wheeler's address is listed as a post office box in Frederick, Maryland. That's about an hour away."

Cobbly shrugged. "She may work in the District and get her prescriptions filled here. Let me see how this was handled." He pecked away again.

"Her birth date shows that she would be ninety next month," Cochran countered. "I doubt that she is still working."

"Well, I suppose you have a point," Cobbly replied as he continued at the keyboard. He then studied the computer screen through his bifocals. "Yes, it was shipped directly from the company to….hum, now that's odd. For some reason the shipping address has been blocked. We do that for celebrities or VIP's, you know, to prevent that sort of information from leaking out to the press. Liability issue, of course. I'm not sure why her shipping address is blocked. I assume it was to the address in Frederick, but I can get that information to you. It will take some time, though."

"Maybe Wheeler is an alias," Dugan whispered to Cochran. He then turned to Cobbly. "May we have a copy of that prescription?"

"Yes, the original is scanned into our data base." He pressed a key and the printer hummed to life again. "Here it is."

The two agents studied the blurred document bearing the crest of Georgetown University Hospital. "The signature is illegible. How do you know it's Hilson's?"

Cobbly pointed to a list of members of the faculty at the top of the form. "The box beside his name is checked off."

"But anyone can check a box," Dugan replied impatiently. "How do you know that this is his signature and not a forgery?"

"If there is any question, we call the physician's office for verification. That is usually done for narcotic prescriptions, though. I don't think any pharmacist would be too concerned about the abuse potential of busulfan." He paused. "Ah, I don't mean to be rude gentleman, but will that be all?" He motioned to the growing line of customers that had formed behind them. "Thank you, Mr. Cobbly," Cochran replied. "Here is my card. If you could please call and let me know where those 300 capsules were shipped, I'd be most grateful." He folded the printout and put it in an inside pocket of his jacket. He turned to Dugan. "Let's go to Georgetown and find this Dr. Hilson."

Forty-eight

Dottie Shane had just dumped a pile of manila folders on her desk when two hulking men in dark suits strode into the office. Still bent over the desk, she looked up and suddenly realized that she was probably showing too much cleavage. She abruptly stood erect.

"How may I help you gentlemen?"

"Hello, ma'am. I'm Special Agent Cochran and this is special agent Dugan. We're with the FBI." They briefly showed their badges and were about to put them away when Dottie stopped them.

"Wait a minute, Hon, not so fast." She retrieved the reading glasses that dangled around her neck on a gold chain. After putting them on the end of her nose, she leaned over the desk and carefully studied the badges.

"I see." She removed her glasses and straightened up again. "What can I do for you, Hon?"

"We need to speak with Dr. Peter Hilson immediately!" Dugan replied.

Dottie raised her eyebrows, puckered her lips and shook her head. "I'm sorry, Hon, but Dr. Hilson is not in."

"We are on official FBI business, and this is a matter of life or death."

She swallowed hard and picked up the phone. "I see. Let me try his cell phone." She punched in several numbers and waited. "It's ringing," she said, holding her hand over the receiver. The phone rang several times before switching to voice mail. After the beep sounded, Dottie spoke. "Hello, Dr. Hilson, please call the office as soon as possible. It's very urgent that the FBI reach you." She hung up. "That's strange. He always answers his cell phone." She started to dial again. "Let me call his home." She punched in more numbers and after a brief conversation, hung up. "That was his housekeeper. She doesn't know where he is and apparently he has not been home for over a week." She pursed her lips again. "Hmm."

Dugan spoke up. "We'd like to talk to him about one of his patients, Ma'am. Maybe you could help."

"One of his patients?"

"Yes," Dugan continued. "He wrote a prescription for a patient recently."

Dottie grabbed her chin, showing her bright red nails. "Are you sure, Hon?"

"Yes, Ma'am," he replied. "We're certain."

She looked about her desk as if searching for some explanation. "But he hasn't seen patients for months. He's been working on grants and research protocols."

"Protocols?" Cochran asked.

"Yes, protocols." She noticed the blank expressions on the mens' faces. "Research protocols are treatment studies that patients are enrolled on to see if drugs are effective, Hon. Maybe this patient was one of his research subjects." She paused. "Hold on just a second."

She sat down at a computer on the credenza beside her cluttered desk and reapplied her reading glasses. "Why don't you give me the name of the patient, and I can see if I have any information on them. I won't be able to give out any information, though. Not without the patient's permission."

"I understand," Cochran replied. "The patient's name is Ethel Wheeler."

"Ethel Wheeler? Hmm." Dottie worked the computer keyboard, making clicking sounds with her long red nails. "I'm not showing an Ethel Wheeler in the system, sir. Are you sure she's been seen by Dr. Hilson?"

Cochran hesitated. "I'm not sure she's been seen by him, but it was certainly his name on the prescription."

With her fingertips on her lips, she stared at the screen and shook her head. "In fact, I don't see her even listed at all. It looks like she's never been a patient here before."

"Never admitted to the hospital?" Dugan asked.

"Nor seen in any of the clinics. That's the best I can do, gentlemen." She looked up and removed her glasses. "Is there anything else I can do for you?"

"We would like a sample of Hilson's hand writing, if you have that available, specifically of his signature," Dugan said.

She looked about, held up her finger then rolled over to the file cabinets behind her desk. After pulling a drawer open, she produced a thick file. "Everything is so computerized these days that handwriting is becoming obsolete, isn't it?" She opened the file and pulled out a page. "Here is the title page of his last grant. It has his signature on it. You may have this as there are several copies of it." She handed it to Dugan. "Is there anything else you need?"

"Ah, yes, one more favor, if you don't mind," Cochran said politely. "Could you Google Ethel Wheeler and see what you come up with?"

"Sure, Hon." Dottie returned to her chair and began to peck away at the keyboard. Seconds later the screen was filled with information about Ethel Wheelers from all over the world.

"Whew, look at this!" She exclaimed. "Who knew there were so many Ethel Wheelers?"

The agents leaned over Dottie and scanned the screen. "There, the one in Frederick, Maryland," Cochran said. "Could you click on that one?"

Dottie obliged, and a picture and write up appeared on the screen.

"It's an obit," Dugan mumbled. "She died over ten years ago. You think it's the one we're looking for?"

"It's got to be," Cochran replied. "The birth date's the same. Could you print that, please?"

Dottie tapped a key, and a page rolled out of her desktop printer. "Here it is, Hon."

Cochran scanned the document. "It says she died of a stroke." He continued to read and when he got to the end of the piece did a double take. "It says her sole surviving relative is a grandson, whose name is......Leander Murray."

"So?" Dugan asked, scanning the paper.

"Her grandson is Dr. Leander Murray!"

"Wait. I know that name. We met him the other day. He's now head of the FDA."

Cochran nodded. "Exactly. And I have a feeling that prescription Hilson wrote was not intended for a woman who's been dead for ten years."

Dottie cleared her throat. "Is there anything else I can do for you gentlemen?"

"No, Ma'am, but thank you. You've been extremely helpful,"

Cochran said as he handed her a card. "Here is my name and number. Please have Dr. Hilson call me as soon as he comes in." He motioned to Dugan. "Come on, we need to pay Dr. Murray a visit."

As the two men started to leave the office, Dugan's cell phone chirped to life. He pulled it from his belt and lifted the cover. "Dugan."

"Where are you guys?" It was Grace Love.

"Grace! What up?" He winked at Cochran.

"I have some interesting news for you," she replied. "We got the psychiatric file on Stanley Wright from Phil Sizemore."

"They have the psychiatric file on Wright," he said to Cochran, holding the phone away from his mouth. He then brought it back. "And?"

"You're not going to believe what we found. We have it down at the precinct if you want to take a look."

He glanced at his watch. "We can be down there in about ten minutes."

As Dugan hung up, Cochran's phone began to vibrate. "Busy day." He pulled it from his belt as they headed down the hall toward the elevators. "Cochran. Yes, Mr. Cobbly." He looked at Dugan. "Let me borrow your pad." The other man handed over the pad, and Cochran began to scribble as they walked. "Okay, go ahead."

"Uh huh," Cochran muttered as he scribbled. "Well that's very interesting. Thank you very much. You've been a great help." He closed the cover of the phone and clipped it to his belt. "Well Dugan, this day has been very productive."

The two stopped at the elevator bank, and Dugan pushed the down button. "Why. What did the pharmacist have to say?"

Cochran handed the pad back to him.

"It says Dirkson Senate Office Building," Dugan said scanning the page as they waited. "What's this mean?"

Cochran grinned smugly. "It means we've just found that black Suburban we've been looking for."

Forty-nine

Jane slowly opened her eyes against the harsh glare of an overhead light. The regular chirping of an electronic signal could be heard somewhere above her head, and a hard object filled her throat. She slowly realized that she was intubated – a long, plastic tube had been inserted through her mouth, into her trachea. The end of the tube protruded from her mouth and was attached to another long ribbed tube, much like a vacuum cleaner hose, that was in turn attached to a ventilator or 'breathing machine.' Because she was too ill to support her own respiratory function, the ventilator, or 'vent' in medical jargon, was keeping her alive by forcing oxygen-filled air into her lungs with each life-giving hiss. But the tube was irritating her already raw throat and, in her semi-conscious state, she wanted it out, not fully realizing its life-sustaining function.

The concept of time had become a foreign one. How long had she been in this place with this thing down her throat? A day? A week? Longer? And didn't she have some work to do? She knew she had a job of some sort, an important job at that…but…what exactly did she do?

She tried to reach up and pull the tube out, but her arms were restrained at her side. Panicked, she tried to scream, but the tube was blocking any air movement over her vocal cords.

Let me out of here! She howled, only no one could hear her.

Tears began to well in her eyes. She felt trapped and helpless.

*　　　　　*　　　　　*　　　　　*

　　*　　　　　*　　　　　*

"She's fighting the vent," Abelman noted as he stood with Josh and the residents at Jane's bedside in the intensive care unit.

Josh frowned, noting her obvious discomfort. "Go up on her sedation."

Abelman wrote the order and handed it to the nurse.

"I'm cautiously optimistic," Josh announced.

The glass enclosed ICU cubicle was humming with activity. A monitor hung from the wall above her head and displayed a continuous readout of her blood pressure, heart rate, and blood oxygen levels. Her heart rhythm danced continuously across an adjacent screen.

"Her condition has stabilized with the white cell transfusions," he continued.

The bacteria-fighting white blood cells had cleared the bacterial from her blood, and her condition, while still precarious, had markedly improved.

"Unfortunately, the transfused cells only live in the body for about seven hours. As a result, she will require daily transfusions at least for several days."

"Her fevers are down. That's a good sign," Abelman said, studying the vitals sheet. "She's still pretty sick, though."

"Oh, she's very sick, I assure you." Wilton Roth suddenly appeared behind the residents in his starched white lab coat and bow tie.

"Dr. Roth, are you joining us for rounds this morning?" Josh asked coolly.

"No, I'm here to see how your patient is doing, and my experienced eyes tell me not so well." He walked up stood beside Josh, being a full head taller.

"Of course, she's not out of the woods, yet," Josh continued, his eyes glued to the monitors above her bed. "But she's definitely better."

"For now," Roth intoned ominously. "I'll be surprised if she pulls through." He turned to the residents and began to pontificate. "She has at least another five days before we can expect to see engraftment, and it could be even longer than that."

"Yes, I'm well aware of how long it takes for stem cells to engraft, and on top of that, the graft could fail, Dr. Roth," Josh added, turning to him. "We're all well aware of these issues."

Roth put his hands behind his back and stuck out his chin. "I certainly hope you know what you're doing, but of that, I am not so sure. Didn't I tell you to observe her a little longer? I certainly hope she pulls through this predicament you've put her in." He hesitated then added: "I think it's going to take nothing short of a miracle. You should have left her alone. Now she has to contend with graft versus host disease on top of all this."

Josh's throat tightened, and his armpits became damp, but he remained silent, not wanting a repeat of his prior interaction with the man, especially in front of the residents.

At the university, the faculty and residents were encouraged to challenge the opinions of others, regardless of rank. It was all part of the learning process. However, Josh was becoming irritated at his mentor's lack of faith in his judgment and making it painfully obvious in front of the fellow and residents. He was just waiting for Roth to emphasize Josh's lack of an Ivy League education by dropping the 'when I was at Harvard' bomb, when the ICU nurse walked in.

"Dr. Hanley, here are her labs from today." She handed him a clipboard.

"Look at this, her white count is up today, higher than it's been since she was admitted!" he exclaimed.

Roth shook his head. "That's impossible. This just reflects the white cell transfusion from today. Any first year medical student would know that."

"No," the nurse cut in. "She hasn't received a white cell transfusion today yet."

Abelman looked squarely at Roth. "Well, Dr. Roth, it appears that Dr. Hanley is right after all. Her marrow is beginning to recover. Don't you agree?"

"Oh," Roth said, his cheeks turning pink." Well…we'll just see about that."

He left the cubicle as abruptly as he had entered, and the whole group let out a collective sigh.

Abelman wrinkled his nose. "What's up with that old fart?"

The residents and students snickered.

"Marc, please," Josh said calmly. "Let's keep this on a professional level."

Abelman folded his arms across his chest. "I'm sorry, but who does he think he is? He shows up out of the blue and thinks he can start running the show?"

Josh smiled. "That doesn't matter Marc. What matters is that Dr. Riley is getting better. It looks like her brother's 'hard headed' cells are engrafting a little earlier than usual!"

Fifty

Ellen Downs glanced over her glasses at Bill Dugan and Jeff Cochran as they came bursting through the double glass doors into the reception area.

She removed her glasses. "What can I do for you two gentleman?"

"We need to talk to Dr. Murray at once!" Dugan announced.

"This is an urgent matter, Ms. Downs," Cochran added.

She stood and came from behind the desk. "Oh, my goodness, I see. Well, he's not in the office at the moment, and I'm not sure where he is. Let me go down the hall and see if I can find him. Why don't you two gentleman have a seat, and I'll be right back."

She hurried down the hall to a suite of offices where several staff assistants were seated in cubicles busily typing away on keyboards or taking phone messages. Deb was at her desk, wearing a headset, pecking away at her computer keyboard.

"Have you seen Dr. Murray?" Ellen mouthed.

Deb removed her headset. "He went to the library a few minutes ago."

Ellen left and took the elevator down to the third floor where the Library of the Food and Drug Administration was housed. After searching through the periodical shelves in the lobby, she went through rows and rows of book-filled stacks where she eventually found Lee Murray seated at a carrel engrossed in a medical journal.

"Dr. Murray! There are two FBI agents in the office who need to talk with you!" she whispered.

He closed the journal with a start and looked up. "Those FBI agents are back? What do they want with me?"

She shrugged. "I don't know, but they said it was urgent."

He looked about nervously. "Did you tell them I was here?"

"Well, yes, they know you are here, in the building. I didn't tell them specifically that you were in the library."

"Ah....okay…ah…tell them that I'll be up in a bit."

"Dr. Murray, they want to talk to you now!" She then noticed that his face had gone white. "Are you okay, sir?"

"Yes…yes…I'm fine. Tell them that I'm on my way, but I had to do something first."

"But Dr. Murray…."

"Just tell them!"

She pursed her lips. "Okay, sir, I will let them know."

When she returned to her office, Dugan was pacing back and forth in front of her desk while Cochran leaned against a file cabinet. "I found him in the library. He said he'd be right up…he said he had something to do first."

Cochran stood straight. "Where is the library?"

"On the third floor."

"And where does he park?"

"In the garage, on the first floor, why?"

Dugan motioned to his partner. "Let's go!" The two abruptly pushed through the glass doors, sending them swinging against the wall. The stairwell sat near the bank of elevators, and after taking the steps two at a time, the two men reached the first floor of the garage just in time to see Lee Murray streak by in a dark blue sedan. Dugan pulled out his service revolver, but the car rounded a corner, its tires squealing on the concrete, and disappeared behind a support pylon.

"He won't get far in the traffic," he said, re-holstering his firearm, as they raced back up the stairs to the lobby, dodging through the crowd and out of the building.

"Hey, you guys need to sign out!" a security guard futilely called after them.

Cochran pointed down the street as he plunged into the passenger's seat of their unmarked car. "He's at the light!"

Dugan got behind the wheel, gunned the engine and pulled the sedan away with a squeal, weaving it between the slow moving traffic. Just as he reached the intersection, the light changed, and Murray's car turned left, heading west onto a busy parkway.

"He doesn't know we're behind him, yet," Dugan said. "We might be able to tail him for a while and see where he's going."

From the parkway, Murray made another left onto the heavily congested Rockville Pike, and Dugan followed, using the vast numbers of vehicles as subterfuge. After about a mile, the car made a right turn and headed to Interstate 270, the major thoroughfare from the Maryland suburbs to the District line. The sprawling highway split into north and south directions to become the Capital Beltway, an eight lane super highway that encircled the District and its surrounding suburbs in Maryland and Virginia.

At the fork in the interstate highway, the sedan veered to the right, toward Northern Virginia, and picked up speed as it entered the Beltway. After the agents had trailed it for several miles, the sedan began to recklessly weave through the heavy traffic.

Dugan pressed the accelerator and flipped on the dashboard strobe lights. "He's on to us."

Cochran glanced at the speedometer. "God! He's doing at least 90!"

The agents followed the sedan as it crossed over the American Legion Bridge into Virginia and veered off the first exit, making the tight loop onto the George Washington Memorial Parkway. The car swerved around slower moving vehicles, with the FBI agents in close pursuit. Within minutes on the heavily patrolled parkway, a Park Police cruiser trailed the two cars with its lights flashing and siren whining.

Dugan adjusted the mirror. "It's a fricken parade."

Cochran squinted. "Where in the hell is he going? He knows we'll catch him sooner or later."

Just as he said this, the sedan suddenly slowed its pace and pulled onto the grassy median that separated the inbound and outbound lanes. Dugan pulled in behind Murray's car, and the cruiser followed suit. The two men jumped from the car, and Cochran flashed his badge.

"FBI! Get the traffic stopped on both sides," he barked.

The patrolman nodded and picked up his transmitter while his partner eased into the traffic with his hand held high. Just then another park police cruiser with lights and sirens raced up the outbound lanes. It straddled the road, and immediately staunched the flow of traffic on the other side of the parkway. After the inbound and outbound traffic slowed to a trickle and eventually stopped, Cochran nodded to Dugan, and the agents approached the sedan, one on either side, with service revolvers held stiffly at arms length.

"Dr. Murray, we just want to ask you some questions. Please

get out of the car!" Dugan shouted. "Dr. Murray, we're ordering you to get out the car now!"

With an electronic whirl, the window slowly spun down. A catatonic Lee Murray sat in the driver's seat staring straight ahead.

"Dr. Murray, step out of the car, we just want to ask you some questions," Cochran pressed. He squeezed the gun with both hands, glanced at Dugan, then back to the car. "Dr. Murray, are you all right?"

Murray turned his head slightly. "Yes, I'm fine." His voice was calm, almost inaudible.

Cochran relaxed a bit and motioned to Dugan. The two men lowered their weapons and carefully approached the car, Cochran on the driver's side and Dugan on the passenger's side.

"Dr. Murray, please get out of the car," Cochran repeated.

Lee Murray turned to look at the agents. "You don't understand. None of you do. Do you know what it's like to work your ass off reviewing all the data for drug approval only to have others get rich from it? I've bent over backwards so those blood sucking drug companies can make their obscene fortunes."

"Dr. Murray, please follow my order now," Cochran repeated slowly.

"Fifteen years of this," he continued to ramble. "All for the presumed good of the American public. But what do I have to show for all this? Not a thing." He continued to stare straight ahead.

"Dr Murray, please," interjected Cochran yet again.

"The Inverness Protocol was supposed to make us all rich." He turned to Cochran and smiled. "What bullshit. I was such a fool to think that we could get away with something so revolutionary." His smile then faded. "And I'm so sorry for what we did to Jane." He then calmly reached down and drew up a revolver.

Cochran reared back and raised his weapon. "Watch out! He has a gun!"

Before the two agents could react, Lee Murray put the gun to his right temple and pulled the trigger. The blast was followed by a bloody torrent of tissue and bone that sprayed Jeff Cochran as he fell back from the car.

Fifty-one

A glum Bill Dugan sat on the other side of the desk. "Sorry to bother you again, Dr. Hanley, but it is very important that I talk to you in person. I suppose you've heard the news about the acting Commissioner's untimely death."

Josh nodded. "I've haven't had a chance to read the *Post* yet, but I've heard snippets about it." He leaned back in his desk chair. "What a tragedy. First Jane, then her staff assistant, and now this. They all must obviously be related in some twisted way."

"Yes, that would be a valid assumption." Dugan took out his pad. He was alone on this visit because Jeff Cochran had stayed at the office to complete a report on the Murray case. "Did you know Dr. Murray?"

Josh thought for a moment. "No…well, for what it's worth, I remember when he was on faculty here in the Department of Behavioral Medicine and Psychiatry, but that was years ago, when I was in training."

Dugan nodded. "Uh huh. And how well did you know him back then?"

Josh shrugged slightly. "We had rare interactions on patient-related matters. He was very competent at what he did, and everyone seemed to like him. Why?"

"Just following some leads. How well do you know Dr. Peter Hilson?"

Josh was taken by surprise. "Very well, of course, he's my boss. I've known him for years. He's head of the Cancer Center and has the ultimate say in what goes on here. What does he have to do with anything?"

Dugan tapped the end of his pen on the pad. "Would you call him a friend?"

Josh started to nod affirmatively but stopped. Was he really a friend or just a colleague? He tried to recall any social interactions outside of work related parties or fund raisers that he and Hilson had attended and couldn't think of any. After many years of being colleagues, he really couldn't call Hilson a 'friend' in the truest sense of the word. "We're....friendly. Friendly colleagues, I guess you could say." He then recalled all the times that Hilson had dumped his patient responsibilities on him and wasn't even sure that was true.

"Have you seen him recently?"

"No. As far as I know he is out of the country. I can't keep up with him. All I can tell you is that he drafted me to cover his inpatient attending responsibilities while he was gone."

"Does the term 'Inverness Protocol' mean anything to you?"

Josh grabbed a piece of scrap paper. "What was the name of the protocol?"

"Inverness Protocol," Duggan replied, spelling it out.

Josh scribbled it down and then turned to his computer. "All protocols are computerized here at the university." He found the research protocol folder on his desktop and opened it with a click of the mouse. "Hum. No. There's no Inverness Protocol listed here. Why, what is it?"

"We're not sure, yet. How well did Peter Hilson know Leander Murray?"

Murray had been on faculty when Josh was a medical student. He tried to recall if he had ever seen them interacting. "I'm sure they must have interacted when Peter was attending on the Transplant Service. You see, transplant patients and their families typically suffer with anxiety and frequently depression. Dr. Murray was one of the psychiatrists who used to consult on our patients. I think his primary focus was on adolescent psychiatry, though." He was wondering where this line of questioning was leading. "Why?"

Dugan nodded and wrote. "How well does Peter Hilson know Jane Riley?"

"I suppose you could call them fairly close friends. They've known each other for years. They trained together and were on faculty together here at the university before Dr. Riley was appointed Commissioner. In fact, they saw each other the night she had a seizure at the Kennedy Center. I know that because I was there. They were engaged in conversation shortly before the program started."

Dugan looked up from his pad. "Really? What did they talk

about?"

"I wasn't privy to their conversation. They hadn't seen each other in a while, and they spoke privately, off by themselves. Why is all this so important?"

Dugan pulled a piece of paper from the inside of his pocket. He unfolded it and handed it across the desk. "Hilson's name is on this prescription for busulfan for a patient by the name of Ethel Wheeler."

Josh examined the photocopy as Dugan continued. "Ethel Wheeler is the grandmother of the now deceased Leander Murray, but she had been dead for ten years when this prescription was written for her by Dr. Hilson."

Josh was instantly confused. "Wait. What is this?" He scanned the document again trying to concentrate as his mind began to pull the pieces together. "Peter Hilson supposedly wrote a prescription for busulfan for someone who has been dead for ten years?"

Dugan shifted in his seat. "Yes, Dr. Hanley. Unfortunately, the investigation has reached a high level of security, and I can't elaborate any further."

"Three hundred capsules," Josh whispered as he scanned the prescription. "That's enough to kill....several horses. Have you authenticated his signature?"

Dugan nodded. "The signature is authentic."

Josh examined the prescription closely. "Hum, that's funny."

"What's funny?"

Josh leaned over his desk and pointed to the top of the paper. "Though Peter Hilson signed this, the name of the patient was written by someone else."

"What is the significance of that?" Dugan asked.

"Well, it could mean that a helpful nurse wrote the name of the patient for him before he wrote the actual prescription, or he wrote and signed this prescription but did not put the name at the top. That would be very odd, though."

Duggan nodded. "I see. Would a pharmacist pick up on something like that?"

"Probably not. That sort of thing happens frequently. It's still a legitimate prescription." He paused. "And I also take it, since you're asking me all these questions, that you haven't been able to locate Peter yet."

Dugan shook his head. "He's out somewhere and no one,

including his assistant, Ms. Shane, knows where he is. He took a trip to Scotland earlier this year, but according to passport control, he's been back in the country for quite some time. After he landed at Dulles, we're not sure where he went."

The whole thing didn't make sense to Josh, but then again, none of the recent events in his life had made sense. Why would Peter Hilson want to harm one of his closest friends and colleagues?

"He would have no motive for harming Jane. When Peter gets back, he'll clear this whole thing up." Josh handed him the photocopy. "He's probably off writing a grant or an article or something like that. He works all the time. The whole notion that he is somehow involved in all this is preposterous!"

Dugan returned the photocopy to the inside pocket of his jacket. "I certainly hope you're right, Dr. Hanley." He stood and extended his hand. "Thank you for your time. Please call us if you can think of any other information."

"I will do that." He stood and took the agent's hand.

After Duggan had gone, Josh walked to the window and stared out at the traffic below. It had rained all afternoon, and the cars on the street below went hissing by on the wet pavement, throwing clouds of mist behind them.

As he contemplated his discussion with Bill Dugan, his thoughts began to dwell on motive. Was Peter's research somehow affected by a decision or decree from the FDA? After all, the FDA had to approve all research trials involving patients and had the power to shut down research deemed dangerous or scientifically unsound. He recalled the story of a research scientist who inappropriately enrolled patients on an experimental drug that caused several deaths. The ensuing investigation had found him liable for significant protocol violations, and the FDA had subsequently shut down his laboratory operations. The investigator was fined and removed from his position. The family of one of the victims sued. His research career had been destroyed by the incident.

Josh then recalled a conversation he had with Nick Perrone weeks earlier about Hilson's research. Nick had learned through Dottie Shane that Hilson had another lab at some undisclosed location. Josh wanted to pursue it with Dottie, but at the time his busy schedule and Jane Riley's admission to the hospital had vanquished any thoughts about it. Now seemed a good time to see how much Dottie actually knew.

He sauntered down the hall and found her sitting outside Peter Hilson's office, working away at the computer with a headset wrapped around one ear.

"Dottie! How are you?" he mouthed.

She looked up and pulled out the earpiece. "Hi Hon! What can I do for you?"

"I was just wondering when Peter will be back?"

She shrugged. "I don't know, Hon, but that seems to be the question of the month, doesn't it?"

"C'mon, Dottie. You're his staff assistant. Shouldn't he be telling you where he'll be and when he'll be back?"

She leaned forward and looked around before speaking. "I don't know. You see, he has this other lab that I'm not supposed to know about." She lowered her voice. "No one's supposed to know about it. I don't even know where it is. I don't think he wants me to know so, you know, Hon, I won't be able to tell anyone else, including you."

"Other lab?" Josh asked with feigned surprise. "He has *another* lab?"

"That's the rumor, Hon," she mouthed. "He has a secret lab."

"Peter has a *secret* lab?" Nick had not indicated that the other lab was a 'secret lab,' rather that Hilson was working on a 'secret' project. His intrigue was tempered by the fact that Dottie had a penchant for embellishment.

She winced and put a finger to her lips. "Shhhh, Hon, not so loud." She looked about and then leaned closer. "I don't know if that's the proper term. You know how these researchers are about their work. So afraid they'll be scooped by someone else. The research world is tough, Hon, and Dr. Hilson is under so much pressure these days to get grants, publish, and raise money for the cancer center. The poor man works all the time, and I suppose his other lab is a kind of refuge where he isn't disturbed by anyone."

"Not even by the FBI?"

Dottie frowned. "How did you know about that?"

"Because Agent Dugan just told me. He said that you don't know where Peter is."

She put her hands on her hips. "Well, I don't. As I said, I don't even know if this lab really exists, and I wasn't about to send them on a wild goose chase. Then I'd be in trouble – with

and a boxed message popped up on the screen indicating that the login ID and password did not match.

"Damn," he said. "Peter changed his password."

He thought for a moment and then typed in 'Hilson.' The metallic thud and box reappeared. He typed in Peter, then skiman, skibunny, and skifreak, all of which were followed by the same thud and box. The computer would soon get tired of his games and shut down. He started to turn the hard drive off when a thought entered his mind. He then typed 'Inverness' into the password box. Instantly, the computer jumped to life, making the usual melodious noise as flashing lights on the hard drive indicated that it was opening all its programs. "Pay dirt," he whispered.

The desktop wallpaper flashed onto the screen, a striking view of the Grand Tetons at sunset as viewed from Jackson Hole, followed by the appearance of numerous desktop icons.

With his finger, he carefully went over each one, but the titles beneath were for the most part meaningless. Then he saw the word 'InvnssI' below one of the tiles. His heart pounded as he double clicked and waited. The document was apparently huge as it took what seemed like minutes for it to open. The first page flashed onto the screen, and Josh began to read:

Protocol 33: The Inverness Protocol, Stage I: DNA Methylation Sequencing Following Human Nuclear Transfer.

"Methylation sequencing? Human nuclear transfer?" he whispered. "So this must have been the project he was working on the day I interrupted him." He read on: 'Sponsor: The Wever Foundation; Principal Investigator: Peter Hilson, MD, PhD., Professor of Medicine. Sub-investigator.....' Here he stopped, and his heart skipped a beat. "Wilton Roth?"

From behind the door, Dottie's piercing voice echoed down the hall. Panicked, he abruptly turned off the computer and nearly threw Hilson's coat back on the door. A single sheet of paper lay face down on the FAX machine, and on impulse, he grabbed it on his way out. A row of file cabinets behind Dottie's desk shielded the door to Hilson's office, and he managed to exit just as Dottie came around the corner.

She grasped. "Dr. Hanley, Hon, you scared me to death!" She was hugging a large bundle of mail to her chest and dumped it on the desk. "What in the world were you doing back there?"

"Just dropping off monthly evaluations of the residents." He held up a small stack of papers. "I just thought I'd bring them over before they get buried in that black hole known as my office."

Dottie took the evaluations and gave them a pitch on her cluttered desk. "Fine, Hon, you don't have to give me a heart attack in the process!" Josh wondered how long it would take for her to realize the pages were blank. He was reassured when she ignored them and began sorting through the mail with her long, red fingernails. He started to squeeze past her when she stopped him.

"So how's your time on the inpatient service? I hear you're the hero taking care of Jane Riley."

Josh chuckled nervously. All he wanted to do was get back to his office. "I wouldn't exactly call myself a hero. By the way, did Dr. Hilson know Jane was in the hospital?"

She shrugged, her gaze still fixed on the envelopes in her hand as she continued to sort. "I don't really know, Hon. Everyone else seemed to."

"Yeah, don't I know it? The news media has given an almost daily report on her condition."

She stopped what she was doing and looked up. "That must be a lot of pressure."

He nodded. "Yes, it is." He looked at the stack of envelopes. "Is all that mail for Dr. Hilson?"

"Yes. I give most of it to Sherry, one of the postdocs in his lab. She goes through it and filters out the junk then forwards the rest to him."

"Where does she forward it to?"

Dottie squinted through one eye. "Why all the questions, Hon?"

"Oh, no reason," he lied. "Well, Dottie, I need to get back to the office and finish up my work so I can get out of here."

She nodded and went back to sorting. "Me too, Hon."

As he headed back to his office, he drew the paper he had taken from Hilson's personal fax machine out of his pocket. The header of the paper carried the university logo with a large box indicating that the transmission was 'OK.' Below it, another box labeled 'Fascimile Transmittal' showed that Hilson had faxed a memo to The Wever Foundation on the day he had apparently returned from Scotland. Part of the memo was visible below the box, and he quickly scanned it: "I have just returned from

Scotland and have great news. Enrollment on the protocol is not only on track, it is now ahead of schedule and you will soon be seeing great returns on your investments. It is now crucial that we proceed with haste to complete…." Here the fax went off the page. Josh scanned the top of the page and noted the fax number to which the document had been sent. There was also a telephone number listed below it that he did not recognize. He went back to his office, picked up the phone and quickly punched in the telephone number before he lost his nerve.

"United States Senate, Dirksen Building, how may I direct your call," came the pleasant voice at the other end.

"What the hell?" he whispered.

"I beg your pardon?" asked the voice.

"Ah….nothing, wrong number…sorry."

He hung up the phone, and, unsure of what to do with the information, started down the hall toward Hilson's lab, which was located just beyond the clinics. Since space was at a premium at the university, the corridor was cluttered with research equipment, subzero freezers, storage cabinets, tall narrow tanks filled with oxygen, nitrogen, and other gases, and a whole host of miscellaneous items. He found the open door nestled between two large incubators and went in. The laboratory was a labyrinth of laboratory benches, sterile hoods for tissue culture processing, freezers, incubators, and at least one ultracentrifuge. Save for the hum of the incubators, the lab was quiet and appeared to be deserted.

"Is anyone here?" he called out.

He ventured further in, inspecting the state of the art equipment with envy before continuing among the maze of research benches. Hilson had a highly productive research lab and as a result, had garnered significant amounts of grant support over the years. The impressive array of equipment was a testament to this productivity.

"Nice, very nice," he said, surveying a nucleotide synthesizer. "I could really use one of these."

"May I help you?"

Startled, he turned to see an attractive young woman with long brown hair standing behind him. She had on a white lab coat that was two sizes too big with the sleeves rolled up to her elbows and had just emerged from behind the reinforced steel door of the laboratory 'cold room.' Her hand held a flask of pink cell culture medium.

"Oh…hi. I'm Dr. Hanley. I'm a friend…and colleague of Dr. Hilson's. Is he around?" he asked.

"I know who you are, Dr. Hanley, and no sir, Dr. Hilson is away. Now if you'll excuse me…"

"Oh, he must be at the *secret* lab," he intoned grabbing his chin, wondering how far that would get him.

The woman hesitated. "How did you…?" She stopped.

"Know about the other lab? Oh, Peter and I go way back on the Inverness Project…er….Protocol." He saw her eyes widen. "I don't think I've had the pleasure of meeting you before, though." He gave her an alluring smile but her face remained frozen.

"I didn't realize you were involved with the protocol. You weren't listed as a sub-investigator, but I guess I'm the last to know everything." There was now an edge to her voice. "I'm Sherry. I'm one of Dr. Hilson's post docs."

"Oh, so you're, Sherry. Peter speaks very highly of you, Sherry." He had never been this deceptive before but was quite enjoying himself. "I need to speak to Peter. He…ah….left some data for me to review, and I need to discuss it with him."

She gave him a sideways glance. "If you know about the protocol, then you should know about this supposed farm where he is."

"A farm?"

"Yes, he referred to it as a farm once in passing conversation, but that's all I know." He saw her look of suspicion and realized that he was finished. "Look, I don't mean to sound rude, sir," she said. "But I have an experiment to finish up."

She started to leave but he gently held her arm. "Wait, please," he said. She glared at his hand on her arm, and he quickly let go. "Sorry. Look, it's very important that I speak to Peter. The FBI is looking for him, and I understand that you forward his mail to him."

"I had been forwarding his mail to a post office box that is now closed. All his mail has come back in the last several weeks and I have had no contact with him whatsoever. That's what I told the FBI and that's what I'm telling you." Her voice was now full of sarcasm. "If you are involved with the protocol, as you say you are, then *you* should know where he is."

He was appalled that someone at her level would address a

tenured associate professor in this manner, but he kept his cool. "Could you please get a message to him, then?"

She heaved a sigh and rolled her eyes. "Look, my desk is over there by that hood. If you leave him a message I'll see that he gets it when he comes back, but I can't guarantee anything. Now, if you'll excuse me, my gel is going to dry out."

She abruptly grabbed the flask of pink liquid and disappeared into the labyrinth, ostensibly to tend to her drying gel.

"Thanks for your help, you little….." Josh muttered. He looked about. Sherry's desk was a standard issue, gray metal piece, with a graffiti-filled blotter in the center of the top, and a pile of well-worn lab manuals carelessly stacked on one corner. When he failed to find a stray piece of paper, he began to pilfer through the drawers. The top, narrow drawer, just under the desktop, contained an array of pens and pencils and a graph paper pad with something scribbled on the top page. He lifted the top page and tore the next piece off. He started to jot down a note on the pad, telling Peter that it was important to call him as soon as possible, when the scribbling on the top page caught his attention.

"Is everything okay?" Sherry had miraculously taken time from her drying gel to reappear.

He jumped. "Ah…yes. I decided to wait till he gets back. You know, to go over the data set he ah…asked me to review."

She smiled thinly. "Right." She then opened the heavy steel door of the cold room and disappeared inside.

"An appropriate place for you, Sherry," he whispered.

He ripped off the top page, stuffed it into the pocket of his lab coat and quickly exited. Once out in the hall he studied the three lines of print that appeared to be an address. "And I thought my handwriting was bad."

He squinted as he read the first line. It contained two words, the second of which was 'protocol.' The second line was less clear and also consisted of two words. The first was undecipherable. The second appeared to be *Oats*. The third line was very clearly 'Charles Town, West Virginia.' "Hum, not far from Fort Detrick," he muttered. Meandering down the hall, Josh continued to study the address, trying to decipher the illegible handwriting.

"Dr. Hanley, where have you been?"

He jumped and looked up. Dottie stood before him with her

hands on her hips, and he drew the paper close to his chest.
"Ah…I was….just…"

"I've been looking all over for you!" She held several pieces
of paper in her hands. "These aren't resident evaluations.
They're blank pieces of paper!"

"Oh sorry! Gee, what an absent-minded professor I've
become. Um…I'll have to go search my office for them." He
eased himself around her in the tight hallway as she studied the
sheet of paper he held close to his chest. "I'll catch you later,
Dottie." With that, he raced back to his office, closed the door
and began to rummage through his desk drawer, trying to locate
Bill Dugan's number. However, the only card he could find was
Grace Love's. He quickly punched in her number.

"Grace Love," said the voice at the other end moments later.
There was a rushing sound in the background.

"Detective Love, this is Josh Hanley."

"Hey, what's up Doc?" She chuckled. "Sorry, I've always
wanted to say that. What can I do for you?"

"I was looking for Bill Dugan. Do you have his number?"

"I do, but I'll be in a meeting with him and Jeff Cochran later
today. Is there a message I can give him?"

"Yes, well, he asked me about the Inverness Protocol but I
didn't really know anything about it at the time. I still don't
know exactly what it's all about yet but I'm looking into it. I just
wanted to know if you all have ever heard of the Wever
Foundation?"

She hesitated. "Why do you ask, Doc?"

"Well, I was in Peter Hilson's office and I found this memo
that had been faxed to the Wever Foundation, and it mentioned
The Inverness Protocol. When I dialed the number…."

Grace Love cut him off. "Don't go snooping around Hilson's
office anymore. You could get yourself killed."

Goose bumps arose on his arms, and his scrotum grew tight.
"Killed?"

She hesitated. "Just remember what happened to Stanley
Wright….and Father McBrien for that matter. Anyway please
don't mention that you know about the Wever Foundation to
anyone else, okay? Not even your closest colleague, your best
friend or your girlfriend. And please don't mention this to Ms.
Shane."

"Dottie?"

"That's right. You've been a big help, Dr. H, but you better stick to doctorin' and leave the investigating to us." There was a distinct warning in her humor.

He wanted to tell her about Wilton Roth's involvement with *Inverness Protocol* but realized it probably wasn't necessary. "Oh, okay, perhaps you're right. Thanks."

He hung up the phone and stared at it for several minutes. "They're on to something," he said.

Fifty-three

Immersing himself in work, Josh concentrated on finishing his charts, making sure the housestaff were on top of the patients under his care, reviewing laboratory work and other diagnostic testing that had been ordered that morning. At one point, late in the afternoon, he decided that is was high time to catch up on his reading. A major article on the treatment of acute leukemia had appeared in the *New England Journal of Medicine* that week and was now staring him in the face. He had re-read the first paragraph multiple times and realized that his mind was not processing the text. All the words were familiar to him, but no matter how hard he tried, he couldn't seem to combine them all into a cogent thought. He gave the journal a toss back onto his desk, sat back in his chair and closed his eyes, letting his mind drift.

*　　　*　　　*　　　*
　　*　　　*　　　*

When Alex failed to show for class the next day, Josh was disappointed but also a bit concerned. He tried in vain to concentrate as Woodward droned on and on, apparently attempting to fill his students with every last bit of vital information before finals week. Joanie soon became annoyed with Josh repeatedly asking: "What was that? What did he say? I missed that."

"What's with you?" she asked when the lecture was finally over. "You're obviously distracted about something."

"Do you know where Alex is?" he blurted out.

She gave him a sour look. "Why would *I* know where Alex is?"

He sighed. "Never mind."

"Is everything all right?" she asked, collecting her things.

Josh nodded unconvincingly. "Yeah, sure. Ah…I might be late for chemistry, can I borrow your notes?"

"Late for chemistry? Josh, that's not like you! What's going on? Finals are next week and…."

Before she could finish, he abruptly stood and started to leave. "Josh?"

He left her standing there dumbfounded and quickly made his way to Alex's dormitory while subconsciously checking his watch every few steps.

Stutzman Hall, the oldest dormitory on campus, had traditionally been reserved for male athletes. Although that tradition had long been abandoned, there were many who held on to it, particularly the sons of 'Hall of Famers' at the college. Since they had always met in the library or an empty classroom throughout the semester, this would be Josh's first visit to Alex's dorm room.

When he reached the building, he hesitated, studying the stone structure with its decorative cornices and turrets before mounting the steps. Feeling as though he was about to enter a forbidden zone, he tentatively reached out to pull open the highly decorated entrance door when several members of the football team, clad in letter jackets, careened out, nearly knocking him back down the steps. One of them snickered as they bounded past him. Steeling himself, he went in. When he finally found Alex's room, the ever red-faced Nelson greeted him at the door.

"Oh, it's you, Hanley. What do you want?"

Josh sensed the sting of disdain and wondered if perhaps Nelson somehow knew what had happened the night before.

"Is Alex in?" he asked meekly. He was now on Nelson's turf, surrounded by Nelson-like men who harbored Nelson-like mentality. Anything could happen.

"He's still asleep….or dead. Come back later."

He started to close the door, but Josh caught it with his hand.

"I need to see him now," he pressed.

Nelson snorted. "What about?"

Josh's meekness suddenly gave way to annoyance at having an intellectual inferior address him with such condescension.

"So what are you? His personal secretary or something?"

Nelson's eyes narrowed. "Watch it, Hanley."

"In case you haven't heard, finals are coming up next week, and Alex's career here may be at stake," Josh continued. "I suggest you step aside."

"What's all the racket?" Alex was now awake, sitting up in

bed, his eyes in an obviously painful squint.

"Your little…tutor is here," Nelson replied sarcastically.

"Alex, I have to talk to you," Josh said, craning his neck to see over the taller Nelson.

"Let him come in," Alex intoned, falling back on the bed.

Nelson scowled but stepped aside. "Don't try anything funny," he mumbled.

"I wouldn't want to make you jealous," Josh shot back as he eased past him into the cluttered room.

"Hanley, I'm warning you…" Nelson began.

"Leave him alone," Alex groaned, his eyes still shut.

"You're lucky I have a class now," he said, stomping out and slamming the door behind him.

Josh dropped his knapsack on the floor and looked about. The room was small with two narrow beds separated by a window. The flaking plaster walls were hung with posters of sports figures and scantily clad starlets. Clothes cluttered the scarred wooden floor, and the air was musty with the unmistakable redolence of dirty socks and underwear. He spied a sink in one corner - the dormitory obviously predated en suite bathrooms - and wetted a washcloth with cold water. After wringing it out, he went over to the bed and gently placed it on Alex's forehead.

Alex grabbed at the towel. "What the hell? That's cold!"

"Oh, sorry," Josh intoned contritely. "I thought it might help. Are you okay?"

"I will be….eventually." His eyes remained shut as he spoke.

"I guess that slime mold really got you, huh?"

Alex managed a grin. "Yeah. The slime mold. What time is it, anyway?"

"It's after two."

"I'm missing all my classes." He pulled the cloth over his eyes. "I feel like shit."

"Don't worry. I'll give you my notes." He then realized that he himself was missing his chemistry class. He tentatively sat on the end of the narrow bed. "I…ah…wanted to talk to you about last night."

"What about it?" Alex mumbled.

"About what I said….and what you…we did?"

Alex sat up abruptly and the towel fell from his face to his lap. "Shhhh….don't talk about that here! I...we were drunk."

His voice trailed off as he fell back to the bed.

"But…but…."

"Just….go," Alex moaned.

Fighting back tears, Josh retrieved his knapsack from the floor and threw it over his shoulder. He quickly moved to the door and threw it open.

"Wait!" Alex jumped up from the bed. He was completely nude.

Josh reflexively closed the door, then looked about the room, to the walls, the window, the floor, anything to avoid looking in Alex's direction.

"What happened is all so….confusing for me." Realizing he was naked, he grabbed the nearest piece of clothing – a tee shirt – and held it to his crotch. "You just need to give me some time," he said, walking toward him. He then looked at the shirt as if wondering how it got there and gave it a pitch back on the bed. "I didn't realize it would be like that. I just need time to…process it all."

Josh finally exhaled. "Okay. Fine. Take all the time you need."

"We're cool, then?" Alex asked.

He nodded. "Yes, we're cool."

"Okay, good. I'll see you tonight in the library."

*　　　　　*　　　　　*　　　　　*

　　*　　　　　*　　　　　*

"Do you have a minute?"

Josh sat up abruptly and found Alex, with his hands on his hips, standing at the door to his office.

"Ah…oh…Alex? Ah…please come in and have a seat." He motioned to a chair across from his desk. "Where's Beth?"

"I sent her home to clean up and get some rest." He plopped into the chair.

"Perhaps you should do the same," Josh said softly. "Jane is improving every day. She's not out of the woods yet, but she's stable enough now for you to go home and get some rest."

Alex put his head back and looked at the ceiling. "She's going to make it, isn't she?"

"By all indications, she's going to make it," he replied.

Alex looked at Josh with glassy eyes. "She has to make it, Josh. I have to tell her how sorry I am." Tears began to roll down his cheeks and he wiped at them with the back of his hand.

Josh came around the desk and put his hand on Alex's shoulder. "Alex, you're exhausted. You need to go home and get some rest."

"No, I need to be here when she wakes up." He looked up through tear filled eyes. "I need to tell her how sorry I am."

"What could you possibly have done to be sorry for? You saved her life."

"You know what a bad person I am."

"Alex, please."

"I've done so many rotten things. You know I didn't even go to Mark's funeral. Do you know that? I wasn't even there for her when her husband died," he managed choking back tears. "I made up some excuse because I didn't want to cut my vacation short."

Josh flinched. "Really? Well…I'm sure that's water under the bridge now."

Alex shook his head. "No, there's more to the story than that."

"You don't have to go into all this," he replied.

"Then there's what I did to you. I'm sorry for that too."

"Alex, please stop."

"You remember the night we drank that bottle of Dom Perignon?"

At that point, Josh's emotional state was somewhere between profound sadness and extreme anger. "Of course."

"Do you remember the vintage?"

"The vintage?"

"Yeah, the year it was bottled," he replied impatiently.

"I know what vintage means, Alex. It was 19…"

"76," he finished.

"Yes…1976."

At that point, Dottie stuck her head into the doorway. "Oh, sorry Hon, hope I'm not interrupting anything serious. A physician by the name of Dr. Smithson wants to refer a patient for admission. He says it's urgent."

"Okay, Dottie, send it through." Josh stood and went back around the desk where he sat down and waited for the transfer.

"Am I loosing it, Josh?" Alex asked quietly.

"No, Alex, you're stressed out and exhausted." The phone rang, and he picked up the receiver. "Dr Hanley."

"If you value your life, you'll stop poking around in matters that don't concern you." The voice was raspy and unrecognizable.

Adrenaline stabbed Josh in the gut. "Who is this?" He demanded.

"None of your damn business. Just do as I say, and you won't get hurt or worse."

"You listen here, I'm…" Before he could finish, the line when dead. "Hello? Hello?" He remembered Grace Love's warning, threw down the receiver and jumped up. "Dottie! Dottie!" he yelled.

She instantly reappeared in the doorway. "I'm here Dr. Hanley. I'm not deaf."

"Who was that on the phone?"

"As I told you, Hon, he said his name was Dr. Smithson."

"Don't play dumb," he replied angrily. "You know exactly who it was, don't you?"

She looked at him over her glasses. "I beg your pardon?"

"Who was it really?" He came from around the desk, his fists clenched.

"Josh, what happened?' Alex asked, his reddened eyes going back and forth between the two.

"I just got a threatening call telling me not to poke around in matters that don't concern me or I'm going to get hurt. I suppose that has to do with all the questions I've been asking about Peter Hilson, doesn't it, Dottie?"

 She bristled. "I have no idea what you're talking about, Dr. Hanley. But if you got a threatening call, we need to let campus security know."

"Oh that's just great. Play it cool why don't you. Well, you can tell whoever that was that I'm not afraid of them."

Alex stood. "Josh, what the hell is going on?"

Dottie let her glasses fall to her chest. "Hon, are you implying that I had something to do with that call?"

"Don't you 'Hon' me! How else would they know that I have been asking questions, unless…" He stopped and suddenly thought of Sherry. "Why that little…" He pushed past Dottie and headed for Hilson's lab with Dottie and Alex in pursuit. When he got there, the door was locked, and he banged on it several times with his fists. "Open up! Open up, damn it, I know you're in there!"

"Hon, er, Dr. Hanley, are you all right?" Dottie asked, her

hand to her mouth.

Josh rested his head against the door and took several deep breaths as he fought back tears. He had been denying how much the stress of the last several weeks was affecting him mentally, physically and emotionally. As a physician, he thought he could handle it, because physicians were supposed to somehow be super humans, able to work days at a time without rest or even regular meals. Physicians didn't take breaks like everyone else did. Wasn't that ingrained in him during his medical training and wasn't that the prevailing perception among his peers? Yet he had no one to talk to, no one to unload his anxieties, and no one's arms to fall into when he went home at night. And now the threatening call had seemingly crushed him.

"I'm sorry Dottie," he said weakly, his voice cracking. "Please forgive me for what I said to you. I'm so sorry."

"It's okay, Hon," she said hoarsely, her hand on his shoulder.

Then Alex gently pulled him from the door and walked him back to his office.

Fifty-four

Jane did not feel the microscopic war that had been waged within her body. The transfused white blood cells had immobilized the life-threatening bacteria with poisons and gobbled them up like hungry wolves. The short lived warriors were beating back enemy lines long enough for the donor stem cells to take root. It had taken several weeks for the transplant to restore marrow function, and the cells that now coursed through her blood vessels were mostly her brother's. What she now felt, however, was the hand that squeezed her own. In a haze induced by medicines that allowed her to tolerate mechanical ventilation, she squeezed back.

"Jane!" The voice belonged to Alex. "Jane can you hear me?" He squeezed her hand tighter.

She nodded weakly and opened her eyes. The tube that connected her to the ventilator felt as though someone had thrust a broom handle down her throat.

"We're decreasing her sedation so we can wean her off the ventilator," Josh Hanley's voice said from the other side of the bed. "But it may take time."

"You hear that Jane?" Alex said excitedly. "They're weaning you off the breathing machine. I'm going to go tell Beth. She'll be so excited."

The stem cells had coursed through Jane's blood stream on the day of the transplant, homing to her bone marrow like salmon to a spawning stream. Once there, they had found the environment hospitable and had begun to thrive. Like seeds, they had germinated and were rapidly multiplying, producing scores of oxygen-carrying red blood cells, infection-fighting white blood cells and blood-clotting platelets.

As the effect of the medication waned, she was ever more aware of the bedside vigil that was being kept by Beth and more unexpectedly, Alex. She never dreamed that her self-absorbed brother would ever be so dedicated to her. But now a part of him was an integral part of her. He had saved her life and for that she could forgive him of any past transgressions. But the bond that was now forming between them went beyond the physical, and the increasing affection she had for her brother seemed to impel her recovery.

As the normal blood-making cells repopulated the once empty marrow, Jane's condition began to slowly improve. The sores in her mouth were less painful, and her fevers had resolved. But despite this remarkable progress, she remained very weak.

"Why is her skin so red," Alex asked.

"She has graft-versus-host disease," Josh replied. "Your cells don't like her skin. We'll have to dial up her immunosuppressive drugs a bit."

"Sis, I know you're going to get through all this." Alex said encouragingly.

Although she had comprehended everything, Jane could only blink and nod.

*　　　　　*　　　　　*　　　　　*

　　　　*　　　　　*　　　　　*

Weeks later, after she had been transferred to a regular hospital room on the transplant unit, Josh brought Cochran and Dugan to Jane's room where they found her propped up in bed. She was dressed in a white gown and her head was covered with a white turban. The blinds were open and sunlight was streaming in, reflecting off her pale skin and white apparel, giving her an almost ethereal appearance. Alex and Beth sat on opposite sides of her bed.

"I don't know whether to examine you or genuflect." Josh smiled. "These are the FBI agents I told you about. Special Agents Jeff Cochran and Bill Dugan."

She nodded to them but did not offer her hand. "Pleased to meet you." Her voice was still hoarse.

"They have a lot of things to discuss with you and have many questions. Are you up for this?"

"Yes, of course," she replied.

Dugan proceeded to fill her in on the details about Stan Wright, his murder, and his connection with her illness. He also mentioned the attempted murder of Father McBrien but avoided telling her about Lee Murray's suicide.

Her face had gone ashen. "My God," was all she could say.

"We've reviewed your dockets from the last several months with your executive assistant, Ellen Downs, who, I might add, has been extremely helpful," Dugan continued. "We have several questions about your professional dealings. Do you know of anyone who may have wanted to see you harmed in any way?"

She looked at Josh briefly then back to the agents. "When Dr. Hanley asked me that weeks ago, I thought he had gone mad. But the answer is still the same: not that I am aware of."

"Surely the commissioner of the FDA must have some enemies," Cochran stated as he leaned against a wall.

"Well of course but *enemy* is such a strong term. I work with professionals. There is a certain code of ethics."

"We understand that Dr. Riley, but you'd be surprised what people are capable of doing regardless of their educational background or code of ethics. Now, try to think."

She looked down and took in a deep breath. "Well, there are so many people that I....oh...disappoint, I guess is the correct term. Drug company executives, congressman, sectors of the public. The list is long."

"Anyone in particular?" Dugan pressed. "Any threats?"

"Threats? Well, once in a while you'll hear something, but I just blow it off as hyperbole."

"Death threats?"

"No, not death threats!" She paused. "Well, nothing serious."

"What do you mean by that?"

She looked into space. "I vaguely remember someone wanting my head on a platter. Then there are the members of the CanActUp Group who would probably like to see me strung up. But other than that, I can't recall anything else, at least that I would take seriously."

"Tell us about Stan Wright," Dugan continued.

She grabbed her forehead and began to message it. "He is…was one of my assistants, who carried out various tasks, Xeroxing, filing, and the like. He's been in the Commissioner's office for quite some time so the staff assistants probably know him…knew him better than I."

"Did he have any grudges against you?"

Jane thought for a while and then shrugged. "If he did, I wouldn't know why."

He then showed her the computer-generated photo of the man

with slicked back hair. "Do you know this man?"

She took the picture and studied the grainy image of the man's profile. "Who is this?"

"This is our prime suspect in the slaying of Stanley Wright."

She shivered and handed it back. "No, I've never seen him before."

"How well do you know Dr. Peter Hilson?"

She arched her eyebrows. "Peter? What does he have to do with any of this?"

"We're just asking, Ma'am," Dugan replied.

"Peter is a friend and colleague. He's a brilliant researcher and one of the most decent human beings I know. Why do you ask?"

"I'll get to that in a second. Do you remember a company by the name of *CloneScience*, Dr. Riley?"

"*CloneScience*? Yes, I think they were the ones who made that comment about having my head on a platter. We closed them down months ago," she replied. "Why?"

"Why were they closed down by the FDA?" Cochran asked.

"They were engaged in human cloning experiments."

"Is that illegal?" Dugan continued to write.

"Not officially, but it does fall under the jurisdiction of the FDA, and therefore, all experiments have to be approved by the agency. They had not followed any of the proper procedures required to conduct research."

"Is anyone else engaged in this sort of research?" Cochran asked.

She shook her head. "No. We presently are not allowing such experimentation until all the scientific and ethical issues are resolved."

"Are you aware that Dr. Hilson was recently in Scotland collaborating with scientists who are planning exploratory human cloning experiments?"

"No, I wasn't." She studied her hands. "That's not his area of expertise. I'm not sure why was he doing that."

Dugan nodded and continued. "When was your last interaction with Dr. Hilson?"

"At the Kennedy Center, the night of the first seizure. He said he wanted to talk to me about something." Jane shifted uneasily on the bed. "Just after he gave me some champagne." She hesitated, closed her eyes and then shook her head. "And then I saw him briefly the following day when he came to my room for a visit. That's when he said he was going out of town for a while. It was something related to his research."

"And how well do you know Dr. Murray?"

Jane shook her head. "This is getting a little spooky, gentlemen. Why all these questions about decent, law abiding citizens?"

"Please, bear with us, Dr. Riley, and answer the questions to the best of your ability," Cochran said.

"Okay. He's been at the FDA longer than I have. He's well respected and has been a great help to me. He was also on the faculty at the university when I was a resident and fellow, but I knew him only peripherally back then."

"Wasn't he considered the likely candidate for FDA Commissioner before the President nominated you?"

She frowned. "He was a leading candidate, yes."

"And he succeeded you when you got sick, correct?" Dugan asked.

"He really didn't succeed me. He's just acting on my behalf until I get back."

"And if you didn't ever go back?"

"The President would have to appoint another Commissioner."

"And that process could take months, correct?"

"Probably. The confirmation process has become so politicized recently."

"So Dr. Murray could have effectively run the agency for quite some time, correct?" Cochran asked.

"Really gentleman, this is so preposterous!" Jane replied. "I refuse to believe that one of my colleagues could have had a hand in all this."

Cochran looked at Dugan and then back to Jane. "Dr. Riley, do you remember a new drug application for a compound known as LNC33?"

Jane thought for a while. "Ah…yes. It's an anti-cancer drug."

"That drug was granted approval over the objections of the Director of the Office of New Drugs."

She sat up in bed. "What? How did that happen?"

"Dr. Leander Murray issued the approval himself. The staff at the FDA were all quite shocked by it, according to Ms.

Downs."

Jane shook her head. "That's highly irregular and I'm going to look into to this immediately."

Josh could now see the familiar fire of Jane Riley's personality and was relieved. She really was back from the brink and would soon be back in command.

"Dr. Riley, have you ever heard of *The Inverness Protocol?*" Dugan asked.

The question jolted Josh and his heart jumped as he remembered Grace Love's warning.

"*The Inverness Protocol?* No, why?"

"Dr. Murray recently issued an Investigational New Drug number for this protocol."

"He issued the number?" Jane asked. "He personally?"

"Yes, and according to Ms. Downs, that's not the way things are usually handled," Cochran responded.

She nodded and raised her eyebrows. "It would be unheard of for the Commissioner to issue an IND over the heads of the deputies and center directors. What was the IND for?"

"We're not sure," Dugan replied. "Ms. Downs could not locate the file in the computer system."

"I don't understand," Jane said. "It has to be there. I am going to call Lee Murray as soon as we're finished here."

The agents looked at Josh Hanley yet again, who nodded 'yes.'

What's going on?" Jane demanded.

"Dr. Riley," Cochran began. "Lee Murray is dead."

"What?" Her voice was almost inaudible.

"He committed suicide. We think he was involved in the conspiracy to murder you."

She put her hand to her mouth and began to quake. "There must be some mistake. Lee Murray respected me. We had a wonderful working relationship." As tears flowed down her cheeks, Alex stood up.

"I think she's had enough for one day, gentleman." Frowning, he looked at Josh. "I think she needs some rest now."

Dugan flipped the cover of his pad and put it in his front pocket. "Thank you for your time, Dr. Riley. You've been most helpful. I'm sorry we've upset you."

Jane nodded and continued to cry softly as Beth held her.

"Dr. Riley, I just want you to know that the FBI is working

vigorously to find the perpetrators of this crime against you," Cochran stated.

Alex followed the agents and Josh out into the hallway.

"I think you went too far," Alex whispered to them harshly. "She wasn't ready to hear all that. You should have known better, Josh."

Josh crossed his arms over his chest. "Look, Alex, she was going to find out about it sooner or later. She was going to try to call Murray! These agents are trying to find out who is behind the conspiracy to murder her, for heaven's sake."

He wagged a finger at Josh. "I'll tell you when she's ready to talk again!"

"You will? Based on all your clinical experience, I suppose? You haven't changed a bit, have you Alex? You always have to be the man in charge."

Alex's face turned deep red, and he clenched his fists. "What's that supposed to mean?"

Cochran stepped between the two men as they glared at one another. "Ah, gentlemen, let's take it easy now. One of you can give us a call when Dr. Riley is ready to talk with us again, okay?"

"Talk to Mr. Byrne," said Josh. "He seems to be in control now."

With that, he stormed past them and left the unit.

Fifty-five

After months in the hospital, Jane's first night home proved to be a restful one. The nurses were not interrupting her slumber to take vital signs, there were no IV pumps alarming in the middle of the night, and there was no one barging in at five in the morning to draw her blood.

She had nearly broken down in tears the evening prior when she entered the front door and saw all her familiar surroundings: the black and white marble checkerboard of the front hall, the elegant staircase rising along the wall, framing the hanging lantern and the old grandfather clock in the corner.

That morning, once downstairs, she went straight to the first floor study, a room wedged between the kitchen and dining room. It was a room lined with tall built-in shelves stuffed with books and a lifetime of memorabilia. Once her father's domain, it had become her own private cocoon and at one point during her illness, she felt certain she would never again lounge on the over stuffed furniture or savor the redolence of old books and leather. An antique mahogany desk occupied one corner of the room near a window that overlooked the garden at the back of the house. The thick Persian rug that covered the wide oak flooring had faded with age and even now sunlight filtered through the shutters on the windows casting bright parallel lines across it. As an antique clock ticked away the minutes on the mantle piece above the fireplace, she surveyed the room and smiled.

"I am really home."

She made her way over to the desk, and eased herself into a chair near the window. The garden in back, bright with sunshine at that time of the morning, was in shambles following the winter storms. They were now several weeks into Spring and ordinarily, she would have cleaned it out by now. She frowned and shook her head. Fortunately, there was still time to bring the beds back to her meticulous standards.

The front door buzzer suddenly interrupted her revelry.

"Estelle?"

There was no answer.

"Estelle, can you get that?"

As the buzzing continued, Jane slowly walked into the hall to the door. Through the Federal fan that surrounded the front door, she saw a man in a white uniform with a cigarette wedged in his mouth standing on the porch, peering at her through the side window.

She opened the door. "Are you from the home health agency?"

"Yeah, Physical Therapy." His accent was New Jersey or maybe Brooklyn, she wasn't sure. He took one last drag from his cigarette and threw it to the flagstone. For some reason, he looked vaguely familiar to her but she could not place his face.

"I thought PT was supposed to start tomorrow."

He shook his head. "No lady, I have my orders. I'm supposed to take care of you today."

"But I haven't showered yet. I haven't even had breakfast."

"Doesn't matter, lady," he said, pushing the door open and stepping across the threshold. "This won't take long."

"Well, okay." She closed the door behind him. "I didn't catch your name."

"Jim," he said, extending his hand.

"Nice to meet you, Jim." She took the sweaty palm. "So where shall we start. I guess my legs are probably the weakest part of my body."

He nodded. "Sure, lady, we can start with your legs. Why don't we start with walking up the steps?"

"Oh, okay, I'm a little weak on the stairs. I had to have help coming down them this morning."

Just then, the phone began to ring.

"If you'll excuse me." Holding onto furniture, Jane went back into the study and picked up the receiver.

"Hello."

"Hello, Dr. Riley, my name is Julie Summers," said the pleasant female voice at the other end. "I'm the physical therapist who will be making an initial visit tomorrow to assess your needs. I just wanted to let you know that I'll be coming around…."

"Wait, there must be some mistake," Jane interrupted. "A physical therapist just arrived. He says his name is Jim."

There was a pause at the other end. "We don't have any physical therapists by the name of Jim," the woman replied. "Is he in the house now?"

Jane's heart began to pound. "Ye...yes." She turned and saw the man standing in the doorway staring at her. A chill went down her spine as she now recognized the face from the photo that Bill Dugan had shown her!

"Dr. Riley, are you okay?" Summers asked.

"No, no I'm not," Jane replied trying to remain calm.

"Would you like me to call the police?" Summers asked with urgency.

"Yes...yes please do that. Please take me off your list." She put the phone down. "Those pesky telemarketers."

"God, I hate those bastards!" Jim replied as he smacked a fist to his hand.

"Oh, they drive me nuts, too. Now, where were we? Ah yes, you were going to take me up the stairs."

"Yeah, lady, right this way." He stepped aside and she gingerly stepped past him, eyeing the front door. She then surveyed the objects between her and the door. A table near the stairs held an antique Waterford vase and there were two umbrellas in a rack by the door. One of the umbrellas had a pointed tip. Otherwise, there were not any other useful weapons. Her mind kept pace with her heart rate, wondering if she could somehow make it to the umbrella stand.

"Estelle...my housekeeper, is in the kitchen...and...and...." She pointed behind her.

"No she ain't lady. I know you're here by yourself."

Struck with blinding fear, Jane limped down the hall toward the door, but he lunged for her, grabbing her robe. In an instant, his strong arm had encircled her waist. She let out a scream, but it was soon muffled by a rough, calloused hand over her mouth. He held her tight against him, and she could feel his hot breath on her neck as she struggled to break free.

"Don't move, lady, okay?" His voice was deep, throaty, and his breath reeked of tobacco. The grip he held on her face was so tight that she could hardly breathe. Waves of adrenaline rushed through her, sending her pulse soaring. She realized with despair that despite the heroic effort put forth to save her life, she was probably going to be murdered in the next few minutes. She then pictured Beth finding her dead in the hallway of her own house, and an intense rage rose within her.

"Now lady, let's just start again. This is supposed to look like an accident."

With his hand still firmly planted over her mouth, he awkwardly dragged her toward the staircase. She resisted, hooking her foot around the hall table, pulling it with her and, in the process, sending the antique vase plummeting to the marble floor where it broke into several large chunks.

"Now look what you done, lady. You done broke your good vase. If you'd just cooperate....."

She bit into the thick skin of his palm, and he screamed out, releasing his grip, while shaking his hand in pain.

"You bitch, you bit...!"

She delivered a sharp, elbow thrust in his midsection. Momentarily stunned, he let go of her and grabbed his belly. Jane then sent a foot into his crotch. He yelped again and doubled over in pain. She shoved him backward, and he lost his balance. His boots skidded on the slick marble floor, and he fell back, grabbing for air before landing on his buttocks, blocking the front door.

Gasping for breath, Jane staggered toward the study, but the intruder quickly recovered. He lunged across the floor, hooking her foot with his hand. She fell hard on the marble, her left arm absorbing much of the blow. Before she could move, he had straddled her, his rough, hands clamping her neck in a vise grip. She saw the hate in his dark eyes.

"Just relax, lady, it will all be over in a matter of seconds."

The pain in her neck intensified as he held tighter. Her arms flailed about in panic, and she futilely grabbed at his well-muscled arms. The lack of oxygen had begun to darken her vision and just as she was about to loose consciousness, her hand fell on a cold, formless object on the floor beside her. She grabbed it and swung with what strength was left, aiming recklessly for his head. The large shard of crystal easily found its mark in his soft, fleshy neck, and blood began to gush over her hand and down her arm.

He let out a grunt and fell back, releasing his grip, allowing precious air to rush back into her lungs. She rolled on her side, choking and gasping. The man lay near her, grabbing at his neck with both hands, as blood gurgled between his fingers, and spattered the walls.

On hands and knees, she pulled herself toward the study.

"You bitch!" His voice was hoarse and full of rage. Despite the rush of blood, he rose up like a tiger ready to strike, while one hand tried to extract the crystal spear. But is was slick and covered with blood; the more he tried to pull it out, the deeper it went. "I'm going to kill you if it's the last thing I do!"

He grabbed her foot, but she managed to kick free and crawl into the study. Using the knob for support, she pulled herself up and tried to shut herself in, hoping the police would soon be there. The man pounced and collided with the door, sending it banging against the adjacent wall. She was thrown back against the mantle piece, into a rack of fireplace tools that clanged against the brick as they cascaded to the floor. He staggered toward her with outstretched hands as blood gushed from his neck wound. Her hand found the cold metal of a fire poker, and she swung it upward as hard as she could. The pointed tip clipped his jaw, and sent him careening backward. He fell against the bookcase and collapsed to the floor as several large tomes came raining down on him.

"What the hell? Where did all this blood come from?" Alex's voice came from the front hall. "Jane? Jane, are you all right? Where are you?"

"Alex!" she managed. "In the study!"

He raced to the room and stopped in the doorway, holding the frame for support. "What the hell happened? There's blood all over the hallway?" He then saw the man lying near the bookcase in a semiconscious state with a steady stream of blood oozing from his neck. "Who the hell is this?"

Jane collapsed into a chair, gasping for breath, still holding her neck. "Alex, call 911. Get the police and an ambulance here at once." Her voice was hoarse, just above a whisper. "Get a towel and put pressure on that wound in his neck before he bleeds to death."

Alex pulled out his cell phone and disappeared into the hall. She could hear him talking into an earpiece to the 911 operator as he returned with several decorative hand towels from the powder room. By now, the man was unconscious as he knelt beside him.

"What in the hell? He's got half of Grandma Byrne's vase sticking out of his neck!"

She waved her hand. "Don't pull it out, whatever you do. Just put pressure around it. But try not to get blood on yourself!"

He put the towels to the man's neck wound. "Would you please tell me who the hell this is?"

"Let's just say," she said between gasps, "He's one hell of a physical therapist."

Fifty-six

The dull gray paint on the cinderblock walls of the prison unit of the District of Columbia General Hospital was beginning to peel in several places. The only window in the unit was high up in the wall, above the nursing station, barred and inaccessible. Reminiscent of the locker room of a gym, it consisted of multiple frosted panes with embedded chicken wire allowing only a hint of light to filter through the accumulated grit. The prison unit itself was a ward of 12 cell-like rooms, most of which were occupied by inmates with injuries from prison yard scuffles.

With Jeff Cochran leaning against the wall behind them, Grace Love sat next to Special Agent Dugan at the foot of the bed of 'Mr. Slick' with a video camera perched between them. The patient lay stiffly in bed, propped up on a pillow, his head immobilized by a bulky dressing encircling his neck. Beside him sat a tall balding man with a gray goatee and wire rimmed reading glasses perched on the end of his nose. A yellow legal pad sat on his crossed leg.

"I hope you're up for this today, Mr....ah.....Leppo?" Grace referred to a yellow legal pad on the table in front of her. "Did I pronounce that correctly?"

"Yeah...Leppo. Jim Leppo," the patient replied, his eyes fixed downward to look at her.

"I know you've been through a lot recently, Mr Leppo." The sarcastic edge still carried some vestige of professionalism.

Leppo had been apprehended at the Riley house by the DC police force and taken to D.C. General Hospital for emergency treatment of his injuries. The crystal shard had sliced through the jugular vein and barely nicked the carotid artery, but the resulting puncture had been enough to cause significant blood loss. The deep puncture had required several layers of sutures. A series of x-rays had ruled out a fracture of the jawbone from the impact of the fire poker.

Jane Riley had also been taken to the emergency room at Georgetown and admitted for overnight observation. She was now resting at home under the watchful eye of police protection.

"Yeah. That broad really did a number on me. When I get outta' this place, I'm going to beat the....."

"Mr. Leppo!" the man with the gray goatee interrupted. "As your court appointed attorney, I would advise you to just answer the question." His frustration was unmistakable.

"Sh…," Leppo hissed. "Can I at least have a cigarette?"

Grace's eyes narrowed. "No, you may not. Now, as you know, we will be videotaping this conversation."

She pushed the 'record' button on the camera. "Now, please state your name, sir." Jim Leppo complied. "Now, Mr. Leppo, who sent you to kill Jane Riley?"

The patient rolled his eyes. "Jeez, you guys have this all wrong. I wasn't going to kill her."

"Then what were you doing there?"

He tried to move his head and winced. "I…don't remember."

Grace grabbed her chin. "And Stanley Wright? Do you remember him?"

"Who?"

"Look Leppo, we have you on tape." Jeff Cochran interrupted abruptly, walking to the side of the bed. "We know you abducted Stanley Wright from the Brookland Metro Station, and you can plead ignorance all you want."

Leppo's eyes followed him. "You don't have shit on me! None of yous do."

"Oh, but we do!" Grace said. "Metro surveillance cameras are everywhere. Now you either start talking or you will become the fall guy for whoever made you do this job."

He closed his eyes. "Could I please have something for pain?"

"You're going to prison for a long time, Jim," Grace said, ignoring the request.

Leppo opened his eyes, glanced at his attorney and then back to Grace. "What's on the tape?"

She raised her eyebrows and sighed. "You. Stan Wright. Need we say more?"

He looked at his attorney again. "I need to talk to my attorney before I answer any more questions."

She looked at Dugan and then to Cochran who nodded to the

door.

"Okay, Mr. Leppo, we'll give you a few minutes with your attorney."

She turned off the camera, followed the two FBI agents into the hall and closed the door.

"This guy actually has an FBI file already," Cochran began in a hushed tone. "He has been the suspected hit man in several murders. He did some time a couple of years ago for armed robbery. He may be our key to solving who is behind this conspiracy."

"I don't negotiate with scum like this," she said bitterly.

"He's just a pawn, Grace," Dugan said. "A dangerous pawn, but a pawn nonetheless."

She crossed her arms over her chest. "You want the big fish, but I want this bastard, too. Call it a woman's intuition, but there's something about him..." Her voice trailed off.

"What do you mean?" Cochran asked.

She shook her head. "There's some alarm going off in my head about this guy. I just have this feeling."

After several minutes had passed, Leppo's attorney opened the door. "He's ready now."

The three entered the room and re-assumed their positions. Grace turned on the camera.

"Now, Mr. Leppo, I have this feeling that your memory has made a miraculous recovery and you're ready to talk," she said.

He avoided her gaze. "Okay, look, I really don't remember being in that house with that commissioner woman."

Grace rolled her eyes and sighed. "Go on."

"As far as the fat kid goes, it was an accident."

"Oh? An accident, how unfortunate."

His gaze was fixed down at her again. "No really. There was this abandoned house not far from the metro station, you know, boarded up and all." He paused. "You sure I can't have a cigarette?"

She nodded. "Yes, I'm sure. So you took him to an abandoned house. A crack house where you usually deal, perhaps?"

"Please, let's keep the questioning to the matter at hand," his attorney interjected.

"Okay, fair enough. Go on."

"Like I said, I took him there, you know, just to ask him a few questions, that's all."

"And to rough him up a bit?" Cochran had begun to pace.

"Just a little. Just enough to put the fear of God in him."

"What questions did you ask him?" Grace asked.

Leppo stared at the sheet of his bed as if the answer were written on it. "I was supposed to ask him who all he told about some powder he was supposed to have. I just assumed he had stolen it from them. Drugs or something like that." His eyes darted back and forth from Grace and Dugan who was scribbling on his pad.

"They didn't tell you what the powder was?" Dugan asked.

He shrugged. "I obviously wasn't told what the hell the powder was so I wouldn't be able to tell yous guys."

Grace toyed with her pen. "So what did he tell you?"

Leppo shut his eyes and winced. "He said he had told a priest," he said through gritted teeth. "A Father McBrien."

"Was that the only person he told?" Grace asked.

"That's what he said. Look, can I have some pain medicine now? My neck hurts."

Grace ignored the question. "And then what happened?"

He took a deep breath. "When I was taking a piss, the kid panicked and ran through the house. When he got to the back of this house…well….you see, there ain't no floor in the back of this house. It rotted and caved in. It's true. I ain't shittin' you. Check it out for yourself. I can give you the address."

Grace stared at him, picturing a panic-stricken Stanley Wright running for his life through the house. She also pictured herself pistol whipping Mr. Leppo and then hanging him up by his scrotum. Instead, she maintained her façade of professional calmness. "Go on, please."

"It was dark, and he fell. Splat! Right on the concrete floor below. I think he hit his head on a rock or brick, something like that. Anyway he didn't move after that."

"So how did he end up in the Potomac River, Mr. Leppo?" Dugan asked.

"I loaded him in the back of my car and dumped him in the river. I thought he was weighted down enough, but I guess he wasn't." His eyes continued to dart back and forth between Grace and Dugan, but the two remained unmoved. "I swear, that's the truth," he continued. "It was an accident. I'll take a lie detector test to prove it."

"What were you supposed to do with him after you got the information?" Cochran asked.

"I was….just going to rough him up a bit and let him go after that. I swear."

Grace gave Cochran a sideways glance. "Right."

"So what did you do with this information?" Dugan pressed.

"I just….dropped it off somewhere."

Grace made a note on her pad. "Where did you drop it off?"

"One of those planters on the mall somewhere around the Lincoln Memorial." His gaze was now fixed to the ceiling. "And that's all I know."

"And the drive by shooting? What was that all about?" Grace asked.

He knit his brow and looked to his attorney. "I don't know nothing about no drive by shootin'."

"Are you sure, Mr. Leppo?"

"I'm positive. Now can I please have a cigarette or some pain medicine?"

"So who hired you to do this job?" Cochran began to pace again.

"Look, like I've already told you, I don't know the guy's name. He said he worked for someone else. You know, layers of protection, I guess. But the money. Geez, the money was *real* good."

Cochran stopped pacing. "Can you describe this man?"

"Big, burley kinda' guy. Bald head. I don't know. He looked like he could have been a football player. I don't remember too much else about him.

"Do you suppose you could contact him again?"

He smiled, revealing two rows of nicotine-stained teeth. "Maybe. What's in it for me?"

Grace shut off the recorder. Despite the disgust that boiled within her, she managed a smile. "We might be able to work something out."

"Ah, a deal. I like the sound of that. But first, you gotta get me out of this place. It makes me sick just being here again."

"Again? You've been here before?" Grace asked. "When?"

"Two years ago. I had cancer…Hodgkin's disease. I got chemo….from a doctor at Georgetown."

Grace felt her pulse quicken. "You were treated at Georgetown? By whom?"

"I don't know. Some young kid. What was his name? Joe or John something."

"Josh. Josh Hanley?"

He shook his head. "Yeah, yeah, that's it. I would stay here between treatments. I only went to the university for outpatient chemotherapy, then I'd come back here and barf my guts out. Please, I'd rather be in a regular cell than in the medical unit. Just the smell of a hospital makes me sick all over again."

Grace exchanged looks with Dugan and Cochran. "Hum, that's interesting. I need to give our friend Dr. Hanley another call."

*   *   *   *
      *   *   *

Josh's direct line buzzed, and he grabbed the receiver. "Dr. Hanley."

"Hi, Doc, it's Grace Love."

"Yes, Detective Love, what can I do for you?"

"I understand we have a former patient of yours in custody."

"You do?"

"Do you remember Jim Leppo? He tells us that you treated him with chemotherapy for Hodgkin's disease about two years ago."

Josh vaguely recalled the burly prisoner from the prison unit at D.C. General who was brought to the clinic every other week for chemotherapy. The guards would sit him in a wheelchair and place a coat over his hands to hide the handcuffs so as not to disturb the other patients - as if the bright orange jumpsuit wasn't enough evidence of his penal status. "How could I forget him."

"There's a story in the *Post* today that you should read. He's the one who tried to finish off Jane Riley."

"You're kidding! Really? As I recall, he was paroled before treatment ended and failed to return to complete chemotherapy. I had assumed that he died of Hodgkin's disease due to inadequate treatment."

"Hey, believe me, he's way too mean to die, Doc," Grace responded. "I have a question for you. The chemo made him loose his hair, right?"

"Well, yes."

"All of it?"

"Yes, all of it."

"Everywhere?"

Josh wondered why all this seemed so interesting to her. "Yes, everywhere."

"And I guess I'd have to get permission from the patient to get those records, wouldn't I?"

"Yes, of course." Josh shifted the phone from one ear to the other. "Unless you subpoenaed them, but why would you want his medical records?"

"Just a hunch," she replied. "How is Dr. Riley doing?"

"She's getting stronger every day. She's a tough cookie. If she can do what she did to Jim Leppo when she's sick, think about what she can do when she's well."

Grace chuckled. "I wouldn't want to get on her bad side."

"If you need Jim Leppo's records we can certainly get them for you."

"That would be great," she replied. "I think I'm on to something."

Fifty-seven

Josh headed across campus on his way home. It was now June, and summer had fully enveloped the Capitol City. Healy Hall was bathed in the waning glow of the setting sun, with its tower rising majestically above the trees. The campus lawn was green from a recent rain, and the beds surrounding the statue of Archbishop John Carroll, the founder of the university, were filled with a mix of yellow and white flowers.

Alex was sprawled on a bench facing an expanse of lawn to the north side of the Carroll statue. Dressed in shorts and a tee shirt, he was watching several young men engaged in a game of touch football. Josh's first impulse was to slip quietly past behind him, but he knew that at some point he would have to make peace. He stood there, his shirt unbuttoned and his tie askew, with his eyes on Alex but his mind somewhere else.

*   *   *   *

*   *   *

Alex headed for Paris soon after finals to spend the Christmas Holidays with his family. For Josh, the holidays spent at home were nothing short of torture. He was restless and irritable, waiting impatiently for a postcard, a phone call or any word from Alex.

But neither a call nor postcard ever materialized. When classes resumed in January, Alex acted as if the night on McMurran Hill had never taken place. To make matters worse, he announced that he and Nancy had gotten back together (as luck would have it, her family was also in Paris for the holidays). Although Josh and Alex had maintained a tutorial relationship early in the term, their friendship began to cool as Alex became more involved with his fellow athletes and their sporting events. In fact, Nelson had become so protective of Alex that Josh began to suspect that Nelson had a 'thing' for him as well. Alex's athletic efforts had been rewarded with the Most Valuable Player

Award at the end of the baseball season. Unfortunately, as he spent less and less time with Josh, his grades had suffered, forcing him to drop all the difficult science courses.

Josh's response was to throw himself into his studies and commit himself with an almost religious zeal to clubs and organizations. At the time, he was unaware of what 'sublimation' was but had become a master at it nonetheless. It had been a successful year for him. He had done extremely well in all his courses and was headed for a summer internship at the world-renowned research facility in Cold Harbor, New York. At the end of the second semester, he felt as though he had finally moved on, despite the memories of McMurran Hill, which returned now and then with a gnawing sense of loss.

In the stillness of a late May afternoon, days after the school year had officially ended, Josh was packing up the last of his belongings when the clatter of footfalls echoed through the empty corridor outside his dorm room. Most of the students had already left for the summer break, and with the dorms vacated, the campus had quickly become a ghost town. Being a research assistant, however, Josh had stayed after final exams to help prepare the labs for the summer session. He wondered if the housekeeping staff had finally come to throw him out but was startled to see Alex standing in the doorway.

"I thought I might find you here," he said.

Josh put the last of his things in a duffle bag and pulled the zipper closed.

"What are you still doing here, Alex? I thought you were long gone."

"I had some things to take care of, and I…well…I wanted to see you before the break."

Josh had been inspecting the area under his stripped bed for errant socks but looked up with surprise. "Oh?"

"Yeah. Ah…when are you leaving for Cold Harbor?"

"Next week. I'm going home to see my folks first." Josh surveyed the rest of the room for any missed objects. "I hear you're biking through Europe this summer. That should be cool."

"Yeah, can't wait." Alex eased into the room with his hands behind his back. "I have a surprise for you."

"A surprise? What it is?"

"Well, actually two surprises. The first is that I'm changing majors."

The news made Josh feel as if someone had just died. "That's not much of a surprise," he said weakly. "What are you changing to?"

"Business and Finance."

"So I guess you won't be needing my help next year."

Alex frowned. "Well, we'll see." His face then brightened. "The other surprise is this."

He produced a dark green bottle from behind his back and held it up. The label on it was a burnished gold shield that glistened in the light filtering though the window blinds.

Josh took it and carefully cradled it with his hands. "Dom Perignon? And it's even chilled!"

"Vintage 1976." Alex had plunged his hands deep into the pockets of his jeans and beamed.

"Wow," Josh said. "Where in the world did you get this? It must have cost a fortune."

"It was left over from my sister's wedding. I've been saving it for a special occasion."

"And what's the special occasion?"

Alex hesitated. "Well, the school year's finally over, and you did well academically. I did well in athletics at least." He paused and rubbed the back of his neck. "Did I mention the school year's finally over?"

The two chuckled in unison.

"I just thought we should celebrate." Alex kicked the door shut behind him.

Josh looked over Alex's shoulder at the closed door. "Um…we're not supposed to have alcohol in the dorm." He paused. "But what the hell? We must be the only two left on campus."

"That will make it taste all the better," Alex said with a devilish grin.

Alex took the bottle from him, and, after unwrapping the foil and removing the wire cage, eased the cork out. The bottle opened with a loud 'pop' that sent the cork sailing across the room. It ricocheted off the ceiling, bounced on the floor and rolled under the bed. The two snickered as the champagne bubbled over the side of the bottle and onto the floor.

Alex handed the bottle to Josh. "You first."

He took a sip. "Ummmm, very nice." He then took another.

"Hey, save some for me," Alex protested as he fell onto the bed and propped himself on the bare pillows.

Josh sat down beside him and handed him the bottle. Alex took a slug and then handed it back.

"So, how long will you be in Cold Harbor?" he asked.

"Eight weeks," Josh replied. He took one sip and then another. "And you in Europe?"

"About six weeks. I sure hope my butt holds up."

This time, Josh took a large gulp and swallowed hard. "Umm. From what I've seen, it should."

"Are you getting drunk already?" Alex asked.

Josh frowned. "No!" He then put his hand to his mouth and hiccoughed. "Maybe!" The two giggled as he handed the bottle back.

Alex took a drink. "If we don't watch out, we're going to have a repeat of what happened on McMurran Hill."

Josh stared him in the face. By now, he felt very relaxed and uninhibited.

"Is that why you're here?" he asked.

Alex let out a nervous chuckle but then became serious. "I…I think so."

Josh's heart was pounding. He took the bottle back and drank again, thinking he must be dreaming. "You know," he began softly, moving closer and resting his arm on Alex's chest. "I've been thinking about something for a long time."

"And what's that?" Alex whispered.

"I always wondered what it would be like to kiss you right where your sideburn meets your ear." He had gaped longingly at that area for almost a year as they studied together.

Alex was now noticeably flushed, his breathing rapid. "I've read that it's an erroneous zone."

"Erogenous," Josh correctly gently.

"Yeah, that. Why don't you try it and see what happens."
"Really?"
Alex nodded.

Josh took another gulp from the bottle and leaned in close. A residual hint of shampoo mixed deliciously with Alex's own masculine scent. His breath was hot as he lightly kissed the spot. Was this really happening? Then his tongue began to explore the length of skin between the edge of Alex's sideburn and the smooth cartilage of his ear. When he gently grasped the earlobe with his lips, Alex let out a soft moan.

Josh lifted his head, breathing hard, sure that Alex was going to change his mind at any second. Instead, he sat up, grabbed Josh's free hand, and placed it over the bulge that had risen in his jeans. Josh thought his heart was going tear through his chest. He swallowed hard.

"Wow, I guess you were right about it being an eron…I mean …erog..."

Before he could finish, Alex had pulled him close, and together they fell back on the bare mattress.

*   *   *   *
        *   *   *

"Touchdown!" one of the young men yelped.

Josh startled and looked about. His eyes fell on a statue of the Blessed Virgin Mary that stood in a nearby alcove, and he reflexively pulled his briefcase in front of him. After taking several deep breaths, which he blew out through pursed lips, he slowly skulked over to the bench.

"The weather has gotten pretty hot already, and it's only June," he said nonchalantly.

Alex looked up and held his hand to his forehead to shield his eyes from the setting sun. "The temperature reached 80 degrees today, but I guess you were stuck inside all day." He put his hand down. "I'm sorry I've been such a jerk. I'm so embarrassed that I've been avoiding you for weeks."

"It's called transference, but apology accepted nonetheless. And I'm sorry I responded the way I did, too. It was unprofessional of me." He dropped his briefcase and sat down. "Who's winning?"

A whoop went up as one of the young men made a touchdown. He grabbed the ball in one hand and raced wildly around the lawn, teasing his opponents with mock insults, and kneeling irreverently before the statue of the Blessed Virgin.

"I think that kid there maybe. I haven't really been paying attention."

"Jane seems to be doing well," Josh said. "I saw her in the outpatient clinic the other day."

"Yes, she's resting comfortably at home now that the police are watching the place."

"Well, that's good." Josh took in a deep breath and savored the earthy air. "Did she forgive you?"

Alex was silent for several minutes. "Yes. She said I have more than made up for it."

"I'm glad to hear that." He stretched. "You know, I'm off this weekend, and I was thinking about taking a drive to the country tomorrow to do some investigating."

Alex turned to him and squinted. "What are you talking about?"

"I just want to go see Peter Hilson's farm."

Alex glanced at the football game then back again. "Peter Hilson has a farm?"

Josh looked at him. "I'm not supposed to tell you this, but there's some clandestine research going on at this university right under my nose, and it involves Peter Hilson, Wilton Roth and God knows who else. I don't know who I can trust anymore. Apparently, I can't even trust my secretary, Dottie Shane. And it's all being funded by Wever foundation, which I'm not supposed to know about either, that somehow involves the U. S. Senate."

Alex sat up and looked at him. "So that's why you're getting death threats? How did you find out about all that?"

"I did some research of my own." He looked Alex in the eye. "The attempt to kill Jane is obviously tied to a conspiracy, and there has to be a very good reason for those involved to have taken so much of a risk. There is something huge at stake, and it's this *Inverness Protocol*. Apparently, Stanley Wright and Leander Murray were just the tip of the iceberg."

Alex exhaled with a low whistle. "Wow. So what is this Inver...what?"

"*Inverness Protocol*. I have my suspicions." He paused. "I want to find out what's going on at this 'secret lab' of Peter Hilson's."

"Secret lab?"

Josh produced a crumbled piece of paper. "Would you be interested in a free trip to the countryside?"

Alex regarded the paper but did not take it. "I don't know if that's such a good idea."

"Wow, did you see that pass?" Josh's eyes were fixed on the game now. "That kid can really throw a ball. Reminds me of someone I knew in college."

Alex chuckled. "At least it didn't land in your lap and ruin your books."

"Yeah, look what that started," he replied wistfully.

The two became quiet. "I suppose you'd like to forget about all that, wouldn't you?" Alex asked.

Josh paused. "Would you?"

The football suddenly came crashing to Alex's feet, and he bent down to retrieve it. "Go long!" He stood and with one quick snap, sent the ball sailing in a perfect arc over the lawn where a sprinting young man reached up and plucked it from the air.

"Nice toss, sir!" the smiling youth shouted. He then turned to his colleagues. "Did you see the pass that old guy threw?"

Alex turned to Josh. "Did you hear that? He called me 'that old guy!' Hell, that's it. I'm in. Let's go find this bastard!"

Fifty-eight

It was mid-morning when the phone rang. Jane was excised from a deep sleep and rolled over expectantly in search of the phone.

"I'll get it!" Beth called from the down the hall.

"I've got it!" Jane said drowsily, bringing the headset up. "Hello."

"Dr. Riley?"

"Yes."

"This is Detective Grace Love."

"Yes, Detective Love, what can I do for you?" she asked.

"So sorry to bother you like this. I hope you're feeling well?"

"Better every day."

"Great. Glad to hear that. I was wondering if your brother Alex was in?"

Jane sat up in bed and looked at the clock. "One minute please." She held her hand over the receiver. "Beth, has Alex left yet?"

"Yes, about an hour ago," she called back.

"I'm sorry, he's not in. He left about an hour ago. Have you tried his cell phone?"

"I have," she replied. "But I'm really looking for Dr. Josh Hanley. I've tried his home and his cell phone, too. I even had him paged. I just thought your brother might know where he is."

"They actually left together this morning for a drive out to the country somewhere. Alex said something about looking for a farm."

"What?" Grace Love's voice resounded in her ear, and she held the phone back.

"I said, they were driving out to the country…"

"To look for a farm? Where?"

"Just a minute." Jane put her hand over the receiver again. "Beth, where were they headed?"

"Somewhere in the Eastern Panhandle of West Virginia." Beth appeared at the doorway in her robe with a towel wrapped around her head. "Charleston or Charles Town. I don't recall exactly where."

Jane spoke into the receiver again. "Somewhere in West Virginia."

"Charles Town?" Grace asked with urgency.

"Yes, that's it, Charles Town."

"Good Lord, what are they thinking?"

"Is something wrong, Detective Love?" asked Jane.

"Not yet, but I gotta go. You take care of yourself, Dr. Riley, hear?"

With that the line went dead. Jane looked at the phone. "Who was that?" Beth asked.

"Detective Love," she replied quietly. "I think Josh and Alex may be in trouble."

Fifty-nine

"I forgot my cell phone!" Josh said examining his belt where the phone was usually clipped. They were sailing up the interstate highway at seventy miles an hour past suburbs and farmland. "I left the house in such a rush I forgot it."

"I have mine," Alex volunteered, pulling his off his waistband. "Oh, except the battery is dead. I forgot to bring my charger from home and I've been using Beth's phone. Do you have a charger in your car/"

"Not one that would fit that phone," Josh replied with exasperation. "Damn. We're cellphone-less."

"We'll just have to call the old fashioned way. By pay phone if we need to." A New York Yankees baseball cap was pulled down over his head with the bill nearly resting on the top of his Raybans. He wore a Giants jersey and jeans.

"Your hair has gotten pretty long. You look like you did in college," Josh remarked.

"So has yours," Alex responded.

"Who has time to get a haircut?" they both said in unison and then began to laugh.

"Anyway, I forgot to ask an important question yesterday before I agreed to take this little trip. Where exactly are we going?"

"Charles Town, West Virginia."

Alex nodded. "Okay, maybe we can at least bet on a horse race if nothing else."

They passed though Frederick, Maryland, with its church steeples like copper-clad stalagmites rising above the town that inspired the Revolutionary War poem, *Barbara Fritchie*. The city was also home to Fort Detrick, a government-operated facility used for biological weapons research during the Cold War. Virulent organisms, including anthrax and plague were still housed in high-level security labs on its campus.

Josh kept his eyes on the road. "So when are you going back to New York?"

"Leaving tomorrow. I have to get back to my company before it goes under." He tipped his cap and ran a hand through his hair. He then hooked the cap on his head and pulled it back in place. "New York's not that far away, you know."

Josh wasn't sure if that was an invitation to visit. "I certainly love New York," was his neutral reply. He took his eyes off the road briefly to look at his passenger and then quickly looked back at the expanse of highway in front of him. "Now that we have some time to kill, I guess we could catch up. You said you'd tell me what happened to your marriage to Nancy."

Alex stared out at the rolling farmland. "Don't beat around the bush, Josh, get right to the point, please!" he jibed. "Anyway, that was a disaster."

Josh sensed that he was out of bounds - that he had opened a wound for the sake of making small talk, and felt uneasy. What business was it of his anyway? "We can talk about something else," he said.

Alex turned to him. "No, not at all. I suspect it might even be therapeutic." He removed his sunglasses before continuing. "We just never really got along. She wanted different things, and she *always* got what she wanted."

"Including you?"

He nodded. "Of course. And after a couple of years, I finally couldn't take it anymore. I wanted my space, my freedom, but Nancy wouldn't hear of it."

"So what made her finally give you a divorce?"

He winced and hesitated. "Well, something really awful happened. She came home from a tennis lesson early one day and..." He stopped.

"And....what?"

Alex exhaled. "Well...I was in a compromising position with...someone."

"Someone? Who was she?"

"He," he said meekly. "The...ah...pool man."

"Oh," Josh replied, keeping his eyes fixed straight ahead. "I suppose that would do it."

"Right. Anyway, she became hysterical, of course, saying that I had deceived her. And then things got real ugly real fast. Her old man was this powerful investment banker in New York, and well, he basically blackballed me after the divorce. No one would hire me; I had no house anymore, and I was in debt up to my ears. It was darkest period of my life. I even thought about ending it all." He grew quiet and began to stare out of the window at the darkening sky.

"I'm sorry," Josh said quietly. "I had no idea."

He nodded but did not take his gaze off the churning clouds. "Looks like we're heading into a pretty nasty storm."

Realizing that the sun had disappeared quite some time back, Josh unclipped his sunglasses. "Why don't we change the subject?"

Alex abruptly turned toward him. "No, I'm fine. This *is* actually therapeutic."

"Are you sure?"

"Uh huh. Anyway, her family kept everything hush-hush. They didn't want polite society knowing that their daughter had married a queer -he made air quotes around the word- I guess. My father would have disowned me, but he was spared the embarrassment of it all. He died shortly after Nancy and I married. One of the hardest things I had to do was tell my mother what happened. She actually took it better than I thought she would." He turned to Josh. "But for the record, I want you to know that I did care for Nancy."

Josh noted the word 'love' had not been used when referring to feelings for his former wife. He shrugged. "I believe you."

"I didn't marry her just because her father had all the right connections," he continued. "Which is probably what you're thinking, right?"

Josh shook his head. "The thought never crossed my mind."

Alex signed. "Who am I kidding? Of course that was a factor in marrying her. There I said it. I know it sounds unscrupulous but at least I've finally admitted it."

Josh looked at him and smiled. "I'm not a priest, Alex, although lately I have the celibacy thing down quite well. And what about Jane?"

Alex shifted in the seat. "I never told Jane *why* I got divorced but she never really liked Nancy anyway so it wasn't a big deal for her. Nothing gets past Jane, and I think she probably figured it out on her own."

"You said in my office that you didn't go to her husband's funeral but that there was more to the story."

"Oh, right. Well, you see, our mother helped me financially to get my consulting business started, which has now gone international. She always said that I didn't need to work for any of those establishment types. She felt that I could make it on my own and I have. Without her help though, I would never have been able to get my business off the ground. Jane resented that because it essentially burned up a lot of our inheritance."

"Did you pay your mother back after you made it big?" Josh asked.

"I tried to, but she refused," he replied. "So when my mother passed away, Jane got screwed out of a lot of her inheritance."

The two were silent for several minutes.

Alex sighed. "There's also something I brought up the first night I was in town."

"About what happened in my dorm room at the end of the year?" Josh asked.

"Yes, how did you know...?"

"I just did." Josh eyed him briefly. "And what I told you afterwards."

Alex looked away. "Yes."

"That I...loved you," Josh said quietly.

Alex turned back. "No. That you were 'in love' with me."

"Wow, you remembered the exact words?"

For several minutes, the only sound was the hum of the engine as it propelled them toward an uncertain destination.

Josh finally broke the silence. "You sort of freaked out about it, didn't you? I didn't hear from you all summer."

Alex hesitated as he toyed with the latch on his watchband. "Yes, I was...confused. I was dating Nancy at the time, and I just didn't know what had happened."

"And when the fall term started, you avoided me like the plague." Josh recalled going to Alex's room again, but being turned away by Nelson. "And you told that moron roommate of yours," he said harshly.

Alex looked up. "Hey, I never told Nelson what had happened. He just figured things out, I guess. Besides, the last message I got from you was that you never wanted to see me again anyway!"

"Could you blame me? My life was hell, Alex, while you stood back and did nothing." Josh tried to control his anger as he recalled the almost daily taunts. After that one encounter, they had gone from being friends to enemies. Alex had not returned his calls and even refused to acknowledge him when they ran into each other on campus. "Luckily, I got into med school after only two years of college. That was my only escape."

"Josh, I'm sorry," he said earnestly as tears welled in his eyes. "Nelson took it upon himself to 'protect' me, and before I knew it, things had spiraled out of control. You know that times were different back then." He hesitated. "I know I was a coward about the whole thing. I freely admit that now. I've always regretted what happened between us, and I am truly sorry. If there was some way I could make it up to you I would, especially now. I hope you can forgive me."

Josh took a deep breath and cleared his throat. "Look, I didn't mean to drag you along so I could lay a guilt trip on you," he said, contritely.

"I'm the one who brought it up," Alex countered.

"It doesn't matter. I'm...sorry, Alex. As I said before, it's ancient history. We're both older and wiser now. I appreciate and accept your apology... and of course I forgive you. Now, let's just forget we ever had this conversation and move on."

Alex let out a sigh. "Ok, if that's what you want."

Large drops began to spatter against the windshield, and before long, the rain fell in torrents. It hammered away on the roof and ran down the windshield in sheets. They rode together in silence as the rain droned on and the wipers continued to thump back and forth in a futile attempt to clear the windshield. A half hour later, they entered Charles Town. By the time they approached the center of the historic town where John Brown's trial had been held over a century earlier, the rain had continued in a steady drizzle and lunch time had long since passed.

They stopped at a small diner called 'Shirlutz's' that was basic - beige Formica booths, paneled walls and white linoleum; Patsy Cline's *Crazy* filtered through the greasy air. An overweight man, dressed in soiled overalls and a hardhat, sat at one end of the counter, and a young woman with dark hair hanging about her face in long, oily strings sat at the other end, nervously sipping coffee. They both looked up and stared when Josh and Alex entered. The two men shook off the excess water and sat down in a booth. Josh grabbed the cracked plastic menus from behind the napkin holder and handed one to Alex.

"Looks like this place was a victim of the great paneling

epidemic of 1972," he said grimly.

A tall, thin waitress with thick black hair piled high on her head came over with two glasses of ice water, her shapely figure evident in the tight fitting yellow dress. She introduced herself as 'Norma' and took their orders. During lunch, their conversation had shifted back to Peter Hilson, his ties to Jane's illness, and the secret lab located somewhere in the vicinity. After they had finished eating, the waitress returned to clear the table.

"Norma, we're looking for a farm somewhere around here," Josh said. "Something with oats or oaks in the name."

"Hum, they's a lot of farms around here. Let's see…oats or oaks. Oh I know, there's a *Whispering Oaks* off of route 9," she said, putting their dishes in a tub nearby.

Josh looked at Alex. "That must be it."

"From what I understand, it has a new owner. Sets back from the road. First thing he did was put up a gate across the driveway," she added, as she wiped the table.

"The place is pure evil!" The young woman sitting at the end of the counter had overheard the conversation and her eyes were wide with fright. "They do evil things, there. Eeeeevil, I tell ya! If you know what's good fer ya, you'll stay away from that place!"

She jumped from her stool and headed for the door, putting on a plastic rain bonnet as she went.

Josh partially rose from the booth. "Ma'am? Ma'am, could we ask you a……"

Before he could finish his sentence, she leapt out into the pouring rain and was gone. The construction worker seated at the counter began to snicker.

The waitress put her hands on her hips and looked at him. "Cut it out, Tommy!"

"What's wrong with her?" Alex asked.

Norma waved her hand. "Oh, that's Millie Beattie. She's a little tetched in the head if you know what I mean." Using her index finger, she made a swirling motion near her ear. "People call her Batty Beattie. They're always making fun of her, but she can't help it."

Josh moved to the edge of the booth. "Do you know what she was talking about?"

The waitress shrugged. "Last year she kinda' disappeared for a while. When she reappeared, she started sayin' crazy things like she'd had the devil's baby, or something like that. Anyway, did you boys save room for dessert?"

"No, I think we'll take the check," Josh replied. He turned to Alex. "Would you mind getting this? I need to talk to her."

Before Alex could respond, Josh jumped from the booth and bounded out into the rain. He searched the sidewalk as rain pummeled his face until he saw the woman get into an old pickup truck parked down the street. With rain lashing against him, he sprinted down the sidewalk towards it. Just as she started the engine of the old Ford and turned on the lights and wipers, he pounded on the driver's side window. Millie frowned and angrily waved him away.

"Ma'am, I really need to talk to you!" he shouted, squinting through the rain-splashed window. "Do you know Dr. Peter Hilson?"

Her eyes widened once again and she drew back.

"I'm looking for Dr. Hilson," he shouted above the din of the rain. "Do you know where he is?"

She cracked the window. "I hope he's in hell where he belongs!" she shrieked. With that, she put the truck in gear and pulled away from the curb. Josh jumped back as the tires sprayed him with water and narrowly missed his feet. He sprinted back to the diner where Alex was waiting just inside the door.

"You're soaking wet!" he cried. "Does she at least know anything?"

Josh tried to wipe his glasses on the sleeve of his jacket and attempted to straighten his matted hair.

"She obviously knows Peter Hilson quite well."

Sixty

Jenna walked down the brightly lit corridor to one of the wooden doors and knocked softly. Much to her relief, the contractions that her patient had suffered with weeks earlier had turned out to be nothing more than false labor. Tanya had been able to continue on with the protocol injections and appeared to be tolerating them well.

When there was no answer, she gently pushed the door open. "Tanya?"

The bed was unmade, and a movie was roaring on the television. Jenna stepped in and inspected the room. There were bags of partially eaten chips on the nightstand along with empty soda cans and carelessly stacked celebrity rags. She went over the bathroom door and knocked. "Tanya? Are you in there?" She opened the door; the lights were on, but the small room was unoccupied. She flipped the switch off and went over and turned the television off. Becoming concerned, she checked the closet and noted that Jenna's overcoat was gone.

"Oh no," she breathed. The image of Millie Beattie running through a snowy forest instantly flashed in her mind. She bolted from the room and nearly collided into Peter Hilson; his wife Suzy Fischer was close behind him.

"How could you do something so irresponsible?" Hilson said to his wife.

"But she needed to take care of things at home. She needed to pay her rent. She was going to be evicted," Fischer pleaded.

"Tanya's missing!" Jenna exclaimed.

"So she's not back yet?" Fischer asked.

"No. Why, what happened?" Jenna asked.

"My brilliant wife let her go out because she had some things to take care of," he said sarcastically, making air quotes. "And how was she going to pay her rent when she didn't have any money yet?"

"Well, I….sort of….gave her an advance," Fischer said meekly.

"You what?" Hilson bellowed.

"She was going to be evicted!" Fischer repeated.

"But Dr. Fischer, she's due at any minute," Jenna said urgently.

"Of course she is!" Hilson spat. "You should know that more than anyone else here. Now what if she goes into labor and ends up in the hospital in town."

"We'll just transfer her here," Fischer replied.

"How would we explain to an outside emergency room physician who we are and what we're doing here? We're not even a recognized hospital. No physician's going to transfer her here!" Hilson turned and started down the hall.

"Peter, I'm sorry!" she said after him.

Hilson stopped and slowly turned around. "I know you meant well, Suzy," he said evenly. "I'm sorry for being so harsh, but you may have compromised the whole project." He turned and continued down the hall.

"Where are you going?" she asked, brushing a tear from her cheek.

"To find her, of course," he replied calmly.

Sixty-one

"We still have him in our sights but we're following at a safe distance," Dugan intoned as he drove the white van west on Interstate 70 in Maryland. The van sported a sign on its side which announced that it was owned by the 'Magic Floors Company," which specialized in the refinishing of hardwood floors. Dugan himself was clad in gray overalls with an oval nametag over the right breast pocket bearing the name 'Jim' embroidered in red cursive lettering.

"Can you tell how many are in the vehicle yet?" Cochran's voice came through the micro receiver wedged in Dugan's ear.

"Negative," he replied. "The windows are tinted and I haven't been able to get close enough to use the infrared."

The Suburban continued on Interstate 70 until it veered right, decelerating onto an exit ramp and then making a left turn onto route 325. Dugan followed suit and ten minutes later they crossed the south branch of the Potomac River into West Virginia. Passing by Harper's Ferry, the Suburban made another left onto a curving two lane highway that connected Harper's Ferry to Charles Town.

"We've turned onto Route 9, heading towards Charles Town," Dugan said, managing to keep several cars between them. Luckily, the traffic had been relatively heavy that day. "We're heading into the heart of town."

"Keep your distance, I don't want to spook this guy," said Cochran. "We're about three miles behind you."

The two agents had received a frantic call from Grace Love earlier in the day alerting them that Josh and Alex had gone out that morning in search of Hilson, thus potentially compromising the investigation. Although the agents had intended to close in on the lab after they had collected sufficient evidence, Josh and Alex's foray into the investigation had made finding the facility ever more pressing. As part of a plea bargain with Jim Leppo, they had located the black Suburban and had kept it under surveillance in hopes that it would eventually lead them to Hilson and his laboratory. Today had been their lucky break.

Dugan followed as the Suburban eased into the heart of the small town, past the domed town hall that had been built in the early 1800's. To his dismay, the Suburban pulled into a gas station several blocks further down the street.

"Damn!" said Dugan. "We're getting gas."

"Stay cool," Cochran said. "We'll hang back until we get the signal."

A man with a shaved head extracted his large frame from the SUV just as Dugan drove up to the pump on the opposite side of the concrete curb. After swiping a credit card, the man opened the gas cap and grabbed a nozzle. Dugan got out of the van and proceeded to open his gas cap as well. He gave a sideways glance in the man's direction and accidentally caught his eye. For a moment, the two stared at one another.

"Howdy," Dugan said in a Southern drawl. "Turned out to be a nice evenin' despite the rain."

The balding man nodded, then rolled his eyes and looked away. It took several minutes longer to fill the tank of the Suburban than it did the van and in the interim, another car had pulled up behind Dugan, waiting for him to finish. It was an older model Camero that had a racing stripe running down the middle, a spoiler on the back and jacked up rear tires. A young man with slicked back blond hair was behind the wheel. He wore a tank top that revealed colorful tattoos decorating his shoulders and arms. Dugan began to clean the windshield then proceeded to do the windows, all the while discretely trying to get a good look inside the Suburban.

The young man behind him began to beep his horn. "Hey buddy, you going to wash the whole damn van?" he asked as a cigarette dangled from his mouth. He grabbed the butt between his thumb and index finger and blew out the smoke.

"I'm almost done, sir," Dugan replied pleasantly, maintaining the Southern drawl.

"What's happening?" Cochran asked into the earpiece.

"Unwanted company," Dugan muttered.

The young man beeped the horn again. "Com'on asshole! You've been done now for ten minutes!"

Dugan smiled and glanced over at the bald man who was still

pumping gas. "Just a few more minutes."

At that, the young man jumped out of the car. "Move it buddy or I'm going to move it for you," he said as the cigarette bobbed with each word.

"Get back in your car, kid," Dugan said quietly. "If you know what's good for you."

By then, the bald man had finished and was replacing the gas cap.

"Are you threatening me, piss ant?" the young man asked, drawing his hands into fists as he towered over Dugan.

The bald man got into the SUV and started the engine.

"I'm warning you...." Dugan intoned as he watched the Suburban pull onto the street.

The young man spat out his cigarette and threw a punch. Dugan quickly dodged it, then hooked the man's arm around and threw him chest first against the side of the van.

"Owww, that hurts," he whined as Dugan pinned his arm against his back.

"Listen punk, get back in your car now or I'll knock your teeth out."

"Okay, okay, let go of me," the young man pleaded.

Dugan pushed him toward his car then hoped into the van and gunned the engine. The van lurched out onto the street, but the Suburban was nowhere to be seen.

"Damn!" he said into the headset. "I think I've lost him."

Sixty-two

By the time they found the property, the rain had stopped but the sky was deep blue and dusk appeared to be rapidly approaching. A tall, vine-covered brick wall surrounded the densely forested property, and an imposing gate of steel bars guarded the entrance. The shaded road on the other side of the gate cut through the trees and curved out of sight. A security camera was perched high on a pole but they managed to stay out of its range of sight.

Alex glanced up at the camera and pushed his hat back. "Looks pretty secure. Maybe there's another way in."

As they walked in the knee high wet grass along the wall, the provenance of the property's name became evident as a warm breeze hissed through the oaks, turning the leaves up and exposing their silvery underside. Further down the road, they came upon a twisted tree that had grown into the wall, buckling the bricks and causing its branches to hang low to the ground. Josh surveyed the mammoth oak, and after mounting the lowest branch, began to climb. Alex took the cue and followed close behind.

"I hope you know this Peter Hilson pretty well," he said grabbing for a branch. "Does he own a gun?"

"Probably several," Josh replied. He carefully scaled the wall with the help of the tree branches and eased his way down the other side, jumping to the soft earth below. Alex soon followed. The forest floor was thick with vines and low lying vegetation, and the closely packed trees limited visibility to only several yards. Josh bent down and tried to see through the tangle of limbs.

"It's too early for snakes," he said reassuringly.

Alex nodded. "Let's hope so. The driveway should be this way."

Josh followed Alex through the thick underbrush as prickly

vines tore at their exposed skin and clothes. It wasn't long before they broke through to an old paved driveway with its asphalt crumbling at the edges. It curved through the trees and disappeared. The steel gate was several yards behind them, and the surveillance camera faced away toward the other side of the gate.

They followed the driveway around a bend to a grassy clearing on which sat a stately mansion made of fieldstone. A Federal fan transom framed the front door, and Palladian style dormers jutted from the roof. Lamps burned in several of the English pane windows. The boxwood-lined driveway made an elegant circle in front of the house and then continued off to the left, disappearing around the corner. The two stopped behind a tree, and Josh eased himself out just enough to have a look.

"Holy Moly! Peter must be making a bundle to have a place like this! I wonder where that driveway goes?"

The mature hedge provided adequate cover around the driveway to the back of the house. The storm had left the evening air humid, filled with the pungent scent of boxwoods and the chattering of crickets. It had gotten progressively darker, and the streetlights that stood along the remaining stretch of driveway began to flicker a fluorescent pale green.

They followed the driveway to a stone carriage house that was architecturally similar to the mansion. It had three vintage garage doors at the front with an entrance to the left of the doors. Several cars were parked in front of the house on a small paved lot. A one-story addition constructed of cinderblocks painted white stretched beside it to the right with exhaust fans sprouting from the roof like giant steel mushrooms, their mechanical hums blending with the sounds of nature.

"That must be Peter's other lab," Josh whispered. "It's not as impressive as I thought it would be."

He motioned to Alex, and the two crept toward the carriage house, using the hedge and subsequently the trees, as cover. They hid behind a large yew that was planted under a window on the side of the carriage house just around the corner from the front entrance. Josh stood on his tiptoes and peered through the window, then immediately sank back down.

"Just a bunch of boxes," he whispered. "Looks like some sort of storage area. Let's go around back."

He led Alex to the back of the carriage house where they

found an old wooden door, the upper half of which had three rows of frosted panes. Josh tried the knob, but it wouldn't turn.

"It's locked."

"I'll fix that." Alex looked about and picked up a large rock. "Stand back."

"Before you go breaking and entering, I think you ought to know one thing."

"What?" he replied, sizing up the rock.

Josh pointed to a small decal in the lower corner of one of the glass panes.

"A security system decal. You think it's real?" Alex asked.

"After seeing the level of security at this place, me thinks it's real."

"Okay, okay...you're right." He dropped the rock and started back toward the front of the building. "We've got to find some way to get in there."

A brown delivery van roared up the driveway and into the parking lot. The two plastered themselves against the wall behind the yew just as its headlights briefly splashed the end of the building. The van stopped and idled in front of the carriage house just yards away. A deliveryman in a brown uniform and bearing a clipboard in one hand jumped from the driver's side. The light on the back porch of the house flickered on, and shortly thereafter, Suzy Fischer opened the door and bounded down the steps at the back of the house. Josh could hear the two conversing but could not discern the dialogue above the roar of the van's engine. The conversation ended abruptly, and Fischer walked toward the carriage house. Josh and Alex fell back against the wall again, barely breathing, as she unlocked the front door only a few feet away on the other side of the yew. Fluorescent lights blinked on through the windows and at the same time one of the garage doors at the front of the carriage house began to slowly open.

"That's Suzy Fischer, Peter's wife," Josh whispered. "This must be the right place but I thought they were splitting up."

The deliveryman hopped back into the idling van, made a sweeping turn with the vehicle, and then slowly backed it up toward the garage door, stopping just short of the opening. The headlights went out as the engine died.

"This is our chance!" Josh whispered. "Let's go!"

He eased past the yew toward the opening as Alex followed

and peered around the corner into the building. The garage was large and brightly lit, with a concrete floor and towering rows of wire racks filled with boxes bearing the names of scientific supply companies that he readily recognized. The deliveryman was using a dolly to unload several boxes at a time, which he stacked in the middle of the floor. When he was finished, he grabbed a clipboard and disappeared through a doorway that led into the cinderblock addition.

"That door must lead into the lab." Josh slid between the van and the garage opening and began to inspect the boxes.

Alex followed reluctantly. "We can't just walk in here. That deliveryman will be coming back at any minute," he whispered.

Before Josh could reply, he heard voices coming from beyond the door.

"Over here!" Alex motioned to him, and the two ducked behind one of the shelves just as the door opened. Suzy Fischer came through carrying the clipboard with the deliveryman trailing behind.

"Let's see if everything is here." She surveyed the boxes and intermittently glanced at the clipboard. "Okay, everything checks out. I guess that will do it for now." She scribbled on the clipboard and then handed it to the deliveryman who took the clipboard, tore off a pink slip from beneath the top sheet and gave it to her.

"Thank you, ma'am. Have a nice evenin'"

"Thank you." She took the slip, folded it, and threw it on a desk inside the laboratory.

The deliveryman pulled on the rear door of the van, causing it to close with a loud rattle and bang. He then jumped into the driver's seat, and the engine roared to life. In a toxic cloud of blue, the van pulled away and disappeared around the house. The garage door began to close, and the lights went out as Suzy Fischer left the building through the outer door, leaving Josh and Alex standing quietly in the burgeoning darkness.

"Now what?" Alex whispered.

Josh hesitated. "Let's have a look at the lab."

The two moved among the shelves to the interior door that ostensibly lead into the laboratory. The door was unlocked and opened into a windowless room, an antechamber of sorts, only large enough to accommodate a desk and a chair. Josh approached the cluttered desk, which was lit only by a low watt lamp, and began to rifle through pink invoices, eventually finding the one for the recently delivered supplies.

"Culture medium, flasks, Petri dishes. Nothing too exciting."

Alex studied the invoice over his shoulder. "Look who it's made out to."

"The Wever Foundation!" Josh laid the invoice back on the desk and surveyed the room. Another door occupied the opposite wall, and he pulled it open instantly flooding the antechamber with light. A modern laboratory stretched before them with white tiled floors and rows of laboratory 'benches' upon which sat some of the most sophisticated equipment Josh had ever seen. Several glass-enclosed hoods lined one wall emitting soft lavender glows from the ultraviolet lights inside.

He stood and stared, his mouth agape. "Wow! Where did he get the funding for all this?" he asked, finding his voice.

"What the hell are those?" Alex nodded to the hoods.

"They're sterile hoods. The ultraviolet light inside kills bacteria when it's not in use."

"What are they used for?" he pressed.

"Doing sterile work, like mixing drugs for injection or performing tissue cultures."

"You mean like human tissues?"

"Human or animal; could be either. If your cultures become contaminated with bacteria or fungi, your experiment is ruined."

"Wow," Alex whispered. "What next, double oh seven?"

"I'd just like to look around a little. I don't yet understand what it is he's doing here."

He leisurely made his way among the benches, assessing the equipment as Alex stood at a distance.

"I hope we're not going to inspect every gadget in this place," he said.

"I'm just fascinated by all this stuff. It's the best....state of the art." He ran his hand over a large white boxy piece of equipment.

Alex grinned. "I think you have lab envy, Dr. Hanley."

Josh ignored the comment. "I feel a little odd, snooping around like this. I almost feel like I'm invading his privacy."

"Until we find out how he's involved in Jane's illness, I don't care how much of his privacy we invade."

Two stainless steel doors with small square windows set at eye height were located at the far end of the lab, and lights glowed in the area beyond. Josh started toward them.

"I wonder what's over here."

The two crossed the lab and peered through the windows. A well lit corridor with white walls and gleaming white tile floors lay on the other side. The corridor was lined with wide oak doors, spaced at regular intervals, and there was a similar set of double metal doors at the opposite end of the corridor. A red sign above the doors announced that the area beyond was 'Sterile.'

"It looks like a hospital," Alex remarked.

"It sure does." Josh pushed open one of the doors and a rush of warm air greeted his nostrils. "And it smells like one too."

The two started down the hall as their wet sneakers made soft squeaking sounds on the waxed floor. The first door was locked and so they did not try the others. Instead, they tiptoed to the sterile area at the opposite end of the corridor and peered through the windows in the doors. There was an antechamber on the other side, which contained a row of stainless steel sinks. The walls and floors were covered in a light green ceramic tile. Beyond it was an open room, similarly tiled, with a surgical table in the center. A large surgical lamp hung from the ceiling above it.

"It looks like an operating room," said Josh.

"Someone just came into the lab!" Alex whispered. "I can hear them."

Josh's heart pounded as he tried the door nearest to the sterile room and found that it was unlocked. "Quick, in here!" he whispered, throwing the door open. Alex sprinted down the hall, and the two hustled into the darkened room. Josh left the door slightly ajar and peered into the hallway. Voices emanated from within the lab and became progressively louder. Suddenly, the metal doors at the end of the corridor burst open, and Josh quickly pulled the door shut. The squeaks of multiple shoes on the floor moved down the hall toward them, and a woman's moaning could be heard as the fracas passed by the door.

"I wonder what's going on?" Alex said in the darkness.

Josh opened the door just enough to see three people dressed in green scrub suits push a gurney through the metal doors of the sterile suite. The doors then slowly swung shut behind them, muffling the woman's cries.

"What is it?" Alex stood behind him craning to see.

"I'm not sure." He closed the door and ran his hand along the wall, finding the light switch. The overhead lights flickered on, revealing a tall, narrow closet with shelves on either side containing a variety of supplies. He looked about and then began to kick off his shoes as he wrenched off his jacket. He then pulled the tee shirt over his head.

"What in the hell are you doing?" Alex asked.

"I have an idea," he whispered. "Get undressed."

"What?"

"Get undressed and put on one of these." He handed Alex a scrub suit. "This should fit you."

Alex grabbed the suit. "Are you crazy?"

He undid the button on his jeans and pushed them down. "Do you want to stay in the closet?"

"Now's not the time to have that conversation," Alex replied.

"Very funny. Just put on one of these." Josh stepped out of his jeans and pulled on a pair of scrub bottoms.

Alex threw off his cap, pulled off his jersey and donned a scrub top. He pulled off his jeans and began to struggle into a pair of bottoms. "Got anything larger?"

"This isn't a fashion show, Alex, now put these on." He handed him a scrub cap, mask and paper booties.

"Whoa, wait a minute! We're not going in that operating room, are we?"

Josh stepped into his sneakers and then covered them with the paper booties. "I'll do all the talking. You can be my assistant." He put on a gauzy hairnet and began to tie a surgical mask behind his head.

Alex raised his eyebrows. "Your assistant? At what?"

"Just follow my lead," he replied, adjusting the mask to conform to the bridge of his nose.

Alex shook his head as he began to apply the booties to his sneakers. "Okay, I'll just follow your lead," he mocked.

Josh helped him with his cap and mask then led them out into the hallway. With shaking hands, he pushed the plate that opened the doors to the surgical suite. As the doors slowly opened, they could see a woman lying on the operating table, her legs up in stirrups. Intermittently, she would roll her head from side to side and moan. Two masked women were standing at a stainless steel sink scrubbing their hands and arms as water hissed from the spigots in a steady stream. An obese woman in mask, gown and gloves - a scrub tech, Josh surmised - was in the operating suite, preparing a table of instruments.

One of the women at the sink turned but continued to scrub her hands and arms.

"Who are you?" Suzy Fischer asked.

Josh nearly froze, hoping she would not recognize him. "Ah....we're from neonatal." Josh's voice was muffled by the mask.

"Neonatal?" Josh detected a hint of suspicion in her voice.

"Yes....ah, Dr. Hilson called us in," he replied. He looked behind and saw Alex cowering in the doorway. "This is my assistant." He grabbed him by the arm and pulled him in.

"I guess I'm the last to know everything." She looked over at the woman standing at the adjacent sink who shrugged. Saying nothing more, she bent over the stainless steel basin to rinse the foamy yellow soap off her arms and hands.

The woman at the adjoining sink had finished rinsing and with dripping arms held aloft, approached the scrub nurse. She was thin and shapely. A few strands of blond hair stuck out from under her cap. She looked over at Alex and Josh as the scrub nurse helped her don a sterile gown.

"You guys must be new." Only her gray eyes were visible above the mask.

"Yeah, haven't been...ah....involved until recently," Josh said.

"Well…welcome!" she exclaimed. *The Inverness Protocol* is quite exciting. I'm Jenna. That's Dr. Suzy Fischer."

Fischer came toward the scrub nurse and began to don a sterile gown and gloves in like manner. She looked at them out of the corner of her eye and nodded briefly.

"I'm....ah....Joe....and this is....Fred." Josh knew that Fischer must be on to them.

"Pleased to meet you both! I'd shake your hands but…." Jenna motioned to her now gloved hands.

"Understood," Josh replied.

Alex gave a stiff nod.

The woman on the table moaned again.

"This is going to be a big one," Jenna said, as she and Fischer began to drape the patient with sterile sheets.

"A big one, huh?" Josh's pulse began to race as panic rose within him.

"Yes. Aren't you going to get the warmer ready?" Fischer

asked suspiciously.

He glanced around the room and spotted an infant warming bed equipped with overhead lamp and oxygen tank. He motioned to Alex, and the two went over to it as Fischer's eyes followed them. He found the switch, and the overhead lamp flickered on. He then opened the valve to the oxygen tank, and readied the suction equipment.

"I'm glad you know what you're doing," Alex whispered.

"It's been a while, but I think I remember most of this from medical school. The equipment has certainly gotten fancier in the last several years."

Alex jumped as the woman let out another wail. Fischer positioned herself between the outstretched legs. "She's crowning!"

"We got her here in the nick of time!" Jenna said.

"Okay, Tanya, you can push now! Push hard!" Fischer ordered.

The woman, now bathed in sweat, held her breath and bore down with all her might, her face becoming a deep red. Josh moved slightly to see what was happening, but Fischer blocked the view.

"I think I'm going to be sick," Alex whispered.

Josh grabbed him by the arm. "Hold it together Alex! Remember your football days. Buck up and take it like a man!"

Tanya's agony went on for several more rounds of contractions as the birthing process continued. Finally, she let out a large grunt and Fischer caught a screaming infant in her arms. Jenna leaned in with two clamps and then severed the umbilical cord. Tanya relaxed on the table, her bleached blond hair dripping with sweat. A smile spread across her face as her breathing slowed.

"Is it a boy or girl?"

Jenna looked at Fischer, her eyes wide. "Just relax, Tanya," she said calmly. "It's all over."

Fischer carried the bundle to the warmer and deposited what appeared to be a perfect male infant onto the table. As it wriggled and squirmed, Josh suctioned the infant's mouth and nose with a bulb syringe, dried him, and then wrapped him in a warm blanket. By now, Fischer had returned to the patient to deliver the placenta, and Jenna approached the warming table in her gown and gloves.

"He's beautiful," she cooed. "What an historic moment this is."

The metal doors suddenly opened, and Peter Hilson strode into the suite dressed in a white lab coat with scrubs underneath and wearing a mask. Josh felt a surge of panic and his first impulse was to run from the room.

"I heard you got her back here just in time. How does he look?" The excitement in Hilson's voice was obvious.

"Come see," Jenna gushed. "He's beautiful."

He went over to the warmer, and Josh lowered his head, thinking that his heart was going to rupture at any moment. Hilson then grabbed a stethoscope from the pocket in his lab coat and listened to the infant's chest. He examined the extremities, and looked in the eyes and mouth as the infant whined.

"Success at last!" he bellowed.

Fischer came over, pulling off her bloody gloves. "Congratulations, darling," she whispered through tears.

"I couldn't have done it without you," he replied. He then went over to Tanya and grabbed her shoulder.

"Did I do good?" she asked.

"You did spectacularly. I'm going to give you an extra bonus! We should all celebrate with champagne. Everyone!" He looked about the room and his eyes fell on Josh and Alex. He cocked his head and his brow furrowed. "And who are you two?"

"That's Joe and Fred," Jenna said helpfully.

"Joe and Fred who?" Hilson asked, searching their eyes.

Jenna motioned toward Josh. "That's Joe, the neonatalogist you sent in."

Hilson wrinkled his forehead and looked first at Josh, then to Alex. "I didn't send anyone in."

She reared back. "Well then who…?"

Everyone was staring at Josh and Alex, including the scrub tech and even Tanya who had lifted her head off the table.

"I knew these guys were phony," Fischer intoned as she continued to stare. "You're from the press, aren't you?"

Josh and Alex slowly backed away from the warmer, toward the door.

"What's going on here?" Hilson moved toward them. "Who the hell are you and what are you doing in here?"

Without uttering a word, the two went crashing through the

metal doors sending them banging against the walls as they burst from the suite.

Sixty-three

Al King ambled into the cavernous precinct office bearing several overstuffed manila folders. He made his way among the empty desks to where Grace was seated and deposited them her desktop with a thud. This being a weekend, the office was deserted.

"What the hell is this?" she snapped, grabbing her coffee mug before it went crashing to the floor. King knew that she was still upset about Josh and Alex.

"What you ordered," he huffed. "Medical records on Jim Leppo fresh from Georgetown. Dr. Hanley authorized their release, and it has taken me all day to get them. I have no idea what you expect to find in them, but I thought it would at least improve your mood."

Grace's eyes lit up. "Thanks partner. Dr. Hanley came through for me so I guess I'll have to forgive him for playing detective today, that is, if he doesn't get himself killed."

She grabbed the first folder, tore it open, and began to pour over its pages, taking them one at a time. She felt King's eyes on her and looked up. "Well, don't just stand there! Grab a seat and start going through these folders with me!"

"For what Grace?" he said with exasperation.

She looked at him. "Al, I need to find out when Leppo was treated and when he got paroled. These dates will be very important." She then went back to flipping through the pages.

"Why?" he asked.

"Just find it," she said without looking up.

King shook his head, pulled up a chair and grabbed one of the folders off the pile.

"My wife expected me home an hour ago," he muttered as he began to read through the voluminous medical record.

The two read silently for close to an hour before King finally spoke up.

"Okay, here is what you want. It says simply that Leppo was treated on these dates." He paused to run a finger over the page. "And was then paroled on this date. Following that, he did not return to complete his therapy and was lost to follow up."

Grace had leapt to her feet and was reading over his shoulder. "And he was suffering from alopecia and retrograde ejaculation!" she said excitedly, pointing to an earlier part of the text.

"Alopecia?" King asked. He then winced. "And retrograde ejaculation?"

"Hair loss from the treatment," she said. "And the second one means that his ejaculate was dry. And look at the date he was paroled!"

"Yeah, so..."

Before King could finish, Grace had picked up the phone and was punching in numbers.

"Grace?" King mouthed to her. "Who are you calling?"

"Hey, Bev, this is Grace Love. Is Dr. Almazy in? I need to talk to him now. This is an emergency," she said into the phone. Then to King: "D.C. General."

"Why are you.....?"

"Dr. Almazy, this is Grace Love," she interrupted. "I need a DNA sample on Leppo as soon as possible."

Sixty-four

Dugan decided that the best course of action was to drive down the main thoroughfare that sliced through the town and head out to the surrounding countryside. He deduced that if Hilson did have a secret laboratory, it would not be located in the town proper but likely in a relatively remote or deserted area. As he took Route 9 through the small village, he scanned the narrow side streets just to be sure. There was no trace of the Suburban, or even a vehicle that vaguely resembled it, anywhere in the town.

Route 9 wound lazily through the countryside past rolling farmlands anchored by a variety of homesteads, from stately antebellum homes made of fieldstone, some of which had fallen into disrepair, to brick ranch houses and even the occasional ramshackle mobile home. He passed by one estate with a sign indicating that the 'historic' property had once belonged to George Washington's cousin.

"Any luck?" Cochran asked through the tiny speaker embedded in Dugan's ear.

"Not yet," he sighed. "But it sure is beautiful out here."

On a whim, he decided to make a left off Route 9 onto a rather well paved road. It made a hairpin turn then became a long stretch of highway that ran through a valley. Dugan's heart skipped a beat when he saw the taillights of the Suburban turning off the road about a half a mile in the distance.

"I've got him again!" he yelped.

"Excellent," came Cochran's reply. "Where are you?"

"Take a hard left off Route 9 onto Summit Point Road," he replied. "The vehicle has just made a right turn off the road but I am approaching the point of exit with caution and keeping my distance."

Dugan pulled the van past the turnoff just as the mechanical steel gates guarding the entrance to *Whispering Oaks* slowly closed. Seeing the security camera, he drove on past about a quarter of a mile further down the road before pulling the van into a stand of trees on the opposite side.

"He went into a property called 'Whispering Oaks.' It has a security gate and surveillance system. I'm going to take a look," Dugan said, pulling off the overalls to reveal a black form fitting jumpsuit with bulletproof padding.

"Okay, we're right behind you," Cochran's voice crackled into the earpiece. "Be careful, my friend."

Dugan grabbed a backpack and sprinted across the deserted highway. He plunged into the tall grass that grew alongside the road until he came upon the tree that had grown through the brick wall. There in the soft dirt at the base of the wall, were two distinct sets of footprints.

"I think I've found Josh and Alex's trail."

He mounted the tree, hoisted himself up through the branches and eased himself down into the dense undergrowth on the other side. The clouds had cleared, but the sky had gradually turned a deep shade of cobalt. In the darkness under the thick canopy of tree branches, Dugan extracted a set of night vision goggles from his backpack and pulled them over his head.

"I'm going in," he intoned, adjusting the lenses.

Following much the same path as Josh and Alex had taken earlier, he came upon the mansion, but seeing that a light burned in only one of the windows, soon discovered the carriage house to the back He passed behind the boxwood hedge to the carriage house and crouched under the same window where Josh and Alex had been thirty minutes earlier, their telltale footprints still fresh in the dirt. Not seeing much of interest in the garage, he slithered around to the back of the complex just as the unmistakable thump of a helicopter motor caught his attention. The sound of the engine grew progressively louder as the low flying aircraft slowly appeared over the trees above him with its spotlights blazing.

"Did you send in a chopper?" he asked into the hidden microphone.

"Negative."

Dugan quickly ducked around the side of the building as the chopper came in low, first over the house and then the carriage house.

"We have more company then," he whispered.

"What's happening?" asked Cochran.

"I'm not sure yet."

"Hang back. We'll be there soon."

"Roger that."

He watched as the helicopter glided to a clearing just beyond the lab, hovered for several seconds and then slowly descended, sending flattening waves over the grass in the clearing and causing the surrounding trees to shake and sway violently as it gently touched down.

The helicopter was large with a white cab and red tail. The words 'FlightForLife" were emblazoned on the side with blue stars toping the 'i's instead of periods.

"What the hell is going on here?" Dugan said more to himself than to Cochran.

After several minutes, the engines were throttled back to a low hum as the blades continued their methodical sweep albeit at a slower pace. The door opened and the pilot, a large beefy man in an olive drab flight suit and helmet, quickly scaled the short stairway to the ground. While still slightly stooped, he helped a young woman, who maintained a similar stance, out of the cockpit. With the aid of the night vision goggles, Dugan could see that she was dressed in a lab coat under which was a scrub suit. A similarly clad man followed her out of the chopper. The pilot then carefully helped a third person down the stairs. He appeared to be an elderly man dressed in a well tailored suit and sporting a fedora atop his head. He grasped the pilot's arm with one hand while the other clutched a cane. Their trek down the narrow steps took about three times as long as it had for the other passengers. The man stopped at the bottom of the steps where the pilot's large frame obscured him from view. As far as Dugan could tell, he appeared to be conversing with the man in the lab coat.

"Com'on," Dugan whispered as the automatic focus on the goggles made a continuous almost imperceptible buzzing noise. Seconds later, he stared in disbelief as the man stepped from the pilot's penumbra and his face finally came into focus.

Sixty-five

The two skidded down the corridor toward the laboratory, the booties over their sneakers giving them almost no traction on the polished floor. They were halfway down the hall when the doors to the laboratory opened, and two men in white lab coats stepped into the corridor. Alex slid to a stop, and Josh plunged into him.

"Stop them!" Hilson shouted from behind.

Alex looked about and grabbed the handle of a nearby door. It gave way, and he pulled Josh in with him, slamming it shut behind them. The door led into a dimly lit stairwell with a metal staircase descending into darkness. Alex bounded down the stairs with Josh at his heels.

"I sure hope this place has an emergency exit!" he exclaimed.

Just as they entered a dimly lit corridor at the bottom of the steps, the stairwell door burst open above them, and the pings of an army of shoes on metal followed them down the stairs. The corridor, which ran the length of the lab above, consisted of cinderblock walls that had been painted white and a floor of sealed concrete. A reinforced metal door stood at the far end of the hall.

"This doesn't look too promising," Josh mumbled from beneath the mask.

"Let's just hope it's the way out," Alex said as they sprinted toward it.

They could now hear the others behind them at the bottom of the stairwell. "Stop or I'll shoot!" one of them shouted in a deep throaty voice that was not Hilson's.

Josh glanced over his shoulder and saw a small army in white lab coats, lead by a large balding man dressed in black with a pistol in his hand.

"He has a gun!"

Alex grabbed the knob, and threw his shoulder into the door causing it to swing hard. He pulled Josh in with him and slammed the door shut on the advancing group of scientists.

Panting, the two leaned on the door, putting their combined weight against it. In the darkness, Josh quickly found the locking mechanism imbedded in the doorknob and turned it as the army of white coats came thumping down the hall. He frantically groped the wall and found a switch. The overhead fluorescent lighting flickered to life revealing a room covered floor to ceiling in white ceramic tile. A metal table resembling a shallow bathtub with a sink at one end was situated in the middle the room. Gray metal cabinets with glass fronts lined the walls revealing a variety of flasks, solvents and other laboratory equipment. The heavy metal door of a cold room dominated the far wall with another wooden door next it. Josh pulled his mask down.

"Hopefully that door beside the cold room is the way out."

Alex removed his mask and took a breath. "We have to do something fast. I'm sure Hilson has a key!"

"That looks like an autopsy table." Josh motioned to the stainless steel table in the center of the room.

"Great. How appropriate!" Alex said, putting his weight against the door.

Josh sprinted over and tried the handle of the door near the cold room, but it was locked. "I think this is a dead end. No pun intended."

Several metal IV poles were propped nearby, and Alex grabbed one of the more sturdy ones. He then wedged it between the entry door and the adjacent wall.

"This should give us some time to figure out what to do next," he whispered. They could hear a commotion outside, and then someone unlocked the knob. A thrust came from the other side but the door did not budge.

"Open this door at once!" Hilson shouted.

As the thrusting continued, the rod began to buckle slightly. Josh raced back to the door and helped Alex steady the pole. "I'm sorry I got you into this."

Alex shrugged but said nothing.

"I just thought of something," Josh said. "Can you hold them off a bit longer?"

"I'll try," Alex replied through gritted teeth.

Josh began to open the drawers in the cabinets.

"What the hell are you looking for?" Alex jerked with each thrust as he spoke. "There must be ten of them out there!"

After rifling through several drawers, Josh pulled out a white plastic baton with a serrated metal edge at one end. "This."

"And what is that?" Alex asked frantically between each blow.

"A bone saw." He moved toward the locked door at the other end of the room.

"A bone saw?"

"Yes, it's used for cutting open the skull so the brain can be extracted." He found an outlet near the door and plugged in the cord.

"Yuck! What the hell are you going to do with it?"

"I think this just might work. Put your mask back on. If this is the way out, I would like to keep our identities unknown." The saw came to life with a high-pitched whine. After repositioning his mask, Josh grasped the handle firmly in his hand. He then held the saw to the wooden door and began to cut around the doorknob as splinters of wood showered his face and hands.

Alex pulled the mask up over his nose. "Well, I'll be damned."

The metal pole bent further as the pounding intensified.

"Hurry, Josh! I don't think this pole's going to hold much longer!"

Splinters of wood continued to cascade over his arms as Josh cut around the doorknob. Just as he finished, the metal pole clanged to the floor and the door swung open, sending the pole skidding across the tile. By then, the two had scampered through the back door, thrusting it shut behind them.

The room beyond was completely black and cold, with a hint of mildew filling the air. Josh felt the rough concrete walls until he found the light switch.

"Holy Shit!" Alex shouted as the lights flickered on.

The cave-like room was lined with wire racks upon which sat large glass vessels filled with formaldehyde, each containing the bodies of preserved infants bearing grotesque deformities. Before they could move, the door swung open behind them and the large bald man stepped inside, a pistol firmly clasp between his two outstretched hands. Hilson, Fischer and a small army in white lab coats stood at his side.

"Hold it right there!" the man growled. "Put your hands above your heads!"

The two quickly complied. Hilson then took several tentative steps toward them, reached out and briskly pulled down the surgical masks.

"Josh Hanley? What in the hell are you doing here?" He motioned for the bald man to put the gun down. "You nearly scared the hell out of us and almost got you and your friend here shot."

Josh put his arms down and swallowed hard before finding his voice. "What in the world is going on here, Peter?"

Hilson crossed his arms over his chest as a scowl spread across his face. "What business is it of yours? How did you find this place and how the hell did you get in here?"

"I'm here because of Jane Riley," Josh blurted out. His voice was steady despite his mounting panic.

Hilson cocked his head. "So she does know what's going on." He nodded and pursed his lips. He found a stool, and sat down, his arms still folded across his chest. "And why did she send you? You don't work for the FDA."

Josh recoiled. "What are you talking about? Jane Riley didn't 'send' me. I came here to find you and find out what you're doing out here. I don't know if Jane knows what's going on here or not."

Hilson was silent for several minutes as he studied the floor. He then began to chuckle.

"What's so funny?" Alex whispered to Josh.

Hilson looked up. "Have you figured this out yet, Dr. Hanley?"

Josh looked about and took a deep breath. "It looks like you're trying to clone a human."

Hilson shook his head. "We're not trying anymore. We just did! But the irony of you being here is just so…colossal."

Josh remembered the title of the protocol that he had seen on Hilson's computer, and suddenly everything seemed to make sense. "Yes, I guess it is kind of ironic."

Alex looked from Josh to Hilson and back again. "What the hell is ironic? Could you please let me in on what he's talking about?"

Hilson rose and began to pontificate to those assembled in the room as if giving a lecture to a group of students. "All of this" - he nodded to the preserved infants -"is based on an obscure set of experiments performed several years ago by a bright young physician-scientist. That budding researcher worked tirelessly in the lab and generated some very interesting data that were most unfortunately presumed to be of little significance at the time. Several years would pass and more discoveries made before the importance of these findings were appreciated. Other investigators built on his work, myself included." He was now pacing about the room as he spoke. "I freely admit my work has been derivative in this area. It was eventually discovered that the initial steps of cellular activation, growth and subsequent differentiation into all cell types, from brain cells to heart cells, depends on the activation of DNA in a particular sequence by a process known as methylation." He paused. "In other words, the normal development of the human body in utero depends on activation of genes in a specific sequence that has not until now been entirely duplicated by the cloning process. Does any of this sound vaguely familiar, Dr. Hanley?"

Josh nodded. "Yes. Yes it does."

"I have no idea what he's talking about," Alex whispered.

"I thought it would," Hilson continued, then to Alex. "Methylation involves the addition of carbon and hydrogen groups, called methyl groups, to DNA in order to make it become functional. It would be like putting a bullet in this gun." He pointed to the tall man's pistol that he now held at his side. "Before you add the bullet, the gun doesn't do much, does it Marcus?"

The man shook his head.

"But put a bullet in the chamber, and it becomes a powerful and fearsome weapon with the ability to effect change, make people do what they don't necessarily want to do, cause serious injury, even death, when fired. Do you understand now, friend of Josh?"

Alex nodded. "Yes….sort of."

Hilson sighed impatiently and continued to speak. "That young man's discovery opened up enormous potential for exploiting the activity of not only normal cells, but cancer cells as well. In fact, for those of you who don't know this, the FDA has approved so called hypomethylating agents for the treatment of certain cancers, in an effort to turn off the driving force behind the growth of malignant cells. But, this process is also important in whether cloned animals, and humans for that matter," Hilson made a sweeping gesture toward the specimen jars, "Are normal." He paused and stood in front of Josh. "Do you know who that young man was?"

Josh hesitated. He recalled presenting data he had generated in Jane Riley's lab at a national scientific meeting where a group of prominent researchers questioned the very relevance of his work. "I...I was that young man....wasn't I?"

The whole room let out a collective gasp, and Alex took a step away from him. "You?"

Hilson nodded. "You generated some important data when you were working in Jane Riley's lab. At the time, nobody knew the ramifications that your findings would have on the cloning of human beings, except of course, Jane Riley."

Josh shook his head. "What are you talking about? Jane has no interest in cloning human beings. I doubt that she even thought about it at the time."

A smirk spread over Hilson's face. "She wanted you to believe that. You see, she wanted all of us to believe it. Those data that you generated are the very building blocks for the cloning of human beings, the key that will make cloned mammals completely normal. Jane knows this now and she knew it then. In her brilliant mind, she saw the potential for human cloning, something she has wanted to be the first to do."

"What?" Josh and Alex said together.

"He's out of his mind!" Alex muttered loud enough for all to hear.

Hilson chuckled. "I know it's hard to believe, but why else has she taken such a strong stance against human cloning, at least for others. You see, before she went to the FDA, she and Richard Willgoos, whom I'm sure you know cloned the first farm animal, were engaged in long distant collaboration across the pond as they like to call it. This was all well before her FDA appointment. She was warned by the president of the university to suspend all research involving human cloning, since as a religious institution, Georgetown was and still is opposed to the concept of human cloning, which explains why I have this lab."

Josh searched for words of denial, but truthfully, the whole notion finally made sense to him, based on what he knew of her research. "But is that a reason to poison her?" was all he could manage.

Hilson glared at him. "Poison her? I don't know what you're talking about." He paused. "Is that why you're tracking me down? To accuse me of such a thing?"

Josh maintained his composure. "Peter, she was poisoned with a lethal dose of busulfan."

"A lethal dose of busulfan? And you think I did it? That's preposterous!"

"I don't know, Peter. I don't know what to believe anymore. All I can tell you is that a bone marrow transplant was the only thing that saved her life."

"What makes you think that I had anything to do with that?"

"The FBI. You're wanted for questioning. They want you to explain how your signature, confirmed by a handwriting analysis, got on a prescription for 300 capsules of busulfan for Leander Murray's grandmother who has been dead for ten years."

Hilson knit his brow. "Leander Murray's dead grandmother? You are now making absolutely no sense."

"Does the name Ethel Wheeler ring a bell?"

Hilson paused and the color drained from his face. "I thought that prescription was for ah….someone else."

"Who?" Josh asked.

Hilson was lost in thought but finally answered. "That's confidential."

"Fine. You can tell the FBI who you wrote it for. Now tell me how Wilton Roth is involved in all this?" Josh continued, trying to get as much information as possible while Hilson was apparently willing to talk.

Hilson rolled his eyes. "You have done your homework. I don't know how you know about all this." He stopped. "Dottie, perhaps?"

Josh shook his head. "No, Peter, Dottie is very loyal to you."

Hilson shrugged and continued. "Anyway, the president of the university was getting ready to sack old Wil for lack of productivity. Wil needed to show that he was still involved in research so he came to me, begging to be put on some project. I added his name to one of our stage I protocols, which did not involve the use of human eggs, to save his ass. I doubt that he's even read it. If you ask him, he probably has no idea what the protocol is all about."

"So that woman up there, in the delivery room, just gave birth to a cloned human?" Alex asked.

"Yes, and for you who may not know this, DNA was implanted in an egg that was then placed in a host," Hilson said.

"Host?" Alex asked.

"A surrogate mother." Josh replied without taking his eyes off Hilson. "That woman up there is a surrogate mother."

"You mean, like crazy Millie," Alex replied.

Hilson raised his eyes. "How did you know….?" He stopped and shook his head. "Millie Beattie was paid dearly to be a surrogate. She willingly agreed to do this."

"And apparently it was horribly traumatic for her to have one of these deformed infants! She's literally nuts over it. She apparently thinks she's had the devil's baby!"

Hilson sighed. "Unlike Millie, the other volunteers have been mentally stable. I regret taking her. She turned out to be a horrible candidate."

"Who did you clone, Peter?" Josh asked.

"This is the part where I say it's really none of your business," Hilson quickly replied.

"None of my business? You're using data that I generated to do this outlandish project and you're telling me it's none of my business?"

"Go ahead and tell him." A voice came from the autopsy suite behind them, and the small army of white coats stepped aside. An elderly man with thick white hair stood just beyond the doorway, wearing a raincoat and a fedora. Using one of his hands, he leaned on a cane for support while the other held a pistol pointed at Josh and Alex.

"Why you're.....Senator Hines!" Josh exclaimed. He then remembered the fax. "And you probably have something to do with the Wever Foundation."

The Senator hobbled toward them keeping his pistol trained on first one, then the other. "I am the chairman of the Wever Foundation and the *Inverness Protocol* is mine. And who, may I ask are you, and what are you doing in my lab...uninvited, I might add?"

"Your lab?" Josh looked at Hilson. "You mean this is not your lab, Peter?"

He shook his head. "I work for the Senator. How else could I have built all this? Federal grants?"

"And yes, you just witnessed the birth of the first normal cloned human being," Hines said. "And I'll tell you who it is."

"But Senator!" Hilson protested.

Hines held up his hand. "I was cloned. I have a rare form of chronic leukemia that Dr Hilson has been treating for several years with the drug busulfan."

"So Peter wrote the prescription for 300 capsules of busulfan for you?" Josh asked.

"That's correct. Ethel Wheeler's name was a cover. Murray was the mastermind behind that. I can't have my constituents knowing that I'm sick. They'll never re-elect me particularly since the disease is now accelerating and only a bone marrow transplant is the surest cure. Unfortunately, I'm too old for a transplant and don't have any living siblings anyway. There were no good options for me…. that is until now. In that little baby, I now have a virtual endless supply of stem cells that are perfectly matched to my body. I can have a transplant without getting graft versus host disease, which is what kills us old folks."

"You mean that innocent little baby was created simply because you want to mine his stem cells?" Alex asked.

The Senator bristled. "That's a tad harsh, young man. I shall love this infant for he is after all, just another version of me."

"But it's not *illegal* to clone humans, is it?" Alex pressed.

"It's not illegal yet, but Congress may soon make it that way," the Senator replied. "And getting past the FDA is impossible, but we conquered that problem. This is a legitimate clinical study, and we have a government approved IND on file with the FDA. We will be the first to market this technology and no one will stand in our way."

Josh turned to Hilson. "But how did you get this protocol past the Institutional Review Board?" he asked referring to the internal panel of scientists that had to approve all research protocols at the university.

"If you recall, Wilton Roth is chairman of the IRB, and he gave it an expedited approval at my request. It did not require full IRB review," Hilson replied smugly.

Josh looked about. "But look at all these obviously failed attempts. You're playing with human lives. You're playing God!"

"Whoa, wait Josh, do you know how many attempts it took to clone a sheep before the researchers in Scotland finally got it right?" Hilson continued. "Over three hundred times! We did it using just a fraction of that, thanks in part to you. I've put my whole life into this not to mention the financial stake I have in it.

We had to act quickly, before Congress passes a law banning human cloning."

"We'll be on the cutting edge, and it will eventually be commonplace to clone humans," the Senator added.

Josh looked evenly at each one of them. "Are you aware of the moral ramifications of all of this? These humans you've created and will create...you don't know whether they have feelings....or souls or… whatever. It boggles the mind….I don't know what more to say."

"And what about Jane?" Alex interjected. "Which one of you tried to kill her?"

"Jane Riley!" the Senator said with disgust, still holding his gun on them. "She was determined to make the FDA the arbiter of cloning experiments because of her own agenda. We will be so far behind other countries in this if we don't act now."

"Did you have anything to do with what happened to her, Senator?" Hilson asked.

"Not directly. That was the idea of our late friend Dr. Leander Murray," Hines replied. "I just wanted a new Commissioner, that's all. I think he intended to make her ill. I don't think he actually intended to kill her."

"And Stanley Wright?" Josh asked. "And Father McBrien?"

"Marcus was in charge of their fates," Hines replied, nodding toward the tall, balding man.

"That's my sister's life your thugs have been playing with." Alex stepped forward, his fists clenched.

"Not so fast!" Hines pointed his pistol at Alex. He then motioned to Marcus. "Get rid of these interlopers."

"What's going on?" Josh looked at Hilson. "Is he going to…*kill*…us, too Peter?"

Hilson stood in front of Josh and Alex. "Leave these men alone. There's been enough bloodshed for this project. Right now we need to focus on the new life upstairs."

"That won't be necessary. That child is being transported to an undisclosed location as we speak," Hines replied. "Just listen."

The unmistakable thump of helicopter blades could be heard somewhere above them. After several minutes, its roar slowly faded.

"There's extensive testing to be done on that child." Suzy Fischer, who had been standing with the other scientists still clad in her blood soaked gown, spoke up, her speech pressured. "We don't yet know for sure that he is normal, Senator. The methylation status of his DNA hasn't even been determined. Where have you sent him?"

"I had to get him to a safe place as soon as possible, Dr. Fischer," the Senator replied. "But don't worry, there will be plenty of time for you to do your testing. Now, Marcus, do as I say. Get rid of these intruders."

Marcus stepped forward, revolver in hand. "Get out of the way, Hilson!"

"No! Stop!" Hilson shouted.

Alex lunged toward Marcus, throwing a kick to his midsection and knocking him backward into the army of white coat clad scientists. He then grabbed for the pistol, and the two fell to the floor in a writhing heap as everyone in the room scrambled for cover. A string of loud booms reverberated in the small space with bullets ricocheting off the walls and floor. Several glass jars shattered into pieces, and their gruesome contents went cascading to the floor. Soon the room was filled the acrid stench of formaldehyde.

All at once, a small army in bulky bulletproof vests and helmets invaded the room. They wore night vision goggles and wielded semiautomatic weapons.

"FBI! Everyone, drop your guns, and put your hands on your head. Now!"

Josh recognized the voice of Bill Dugan.

Alex dropped the gun he had wrested from Marcus and prostrated himself on the floor, his hands planted firmly on his head, as the others followed suite trying to avoid the noxious preservative that now coated the floor. "Don't shoot!" he shouted.

Josh looked through the bluish haze that pervaded the air and saw Senator Hines lying face down in a pool of blood.

"Bill! It's Josh Hanley! A United States Senator has been shot," he shouted, raising his head slightly.

Cochran appeared and reached down to retrieve Marcus' pistol from the floor. He then stepped over Alex and Marcus to retrieve the pistol next to the stricken Senator. "Stand down!" He bent over and rolled the Senator on his back, revealing a large bloodied area over his chest. "This man needs medical attention!"

Josh ran to the Senator's side, with Peter Hilson and Suzy Fischer at his heels. They tore through the tailored clothing to find a large gaping hole just below the left nipple with blood frothing out of it like a volcano. Hilson put his hand over the wound.

"We need an ambulance now!" he shouted.

The dying Senator grabbed at Hilson's lab coat. "Peter…." He gasped. "If I don't make it…the baby has been sent…..to……" He began to choke.

"Where? Where did you send him?" Fischer asked frantically.

The man's eyes rolled back into his head and his body went limp.

"We're loosing him!" Hilson shouted, feeling for a pulse. He then began CPR and continued for several more minutes, giving mouth to mouth resuscitation then chest compressions. He looked up at Josh then to Fischer. "Don't just sit there! Help me!"

Fischer started to move but Josh shook his head. He then grabbed Hilson by the shoulder. "Peter…it's through the heart. It's no use."

"No, no! This can't be happening!" Hilson put his head down and then sat back on the floor as Fischer rushed to his side, cradling him in her arms. "After all this hard work, everything is ruined!"

Marcus let out a roar as several agents tried to subdue him.

"Nooooooo!" he screamed as the agents struggled to hold him down.

Josh sat motionless next to the body of the dead Senator for several minutes staring transfixed at Hilson sobbing uncontrollably in the arms of his wife. It was a surreal moment. He had always thought of Hilson as hard and cold, ruthless even, but never emotional. Now, he looked just like an injured child in the arms of his mother.

As the agents escorted the rest of the scientists from the room, he was suddenly aware of Cochran and Dugan standing over him. He looked up.

"How did you find this place?" he asked numbly as Alex helped him to his feet.

"Jim Leppo told us where we could find Marcus. So we put two and two together and tailed him here. We knew he worked for a Senator, but we weren't sure which one. This Wever Foundation was a front of sorts."

"But what about the fax I found? Couldn't you trace the number to Senator Hines?"

"It was a general fax to the Dirkson mailroom which is where Marcus works. It was obviously a cover to protect the identity of the Senator." Dugan said. "We figured he'd at least lead us to Hilson."

Josh went over and helped Fischer and then Hilson to stand.

"Dr. Hilson, you'll have to come with us for questioning," Cochran said grimly. "Right now, you're the chief suspect in the attempt on Jane Riley's life."

Hilson turned to Josh, tears still streaming down his face. "None of this would have happened if you hadn't come here. Why did you have to come here? I swear I had nothing to do with what they did to Jane."

"I...I," Josh stammered unable to find a response.

"You can blame Hines and his thugs for everything," Cochran interrupted, directing his comments to Hilson. "They're the ones you should be angry with. Besides, we were already closing in on you."

When he was finished, Dugan led Hilson through the door as Fischer followed silently behind them.

Frowning, Cochran escorted Josh and Alex out of the room. "Let's get the hell out of here. You two have made quite a mess."

"But I thought you said...." Josh began.

"Never mind what I said to Hilson. I have a notion to run you two in for interfering with an FBI investigation!" He turned to Josh. "I think you should have listened to Grace Love, Dr. Hanley."

"Why?" he countered. "We got here before you guys did."

Cochran's eyes narrowed. "And almost got yourselves killed in the process. No, I think you should stick to what you do best....'doctorin.'"

"I suppose you're right, Jeff," he replied sullenly. "I promise this will never happen again."

Sixty-six

It was a hot evening in July and Josh sat under an umbrella in Jane Riley's garden, sipping Frangelico following a sumptuous picnic. The remaining seats were filled by Alex, Beth, and Father George McBrien. In addition, Bill Dugan and Al King had brought their wives, and a svelte Grace Love had shown up on the arm of Jeff Cochran, their romance just beginning to blossom. It had been several weeks since the cloning lab had been shut down, and Jane was back to work, albeit still on a part-time basis.

"I just want to clear something up, if I may," Josh began, swirling the hazelnut liqueur, his tongue loosened by drink. "Jane, did you really want to become the first to clone a human being?"

She smiled. "At one time I thought it was an exciting idea, but the ethical issues are just too profound. And to set the record straight, Peter was wrong. I didn't shut down cloning labs because I wanted the glory. That's just plain ridiculous."

"So, are the infants in the jars, or life forms I guess would be a more appropriate term, considered to be human?" Dugan asked.

"I guess technically they are," Jane replied after some thought.

"So, what do we do with the data that Peter generated?" Josh directed his question to Jane.

"It actually should be of interest to you since you generated important data on which some of it is based. From a regulatory standpoint, it will be helpful in future debates when it comes time to deciding how far we should go with this technology. And also for the record, when you generated those data, I did not know how significant they would become. Nobody did for that matter. Peter is essentially accusing me of being able to predict the future. I guess I should take that as a compliment."

"I would," Josh replied. "Peter has the highest regard for you."

Before Jane could respond, Alex interjected. "Until now, I had never even thought of the moral ramifications of human cloning."

"It's a complex issue to be sure." Father George retrieved his cup and began sipping his tea again.

"The idea of human cloning is so science fiction. I mean there are lots of movies and novels about this stuff that you think could never really happen." He paused. "Then I saw it first hand."

Josh smiled. "And science fact clobbered you over the head."

"I'm just glad it's over," Alex replied. He turned to Grace and the other detectives. "So will we ever know how Lee Murray convinced Stanley Wright to put busulfan in Jane's food?"

Grace held up her index finger. "Ah, now that's all very interesting. I suppose we'll never know for sure since both parties are now dead. However, we were able to pull Stanley's psychiatric record and found some very interesting information," she began. "You see, Stanley suffered with behavioral problems in school, and he was sent to a psychiatrist to see if he was a candidate for medication to curb his aggressive behavior. That psychiatrist was none other than Dr. Leander Murray, in practice at the time, before he went to the FDA. Hypnosis just happened to be one of Murray's specialties. Under hypnosis, Stanley confessed that he had poisoned his father. Until then, everyone assumed that Stanley's father died of a brain hemorrhage, in other words, a stroke. But Stanley had used rat poison, which contains a compound called brodifacoum, to poison his father."

"Brodifacoum?" Alex asked.

"It's an anticoagulant that is similar to a drug used in humans called warfarin but is much more potent," Josh offered. "It's known as a superwarfarin that inhibits blood from clotting. Rats essentially bleed to death."

"Good god!" Alex winced. "So why did he poison his father?"

"Lee Murray had written in the chart that they didn't really get along. His father constantly was on him about acting up in school. The final straw apparently came when Stanley's father refused to let him get a driver's license until he stopped misbehaving."

Jane raised her eyebrows. "So Stanley poisoned his father over a driver's license?"

She nodded. "Apparently, but Dr. Murray had suppressed that information, due to patient confidentiality issues, much like what you face in the confessional, Father. Our criminal psychologist has concluded that Lee Murray must have confronted Stanley Wright with the truth and thus maintained a pathologic control over him."

"Stanley would do anything for Dr. Murray because he was afraid of being found out by the police," Cochran added.

Dugan nodded. "Post hypnotic suggestion may also have come into play."

Alex turned to McBrien. "So why did Stanley confess?"

"Guilt. I think when he saw what he had done to Jane, the guilt was just too much to bear. Stanley was scared and wanted a way out. When he refused to go to the police and tell them what was going on, I told him to bring the vial of poison to me so that we could at least find out what Jane had been poisoned with. Unfortunately, he had lost the vial of busulfan which, by Providence, I found in his favorite easy chair."

"The mail room staff indicated that Stanley was frantic about finding that vial," Dugan said. "He told them it contained his mother's medicine, and that he needed to find it right away. Ellen Downs had caught him snooping around Jane's office one day. Dr. Murray told her that Stan was looking for the get well card the President had sent Jane, supposedly to show it to his buddies in the mail room. However, when we interviewed the mailroom staff, no one had ever recalled Stanley saying anything about a card from the President. It appears that Stanley was actually looking for the vial, apparently thinking that he had dropped it somewhere at the FDA when in reality it had slipped out of his pocket one night while he was lying in that recliner."

McBrien sighed. "I have felt so guilty about the whole thing."

"There's no reason for you to feel guilty, Father," Jane countered. "It sounds like you did everything you could."

"In fact, you actually saved Jane's life," Josh said. "I had my suspicions of what was going on but when I got your letter, it all fell into place."

McBrien held up his hand in protest, his cheeks now pink. "Please don't minimize your role in saving Jane's life, Doctor."

Josh turned to Grace. "What about Jim Leppo? What did you

find in his medical records that was so important?"

"Grace can now sleep peacefully knowing that she has solved the murder of Dr. My Ting," Al King said, smiling broadly.

Grace nodded gravely. "That's right. You see, My Ting died after Jim Leppo had been paroled. Remember I told you that not a stray hair was found on My's clothes, and that she had been raped but here was no evidence of semen? Jim Leppo didn't have any hair at the time of his parole as a result of his chemotherapy treatments. In addition, Josh, you noted in the medical record that he suffered with retrograde ejaculation due to some of the medications he was taking."

"Retrograde ejaculation?" Alex asked.

"Simply put, his ejaculate was dry," Josh noted.

"That's right," Grace said. "But the clincher was that My Ting had scratched her assailant, leaving his skin beneath her fingernails. The DNA fingerprint, though somewhat degraded, matched our friend Jim Leppo's perfectly."

"Imagine, most people use DNA fingerprinting to get people out of prison these days," Beth noted.

A smile spread across Grace's face. "You can imagine the shock on the old boy's face when I charged him with the murder of My Ting. Yes, Al, I've been sleeping soundly ever since."

"So what has happened to the first cloned human?" Josh asked the detectives, looking at each one of them in succession.

Cochran spoke up after some hesitation. "We have our suspicions but we're not sure. He may have been spirited out of the country, to Canada maybe. I'm sure he'll resurface somewhere, at some point in the future. Right now it's a mystery."

"Wow, this is too much." Josh got up and went to the bar to pour himself another drink and Alex followed.

"Nice party. Jane really knows how to cook." Josh poured some sparkling water into a glass. "So what are your plans?"

Alex dropped his head. "Back to New York tomorrow and then on to Prague."

"Prague...wow. I hear it's really beautiful there." He drained the glass and put it down. "It was nice seeing you again, after all these years, Alex. I hope our paths will cross again soon."

Alex nodded. "I hope you mean that."

Jane called from the table. "Josh! Alex! Come on back to the party."

Josh walked back over to the table, and Alex followed. "I really have to be going, Jane. I have an early day tomorrow."

Jane stood and threw her arms around him. "Oh, you really shouldn't work so hard. When are they finally going to let you go on that vacation you so highly deserve?"

Josh broke the embrace and shrugged. He then extended his hand to Alex. "Don't be a stranger."

Alex pulled him close. "I think you deserve more than a handshake."

Epilogue

Josh was in his office when Dottie came bursting in with a package about the size of a shoebox wrapped in brightly colored paper. "Dr. Hanley, this just came for you...Federal Express, Hon!"

There was no card or other identifying marks, and so he tore through the paper as Dottie stood by, wringing her hands with excitement. The box contained an object wrapped in bulky white tissue paper with a card tucked in beside it. Without lifting it out of the box, he unwrapped the paper just enough to identify its contents then quickly read the card.

"What is it?" Dottie asked craning her neck to see. "I just knew you had some girl you were hiding from us! Hon, are you all right?" she asked after a while. "You look like you've seen a ghost."

He replaced the lid on the box and looked up. "Dottie, would you do me a favor....a personal favor?"

"Sure, Hon. You name it."

"I have to leave town as soon as possible. Could you find a flight for me to Prague."

"Prague?"

"Yes, the capital of the Czech Republic."

"Sure, Hon, I know it's the cap....."

"Here, use my phone." He handed her the receiver, sprinted past her down the hall to Nick Perrone's office and stood in the doorway. "Hey Nick. I have to ask you for a favor."

Perrone looked up from what he was doing. "Anything, Josh. What do you need?"

"I need you to cover for me."

"Sure, you want me to do this weekend?"

"Oh no, I'm taking that long trip that I have needed all these years. We're talking two, maybe three weeks....at least. Could you cover for me?"

"Well, this is short notice, but, sure I..."

Josh didn't wait for the complete reply. Instead he turned and raced back to his office.

"Did you get that plane reservation made yet?"

Dottie was on the phone. She nodded and pointed to the receiver, then began to scribble on a pad. "One leaves from Dulles at nine tonight," she said, holding her hand over the mouthpiece.

He looked at his watch. It was just after three. "Book it for me, please. I have to go home and pack!" He grabbed the piece of paper from her and ran out.

"What was all the fuss about?" Dottie asked as she watched him race down the hall, through the clinic and out the doors, leaving baffled nurses in his wake.

"What's gotten into him all the sudden?" She then spied the box on his desk with the card still beside it and without hesitation, picked it up and read.

"Dear Josh, I'm here in Prague missing you. The content of this box says it all. Alex."

With the same boldness, she gingerly lifted the lid. Inside was an empty champagne bottle, with a noted vintage of 1976, bearing the shield of Dom Perignon.

Acknowledgements

Over the years of writing this book, I have found that formulating the plot has been the fun and somewhat easy part. The story develops and flows out of one's imagination, drawing on years of accumulated experience and knowledge, and materializes onto the page, or, in the twenty first century, the computer screen. There is no limit to character manipulation or plot twists. Anything and everything is possible. I would first like to thank and acknowledge those who read the manuscript and gave their critical appraisals and advice: Linda Cashdan, John Morrill, and Dr. Susan Honig. To them I will be forever grateful. But stories are written only with the love, support, patience, and advice of one's family. It is the countless hours spent editing, rewriting, re-editing and re-writing that is the difficult part. Because I have a full time career caring for very ill patients and am somewhat of a perfectionist, this book has taken more years to write than I'd like to admit. For enduring all that for all those years, I would especially like to thank my partner of twenty-three years, Dr. John Jenkins, who also read the manuscript many times, and our son Nicholas Catlett-Jenkins.

Joseph P. Catlett, M.D.